PERSIA: POWER AND PRIDE
THE GREAT PERSIAN SAGA

BY DR. JEFFREY DONNER
WWW.JEFFDONNER.COM

Copyright © 2018 by Dr. Jeffrey Donner

ISBN Number:
978-1-7320143-0-5

THIS BOOK IS DEDICATED TO ALL THOSE WHO WEAVE TALES OF MYSTERY AND SUSPENSE. I HAVE ALWAYS ADMIRED THOSE WHO CAN TRANSFIX ME, AND TAKE ME AWAY FROM THE BOUNDARIES OF REALITY.

Historical Prologue
Book 1
The Great Persian Saga
Persia: Pride and Power
King of Peoples, King of Lands, King of Kings

The Persian Empire at the time of this story
The Persian Empire

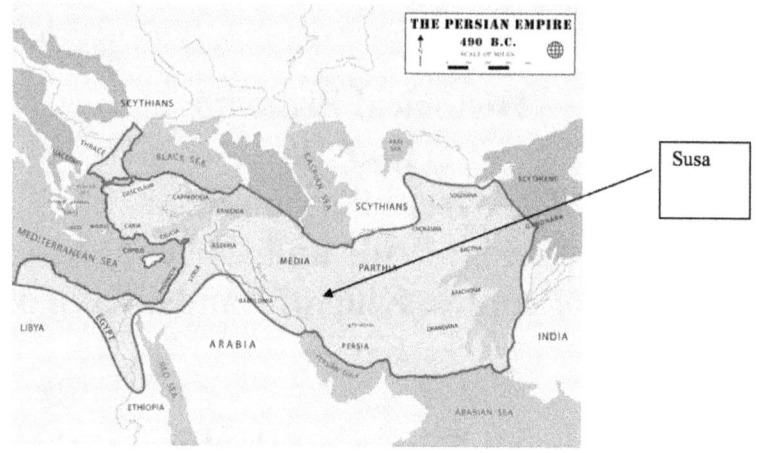

This fictional story unfolds at a very special time in world history. History was in a state of fluctuation, as the great Persian Empire was considering invading the Greek Peninsula. The Achaemenid Empire (The Persian Empire) was larger than any previous Empire in recorded history. It spanned 5.5 million square Kilometers reaching from the Indus valley in the east, to the Balkans in the west, and encompassing Egypt in the southwest.

The Empire was first established by Cyrus the Great, expanded by Darius the Great, and at the time of this story, ruled by Darius' son Xerxes. The Persian culture was notable for the establishment of a centralized government, the establishment of civil services, engineering wonders, exquisite artistic achievements, philosophies of tolerance, and medical advances, to name just a few of its accomplishments.

I hope you enjoy this story. Remember, this book in the first in a series of four. It will be followed by:

BOOK II- GREECE
BOOK III- THE DELPHIC ORACLE
BOOK IV-PRAY TO THE WIND

I hope you enjoy the reads!
Jeff Donner

The Great Persian Saga
Book 1
PERSIA: PRIDE AND POWER
King of Kings

The Major Players In the Story:

Ningizzida-the rogue priest- The Sheshgallu
Xerxes- The King of the Persian Empire
Artemisia-The Warrior Queen of Halicarnassus

Important Players in the Story:

The Persians

Penish- Body Guard to the great King Xerxes
Janlikorven-Persian Spy and Envoy
Mardonius- Xerxes cousin and highest ranking General
Smerdomences- Immortal General- close with the great King
Ummanaldash- Eunuch in the Persian court
Darius- Xerxes father
Hamas- Military Technician and teacher of the great King
Zeba- Xerxes Handmaiden
Zopyros- Persian Governor of Babylonia
Sippar- Persian tracker
Calah- Xerxes personal attendant.
Asanaladace- Chief Engineer of the Persian Empire

Babylonians

Manishtusu- under lord to Ningizzida
Shamah-eriba- Powerful Babylonian land owner
Belshimanni- Powerful Babylonian land owner
Jehoash- convert to the great Sheshgallu- also known as Nin-Nibru
Baldigul-el- famous teacher of Ningizzida

Phoenicians

Ekallatim- Warrior Queen's consort
Cassites- Magi to the Queen
Nabu-na-id- Eunuch and slave of the Warrior Queen
Jyylim- Phoenician spy for the Warrior Queen

Other Important Characters

Herodotus- historian
Delir-el Bar- Leader of the Sand Dancers
Sameron- Lioness- Xerxes' personal pet
Ho of Sebennytos- Xerxes Egyptian step mother
Marduk- Babylonian God
The Monster Tiamat- Internal monster- destroyer of souls.
Ahuramazda- Persian God
Demaratus- Ex-Spartan King
Psusennes- Egyptian—Representative of the great King in Egypt.

Enjoy the read!

PERSIA: POWER AND PRIDE
THE GREAT PERSIAN SAGA

PRELUDE TO THE ANCIENT, FIRST WORLD WAR

BOOK 1

History is shaped by the friction between opposing forces. The world revolves around these conflicts. Each side is convinced of their righteousness and the morality of their cause. The flow of the tides and the wills of the gods give rise and prominence to one side or the other. The zeitgeist continues to evolve. The overpowering will of one side is seen as arrogance from the other.

Jd

PERSIA

CHAPTER I –
SHESHGALLU- THE GREAT
GUARDIAN

His face foretold many years of study, political battle, and anguish. He was a quiet man who rarely betrayed his inner thoughts. Ningizzida was an ancient priest. The elders of Babylonia remembered him as aged and wrinkled from head to toe when they were young adults. Although cherished for his extraordinary abilities, Ningizzida was very much a recluse.

For all his power and esteem, he wore unpretentious clothing, a simple white robe and cap. Ningizzida was the most important religious figure in the great city of Babylonia. To the people, he was the Sheshgallu, or the great guard. This honor was given to the highest-ranking priest. All spiritual and religious decisions went through the Sheshgallu. He was the guardian of all holy rituals and prayers. His word was final in all matters. He had vast power, both because of his exalted religious position and his extraordinary ability to manipulate the behavior and thoughts of other people. He was the ultimate salesman and had the credentials to back up his boasts. Ningizzida was a very proud priest. He believed even Kings needed to pay homage to him. After all, he was one of the few living individuals who understood the Enuma Elish - the creation myth and what it meant. This knowledge hadn't come easily to the old man. He recalled every memory he spent in obtaining and eventually mastering these primeval secrets with anguish. The memories brought tears to his eyes and his body began to sweat with anxiety. "*A small price to pay*" he thought, as it was a cherished prize to have this information for it afforded him great power within both the religious and political circles of the region. Knowing the creation scrolls put Ningizzida in direct contact with God.

* * * *

A silence filled the empty room, but it was a heavy feeling with much tension hanging like rotting leaves on a dying tree. King Sargon, the King of Ur, stood outside the door of the great priest. As he waited, he kept rubbing his neck and scratching different parts of his limbs. The King hadn't eaten in an entire day. With a deep breath and a heavy hand, he opened the door to a shockingly modest room. He paused to evaluate his surroundings. It was not what he expected. The room was dimly lit by a single candle and mostly empty except for an old, large wooden chair with intricate carvings that he could not quite make out from across the room. In a corner of the room was a golden pot, out of which came the smoke that circulated through the room. The air was damp, thick and smelled of frankincense and other sweet lemon scented oils. Sargon knew well of frankincense oil, although it was called levona in Ur. It was a consecrated oil and used by priests with other compounds in religious ceremonies. The exact amount of the resin and the other sweet spices was a closely guarded secret by the local priests, passed down from generations.

Sargon had to wait in this room for a good part of a day. He was told that he had to be cleansed before his meeting with the Sheshgallu. It was explained that the plant from which the frankincense came was a holy tree, as it can grow without soil and in the harshest of environments. Being in this environment would not only cleanse the King but connect him to the essence of all people.

The unease of the long wait caused his mouth to go dry and he worried he wouldn't be able to present his thoughts clearly. As the scents overwhelmed his intelligences, the King felt his chest tightening and he was feeling overheated. He kept running his hands through his hair and he had begun biting his lip. He knew that the future of his city and his people hung in the balance of this meeting. History was about to be determined between he and the great Sheshgallu. Sargon had waited and ruminated over this moment. But as it grew closer, it appeared only farther away.

And then, Sargon began to hear a drum pounding in the background. The first sound of the instrument startled him. Something was going to happen, and the

King's hands became clammy and his lips imperceptively began to tremble. A curtain that he hadn't noticed before began to open and the room immediately became brighter. The guardian of the Great Spirit was arriving. The King's eyes opened as wide as his body could support and his confusion seemed to escalate. Out of character, Ningizzida's white hair was smoothed and reached his shoulders. He wore a light blue cap and gown, the color matching his eyes. The change from what he had heard made the King even more anxious. He had waited many months for an audience with the great one.

King Sargon could trace his lineage to Enki the Great, the ancient ruler of Mesopotamia. Yet, even with his ancestry, in this atypical venue he was edgy. His chest tightened, and his breath shortened. Before him stood the mythical Priest, Ningizzida, the man with whom the boundaries between man and God became blurred. Sargon was not the type of person who was easily intimidated; however, in this moment, he could not swallow, and he feared that he could not speak. His mouth and throat were as dry as the desert at high noon. His brow was wet with anxiety and his hands shook with trepidation. The King began walking slowly towards Ningizzida. Each step felt heavier than the last, until the pure weight of his legs made him stop.

Sargon took two more trivial steps and noticed that Ningizzida's face was heavily wrinkled with history and secrets. As Sargon stared into Ningizzida's eyes, he found they were unreadable, distant and empty. Was he truly in the company of the one who was the direct link to God? Sargon found his courage weaken as he edged forward. His knees finally buckled under the stress and he bowed his head silently in front of this Man God. Ningizzida's eyes now bore down on the King, and the Sheshgallu moved towards Sargon placing his hand on his head. Sargon felt a charged tingling as the great man touched his head. It was a transfer of energy and his arms shook. Ningizzida moved his lips in silent prayer as Sargon knelt in front of him, remaining as still as his trembling body could muster. Finally, the priest turned and walked back to his chair. Ningizzida raised his head. He motioned to Sargon and the King cleared his throat and in a low gravelly voice, void on tone, spoke: *"My Lord, I praise you to the highest. To be in your presence is a great honor for me and the people of Ur. But Lord, I come to you in desperation. My people have lost hope, for they see no happiness in their future and no contentment in their lives. For the last two years, the false King of Kisch has been raiding our traders. We have been patient, Lord. I come to ask for your guidance."*

Ningizzida's name was well known throughout the vast Persian Empire. The Kingdom reached as far east as the Qjang people, and as far west as Egypt. The Persian Empire encompassed many different religious beliefs and languages represented within its borders. There was not a village in all of Persia that did not praise the great Babylonian mystical priest. He was the One, the Sheshgallu. As one traveled to the far outskirts of the civilized world, the only religious icon that was superior to Ningizzida was the Greek Oracle at Delphi, in which priestesses spoke directly to the god, Apollo. Of course, the Sheshgallu never acknowledged the supremacy of the Oracle, and even preached that the Oracle was an illusion of blackened magic. Even the far away Greeks and Phoenicians and their pantheon of gods, knew of the powers and influence of Ningizzida. Kings and politicians feared him, for it was rumored that his understanding of the creation process put him in direct contact with the deity. His reputation brought vast sums of gold and riches from those wishing to seek his favor and insight. When walking through the streets of his beloved city, slaves and nobles alike would humbly bow to his steps and kiss the ground that he had tread upon. He could claim superiority over all other priests and magi. Nobody could or would question him or his decisions, and he knew it. He was Sheshgallu, beyond reproach, the ultimate knowledge of creation itself, chosen by God to be his earthly representative.

Within Assyria and Babylonia, Ningizzida had developed a cult following and most circles spoke of him having divine abilities. His life accomplishments were the stories told to young children by the evening fire. Claims that the old man could leave his body and float throughout villages circulated as wild as the images of the old priest circling above. His power to read the inner thoughts and intentions of others was legendary. It was told that he never slept. Instead at night, he would travel into people's minds, planting both blessings and curses. He guarded those with true beliefs and punished transgressors. One could not think bad thoughts without the fear of punishment against self and family.

Ningizzida cut the King of Ur off while he spoke. He raised his hand and Sargon was immediately silenced. Stillness hung in the air, like the coming of death itself. The priest closed his eyes and breathed deeply, *"I have seen your city as it weeps. Your people are desolate, your children hungry. Their suffering disrupts my dreams."* His eyes seemed to become fiery red as he declared: *"I have visited your city in my dream ventures. I have visited the temple of Ziggurate and spoken with the father of your people, Mesh-Ane-Pada, who has been with the great God for many generations."*

From early in his life, Ningizzida had aspired to greatness. He never played with other children. He would lock himself away and play within his own mind. He paid attention to his inner voices. He was a strange child for he rarely looked another in the eye. He had fits of laughing and anger. He sometimes spoke in languages nobody understood. Some rumored him possessed by forces beyond understanding. Feeling desperate, lost, and to some degree scared of their own child, Ningizzida's parents sent him away at an early age to a religious school. Even within the cloistered setting, the young man was outcast, as other students would torture him and make fun of his strange ways. One afternoon in a fit of anger, the adolescent Ningizzida decided to retaliate against a particular student who had been especially harsh with him. He had been reading old Hebrew texts and brashly put a curse on the young man in front of the entire school. His curse was met with derisive laughter and even physical threats until, by surprise that evening, the boy who was cursed, choked to death on his supper. From that day on, the cursing, taunting and bullying ceased,

22

and the young Ningizzida was viewed with fear, reverence and awe. He immediately began using this newly found command, realizing that if he stared at certain people, they would shrink under his gaze. He was creating his own sense of insuperability.

After the curse and the ultimate demise of the other young priest, the young Ningizzida rose quickly in the ranks of priesthood. He eventually found his way to the celebrated school, the Kussara Monastery, in Mesopotamia.

Upon arriving at the Monastery, the young Ningizzida began privately questioning some of the old traditions and beliefs. He was afraid to voice his skepticism out loud. He couldn't understand why the one god, Marduk, hadn't yet made himself directly known to him. There was another student that claimed that the god had spoken to him on a regular basis. So jealous was the young acolyte Ningizzida, that he planted an asp in the man's bed. The death only convinced the young Ningizzida that the man had lied about his spiritual relationship with the deity. For, if in fact he had communication with God he would have been warned of the impending danger. It was an epiphany for the young priest, as he realized that night that when others claimed sacred connection, it was probably just empty boasting. **"Was it** *always such?"* he wondered during the long nights of meditation.

Ningizzida's teacher was the famous spiritual leader, Baldigul-el, who would school the young priest in every aspect of his craft. Ningizzida spent almost ten years under the master's tutelage, suffering many indignities. Baldigul-el was not an inherently compassionate man and he drove his young disciple with unearthly purpose. Some believed that Baldigul-el's techniques of education bordered on the sadistic. But even so, they went unquestioned and unchallenged.

Baldigul-el once admitted to Ningizzida that he couldn't afford to be easy on him the way he was with the other young priests. This unusual admittance occurred when the old master found the young Ningizzida crying in the meditation room. Baldigul-el explained that Ningizzida's abilities were such that they had to be "molded with fire", like the flawless clay pots that were made by the artisans of the city. Only with sweat and tears could the essential information be transferred, for to know God, one had to appreciate the dirt that he created to blanket his planet. *"One does not reach God by prayer alone. All men pray. One must suffer to reveal their inner strength to the Almighty One. Pain is encompassing. It creates clarity of reality. The god, Marduk, was born*

from pain and so must his children."
Baldigul-el was harsh. His teachings involved both spiritual and physical pain. Ningizzida's personality was washed away as the rain-washed dirt from the stone. His old traits, his inherent weaknesses, and his illusions of life had to be transformed. It had to be such so they could be recreated in the proper way. Ningizzida couldn't always comprehend the need that physical torture played in his religious passage, but for Baldigul-el, it was obligatory. He required not only sacrificial blood, but blood from Ningizzida as well. As he aged, Ningizzida found himself employing the same severe techniques of passage that his mentor used on him. Blood and physical pain were needed to learn humility in the face of God. He eventually learned to relish every scar that crisscrossed his body. When he bled, he would lick his wounds, tasting his own blood.

When he had just begun his studies, it quickly became apparent that Ningizzida was the natural successor to the great man. Baldigul-el also recognized that Ningizzida would eventually eclipse him in both notoriety and power. The jealousy surrounding Ningizzida's status frequently incited violence from other acolytes. At one point he became deathly ill after an assassination attempt by a jealous young cleric. Ningizzida fell into unconsciousness after consuming celebratory wine offered to him by a fellow student. His coma was preceded by violent vomiting, which probably saved his life, ridding his body of some of the poison before it could be fully digested. The event was the first in a series of close escapes that Ningizzida had with death. Each of them cemented his reputation as invincible, protected by the deity. But more importantly, it left the young Ningizzida persuaded of his own supremacy. Six months later, after the young Ningizzida had recovered his strength, the youthful student that was suspected of the attempt, was found hung in an alley with his neck sliced from right to left and back again. Baldigul-el had schooled Ningizzida in revenge and it was rumored that Baldigul-el himself ordered the termination of the suspected assassin.

Early in his career, what separated Ningizzida from the other neophytes, besides his inherent aggressiveness, was that he seemed to inherently understand the pure Apsu. The Apsu is the heavenly space serving as the yoke that gave birth to Marduk. The Apsu was the magical substance that encompassed the universe and gave rise to every living thing. If one understood the Apsu and was in contact with its power, one was part of the continuum that connected man with the god, Marduk. If one was in contact with

Apsu, it was said one could discern the future in every living thing. For in every part of the body, in every muscle, tendon and blood vessel lived one's own individual destiny.

During his meditations and long solitary sessions in the desert, Ningizzida wrestled with the primeval internal monster known as Tiamat, the destroyer of souls. One had to get past Tiamat to understand Apsu and reach the higher level of consciousness. Tiamat was the pseudonym given to one's inner madness, that out of control feature that could encompass one's existence. Reaching Tiamat occurred only after long periods of isolation, physical deprivation and self-torture. It was written that during times of distress, the human psyche was taken over by the monster, Tiamat. Tiamat embodied both fear and desire, two of the under emotions. The monster lays dormant in most people like a destructive seed waiting for the misery of life to enter the soul. Tiamat waited until one's life became blackened by circumstance and visited by the darkness of sickness and despair. The monster then entered the soul in periods of weakness. It was then that Tiamat emerged from one's inner bowels to challenge for supremacy over the body and soul. Once Tiamat awoke and inhabited a human, it took extraordinary internal discipline to cleanse the soul and vanquish the monster. If Tiamat won the battle for the soul, eternal madness and suffering followed. Many people who lost the battle with Tiamat became obsessed with the trivialities of life and became possessed by their fears. People controlled by Tiamat wandered through existence in a dark tunnel of life. They became void of substance and utterly haunted.

In times before recorded history, the monster, Tiamat, laid claim to the heavens and ruled the pantheon of the gods. He was unchallenged for supremacy amongst the godlike creatures. In an epic confrontation, Marduk, the true God, finally defeated Tiamat. Marduk vanquished Tiamat to the depths of human sufferings. His decree for punishment: Tiamat must prove himself by conquering the spirits of both the weak and strong. His order was that the monster would gain little by overcoming the weak willed, but overcome the strong, the priests and the nobles. Then, with every victory, the monster would rise closer to his salvation and be able to return to the heavens.

During the rights of passage all the young priests had to engage in periods of extended isolation in the desert caves. It was a dangerous time and many succumbed to the madness and fear that it brought. Ningizzida had fought the madness and conquered the monster,

Tiamat, regaining and saving his inner soul. The master, in seeing Ningizzida emerge from the caves, proclaimed that he had visions that Ningizzida had crushed the monster, Tiamat, and now possessed the clarity of vision.

According to legend, everyone carries around the monster, Tiamat, within our immature souls. The book of creation reads:

"Tiamat, the almighty, was foremost amongst the deities in the heavens. His rule over the worlds was harsh and there was unrest in the seas and heavens. The warrior god, Marduk, emerged to bring justice back to the heavens. In bowing to the master, Tiamat shamelessly pleaded with Marduk for mercy. The omnipresent Marduk allowed Tiamat to withdraw into the souls of humanity, into the depths of the clouds.

The monster lives within all life. It stays sleeping, only leaving its den for periods of madness. The battle is continuous for the host, for Tiamat will probe for moral and spiritual weakness. The monster is very deceptive, using unusual trickery to accomplish its tasks. If given space in one's mind, it will suck the bones dry of its life sustaining energy. It controls many more souls than it loses. When fear controls one's actions, you become a servant of the monster and you are destined to fail.

Tiamat is the first natural enemy of man for he is raised by the fears of existence. The monster lurks, living on every road, behind every tree, inhabiting every living organism. When Tiamat controls the soul, all advancement ends and action is dominated by the need to vanquish the fear. Green leaves become brown, branches turn brittle and unbending, animals fall easy prey to hunters, rivers dry and fish gasp for breath. No living thing escapes his darkness."

Many succumb to the monster's desires and temptations on their way to their destiny. Who rules the soul is the first obstacle that must be overcome on the trip to succession and eventual understanding of the pure Apsu. It is not until you can vanquish your own inner fears that you see with a clear eye. Until that time your fears and desires rule your life. It is not until you are able to conquer yourself that you could study the Enuma Elish. It was a special honor, to be able to reach the pinnacle and be allowed to learn the secrets that are housed in the seven tablets of creation.

The seven tablets of the Enuma Elish explain the creation of the world and when understood, guided priests to states of nirvana and enlightenment. More importantly the books reveal the underlying solution to every human problem. The Enuma Elish outlined in elusive and nonrepresentational ways, how an individual can communicate with the gods.

The third of the seven tablets explain the use of the psychic smoke. If one knew how to read the smoke, all mysteries of life and death were revealed before you. Special candles were used in these prophetic rituals. And if one could read the future with any accuracy, one could control the world. The Sheshgallu believed that was his destiny. Ningizzida knew that the only thing more precise than the psychic smoke in its predictive power was the Delphic Oracle that lay north of Athens. He instinctively despised the Oracle for it could challenge his own supremacy of the heavens. Even the ancient Hebrew texts did not match the seven tablets of creation.

These old testaments of the Enuma Elish were the foundations of the priest's power over his flock and their hidden secrets which controlled every aspect of life. Understanding the holy smoke gave one access to the future. But accurately reading the smoke took many years. The ability to read the smoke was one of the steps leading to the joy of the Apsu. But the Apsu too had its challenges. Once engulfed by its power, breaking away, back into the world of humans was a challenging accomplishment. For the contentment that the Apsu brought and the world of its illusion was far preferable to any realistic existence.

The King of Ur remained silent as the old priest fell into a deep trance. After an hour, the King himself began to doze, still exhausted from his journey, and overcome by his lack of food and the sensory surroundings. He silently wondered whether it had been worthwhile to bring his problem to this old man. The thought itself, the silent questioning of the Sheshgallu made the King's stomach cramp and he cringed at the thought. His skin was now pale and blotchy, and his heart fibrillated, seemingly wanting to leave his chest. But his city was suffering, and he needed to know whether it would be advantageous to raise an army and attack Kisch. Sargon wanted the great prophetic priest to gaze into the future. He needed to start his journey back to his people, and as he sat while the priest meditated, the people of Ur starved. Suddenly Ningizzida opened his eyes. They looked ablaze again as he glared through the King of Ur. The sudden change almost took Sargon aback. The priest began to speak, but his voice was gravely, and low. ***"Sargon, why are you upset? Your soul is troubled."***

With deference, Sargon looked to the ground, *"Sheshgallu, you see the future. The god, Marduk, has put his faith in you. I have put my faith in you. I sit on your floor and shiver, I am not a man given to fear, but my people suffer and cry. I am not a violent man, Sheshgallu, but my blood is beginning to grow hot. I must know your insight. Please, Sheshgallu, please help the people of Ur."*

"Return to me, King of Ur, this evening," uttered the priest, *"Your future and the future of your people will be determined then."*

After ten years of studying the Enuma Elish, Ningizzida was ready to leave the monastery in Mesopotamia and the protection of Baldigul-el. Baldigul-el was close to death at the time. Regardless, Ningizzida knew that he needed to venture out and establish his own supremacy, his own dominion. Besides, Baldigul-el was worn and his lessons repetitive. The songs of his methods no longer rhymed, and his words rang dry.

After leaving the security of the monastery, Ningizzida wandered for over a year. He was waiting for a delfic sign. Which direction held his destiny? After a year in the desert, Ningizzida eventually became head priest of Ashur, a mid-level city. Although he believed this position was below his celebrated training, his meditations led directly to this place. Ningizzida spent seven years in Ashur. His reputation and power grew exponentially in Ashur as his prophecies and the stories of their accuracy spread over the desert. Then, one night during a hallucinogenic trance, Ningizzida abruptly left Ashur, showing himself at another monastery in Bisitun. He had never been there before, but he knew it was the next step on his path. After two years in Bisitun, his name was being spoken in the same breath as the deities. He was considered God's representative.

After a vision, Ningizzida took a journey to the golden city of Babylonia, the capital of his religious belief. He preached outside of the great white walls of Babylonia that the city was now facing a new threat. It emerged from the incumbent high priest who was old and frail. The threat that Ningizzida prophesied was that the old priest's power had desiccated, and God no longer paid attention to the ranting of the old soul. Then an unexpected event intervened, and the high priest of the golden city of Babylonia died of a mysterious disease. In fact, a plague spread through the city killing many of its inhabitants. Still not in the city, Ningizzida preached that he had foreseen the plague, and that it was God's way of

clearing the path for the new Sheshgallu.
Before long, the great city of Babylonia
came calling, wanting to recruit God's
apparent new representative.

Another life changing event happened
when the young priest was teaching in
Bisitun. His strong and charismatic
preaching reached all the way to Susa,
the capital of the Persian Empire. The
great King Darius heard of this young man
and traveled to hear his words. Darius
was struck by the words and brought the
young priest to his table. The two men
immediately felt a bond and became close
allies.

Ningizzida was offered the position of
high priest in Babylon only after
considerable debate within the inner
circles of the city. It was clear why
Ningizzida met with such resistance
within political circles. The powers
that were fearful of him and worried that
this aggressive priest would eventually
supplant their power. They were not naïve
in their concern. The King of Persia,
Darius, supported Ningizzida and once
Darius made his wishes known, debate
essentially ended. Ningizzida had
already learned about political intrigue
and unknown to anybody, had bribed one of
the lesser priests who was in the group
of elders choosing the person to ascend
in Babylon. In his typical style
Ningizzida did not return a favor for a

favor. The elder priest died under unusual circumstances two years into Ningizzida's tenure.

Once within the power base itself, inside the great City of Heaven, Ningizzida's influence increased geometrically. His command of the interpretation of the smoke quickly became evident, enhancing his power that much more. By reading the smoke from the spiritual candles, Ningizzida had helped many officials make the correct decision within the power struggles of government. With every correct prediction, the official not only paid large sums of gold but were now in debt to the priest. Knowing they were now beholden to him, Ningizzida regularly held this debt over their heads. The ritual and ceremony of the smoke reading was complex and came from primordial scrolls. It was thought that the original basis for the readings came from the Sealand peoples of the southern end of Mesopotamia. The candles were brought from the Ziggurat Temple at Ur. Their scents had a pungent amber rose smell when lit. The candles burned very hot and the colors that the flames produced were dramatic. It was in fact, the colors that the flames omitted in conjunction with the pattern of the smoke that made the interpretation so complex.

For the reading, Ningizzida would sit in the center of the room in total darkness. The person asking for the reading sat opposite the priest. They had to have two cuts on their arms, both of which had to bleed during the ceremony. Ningizzida began chanting almost a half hour before the candles were lit. The path to the gods had to be prepared before the cleric was able to walk on it. Most of the people sitting in front of the priest could not understand the chanting as the language used in the ancient ritual was Akkadian. Eventually the candles were lit while the priest was deep in a sacred stupor. Next to the priest were three small wooden boxes. In the boxes were small clay figures colored in black and red. The priest would caress the figures as the smoke began to rise. The candles produced colored smoke. A person's future was told by which color rose first and how the colors intertwined.

The Sheshgallu was well trained. He had enhanced his knowledge of scriptures in the temple that was known as E-Sharra, the heart of the city of God. He was an expert in the interpretations of the smoke. From a very young age, Ningizzida became aware that he was a natural interpreter of the future that was foretold in the smoke. The old priest now professed that he had the power to keep the gods out of the internal politics of the city by understanding the smoke and how God conversed to mortals. He spent many hours in meditation over these mysteries until he could accurately read their meanings. His epiphany came during one of his cleansing fasts. It happened after the fifteenth day when Ningizzida was close to delirium and dehydration. He was becoming depressed from his lack of sustenance during his isolation. Ningizzida envisioned that he was visited by an apparition sent by the one god, Marduk. The legend would be told that the spirit schooled Ningizzida in the smoke, because when he emerged from his seclusion he had new insight into the desires of the gods.

Ningizzida was not only revered but feared by most. Some even considered him a true dreamer, but Ningizzida knew that his dreams were only hints at what the gods truly wanted him to do. His skill was being able to decipher those messages that were important from those which were incidental and supplementary. Ningizzida knew that the gods sent many false signs as a way of teasing and misguiding men. When he had a dream, he would immediately consult the smoke. The meditations were the key to his destiny. As a young cleric, Ningizzida had spent hours and days in isolation. Many times he crossed the line between sanity and madness. Within his seclusion, Ningizzida saw many apparitions, some of which were the monster, Tiamat. Ningizzida also had frightening visions about the end of the civilized world. During one of his extended fasts, Ningizzida saw the world engulfed in godly flames, burning every soul to cinder. The hallucination petrified the young priest, and it took some time for him to return to his isolation sacraments.

PERSIA

CHAPTER II - MANISHTUSU

Ningizzida was also part of the priesthood that was known as Erib-biti. He was trained in all aspects of the religious ceremonies and how to please the gods. He was thus able to lead the important ceremonies to honor the god, Marduk. Being the Sheshgallu, Ningizzida also had had the role of the Kalu in Babylon. He could exorcise any of the evil spirits that would dare to inhabit his parishioners. It was very unusual that one man could hold all three of these distinctions; a reader of the smoke, a dream interpreter, and a Kalu. These powers were central to Ningizzida's unparalleled reverence within Babylonia. In truth, his power and recognition extended as far as Canaan in the east and to the borders of the Qjang people in the west. And powerful he was. Only the great King of the Empire, Darius, surpassed his influence. Ningizzida was even more powerful than the many politicians and minor Kings that he advised, and they all knew it. They paid tribute to him and they bowed to the God he believed in. The people were more fearful of the powerful priest than of any deity that they could not see. God was transcendent, whereas Ningizzida was tangible.

Sargon, the King of Ur returned to the priest's residence as the sun set. He had been there before, but the room was transformed. The frankincense was gone and there was a stale odor and almost a cloud that filled the air. Sargon was astonished at the change. A small stool was stationed to the left of the King and a naked slave ushered him to it. It took a few minutes for Sargon's eyes to adjust to the dimly lit space. The room was also very warm, and Sargon began sweating almost immediately. There was also a new strange, sweet smell in the room and

Sargon felt nauseated. Within a few minutes, the Sheshgallu entered. It was dark, but Sargon identified him from his posture, as his face was covered with a dark red paste. Sargon could hear the chanting in the background as the protector of souls walked. A second priest entered a few steps behind the ancient one. The second man carried a blue stone dagger. The second priest approached Sargon and reached down grabbing his arm. The King had heard about this ceremony so he was not surprised at the action. With surgical precision the priest cut into Sargon's arm. Blood immediately appeared from the incision. The priest watched how the blood began dripping and turned to Ningizzida and said something in an unrecognizable language. The priest turned back towards the King and grabbed his other arm. He completed the same procedure. The priest then dragged his hands through the bleeding King's arms.

As the King watched, the secondary priest repeated the same cutting procedure on Ningizzida. With his arms and tunic covered in his blood, Sargon was asked to walk to the center of the room. Again, he sat on the stool directly opposite the great Sheshgallu priest. Still chanting, Ningizzida's tone now varied, growing louder with each lament. Having left the room, the second priest now returned with two very thick black

42

candles. As the priest lit the candles, Ningizzida finally opened his eyes and Sargon flinched as he saw white eyes with no pupils. Sargon felt his body go ice cold and began to shiver. He began to unconsciously adjust his clothes and rock in place.

The flames of the candles sparkled and the reflection of the colors in the Priest's eyes created a ghostly image. Finally, in what seemed like an eternity, Ningizzida scolded the King: *"You have lied to me, Sargon. You said your country was under siege from Kisch. The smoke says that your countrymen have been torturing men from Kisch. The people of Ur are not crying, but the people of Kisch are."*

Sargon began stuttering, but the priest held his arm up for silence. He continued: *"You must sacrifice to appease the god. You will decide which of your children will be delivered to this temple."*

Sargon flinched again. But this time anger seemed to rise on his face. He started to stand in protest but Ningizzida raised his bloody arm and the King buckled, falling to the ground in front of the table. Ningizzida rose and walked around the table reaching the prone King. *"You dare question my supremacy!"*

Ningizzida bent over and produced a knife from his sleeve. Without hesitation, the old man swung the blade gashing the King's chest. Sargon attempted to escape, but his legs were lifeless. A smile crossed the priest's face and he grabbed the King's hair. **"Did you know I enjoy blood? It rejuvenates my soul. I will watch you bleed until your body is void of fluid of all life. I will have a good night. You will soon meet the great God and your punishment will continue."**

And with that, the priest buried the knife under the King's ear.

****

The beautiful city of God, Babylonia was a satrap of the immense Persian Empire. The Empire was divided into provinces or satraps. Usually those were independent countries that were merged into the greater whole of Persia. Satraps were kept in line by force or intimidation. When a country allied itself with the great King, the country became one of the many satraps in the vast Empire. In most instances, the reigning King of the satrap could stay in power, as did their provincial religious beliefs. Thus, the term "King of Kings" was used when referring to the Persian monarch. The Persian Empire had many capitals, with the godly city of Babylonia being one of them. However, the true base of power arose from Susa.

Ningizzida's under lord's name was Manishtusu, who was himself a distinguished spiritualist. He was heralded as an interpreter of omens. Manishtusu had a large religious following in a distant satrap called Phrygia. Ningizzida had kept watch over the reports of the young priest's ascension toward greatness. Ningizzida took great pains and used many favors to bring Manishtusu into his service. Ningizzida knew that Manishtusu's skill was also legendary and worth all the sacrifice to bring him under his supervision. In some ways Manishtusu was as learned as Ningizzida himself and the old priest wanted to eliminate him as a rival, using his power in service of his own agenda. From the first day he arrived in the golden city, Ningizzida kept a close eye on his student. Manishtusu was after all, a Baru priest.

It was rumored that the great Baru priests could ascertain the will of the gods through reading sacrificed body parts. Manishtusu also knew the specific sacrifices that would satisfy the gods to cleanse a man's soul. Between Ningizzida's special gifts and Manishtusu's skills, Ningizzida felt untouchable. He organized this alliance with Manishtusu because he believed that with this support, he could even challenge the Persian King himself, if it ever came to that. For once he controlled the King, all Babylonia and Assyria was within his grasp. In fact, the entire Persian Empire would bow at his feet. To reach this level, Ningizzida knew that he had to humble the King of Kings. The King would then have no choice but to recognize his power and eventually bow to him. Ningizzida secretly believed that he had grown past Babylonia. He desired a larger audience. But challenging the Persian King was a very dangerous undertaking, even with the approval of the gods.

Suddenly, and without warning the rules had changed. History had intervened again in the fate of the Sheshgallu. The great Persian King, Darius, now lay dead in Susa. Darius was an ally and a devotee of the Sheshgallu. What Ningizzida had heard through the underground was that the great monarch was poisoned. Using his sources, Ningizzida ascertained that the conspiracy to murder the Persian ruler originated in the deserts of Egypt. This infuriated the Babylonian cleric for it meant that the bastard son of the Persian King, Xerxes, would inherit the monarchy. Ningizzida had gotten to know the young Persian heir apparent, as the great Darius had asked the Babylonian priest to "babysit" his son, Xerxes, whom he was grooming to take over the Empire. Of course, this was supposed to happen many years in the future, not so quickly. Five years previous, Xerxes became the viceroy of Babylonia, representing the Persian King's interests in the heavenly city. In his years in the position, Xerxes alienated Ningizzida with his obnoxious and narcissistic personality. The priest tried hard to teach the young man who seemed to take every opportunity to irritate the Sheshgallu priest. If Ningizzida wasn't fearful of Darius' revenge, he would have taken care of the Xerxes problem himself. And now, the egotistical Xerxes was the King of Kings, a very problematic pill for the priest to swallow.

Xerxes, unlike his father, was ruthless and revengeful. But what was worse was that he considered Ningizzida a charlatan, and the God he represented, a counterfeit deity. This problem now consumed the priest as his plans now had to be significantly altered to meet this inopportune change in fortune.

Within the last year, Ningizzida had decided to partially take Manishtusu into his confidence, revealing to him his broader plans. Upon hearing his grandiose desires, Manishtusu appeared stunned and unresponsive. Manishtusu locked himself away for thirty days to meditate and try to ascertain the future. It was a brutal self-discipline that the young priest had learned in his connection with the Hebrews. During his thirty-day retreat, he would refuse all food as a way of purification for his soul. Only then could he see what lay ahead. His lack of food and his continual chanting left him confused and close to death itself. This ritual, however self-sacrificing, was one also practiced by the Hebrews to speak with their God, and Manishtusu was aware of its power. Manishtusu had spent two years learning from Jewish hakhamim or sages. He learned about the divine realm and the mystical ways to create union with God. His study was called, darash.

On the thirty-first day of the fast, Manishtusu emerged from his self-induced trance to hail Ningizzida as his lord and pledge his allegiance to the old priest. Manishtusu was a very contemplative and quiet individual. It was also very difficult to read his feelings or emotions, but Manishtusu also emerged with a warning for his master. He entered Ningizzida's study and fell to his knees in front of his mentor.

With tears in his eyes he pleaded, *"My dream revealed an eagle, my lord. The bird flew high over the blue sky. Its feathers were elegant and its spread was beyond that ever seen in this world. It hunted for thousands of miles and even the lions feared its talons. When its shadow graced the land, all living things hid. And yet there was one animal that showed no fear to the majestic bird. On the ground, the gigantic arrow viper flaunted its lack of fear when the great bird appeared. By its presence in the open, it challenged the eagle for supremacy. The snake peered into the sky and told the eagle to leave its realm. I will make your eyes bleed, the snake boasted. You might rule the air, but I rule the rocks."*

There was a pause as Manishtusu swallowed hard. He was troubled and his face betrayed his concern.

"Continue," Ningizzida insisted, as his interest now peaked. His voice was graveled and guttural. It was as if his words were passing over hot coals as they left his throat. *"The snake and eagle battled for seven days, my lord. The other inhabitants of the desert were terrified and buried themselves in the sand. The eagle's talons raked the snake over and over. But the great serpent never lost his fear of the raptor."*

Manishtusu stopped his story, *"That is the end lord. It is a talisman, lord, foreshadowing the future."*

Ningizzida did not question the young devotee or ask him how the vision ended.

He turned away and walked to the window. The older priest finally responded, *"I, too, have read the symbols. I spent hours reading the smoke when you were away. I saw a great blue flame before the smoke extended upwards. The blue then unexpectedly turned to red. It has also have foretold the future. The smoke revealed to me the danger involved in challenging the young King."*

Ningizzida turned to face his young student. *"But I have learned that all great accomplishments are complemented by great fear and uncertainty."*

The young priest's face looked anguished. He was not comforted by the older man's words. *"I am anxious master. This course of action is very risky, and neither of us has seen a clear outcome. It makes me anxious to believe that we will not be as successful as we hope. Are you sure that the encounter you are considering is worth the risk? Would it not be better to secure our power first? If you believe that the Archemednian monarch will eventually take his army to Greece, then wouldn't that be the time to press our independence?"*

Ningizzida smiled again and turned towards him. *"You are correct, my young acolyte. But I must point out, that neither of our visions forebode failure.*

Besides, the viper fought valiantly against the eagle, did it not?"

Ningizzida knew that his acolyte was not a gambler as he was. That was another reason he trusted Manishtusu. He was not impulsive or given to impetuous decision making. *"Manishtusu, I will need your help after the Akitu ceremony."*

"You can depend on me, lord." Manishtusu assured.

"Good, Manishtusu, Good."

PERSIA

CHAPTER III - KING OF KINGS

The King was elegantly attired. His long Median robes were made of the finest lambskin and fit him perfectly. The dark gray color was the hue reserved for sacred ceremonies. He only wore this particular garment on special religious occasions. It had a sleeved coat and reached downward to his ankles. It was tradition that the sleeves were long enough to cover his hands. It was a sign of respect to the gods that his hands not be exposed. It showed that only God controls fate. Man is helpless without strength and at the mercy of the deity. The King's robe was fastened by braided, multi-colored cord and hung loosely over his shoulders. His undergarments were gold and perfectly contrasted his robe.

Because he was in a public place, the King's square shaped beard was impeccably tailored. He wore massive amounts of gold ornaments around both his neck and arms. On this occasion, he wore Babylonian earrings as a tribute to his hosts. His hair was tied in tight crisp braids, with white ribbons on the sides. On his head, he wore the Persian tunic which matched in color to his robes, again a sign of respect for the deity. The makeup on his face made him look sculptured. On his wrists, he wore the usual series of gold bracelets and cidaris. It took his adorners hours of preparation to achieve this exactness. Two of these special attendants would suffer the ultimate punishment for not perfecting the exact color that the King had stipulated and imagined in his mind's eye. This young King was very particular about his facial makeup. Before he ascended to the throne, the King had sent for celebrated tattooists from far away African lands. The markings on his face made his eyes look like a person from the far east, and eerily cat-like. The black curves originated at the corners of his eyebrows and curved both up and down forming a wave with both ends curling inward.

The vast Persian Empire spanned almost three continents. It consisted of many semi-independent countries call satraps. Each of these areas, although generally self-governed, were overseen by a Persian governor. Each local King was answerable to the Persian King. He was therefore known as "The King of Lands, The King of Peoples, and The King of Kings". He was more than just a monarch; the great King was accepted as the bridge between man and the heavens. His power was supreme and absolute.

The King of Kings was also adorned with a series of special fragrances. This distinct aroma was a mix of many ingredients, consisting in part of cassia, cardamom, spikenard, myrrh, and the fat of lions. He was spectacular in his elegance from head to toe. He drew attention and he savored it.

The King of Kings stood tall in his stance, daring eternity to strike him down. His stare was stoic and focused. But it was not the stare of a man looking in the distance; it was an icy stare, more reminiscent of a reptile or a raptor than a man. He not only wanted to exude confidence but more importantly, project dominance and invulnerability. He had learned from his father that staring at others was a sign of personal weakness. Your soul can be seen through your eyes. *"The King must be above others."*

His father had taught, **"You are closer to God than any other mortal. Let others stare at you. You must learn to see through others. They stare at you, not you at them."**

The King was a commanding and majestic sight to see. He was like a perfect painting where every color fit to perfection. There were no rough edges. Unlike other rulers, this man was very aware of his body and how he looked to others. He was in excellent physical shape and obsessively practiced his disciplines and exercises. He had one of the quickest swords in the Empire. The King practiced with salves brought in from the farthest corners of his lands. Even against the most skilled practitioners who gave immense effort, this young King rarely lost a bout. He was also quite proficient with a knife. There were many rumors that spread through the Empire about the young monarch, most of them centered on tales about his sexual prowess. Some told about his insatiable desire for young women, others told of his preference for men. In truth, sex was just an afterthought for this young monarch. His thoughts did center around conquest, but not of the intimate nature. This man viewed sex as a waste of his precious energy.

Although very intelligent, this young King was not emotionally complex. Life was black and white, and he spent a good deal of his psychic energy controlling the rage that boiled underneath the skin. He held tightly to what he believed and everything else was depraved.

The King's moccasins were imported from far away Egypt and a gift from what he thought was his ally in the West. They were made of elephant hide covered in part with leopard skin. The King of Kings had only heard of the magnificent trunked beasts that gave their lives for his shoes. He could only vaguely imagine what such a large animal looked like in real life, although he had many colored reliefs of the regal beasts.

The great King had travelled to this city of heaven because of a very special religious event. This observance was a Babylonian tradition of the highest order. Arriving in Babylonia a week before he needed to, the King had already paid homage to the primeval rulers of this glorious city at the tomb of Belitanes. The young King did not believe in the Babylonian deity that this ceremony honored. However, due to the importance of the alliance between the

Persians and the Babylonians, it had become tradition for the Persian monarch to honor the Babylonian god, Bel Marduk. He was told that taking part in this ancient tradition would bring him good luck in his future endeavors.

Everything about the King exuded confidence and his external mask did not betray his underlying apprehension and concern. His lack of inner calm arose from his knowledge that much would be at stake in the future, and the King was astutely aware of both the existing and impending danger, facing him personally and his Empire, which was now his to hold together. He spent an enormous amount of energy making sure that nobody could read this inner strain. He hid his feelings for he wanted others to feel sureness in his leadership. In that regard, Xerxes was a perfectionist which led to his preoccupation with his appearance. He always assumed a pose that drew attention to his attributes. If others they felt his uncertainty, his dominance would be threatened, as if hesitation became known, challenges to his sovereignty would surely follow. And yet, if one was astute enough, they would notice the small squint and the slight wrinkling of the forehead. When one ruled such a large and diverse Empire, any small weakness could be interpreted as an opportunity for those who sought their own domain.

The King had only recently ascended to the throne because of the unexpected and suspicious death of his father, Darius. Unlike the unfaithful and treacherous Egyptians, who were already revolting against his rule, the Babylonians were dedicated to the new Achaemenid King, or so Xerxes assumed. That loyalty was the reason that the King stood in this glorious city about to perform this ancient religious rite.

Babylonia was originally called Ka Dingirra, interpreted as, **"The Gates of the Gods"**, and its reputation for splendor was unrivaled in the eastern world. What made Babylonia special was its grandiose buildings and its unparalleled beauty. One entered the city through the Gates of Ishtar. Although the city was generally tan and lacked color, the Ishtar gate was blue and extravagant. It was marked by animals carved into enamels that offered their ferocity and splendor to incoming visitors. Figures of bulls and serpents were represented in precise rendition. Every tensed muscle, every expression of ferociousness was represented in exacting nature. It was built by Nebuchadnezzar II, who also built the hanging gardens to beautify the city.

The gate opened to the Processional Way and involved over one mile of boulevards ending at the exquisite temple of Esagilia. The shops and taverns that lined the boulevard were splendid and offered diversity to visitors and residents alike. The streets were kept spotless by the many slaves that were continually grooming the area. As impressive as the boulevards were, the Gate of Ishtar was special. It consisted of two dynamic stone pillars with arched entrance ways connecting both structures. Ishtar was only one of the wonders of Babylon. The tower of Babel overlooked the entire city, and the six-hundred-and-fifty-foot structure towered over the city. It had also been built by the Babylonian King, Nebuchadnezzar, as a tribute to himself. As spectacular as the tower was, it paled in relation to the hanging gardens. It was the tradition of the Babylonian rulers to create gardens in the middle of the desert, consisting of both plants and animals from the faraway lands that they ruled or were allied to. Again, slaves from every walk of life were imported to tender these lush biological and zoological gardens. This beautifully white walled city was surrounded by flourishing farmland. The walls that protected the city were multilayered with lush trees and shrubs seemingly growing out of the stone walls themselves.

This golden city with its gates of the gods, was located between the two great rivers of the Tigris and the Euphrates.

It was generally accepted that all life on earth originated in this plush Eden. Canals from the rivers fertilized the abundant countryside. This land supported many types of fruit trees and numerous grains. The Babylonians themselves were very astute traders, and the city was in the perfect place for trade routes intersecting both east and west.

The Persian King had almost grown up in Babylon, having spent many hours roaming the gardens. The young monarch didn't like admitting it in public but being in the solitude of gardens was one of the ways that he could relax his mind. Even though he was envious of some of the wonders of this city, this young King secretly preferred the royal palace at Susa and furtively resented both the people and the culture of this ancient city. Even though the King had lived in the city for years, it was only one of four capitals of his vast Empire, and his winter residence, but Babylonia still felt like a foreign city to this neophyte Persian King.

The King and his father, Darius, were builders, and they both took the creation and building of monuments to their greatness very seriously. The rebellious Egyptians had openly complained about their taxes, believing that much of the new architecture of the palaces in Persia was being procured from Egyptian funds. Egypt was a distant satrap of the Empire and had always been a hotbed of unrest. The King's father, Darius, had mysteriously passed away before he could put down this unexpected and treasonous revolt. The Egyptian priests of Buto had instigated and preached this revolution, becoming more and more vocal in their criticism of the great Persian King. The King of Kings swore that these magi would be punished. Xerxes had strenuously argued with his father about the religious freedoms that could exist in the various provinces of the realm. Xerxes had predicted that giving people such religious freedoms would eventually come back to haunt the Empire. His ominous prognostication seemed now to have been prophetic.

Darius had believed that when conquering a people, it was propitious to allow them their historical religious freedom. He believed that if conquered people could maintain their beliefs, they would have no stomach for revolt. Now that Xerxes was King, this would soon change. When he heard of his father's untimely death, the young King had angrily sworn blood vengeance. He went into retreat for a few days, both to calm his anger and contemplate his future. He would make the Egyptians pay for their insolence. There were even rumors that the Egyptian magi were behind the unexpected death of the former King. Even though Darius was vigilant and had slaves taste his food, it did appear as though he was poisoned. It was now up to the new King to quiet the rebellion and revenge his father's death to cement his legacy. He could not afford to look weak and the difficulty in Egypt would be his first adversity. If he did not respond with strength in putting down this insurgency, then other satraps would start believing that they also could revolt, and the Empire could disintegrate as quickly as snow in the sun. After this week of ceremony, the King of Kings knew that he had to return to his temple at Susa and raise his army of retribution. His thoughts rarely ventured away from this task. He promised the gods that the day of reckoning was near.

Before his sudden ascension, the King had served as the viceroy of Babylonia, which was his father's idea of a working internship the ultimate purpose of which was learning how to rule. Persia was a vast Empire, the largest of the known world. It stretched from the Indus River and the Hindu Kingdoms in the east, to Lydia and the Ionian Peninsula in the west. Because of the immense amount of territory, the King needed to secure the loyalty of the Babylonians for their land, and loyalty was central in both position and spirit to the Empire. He would soon have to prove his mettle and reassert his supremacy over the renegade Egyptians.

Although the new King of Kings stood in this ancient temple awaiting a solemn ceremony, he could taste the revenge in his mouth. When he thought of Egypt his skin flushed and his brow wrinkled. As his jaw was set in a stiff protrusion, his thoughts were being dominated by his need for vengeance, both against the Egyptians and further to the Greeks. Securing the Babylonians was a main part of the plan that prompted the King to participate in this ancient ceremony. They were allies that Xerxes needed for stability.

During his years of learning in this city, the future King had made some enemies. In the beginning, he was an inexperienced and a head strong governor, at times over reacting to rumor and innuendo. Darius was a charmer and converted this charisma to direct power. His son Xerxes did not have the seductive skills of his father. Xerxes inadvertently confused strength and physical power for charm and magnetism. Because of this, he spent many hours showing off and honing his physical skills. The young man couldn't understand why his bodily prowess did not bring him the respect that his father had, and he knew in his heart he deserved. In those early years, Xerxes had trouble controlling his random and capricious comments. Although he had since matured, there were still many in this ancient city who silently prayed he would go the way of his father, and the sooner the better.

Although spoiled and overindulged at times, the young King was nonetheless an accomplished warrior. He was an artisan with weapons. From an early age he was trained in the art of the sword and dagger. When he could control his considerable temperamental anger, the young King was a formidable opponent, directing his strength with precision and accuracy against his foe. As a child, the young prince would throw himself on the ground when frustrated. His face would redden and his bottom lip would curl. Darius was encouraged by this behavior, seeing it as foretelling the young man's strength. With his many mistakes, Xerxes gradually gained control over his emotions as he matured but even now as a young adult, when pressed on certain issues he could become explosive.

The future King was also trained by the most respected military technician and strategist in the Empire. His name was Hamath and he served the King's father, Darius, in all his conquests. Hamath was known for his defensive strategies and his uncanny luck in battle. Hamath was a grizzled, determined man, who was well-tested and tenacious. Three times over the years, arrows had caught his body in various places. Hamath appeared impervious to pain. He fought an endless battle with an arrow protruding from his side. His reputation was enhanced by the report that his side never swelled or turned red from the protrusion.

Darius had put Hamath in charge of the young prince at an early age. His charge for Hamath, known throughout the realm as "The Magician" or "The Teacher", was that if the young prince was not up to the task of ruling, then he didn't want him surviving his education. Darius wanted a hardened, focused and aggressive heir. He couldn't feel or show fear. The young prince passed many tests of strength, concentration and bravery. Hamath was a fair but often brutal teacher, not allowing his young student to rest or take comfort. Over the years, The magician learned to respect the young man for his resolve. During one training session, Hamath thought that he had broken the young man as he had fallen to his knees in exhaustion. Xerxes smiled, looked up at his teacher and spit on the ground. The magician, shocked by the irreverence of his student, smiled to himself taking joy in the inner strength of the young man. The young man was only 12 years old at the time, but Hamath never forgot the importance of the moment.

When the young prince was sixteen, one of his trials was a life-threatening ordeal. The old tradition to hail the emergence of a great warrior was usually saved for a young adult in his ascent to the throne of a tribe. But the young future monarch begged his teacher to allow him to attempt the trial. Hamath couldn't believe the audacity of the young man. He wondered whether his student had lost his senses at the request. At least, Hamath believed that his young apprentice might be delusional. When Xerxes approached him, Hamath was met by the fire of his stare and the rage in his heart. **"My prince, I respect your desire to attempt this trial. I have gained great respect for your heart simply asking for it."**

"You believe me brazen?" The young supplicant questioned, as he turned to face his master.

"Not brazen, lord. However, you place your life in jeopardy by this challenge. You must be alive to rule."

"Do you not believe I will triumph?"

"I do not doubt your aspiration and your strength, but I also value your life."

"Hamath, if you do not have faith in me I will not pursue this quest. The decision is no longer in my hands, it is in yours."

Hamath was stunned by the challenge and the temerity of his young charge. This primeval test could very well sacrifice his young charge's life, or wound him, leaving his disabled. The reason this passage challenge was almost outlawed was that it was so dangerous. And now, this young, brash adolescent wanted to resurrect the ancient challenge to prove his worth. Hamath knew that he had to agree. After all his training, he couldn't place doubt in the young man's mind. Not now, after he had learned so much and come so far, *"I believe you will triumph my prince."*

"So do I Hamath, so do I."

The young man, only sixteen, walked bravely to his teacher with no sign of fear. He leaned over to him and remarked, *"I believe that I can accomplish anything I set my mind on. The gods are with me. I can feel it. I have proven it in all the bouts you have placed me in. Until somebody proves differently, I must believe I will conquer. The world is mine."*

67

Hamath had to bow to this confidence and strength of will, whether he was eventually successful or died in the process.

***

The young prince was placed in a darkened room brandishing only his spear. He also had his ancestral Persian dagger tied to his calf. The knife was forty-two centimeters in length and had his familial tribal markings on the blade. The young prince kept his weapon razor sharp. At its head was the golden eagle pictogram that marked the strength of his purpose and the connection to his family tree. He wore no formal clothes, only a red scarf draped around his head the tail of which reached the floor. The young prince made his way around the room. Xerxes was memorizing every inch of the room. He watched how the little light that existed played on the walls. Xerxes took a few steps and knelt to the floor, smelling the ground. He needed every advantage, every slight bit of information that might tilt the scale to give him an edge. Xerxes instinctively knew that this was a dangerous challenge and he needed to focus his thinking and his strength. The young prince had also starved himself for 24 hours, believing it heightened his senses and directed his anger.

Xerxes knew the rules. He would be given no warning when the challenge would begin. It could be sudden, or he could be waiting for hours. He struggled to calm his emotions and his pounding heart. The prince needed to reach out with all his finely tuned senses and prepare himself for whatever this ordeal entailed. He could feel the perspiration running down his waist betraying his anxiety. Finally, after surveying the entire space, Xerxes stood as still as he could with his back against the wall preparing his defenses for imminent attack. His proprioceptive organs were on fire as he anticipated the start of the test. He felt more alive than he had ever felt. Time disappeared in this vacuum, and even with his eyes adjusting to the darkness, the prince was partially blind. The prince knew that the elimination of time in his mind would allow him to hone his defense. He crouched down, assuming that whatever was going to stalk him also had limited sight. But he was aware that some predators hunted in the dark.

The prince's first warning was the scent. It was a strong odor, clearly that of a wild animal. He could feel the air move as the animal entered the room. He heard the breathing and a low growl, immediately identifying the tendencies of a male lion. The prince knew lions well. However, this would be the first time he was enclosed with one in a small space. The prince had hunted the great beast but was always out in the open, being free to move about and strategize an approach. While hunting, the prince had shown little fear of the great beast, often challenging the largest of the males in the pride. He would hunt them with spear and sword, refusing to use the bow. He said he wanted to be close and feel the animal's sweat. But what he really wanted was to see fright in the fearless beast's eyes.

Immediately the young King evaluated his position and his place within it. **"My task is to outthink and kill this beast before it does the same to me."**

The prince's eyes narrowed.

"There can only be one survivor, and by god, it will not be the beast."

The composed prince could feel the lion moving. He could sense the air moving. The lion's smell was also distinctive. It was a rank smell, reminiscent of rotting flesh. Its odor was pungent and easy to recognize. Xerxes could sense the odor moving, and although it filled the room, he could distinguish its movement. Xerxes also knew that the lion's vision, especially in the dark, was very superior to his, so he wasn't deluding himself that the predator could not see and identify him. He knew that the beast would not wait long to attack. It would pace nervously evaluating the situation. The lion had no fear; he knew the pacing would be followed by a lunge. Xerxes reasoned that the animal had been starved to arouse its energy and its desire for the kill. This was an advantage for the young King, as it meant the beasts strategies would be compromised by his need. The great creature would lunge at his throat trying to knock him down. Once on the ground, the beast would resort to using his formidable jaws to grab his neck and suffocate his lungs.

Surprisingly, the prince was not frightened. He had been trained for these life and death situations. It wasn't his training that vanquished his fear; it was that the young prince didn't believe he could die. He couldn't see it and therefore was immune to its influence. The animal did have a weakness and the prince knew it. His low growl and musty smell was betraying his whereabouts. The animal did not understand that his enemy was blind to him and that his vocal excitement evened the odds for the prince. His lunge would be preceded by silence.

Unbelievably confident, the prince now assumed that he held the advantage. His intelligence and strategy would need to be applied against the brute force of this creature. His strategy was to anticipate the lion's attack and let the beast make the first move.

Xerxes knew that he needed to clear his mind of all other thoughts and focus on the animal in front of him. Every random thought would weaken and slow his reaction. Then it happened. Xerxes sensed movement to his right. He knew the beast had crossed in front of him and was going to attack from the side. He maintained his breathing and wanted to hold his spear until the precise moment. He waited and waited, with each second seeming like an eternity. His ears were focused on the low growls waiting for a pause. His shaking had stopped and he had achieved a singular focus. His senses were heightened beyond any level he had felt before. He heard a change in the animal's breathing and anticipated that the time had arrived.

Instinctively, the prince began the swing of his blade. The prince's guess at the animal's approach was correct. He dropped to one knee and swung where his chest had been. Xerxes felt a blow on his cheek which knocked him to the ground. The animal's claw had caught his cheek. There was little pain and Xerxes tasted the blood in his mouth. Xerxes' reaction was automatic. He rolled to his left as the lion hit the wall that had been behind him. Xerxes heard the bump as the beast caromed off the boundary. As the beast was stunned by hitting the wall, Xerxes swung and slashed the animal's hind quarters. The lion roared in pain and anger at the assault. Xerxes continued to move, rolling again, but this time to the right. Even though he was still dazed, the male lion almost stood up on his back legs and roared his displeasure. Even though wounded and in pain the lion slashed out at the King again cutting him, but this time on the chest. Xerxes fell backwards from the blow. He quickly bounced himself forward ending on his knees. The lion continued to roar with saliva streaming from the sides of his jaw. Xerxes eyes had recovered from the dark and noticed the lion was clearly favoring his right side. Instinctively, the young prince knew that the beast was more injured than he first imagined.

The young male lion again reared back and readied himself for another lunge. The animal could smell the blood from the prince's face and stomach. Xerxes himself appeared to be impervious to the pain, as he readied himself in a crouch position. The lion's tongue began to hang out of the side of his jaw and the young prince knew that he was reaching the end of his energy. Xerxes also knew that although wounded, this animal was still capable of tearing his body apart. A wounded four-hundred-pound animal was like a man protecting his family. Xerxes knew he had to be patient, control his fear and the temptation to overreact. He wanted the lion to make the next offensive move.

After a few minutes of low growling, the noise finally stopped. It was time. The final play would be made within seconds. Xerxes and the lion exchanged glances. Both were breathing heavily. The lion's eyes gleamed with hunger, his mouth open and dripping with saliva, anticipating a meal. The prince tried to stare down the animal. Even in the dark room he believed he could see both anger and fear in the animal's eyes. The silence was followed by what the prince had anticipated - the angry creature jumped toward him with claws outspread. Almost at the exact same moment, the young monarch tumbled forward again under the animal's stomach. In the same motion, he swung his spear upward as the lion passed overhead. The blade punctured the animal's neck, with the beast's own weight cutting his own throat. But the wound was far from fatal. The young lion had flung itself through the air at the adolescent. The prince had thrown his body to the ground as he swung, but the force of the great beast landing on his body and its heavy head knocked the prince into semi-unconsciousness. Though the lion was wounded, his back paw struck the prince on the top of his head as he fell, cutting a gash almost ten inches long in his forehead.

   Although he could taste the blood on his face, the prince's next movement assured that the lion would not recover for a second strike. The animal had underestimated his adversary and it cost him his life. Hunger had dominated its movement. The future monarch had known that the lion was not used to combat with an adversary as deadly as he was. The animal had sharp claws but relied more on his wits and instincts than his speed. Even though wounded, the lion somehow managed to gain its footing. The anger and distress of the beast filled the room with hideous sound. The battle was not over, as the King of the jungle would not easily succumb to this adolescent human, for he knew not of the princely reputation. The animal took a tentative step toward Xerxes. Now with consciousness fully regained the young prince tried to focus on his wounded adversary. The blood dripped over his face partially blinding him. He swung weakly at the beast but missed horribly. The animal now lunged again, but this time weaker and with less strength. Xerxes had also regained footing and gracefully stepped aside letting the animal pass. but as it did, the young monarch thrust the knife again into its neck. But even with this second blow the lion did not relent. The dance repeated itself numerous times, with the lion attempting to reach the Prince and the young monarch avoiding its grasp and striking. For ten minutes, the King of the jungle began losing its legendary strength and stamina. Two single movements were all it took to end this dance macabre. These were practiced thrusts with an exertion of energy that focused lethality. Xerxes now lay dazed covered with both his own and the animal's blood. His mind was transfixed with both fear and adulation. His throat was dry and time had disappeared. The young prince felt no pain even though he watched his own blood flowing.

On unsteady legs, the prince rose from the floor almost falling over a few times. He stood silently against the wall and listened to the last factions of breath leave his adversary. He didn't smile at his success, but he wasn't surprised by it either. As he rested his head, the prince whispered to the walls that he wasn't meant to die that day. He reached up and felt the large, deep gash in his head. Although he didn't feel much pain, dizziness began to overcome him. He took his bandana and tied it over the gash. The prince bent over the now dead lion. He stroked its mane and silently apologized to the beast for his life. But Xerxes knew that the lion's spirit was meant to serve him

PERSIA

CHAPTER III - AKITU

It was the Babylonian month of Nisan, and time to perform the New Year Festival of Akitu. Although the King of Kings was secure in his own unlimited powers, he was by nature a superstitious man. It was part of the reason that he was at this festival. He didn't want to offend any deity. Once he made up his mind he could be decisive and fanatical in his dedication. But until the time that Xerxes could settle his thoughts in one direction, he could appear to others as being diffident and wavering. In private, his advisors had preferred to call it contemplative. The young King had always admired his father's natural command of decision making. When his father, Darius, died unexpectedly, the power void brought immediate questions about Xerxes' rightful accession. After his father's death, the prince had heard the rumors and his advisors had apprised him of the unsettled nature of some of the provinces.

After finding out his father had been murdered, Xerxes, although still in mourning, allowed the teacher, Hamath to enter his room. It was tradition that the prince should isolate himself for three days after his father's death, **"My Prince, my heart is bleeding over your pain."**

Xerxes was sitting with his back to his mentor. He hesitated to turn as his eyes were red with pain and loss. Hamath just sat waiting for the Prince to ready himself. Suddenly Xerxes muttered in a low voice. **"He was murdered Hamath. My father was murdered."**

Hamath remained silent, allowing his young student to vent his frustration.

"I want them dead! I want them to burn. I want them now."

The soon-to-be-King suddenly began pacing. Hamath could see the heat radiating from his head. It was the most uncontrolled emotion that he recalled observing of his young apprentice. Xerxes was having difficulty keeping his body still and his movements were spasmodic not smooth. His gaze was also distant and he avoided direct eye contact. Hamath remained silent as the King vented his bile. Xerxes began picking up objects and throwing them against the wall. *"I feel useless, Hamath."*

The teacher after a great long pause assured, *"I know you are angry my prince. But there are greater issues here than your fear and self-pity."*

His eyes wide open and still teary, the young, soon-to-be-monarch, stared with empty eyes at the only man he trusted in the world. Hamath continued, *"You now have a bigger purpose my prince. You cannot be sidetracked away from your destiny. Unless you focus on taking and holding power, the satraps will fall away from the Empire like rain from the sky."*

Hamath grabbed the prince by the shoulders and looked directly in the red, swollen eyes. *"You **must** secure your ascension."*

The soon-to-be-King knew that he was transcended from eight former rulers, stretching back to Cyrus II. His patrilineal rights to the crown were indisputable, his lineage clear. Others in the Empire, of course, did not accept these conclusions.

His father, Darius, also had a rough road in his ascent to the throne. He had to oust the usurper Gimirraya, who initially threatened his authority. Gimirraya was also a magus, but he was a follower of the Lie, not a follower of the true God, Ahuramazda.

Having heard the stories about his father's experiences, the new King knew that the magi and other religious leaders were lethally treacherous and not to be trusted, for they lusted for power and control beyond their spiritual realm. As precariously as their loyalty was, they were potentially helpful individuals within his realm. Thin ice to walk on. The magi often had the pulse of the people. The King was not afraid of any earthly creature, but the deities had to be appeased, and these priests knew the will of the gods, or so they claimed. Because of his cautious and superstitious temperament, the rumors around the royal palaces were that the new King would become overly influenced by his trusted eunuchs, magicians, and other political and religious advisors. Of course, the truth was that Xerxes trusted very few.

The room in which the young King waited for this current Babylonian ritual was very old and revered. It was eloquently decorated with reliefs depicting sacred events in Babylonian history. Unlike other places in the temple, this room was very colorful, with reds and blues in every corner. Xerxes, for all his faults, loved color. He despised the grayness and sparsity of the desert. The ceiling of the room depicted a violent storm that shook the roots of Sumerian culture. There was a poem written in ancient script:

"On that day, the tempest fell from the sky
The seven winds seared the heavens
Ishkur howled with his anger
Great hailstones blanket the ground
And the backs of the people bled like the river."

The King's father, Darius, had stood in the same place and performed this same ceremony. Having spent the last few days in the Etemenanki Ziggurat, which was the special residence for the ruler of this celestial city, Xerxes was ready to return to his home in Susa. The Etemenanki Ziggurat was a holy place in Babylonian culture as it was believed to be located at the confluence of heaven and earth. The special residence sat at the side entrance of Esagilia, the temple of the Babylonian god, Marduk. Xerxes was prepared to make believe that the Babylonian god had some influence. Such things were necessary for a man who ruled many nations of people.

For this ceremony, the King was surrounded by his entourage, which today did not consist of any of his advisors. This was a ceremonial event, not a diplomatic one. To bring his advisors would be an insult to his hosts. With him stood his three bodyguards, each of whom was sworn to protect him with their lives. The Babylonians reluctantly allowed the bodyguards to attend this event. His father, Darius, had never asked for bodyguards, so why did this young, foolish King need such protection? Was it not sufficient to know that the Babylonian people were his closest ally?

The Babylonians preferred that the King be surrounded only by his handmaidens. They preached their loyalty and felt an underlying uneasiness about this skittish, and some believed, paranoid monarch. There was also a low but noticeable reaction from the crowd at the ceremony when they noticed the beauty of the women that accompanied the King. The King always surrounded himself with the most beautiful of women in the Kingdom, and yet he believed he was ultimately more attractive than any of them. He held that the beautiful women only allowed the world to compare others to his own perfection.

As he stood, the young King felt his jaw beginning to clench. Patience was not an easy discipline for Xerxes. The King did not like the waiting, especially for a meaningless ceremony. Others should wait for him, not he for others. He had to stand perfectly still during this pre-ceremonial time and be careful not to engage anyone's stare. He had learned from an early age not to look directly at others. He was taught that such a weakness would allow others to know his thoughts. He had been warned by his teachers and his father that some were able to gain access to his soul through your eyes.

This was a good test of self-discipline for the emerging monarch, for in the audience on this day sat two of his chief adversaries in this primordial city. Both were large landowners and controlled much of the secular power in Babylonia. If they so decided, they had the influence to foster a revolt against the Achaemenid dynasty. Of the two men, Shamah-eriba was potentially the most dangerous. He controlled the most foreign-born slaves and political influence within the city. Many had mistaken his short stature for weakness, a mistake that had cost many their lives. Shamah-eriba appeared unobtrusive and unassuming, but underneath that placid surface lurked a vicious and revengeful man. On this day he sat in his customary place to the right of the pulpit. Next to him was his impeccably dressed wife and children. The entire right quadrant of the temple was made up of tribesmen and allies of the influential leader. Ningizzida, the influential old priest, was a close ally of Shamah-eriba, but was also a potential adversary of the King. Shamah-eriba was externally quiet and restrained, using his influence behind closed doors and in shrouded alleys. Belshimanni, the other major landowner and powerbroker in Babylonia was just the opposite of Shamah-eriba. He was boisterous, confrontational, and after over consuming wine, quite explosive. His tribe and position were to the left of the pulpit.

Both powerful men claimed descendance from Babylonian royalty. Shamah-eriba claimed that his line could be traced to the great Hammurabi. His Amorite tribe was very proud of this connection. Belshimanni claimed a more interesting historical lineage. His tribe was descended from the great Babylonian warrior, Nabopolassar. Nabopolassar was a fiery commander who rallied the Babylonians against the Assyrians and was the force behind bringing Nebuchadnezzar to power. Belshimanni toasted Nabopolassar whenever he drank, blaming his own touchy disposition on this distant and questionable relative. When inebriated, he would almost claim to be the reincarnate of the old warrior.

The King was unaware that earlier in the week the two power brokers of Babylonia had a secret meeting. Being rivals, it was unusual for Belshimanni and Shamah-eriba to be in the same room. The covert meeting was brokered by the audacious priest, Ningizzida, and occurred at this very temple in a little-known room behind the great podium where, ironically, the young King stood this day. The two Babylonians, both proud and secure in their own power and influence within this city, were very skeptical of the hidden agenda, considering that Ningizzida was very secretive about its purpose. Both knew that the high priest could not be ignored and if he requested such a gathering, they had no choice but to comply. Each had informants within the church and sent messages to their people to find out the hidden purpose of the meeting. Neither heard anything but unusual and preposterous rumors.

Upon entering the temple, neither man was prepared for the scope and the danger of the plan that the priest was suggesting. It was an uneasy situation as both men entered the room. The

Sheshgallu had expelled their compatriots and advisors who accompanied the two leaders. This situation only increased the unease of the tribal leaders. The old priest began the process, *"My friends, we have known each other for many years."*

As a slave entered with drink, Ningizzida stopped his introductory comments. The slave left and Ningizzida followed him out, warning his acolytes not to disturb him again. Upon returning, he composed himself and continued, *"I have recently read the holy smoke and it has foretold a very disturbing future. A horrible pestilence will befall our city, eventually destroying every building and dwelling, until our lovely city is completely swallowed up by the desert."*

"Impossible, we live in the city of God." Belshimanni exclaimed, jumping out of his seat with fear in his eyes.

"Please, sit my friend," Ningizzida urged. *"The smoke foretells that this plague will be brought on us by the Persian imposter to the Median throne."*

Both men felt a chill because they both knew where Ningizzida was heading with this logic. There was quiet as Ningizzida purposely gave both men time to ingest this potentially hazardous information. Before he began again,

Belshimanni gave voice to what both men were thinking. *"Sheshgallu, to rise up against the Persian King is self-destructive, even if that King is young and stupid."*

"Be calm, my friend," Ningizzida said reassuringly, as he went over and patted the man on his back. *"An opportunity is arising soon for us. Our new birth is almost at hand. You can't be fearful of losing what you have for the world is soon to be transformed for us."*

He hesitated again, letting the tension hang in the air as he bent over with his eyes widening in excitement. Both men sat quietly, still stunned about the possibility of revolting against the infallible King.

"This young, stupid King burns inside my friends; it is a fire that will destroy him from the inside out. His anger will blind him as sure as the clouds cover the sun."

Ningizzida continued. *"He burns with hatred and it will undo him. He will test his hatred against our Egyptian brothers. The word that I hear from Samaria is that the priests are rallying against the Persian yoke. The smoke predicts that the Persians will raise an army and march to Thebes."*

"How is this an opportunity for us?
Belshimanni asked in puzzlement.

The priest turned to him and smiled.
"The opportunity for us will bloom like a desert flower after he conquers the Egyptians. The conceit of his triumphs will consume him and urge him to march against his real enemy, the Greeks. This will not be as easy a conquest as the Egyptians. He will need to take all his legions hundreds of miles to accomplish his march to the Aegean waters. This, my brothers, will herald a new opportunity for Babylonian freedom. This King needs us more than we need him. Babylonia is central to his vast Empire. We control the blood of the beast."

The priest now appeared to be locked in a religious daze as his eyes widened and sweat ran down the side of his cheeks.

"We will undermine the Persian government of our city and then align ourselves with the Persian ruler."

After a long while, Shamah-eriba shed his reticence and spoke up. *"So, we become slaves of the Median either way?"*

The priest again smiled *"I have seen the future my friends. The Greeks will destroy the blind King, which will leave a vacuum of power. His blind hatred for the Greeks will eventually destroy him. We will then be in position to fill the void. Don't you see? Our time has arrived! We are in the right place in history for our rebirth. Like Nabopolassar, we will rally our strength against an intransient enemy; and like Hammurabi our star will again become the brightest in the heavens."*

There was quiet in the room. Both men couldn't tell whether they were excited or terrified. Their throats were parched and energy ran through their veins and limbs. Their fate was being sealed. It quickly became evident to them that there was a very dangerous difference between talking and doing.

****

It was the fourth day of the religious celebration. Each day had its own significance and the scripted ceremony was strictly adhered to. The high priest was as ancient as the tradition he celebrated. Ningizzida had a mystical reputation and during this ceremonial time he was in his glory. He had been the chief magus of the city for what seemed like a century. His power was extensive, with its tentacles invading almost every aspect of Babylonian life. All important decisions in this ancient city eventually flowed through him. Ningizzida had spies and conspirators everywhere. But so did the King, having been outmaneuvered enough times by the old priest in his younger years to learn the importance of the secretive art. The priest and the King had conflicted over policy many times before this. There was no love lost between them. When in each other's presence, the two were forced to be ever heedful.

From his first glance upon the young prince when Xerxes was sent to Babylonia as Viceroy by his father Darius, Ningizzida had detested the boy. He disliked his disposition, standing with his nose above all others. He disliked his posture, always as straight as a Lebanese oak. The young prince's movements were graceful and fluid, almost unworldly. He was always perfectly dressed and ornamented. All these traits were diametrically opposite that of Ningizzida who was old, slightly bent, and considered himself the heart and spirit of the people.

After the smoke foretold Darius' upcoming death, Ningizzida had secretly hired the sand dancers to end the prince's life before he had the opportunity to ascend to the great throne. The sand dancers were a secretive sect of assassins. They lived somewhere in the desert and were bred for death. But, this attempt was thwarted by a soldier who had appeared out of nowhere to save the soon to be monarch. This failed attempt only angered the priest more and more.

Ningizzida had secretly supported one of the young King's rivals when Darius passed away. Ningizzida and the King's father, Darius, had established a mutual respect. But this young King was self-centered and irreverent, and never showed Ningizzida what the priest assumed was his due respect. That friction permeated their relationship. Ningizzida had seen this man as a foolish child, watched him make impetuous mistakes, and had outmaneuvered him in every confrontation they had.

This period was the most important observance of the Babylonian religious year. It was the cleansing period in which all sins were washed clean. On the first day of Akitu, Ningizzida arrived at the sacred Euphrates before sunrise, and slowly cleansed himself to become pure enough for the observance period. This was followed by a day long prayer period at the temple. Not only was the Supreme Being, Bel-Marduk honored on this day-long marathon, but his consort, Beltiya, was also paid homage. Her import could not be underestimated, as the scriptures told that she held seductive influence over the God. The priest was careful to give her enough deferential time to appease her soul and deter her wrath, for she could undermine even the most positive of events.

The second day of the ritual involved purifying the temple. Without the proper incantations, Bel-Marduk would curse the priest and the temple, and the year would bring untold hardship. The ancient purification ritual was meant to protect the priest and the ceremony from all evil. In these prayers, the god Marduk's earlier name of Asar-lu-hi was used. Long and prescribed incantations marked the ceremony. Ningizzida was only one of two living people who had memorized these important prayers. The incantations were shrouded in secrecy and circumstance and the Sheshgallu was reluctant to teach his disciples the secrets.

The third day of Akitu was marked by the summoning of the three most decorated artisans in the city. They were showered with gold and precious stones for the design and creation of two godly images. Both Bel-Marduk and Beltiya were elegantly drawn, with the colossus Bel-Marduk holding a snake in his left hand and a scorpion in his right. These images signified the supremacy that the god held over these deadly creatures.

But now the most important day of the holiday had arrived. It was during this ceremonial cleansing of the living deity that the Enuna Elish was recited. This ancient prayer was central to ridding the King and the holy city of spiritual impurity. Ningizzida now was in the unenviable position of having to cleanse and bless a man he despised, and unknown to anybody, plotted against. He was incensed at having to perform this ceremony honoring this egocentric man in front of his god.

This ceremony had been performed in this temple since time everlasting. Many old pictographic images appeared on the clay walls reaching back almost 1500 years before this ceremony appeared. Many monotheistic religious symbols were represented by animals, such as the intertwined serpents that adorned the top of the pulpit. Ningizzida, the Priest-God, lived in a part of the temple called the Egipar.

Finally, the King of Kings was led to the alter. The podium was lifted above everyone else to symbolize the supremacy of the god over all mortals. The King was slowly led up the ramp leading to the lectern. The center of the stage boasted a solid gold stature of Marduk. The rendering was twice as large as a man, with Marduk pictured holding his arms out to welcome his children. On the sides of the stage were three clay bowls of fire that provided the only light for the pulpit. Out of the floor came smoke and steam originating under the lectern and covering the stage in a haze. When the King stepped on the stage, the lower half of his body was covered by the smoke.

The Sheshgallu entered the holy alter from a hidden side door. It was as if he appeared out of nowhere as he seemed to ascend out of the mist. The King had preceded him onto the temple area and showed no surprise at the sudden appearance of the cleric, Ningizzida. The young monarch's forward stare was unflinching, although he felt his stomach tighten at the sight of his old enemy. He couldn't read any expression that suggested Ningizzida was irritated to have to perform this ritual with a King he felt was incompetent. After all, he was Xerxes, King of Kings, and feared nothing living. Since ascending to the throne, Xerxes had lost some perspective. He had become preoccupied with his position. The young King felt like he was indomitable. Not even this ancient priest, whose secret incantations were foreign to him, seemed to faze him. He was assured that his own priests had protected him against the unusual rituals of this ancient cleric. This old, Babylonian, alien faith was strange to Xerxes, and he only half believed in its importance. His father, Darius, the Great King, had taught him to show reverence to the gods, even those of distant lands.

Xerxes was led to the center of the stage as the lesser priests showered the area with petals of flowers. Smoke covered the floor emanating from the fires that burned at the corner of the alter. Zeba, Xerxes' most senior hand maiden, gently touched his shoulder indicating that it was time for him to kneel on one knee. Zeba, an expert in protocol, performed this ceremony with Darius many times before. She orchestrated Xerxes movements ensuring that the King performed all the steps in the correct order.

Xerxes took a step forward staring at the old priest whose wrinkled face was covered by the large hood that shrouded his head. He looked other worldly with a distorted expression. Before kneeling, Xerxes straightened his back and raised his sword to allow everyone in the temple to understand that the King of Kings only bowed to the gods. And even then, he would only give up his weapon only with reluctance. He replaced his sword and knelt in front of the alter. As the Priest raised his arm, an acolyte of his brought in a ram from the right side of the podium. It was a magnificent animal and was paraded around the gathering as the onlookers touched him with their shawls for good luck. The animal appeared to become anxious at this display and tugged at the rope that was firmly tied around his haunches. The ram was led back to the front of the alter and the priest continued his incantations. Again, Zeba touched Xerxes' shoulder. The King rose, and in a fluid motion removed his sword, quickly beheading the animal. The blood from the animal's body seemed to explode outward, covering the King's arms and chest. Xerxes reacted with no disdain, as he fluidly returned his weapon to its holder. This King was an accomplished swordsman. He prided himself on the acumen of his skill.

The old priest himself then fell to his knees. He raised his arms pleading with Bel-Marduk to rid the temple and the King of all evil. Satisfied that the sacrifice was accepted, the priest rose with the help of his subordinates and slowly walked to Xerxes. A second priest entered with a bowl of water. Gently the priest washed the blood from the King's hands and arms as he continued to pray. He did this in a tender, almost seductive manner, taking his time and exaggerating his movements. Their eyes met and the hatred between them seemed to heat the temple mount, again covering the stage with smoke. The priest smiled, released his stare with Xerxes, and gently took the King's crown and sword from him, placing them on the alter as gifts for the god.

Zeba touched the King's shoulder
again, signaling him again to fall to a
knee. The old priest slowly returned to
where Xerxes was kneeling. He then
reached back and slapped the King across
the cheek. The King's bodyguards
instinctively jumped, although Xerxes
quickly held his hand up freezing them in
place. As Xerxes reached his other hand
to comfort his reddened face, the priest
began dragging him to the alter, forcing
him down to bow before Bel-Marduk. By
this time, Xerxes' blood was seething. He
was told this was a ritualistic enactment
and not an actual assault. It took all
his control not to rise immediately and
punish this man. A sneer replaced his
mask of serenity. Even though this was an
ordained ceremony, Xerxes had difficulty
justifying this level of disrespect.
Although Zeba had warned him of the
assault, Xerxes had thought it was more
ceremonial and was outraged at the
strength of the physical attack. Never
in his life had he been struck in this
manner and this was not a ceremonial
touch. And then, while the King was down
in front of Bel-Marduk, the priest struck
again. The King, surprised and shocked
by this second assault, again covered his
face with his hand. He was sure, as he
lay in a crouched position, that this
second attack was not in the ceremonial
program but had been added by Ningizzida.
Xerxes was overcome with anger and fear

that this could be ushering in his last minutes of life.

The priest smiled, keeping his hand on the King's neck as he lay in front of the idol. Ningizzida raised his other hand to heaven and began chanting. The King attempted to move, but the priest had placed his knee in the King's back. Xerxes' guards struggled to maintain their composure watching this beating. Ningizzida struck the King again on the back of his head with his ceremonial staff causing a visible welt with blood spurting to the floor. Xerxes appeared to briefly lose consciousness. Ningizzida stood and faced the audience who appeared stunned by the severity of the events. Some of the parishioners were standing with their hands over their mouths. The faces of the guards were wide eyed in shock.

The priest pronounced, *"Marduk is pleased. He has shown his superiority over all men."*

He pointed down with his arm at the prone monarch. *"Even the Great King is subservient to the Great God. He lies unconscious at the God's feet. We are all at the God's mercy. No one can rise above Marduk, not even the great Persian ruler."*

He knelt next to Xerxes and with his hand on his head he forcefully pulled the King's head up. The audience could see a trickle of blood on the King's head and on his face. Ningizzida turned his head to the audience. ***"The red blood proves the King's subservience. He bows to the Great God."***

Ningizzida smiled, raised his hand and pushed the King's head hard to the floor. The King's guards had seen enough as they rushed to the pulpit.

They heard a rush behind them. The alter was engulfed in smoke and fire. The crowd could hear the great priest laughing as the smoke rose to cover all those on the dais.

With the entire audience standing in shock, Zeba rose and ran with the guards into the smoke. The smoke seemed to open for her. And then it engulfed her for a second. She slid across the floor, ending up by her fallen monarch who was now just beginning to regain consciousness. Xerxes rose to one elbow as Zeba began wiping his forehead and his head. She was crying as she attempted to help him to his feet.

Even in his weakened state Xerxes was reeling with rage. He was embarrassed that this old man shamed him in front of the populace. The thoughts flashed through his mind that here, in his first religious ceremony as the Great King, he was humiliated in this fashion. The fire seemed to explode in his gut and a thought rang through his mind that his entire reign could be colored by this moment, this disgrace. Others wouldn't see him as a self-confident decision maker but subservient, lying on the ground under the pounding of this old man. Xerxes looked around trying to focus his eyes and locate the priest. He grabbed Zeba and pulled her forcibly to him.

"Where is the priest? Give me my sword!"

The King's voice was shaking with rage. He tightened his grip on the young woman and began shaking her.

"Where is the priest?"

"I don't know, Lord, he disappeared into the smoke."

The King unceremoniously released his grip on the woman and in a blinding impulse started to wave his arms trying to fight his way through the smoke. He quickly reached the back wall and searched with his hands to find the secret exit. As he began acknowledging that his search was in vain, the King of Kings began to bang his fists on the stone wall that surrounded the pulpit. He gained control of his emotions turning to Zeba, **"Clear these people from the temple."**

Zeba hesitated, and the King demanded **"Zeba, I said now, I want the temple emptied, before I strike them all down."**

Still in shock from his ordeal Xerxes stood motionless. Although his arms were down his fists remained clinched. He was momentarily unsure of what to do although he knew that he didn't want an audience to report his actions. Zeba had given the order for the evacuation of the temple and the guards had responded with urgency. Xerxes now stood alone in the smoke. Within minutes there were no longer any worshippers in the temple and Xerxes moved forward on the podium. Another thought ran through his mind that he should have killed all the onlookers to ensure that this hideous event would not be spread and gossiped.

For the first time, the other handmaidens noticed his state and made audible comments, having never seen the great King either disheveled or injured. Two of them rushed towards him while the other hastily ran to find water and bandages. Xerxes was motionless. Thoughts were spinning through his mind but the rage continually reasserted control over him. Anger is a great motivator and helps one to focus. He began to realize that his anger for the priest could not be satisfied in this moment, and he began to accept that fact. He felt his limbs shaking a bit, partially from his temper and partly from his ordeal. As he sought to internally gain control of his feelings, he struggled with the desire to strike out at the first thing he saw. Xerxes turned and with his fists destroyed part of the pulpit. His anger was at the point that it needed death to satisfy its longings. Again, he focused and exerted effort at control. He neither saw nor heard the handmaidens attempting to straighten his garments and comfort his wounds. Xerxes began to walk slowly, almost in a trance, his mind whirling between chaos and command. All other senses were blocked as this inner struggle was being played out. His eyes were focused yet blank betraying his state of disorder. Zeba finally returned and took the King by the elbow gently leading him off the alter and towards his residential antechamber.

Midway down the center isle of the sanctuary stood Penish, one of the two guardians who had been allowed to accompany the great King to these proceedings. Penish seemed confused as well, his eyes wildly staring at the monarch as he slowly made his way towards him. As a lieutenant in the Guardians, Penish had not been taught to think. He had, from an early age, been trained without question to obey. A state of uncertainty was very unusual for his mind to comprehend. During battle at least, he felt clarity and purpose of direction.

Penish was a tall man with chiseled features. Although solidly built, he was not overly attractive, sporting a large nose and heavy eyebrows. His droopy eyes gave one the impression that he was regularly tired. Men had died misinterpreting this look which led to hesitation on their part and resulted in the ending of their lives.

Penish had attained a very special and valued state in the hierarchy of the Guardians. Twice in his life he had singlehandedly foiled assassination attempts on the rulers. The first involved the King's father, Darius. The second had occurred when he had been sent to Babylonia by Darius to deliver a message to Xerxes. He had entered the viceroy's residence and had noticed that there was a paucity of guards questioning him about his purpose in his visit. He immediately became vigilant and saw the feet of a guard protruding from behind a post. The man had obviously been murdered, and Penish's training immediately kicked in. As he began sprinting in the direction that he assumed led to the young viceroy's residence, again he noticed other bodies.

One man was groaning slightly and Penish assumed that the assassination attempt was still in play. As he ran, he instinctually drew his fine Persian blade and began preparing himself for assault.

Penish burst through the bed chambers to find Xerxes in a corner of the room also with sword drawn, surrounded by five men inching their way towards him. As the men reacted to the sudden noise of the door opening, Xerxes shoved his sword into the neck of the nearest of the attackers. The man gasped as the blood began spurting from his neck. With cat like quickness, Xerxes removed the blade and again backed into his corner assuming a defensive position.

In a full sprint Penish threw his body in the air sliding on his back across the room. The attackers were surprised by the unusual approach and before they could react, two of them had lost their legs. Penish had swung his blade and in one motion separated the other two limbs from the now screaming men. There was an instant of silence as their screams welled in their throats and they seemed to float for a second in the air. Penish planted his left foot stopping his slide and immediately rose to a crouch. Again, as if the movement was a scripted ballet, his blade swung beheading a third man. There was now only one man standing between Xerxes and Penish. This lone assassin immediately realized the failure of his mission and to both of their surprises lowered his sword. He turned towards Xerxes and bowed as if apologizing for his failure. The future King slightly bowed his head acknowledging the gesture and immediately impaled him with his blade. The blow was intentionally not lethal, and the man dropped his sword and fell to his knees. While this was occurring Penish raised his sword, placing it under the man's throat purposely meeting the young viceroy's eyes. Xerxes raised his hand and Penish froze statuesque. Xerxes approached the assassin now holding his side where the blade had entered. Xerxes, maintaining his distance, used his sword to raise the man's hair off his neck revealing a small red tattoo. It was the sign of the Sand Dancers. Xerxes' eyes widened at the revelation and he briefly met Penish's eyes which responded with recognition.

The assassin began to plead, *"**Please, lord, let your servant end my useless life.**"*

Xerxes walked in front of the man, his eyes focused on him, almost expecting another attack. Penish was also on guard and readied a stroke if the man attempted a move.

Xerxes again demanded, *"**Who hired you?**"*

The assassin was now breathing heavily gasping for air. Life was draining from his body. *"**Lord, I have no knowledge of these things. I am given a task and I carry it out the best I can.**"*

Xerxes shouted, *"**Who hired you?**"*

The man bowed his head in frustration. In his pacing, Xerxes turned to retrace his steps, and surprisingly, the assassin leaped toward the young man with a dagger in his free hand. He was obviously feigning his gasps and even though he knew that he wouldn't survive the day, he was determined to carry out his contract. He flew himself into the air, and as he did, Penish, with the swiftest and most fluid of motions, separated his head from his body. The man's beheaded body landed at Xerxes' feet and continued shaking as if it were doing a macabre dance. The young future King stared down in surprise at the unexpected occurrence, and as if mesmerized by the event, watched the blood flow effortlessly from the man's open neck.

As the young Viceroy stared down at the bloody body at his feet, Penish fell to a knee and bowed his head. It would still be a few seconds before Xerxes noticed him in that position. Finally, the young, would-be King, lifted his right arm which contained his sword and raised it above Penish's head. *"You have saved me warrior. What is your name?"*

Without moving a gross muscle, he responded *"My name, Lord, is Penish, and I am your servant."*

"Penish, do you know what the tattoo on that scum's neck means?"

"I do, Lord. It is the sign for the Brotherhood of the Sand Dancers."

"Sand Dancers, Penish?"

"Lord, the Sand Dancers are an ancient brotherhood of assassins. They are taken as young children from their mothers and trained in their black art. Their only life is that their existence is for one purpose, to carry out their contract. They do not exist as people, Lord. They have no soul. They only have purpose. It was probably true that the young man did not know who bought the contract."

Looking puzzled, Xerxes questioned: *"How can I find these Sand Dancers?"*

"They have never been found, Lord. They are like desert ghosts. It is told that their secret sanctuary is somewhere in the great desert, someplace in the Zagros Mountains."

"*Do we know of no one who has knowledge?*"

"*Lord, the Sand Dancers' reputation is legendary. Some believe that they are not men, but spirits. They are reported to never fail in their attempts.*"

Xerxes sneered and looked at the beheaded body still lying at his feet. Without moving his gaze, he pronounced, "*Well, they are men and they can be killed.*"

His gaze shifted upward meeting Penish's eyes "*And thanks to you Penish, they are not always successful.*"

"*How else might I serve you, my Lord?*"

Xerxes slowly walked to the warrior. As Penish rose by the viceroy's command, the young man bowed deeply to the warrior, startling Penish.

"*I am in your debt, warrior. I will remember your bravery and valor today. When the day comes and I rise to power you will rise with me. But for now, spread the word of the glory of Xerxes. The God protects him from the undefeatable. His skills are as deadly as a pit of vipers. Not even the Sand Dancer can tarnish his bravery.*"

And with that, the young viceroy spat on the dead man's body and left the hall.

* * *

Now in his time of great embarrassment at the religious ceremony, the now King called for his loyal servant Penish. As he entered the chamber, Xerxes gestured for all the servants to leave. He grabbed his friend appearing to stabilize himself on the shoulder of the warrior. Xerxes held onto Penish as the others left the chamber. When they were alone, Penish faced his ruler and said, **"My King?"**

Xerxes, still angered by the events of the past few hours, lowered his voice to address his subordinate. **"Penish, my Empire and my reputation have been tarnished by this insult."**

He swallowed, appearing to catch his breath. His eyes were wild and his face was only inches away from Penish **"I cannot allow this to continue. The satraps in my Empire will read this as my weakness. This day must be avenged. I want the leaders of the city brought to me. They must understand that what happened in that church will be punished. Tell the guards they should destroy three of the priest's churches. I want the tongues of 100 of the priests that follow that renegade. I also want the gold** *statue of their false god melted down and taken to Susa to build our new temples."*

"Yes, Lord."

"Penish, you have exactly two months. I cannot allow this act of defiance to color my rule. I want you to bring me that old man's hands. He will never strike the King of Kings again. "

Xerxes moved closer to the warrior's face. With an intense expression of fury, he whispered, *"You have saved my life before, now it is time for you to save my Empire."*

Penish bowed, and with resolution in his face, left the room.

The next morning, Belshimanni and Shamah-eriba were among those rudely treated as they were dragged in front of the young ruler. The men were forced to their knees with their heads to the floor. The King made them wait in that position for two minutes. Finally, he motioned that they could lift their heads. Penish entered the room and the men were asked to hold out their hands. Penish started dropping bloody tongues in their hands. The ritual continued for at least five minutes, as one hundred tongues of priests were deposited on the two men. Xerxes paced in front of the men with the sternest of looks on his face.

He finally admitted, *"You all know why I've called you here!"*

Again he paced, this time reaching for his scabbard. He pointed the blade at the men continuing his lecture.

"The renegade priest, Ningizzida, will contact some of you as he hides like a rat."

Looking directly at Belshimanni, Xerxes said, *"You will all be tempted by his words when he contacts you. But consider this, any contact with this scorpion I will consider as collusion. In that case there will be no forgiveness. You will pay with your life and the lives of all your family. It will mark the end of your line. I will burn your property and cover the scarred ground with salt so nothing will grow again in that area. It will be cursed. After you are dead, I will have your bodies cut into small pieces and fed to the shit eating fish."*

He now switched his gaze to Shamah-eriba. *"You have two young daughters, do you not?"*

Shaking, the man nodded, *"They are beautiful young things, if I remember."*

A moment of silence filled the space. Xerxes then continued. *"I know a man who prefers pretty young things. But you know it is tragic, because after he has them for a time they cannot stop the bleeding from their ass. It is sad, for they die a very painful death after such treatment."*

Backing away, Xerxes gave the image a minute to solidify in the men's minds. *"I expect any information you have about this renegade priest to be brought before me. When he contacts you, I expect you to tell me. Is this clear enough?"*

After mentioning his name Xerxes, spit on the ground, *"Ningizzida will need the support of the people to hide. And you men have the pulse of the people. I expect answers and I expect them soon."*

With that the King summoned again and five female slaves were brought in from both directions of the room. The two prone Babylonians recognized the women as favored slaves from their harems. The King watched their eyes for recognition. These women who were closer to these two men than their wives. Xerxes pointed at Belshimanni, *"Rise Babylonian."*

Belshimanni's eyes were wide with fear. The King walked to him. Looking at the Babylonian he pronounced. *"You must prove your loyalty to my Empire. You forfeit these five slaves to me. But you must choose one to die.   It must be your choice."*

Belshimanni shook with fear. He could not choose among these people.

"Choose, Babylonian, or they will all die."

After reluctance and hesitation, Belshimanni dropped his head and pointed to a young slave standing on the end on the line. She screamed and fell to the floor. Xerxes summoned, and a warrior immediately beheaded the young girl in front of the others. The same procedure was carried out with Shamah- eriba. The two men were dragged from the hall.

After they left, Penish bowed and questioned*, "Lord, how should I kill the other women?"*

The King smiled and explained, *"You will not kill them, Penish. I do not require their blood, I only require the fear that the assumption of their death brings. We are not murderers. Remove them to Susa."*

Xerxes patted Penish on the shoulder and began walking out. Then he suddenly stopped and turned back to his guard, *"Penish, take which ever slave you would like for yourself."*

PERSIA

CHAPTER IV -
DEMARATUS

The envoy had arrived the day before. Demaratus was pre-warned of the arrival. He knew of the envoy because the ex-Spartan King had taken many precautions when he was granted this new Kingdom. He was placed in charge of his new Kingdom, a Satrap in the western Persian Empire in Lydia, by Xerxes himself. Knowing the importance of understanding the comings and goings in the great palace in Susa, prompted Demaratus to create a series of spies within the palace of Xerxes. He knew from experience that being surprised could easily lead to his downfall, and he preferred not losing his head. Although he was aware of the envoy's coming, Demaratus did not know what news the envoy was bringing from the great Xerxes. Surprises always made Demaratus anxious. Demaratus would see him after his morning meal. A message from the King of Kings could not be ignored for any period, as any substantial delay would be reported back to the King by the envoy. Even delaying a meeting, was taking a mammoth chance. But Demaratus was a very proud man, an ex-King in his own right. So even though he would show deference to Xerxes, he would not totally submit. He had to preserve some self-respect and maintain face. He was, after all, a Spartan, and even though he had been banished by his people, Demaratus was a Greek at heart.

Demaratus instinctively knew that every aspect of his meeting with the envoy would be reported back to Xerxes. From the subtle verbal intonations to the facial expressions. He had only met the King of Kings twice before, but he knew that he was meticulous in his valuation of information. He had no misconceptions about the King's hidden agendas. He knew that Xerxes would test his loyalty to his new Empire. Demaratus knew that the envoy would be interrogated in detail about Demaratus' reactions to the communication that he carried. What was important was what Demaratus reacted to, and even more importantly, what he did not react to. All this information would be reported back to the great King by this envoy. Xerxes was known to use such information in his decisions about the loyalty of his underlings. More importantly, Xerxes had to evaluate the character of those he would one day entrust his army to.

Demaratus also knew that the envoy was under tremendous political pressure, as the job of a messenger was not as simple as the term suggested. Envoys for Xerxes were just spies with other names. They usually knew what the message was that they were delivering, as it allowed them to more accurately judge the reaction of the person receiving the message. To reach the level of a royal envoy meant that the great King trusted this man to a large degree. Demaratus had to be ever

117

present for this meeting. He could not let his thoughts wander or his motions betray his feelings. He desperately wanted to gain the great King's trust, so his reactions had to be carefully measured and scripted. Demaratus had to draw from all his experience over the last thirty years. His efforts and training in Sparta were spent in preparation for this type of meeting. It was almost as important as the first meeting that Demaratus had with the great King when he entered the Persian Empire after his expulsion from Sparta.

Ever since his arrival in the Empire, Demaratus had to assume an unusual position for an ex-Spartan King. He had made a strategic decision to come to Persia after being brutally ousted from Sparta. Even though Demaratus decided on his own to leave his beloved city, he did so only because his rival had brilliantly set him up, politically outmaneuvering him. His fate was sealed and he knew it. He chose what he considered the more propitious course of action and left his beloved city. In his heart though, Demaratus believed that one day he would return to Sparta and reassume his rightful place, as King.

He had carefully chosen Persia after his exile, for Demaratus and Xerxes had many things in common. The central feeling that they shared was their distrust for Athens and more notably, their desire for revenge. Demaratus knew before their first encounter that Xerxes hatred the Greeks, the Athenians in particular. Xerxes' father, Darius, was defeated at Marathon and the young King had inherited the vengeful contract that his father planted in his psyche.

Marathon had been the only defeat in battle that the Achaemenid monarchy had ever experienced. It was a stunning setback for the proud Persians, and the only way to rid the bad taste in their mouths was to punish the Greeks and reassert their dominance. Darius had died before he was able to complete his vow adding insult to Xerxes injury. There was also underlying gossip around the Kingdom that the Greeks might have plotted and been responsible for the unusual and untimely death of Darius.

The rebellion in Egypt, although financially important to Xerxes, was only an inconsequential itch to the King of Kings. The blood obsession for Xerxes was Greece, and more specifically, Athens. Whereas his father was angry and had sworn revenge, Xerxes was preoccupied and fanatical regarding blood vengeance. Xerxes wanted to see Athens burn. Xerxes' advisors were growing tired of the King's tirades directed at his hatred of the Greeks. His thoughts bordered on genocidal.

When Demaratus left Sparta, he traveled many miles incognito to arrive at Susa undetected. He entered the Persian Empire looking for asylum. When told of the Spartan King seeking sanctuary in Persia, Xerxes saw it as a sign from the heavens that his ultimate conquest would be successful. Xerxes needed an edge in his plans to defeat the Greeks and Athens, and he thought Demaratus could be that edge. When the message came to the great King that the disgraced King of Sparta was entering the Empire seeking asylum, Xerxes immediately consulted his most reliable magus, Vernas. Vernas had been one of his father's chief consuls and Xerxes grew up implicitly trusting this man. Vernas argued that Demaratus was a special jewel, delivered to the King from the heavens. But like a flawless stone, it had to be smoothed and shaped into its ultimate form. Most importantly, the stone had to be inserted into the proper setting to enhance and expose its beauty.

Although he trusted Vernas, Xerxes also decided to speak with Hamath, the military genius who trained him. Hamath did not talk in abstractions like the magus. He was very clear to Xerxes.

"My King, I have devoted my life to your training. You have always been above the rest. You have shown strength

in the face of adversity. You are courageous, not fearing either man or beast. It is time, my King, for you to learn foresight. You can only see into the future by planning for it. There is no such thing as luck. There is only preparation and foresight."

"*Be clearer*," the young King urged the old master.

"*I know your feelings, Lord. I know the blind rage that you feel towards the Greeks and their dog servants, the Athenians.*"

The old master walked over to his young student and placed a hand on his shoulder. "*Information, my young monarch, Information will destroy Greece. Yes you can gather a large army and navy and invade their land. Remember what the Greeks did to your father's greatly superior force at Marathon.*"

With anger on his face, he turned the young King to face him. "*Your father and our Empire were embarrassed.*"

The old man withdrew his hand but continued explaining. *It will not be the strength of your sword that conquers the Greeks and allows you to burn their queen city. It will be your cunning and planning. Seeking the disenchanted and disenfranchised from the enemy strengthens your army. You will be able to manipulate others if you know their weaknesses and strengths. In war my young student, you will find that no rules exist. It follows no natural path. The path must be established by the general. A leader must be certain of his direction, his purpose, for in war, our eyes blur and our vision becomes foggy. Your instincts must guide you, but they are guided by knowledge. The more you know of the enemy, the better you can plan strategy. War is chaos, but the true general creates stability within that disorder, to lead his people to victory. He must guide it like a ship on the high seas."*

Xerxes meditated on this advice and decided to insert Demaratus in a province in the western section of the Empire and restore his Kingly manner. Days later he called both Vernas and Hamath to his council. When they entered the chamber, Xerxes began: *"This, Demaratus, this disgraced Spartan King, will be more valuable to me if I can restore his confidence and give him land and people to rule. He was born a King and must be returned to his status. A lion must act like a lion, it cannot act like a lamb. If I can restore his confidence, the fire will be ignited within him. I will give him the cities of Pergamum, Teuthrania and Halisarna. There he will rule as supreme."*

Vernas and Hamath both smiled at the King's logic. He was learning how to rule.

"Vernas, I want you to plant spies in these cities. I also want people in his inner council. The closer they can get to this Spartan the more information they will supply us with. I want to know whether I can trust this man before I have to rely on him."

He turned, *"Hamath, my friend. This man, Demaratus will raise an army from his populace. Your job will be to place people you can trust in his military structure. Not only do I want to know if he is trustworthy, I also want to know if he is a gifted soldier. If he is, he could be very important to us. He understands the Greek mind. They are a dissimilar race from us and think differently. I want to know how they reason. They are shrewd and underhanded."*

****

Sparta had been traditionally ruled by duel Kings. But these two men were by no means partners in their rule as the theory suggested. It was closer to the truth to see these two men as combatants and enemies within one government. Demaratus' co-King was Cleomenes. The two men had a long familial history of mistrust. Their suspicions stemmed from the power of each of their families in the Spartan society. They each came from one of the two royal families of Sparta, the Eurgpontids and the Agiads. Demaratus was a Eurgpontid. Both men were bred into this royalty but came to power in very different ways. When Cleomenes' father, Anaxandridas died, there were tangible reasons why his half-brother Dorieus, should assume power. But Cleomenes was a very deceptive, manipulative and ambitious young man. He would use any means at his disposal to secure what he believed was his rightful place, not his brother's.

Dorieus and his half-brother, Cleomenes, were different in both temperament and disposition. One of the mainstays of Spartan society and education was the Agoge. This system of education for all young Spartan men in this martial society consisted of a rigorous training regimen. The preparation involved learning how to inflict and more importantly, sustain pain. The Spartans considered both to be equally important in the psyche of a young man. Inflicting pain was taught using the ability to fight and use weapons. The ability to endure pain was learned by feeling the lash. Young boys were forced to sustain nasty and frequent beatings. Tears and cries of pain only extended the beating, so the young

Spartans learned to separate pain from the mind. The ability to ignore pain was a conscious training of mental discipline. Those who could not acquire the discipline of controlling pain would perish in the process. Pain had to be absorbed and inflicted without emotion or compassion.

The final test of the Agoge, the graduation test was the most severe of all and was called, "The Release". In "The Release", the young student had to sneak out of the enclosure and kill one of the fighting slaves of Sparta. The Spartans trained their slaves to fight and many of them achieved more proficiency than the Spartans themselves. Their training was not the Agoge but it was rigorous. So "The Release" was not an easy task by any stretch of the imagination. It was made more difficult by the fact that the student had to accomplish the task without weapons. He had to feel the death of his victim, experience it with his hands. Death had to become their comrade in life, for if it was it would not be feared. The student was taught to extend their left hand. Two inches beyond their fingers sat death. The students were taught that death was always present. It sat just beyond their finger tips and smiled at them. It smiled because it understood that it would win in the end. The student was taught that when death smiled

125

at him, his only response was to smile back.

Only the children of royalty were exempt from the Agoge. Because Dorieus only had half of the royal Agiad's blood flowing in his veins, he himself petitioned to participate in the Agoge. It was a highly unusual request, as the training was so extensive and dangerous that to ask to participate showed an inner vigor and sense of self-assurance. Even though he didn't follow his brother, the decision by Dorieus to enter the Agoge made Cleomenes quite envious. Even with such hidden feeling, Cleomenes did not have enough self-confidence or physical strength to attempt the difficult training.

Whereas Dorieus was a warrior by heart, Cleomenes was spoiled and narcissistic. Due to their separate maternal lineage, the two men grew up natural rivals. Cleomenes was never able to compete with his younger brother and it incensed him that his brother was taking such a bold, political step as entering the Agoge. He did understand the implications and believed that he understood Dorieus' hidden agenda. Unfortunately, or fortunately, his lack of physical prowess led Cleomenes to study the delicate black arts of manipulation, exploitation, and bribery. What was worse for Cleomenes was that his innate aggravation, immaturity, and self-centeredness led to gross overindulgences of the flesh. As he approached adulthood his love of alcohol and women grew in proportion to his age and frustration. By the time he was fighting his brother for the throne, Cleomenes was ruled more by alcohol than by any rational, well thought out strategy.

The lack of participation in the Agoge for royal family males had been a point of contention for generations within Spartan life. The Agoge stressed discipline, loyalty, and fearlessness. It was argued that future Kings needed such strengths to rule. Sparta was one of the few Greek cities without external walls for protection. They didn't need such external structures because the young men that were trained in the Agoge became the **"walls of Sparta"**.

Besides the two Kings chosen from the royals, Sparta was ruled by an assembly called the Gerousia. The Gerousia consisted of 28 Spartan Elders, who along with the two Kings ruled the city. The Gerousia elected five of their members to form the Ephor. The Ephors were the elite. Along with the Kings, the Ephors had the true power within the city. The Ephors had the ability to override the Kings, and in extreme cases, even banish him from the city, stripping him of his royal lineage. The Ephors were so powerful that two of its members accompanied each King whenever he left the city, either on political or military matters.

When it came time to determine the Kings, Cleomenes had secretly bribed three of the Ephors. Cleomenes' father had established this enticing relationship and Cleomenes added to it, only cementing his hold over the elite council. So even though his brother was popular with both the people and the Gerousia, Cleomenes knew that he had the unseen advantage. His ascension was guaranteed before the infighting even began. He sat calmly eating chicken as the Ephors discussed the issue of which brother would ascend to the Kingship. And so it was decided, Cleomenes would be King and Dorieus was shunned. After the decision was made, Dorieus was ostracized from the city by his brother's orders and fled in exile, never to be heard from again.

Demaratus, on the other hand, was chosen to rule from the time of his premature birth. He was raised and trained to be one of the duel Kings. When he finally ascended to the throne, he could not anticipate the lengths to which his rival, Cleomenes, would go to have him removed. To his face, Cleomenes smiled and paid due respect to his fellow King. Cleomenes only let his true feelings known to those he completely trusted which could be counted on one hand.

The animosity that Cleomenes felt for Demaratus eventually gave birth to a well-rehearsed and planned lie. When Demaratus' was born only seven months after King Ariston slept with his mother, there were many rumors that the young infant was conceived by another man. Because of political differences, after ridding himself of his brother, Cleomenes immediately set to the task of undermining Demaratus. This rumor served good purpose. Cleomenes brought the issue of Demaratus' right to be King to the Ephors claiming that Demaratus was an imposter. The allegation was a complete surprise to both the Ephors and to Demaratus himself. Demaratus was called before the astute body and asked to defend his right to serve. And although his arguments were sound, no position could carry the day. As with his own ascension, Cleomenes had already bribed the usual suspects to preordain the outcome of this conflict. Being as astute as he was, albeit after the trap had been sprung, Demaratus realized that his fate was sealed, which is why he decided to leave before the verdict was announced.

The exiled Demaratus had slumped into a deep dysphoria after his self-imposed expulsion from his beloved city. Emotionally he bounced between feelings of stupidity stemming from the fact that he did not see this conflict coming, to unbridled rage of having been outsmarted by such a snake as Cleomenes. When he finally recovered his judgment and decided to reinvent himself, the ex-King finally chose to seek out the Persian monarch. Demaratus knew his worth to the Persian King. Their deal was a simple one. Demaratus would accompany Xerxes in his conquest of the Greeks, providing inside information about the nature of the city states that they would encounter, as well as the background about the strength and weaknesses of the various Greek city states. He also knew the terrain which the Persian army would have to transverse. Xerxes, of course, also had a very intricate system of spies and informants which were already in place on the Greek mainland.

But to the Persian King, the ex-Spartan King was an unexpected prize that fell into his lap and had to be utilized. It made him smile to himself when he thought of the fortune that brought him Demaratus. The King of Kings made generous sacrifices at the altar of Marduk to praise the God for this fate. Xerxes knew his destiny rested in burying Greece and regaining Persian dominion. In return, Demaratus was promised to be reinstated on his throne by the Persian

King. The King also implied, but never directly said, that Demaratus would rule the entire peninsula, Athens as well.

In his secret heart, Xerxes knew that Demaratus would never rule over Athens. Nobody would. Xerxes wanted it burned. He would reduce the great Greek city to rubble and then cover the ground with salt so that nothing could grow. Since his ascension to the throne, Xerxes had recurrent dreams of burning grass and stone. The dreams haunted him. His trusted magi interpreted this incarnation as the incineration of the famous Acropolis after his victory. Xerxes was unsure of the truth of this interpretation. The dreams always made him uneasy and he somehow felt that the interpretations were overly positive. He always feared deluding himself.

***

The sun was rising and Demaratus was already in preparation for his meeting with the King's envoy. His informants had prepared him for the message that the man carried in his pouch. There were very few secrets in the Kingdom, and Demaratus was aware of the precautions that had to be taken in order to secure his return to power. He needed to be one step ahead of Xerxes. Having been burned once before, Demaratus knew that he had to depend on more than his shrewdness to secure his future. He was outmaneuvered once before, and it cost him his fortune and Kingdom. It would not happen again he swore to himself. He needed to learn from his mistakes and he concluded his major error was a lack of preparation. Demaratus now assumed that there were underlying currents and hidden agendas. He had to do his due diligence to stay ahead of those hoping to topple him.

Demaratus knew from the moment he entered the Persian Empire that the King would eventually test both his loyalty and his skill. The time was now before him and Demaratus was prepared and ready to prove his worth. His informants told him that the King was going to ask him to lead one of the Persian armies in the reconquest of Canaan and Egypt. He would use this situation to judge Demaratus and his skill as a general.

The envoy wore a black cape and a gray turban. He was a well-traveled, grizzly man who held himself with an air of self-importance. Demaratus had heard of this man. His spies told him he was dangerous and that he should be cautious in his presence. For some reason Demaratus was unmoved by the warning.

Demaratus was seated on a small throne which was positioned two feet above where the envoy Janlikorven, knelt. There was protocol. Demaratus knew of this man, as his reputation for deceit and underhandedness preceded him. Even so, Demaratus let him remain on his knees for ten seconds longer than the required time. He wanted to silently assert his dominance over this scorpion. Demaratus knew that if he showed fear or hesitation this arachnid would strike at his heart when he returned to Susa and reported to the great King. As long as Janlikorven remained in his province Demaratus knew that danger would remain. He had been warned that Janlikorven was known to distort information in making his reports to the King. There were rumors that he would attempt to undermine the person he was reporting on. He would suggest that the individual was in some way irreverent to the King. Demaratus had to be attentive and on his guard.

Being an envoy, Janlikorven had a difficult task. To arrive at this place, he traversed the King's Royal Road. On his journey there would be one hundred and eleven staging posts where the messenger changed horses, got something to eat, and rested for only a few hours. He was called the Angaros or the courier. It was rumored in the east that nothing traveled faster than the Angaros. The sixteen hundred miles that he rode could be accomplished in less than two weeks if he didn't stop at all the locations. But when he was delivering messages to Kings, his time was dictated by the

idiosyncratic responses of these minor
monarchs.

Finally, Demaratus raised his hand
indicating to Janlikorven that he could
rise. In response Janlikorven slowly
rose keeping his eyes frozen on the King.
Janlikorven was a dark-skinned man with
smallish eyes that appeared sunken deep
in his forehead. His eyes were slightly
crossed which made his stare look even
more ominous. He had heavy eyebrows and a
dark beard that looked as if it was often
shaped. The amount of extra time that he
spent on his knees did not escape him.
His dark eyes focused directly on
Demaratus, as if he were burning a hole
through the King. Demaratus felt a
silent shiver proceed up his back, but he
tried hard not to let his face betray
those feelings.

"*My Lord,*" Janlikorven began. His
voice now was much more conciliatory than
his stare. It struck Demaratus that this
man was frequently not what he presented
to the outside world. "*It is an honor to
be in your presence.*"

Demaratus nodded his head accepting
the compliment but knowing it was smoke.

"*My lord, I have been sent to you by
my master, the King of the world, the
great Xerxes. My King hopes that this*

message arrives safely and finds you in health and prosperity."

Demaratus rose from his seat in deference to the great King's name. He responded to Janlikorven. *"I am, and forever will stay, servant to the King of Kings. He is, and will always remain my sovereign, and my loyalty to him is beyond reproach."*

Demaratus slowly turned to the East, facing the King's temple at Susa and bowed. He then returned to his seat. It was an unnecessary gesture, but it would be remembered.

Janlikorven continued, *"Lord, I have in my purse, a written message from the Great Xerxes. May I approach?"*

Repeatedly, Demaratus nodded his head and put out his hand. Janlikorven proceeded to the King and handed him the purse. Demaratus took the envelope but didn't open it. He placed it on his lap and spoke directly to the envoy. *"Janlikorven. As you are the King's representative in my city, I would be honored if you join me for supper."*

The wily Janlikorven bowed his acceptance to the invitation. It was unusual for Demaratus to present such an invitation to someone who was beneath

135

him, but this man was powerful by his representation of the King.

A servant appeared out of the shadows. The first meeting between the courier and Demaratus was over. Janlikorven was escorted to his room by the servant. The room where Janlikorven was taken was a place for him to rest, and after supper with the King, a place to sleep. Although the room was small, it had beautiful red carpets and a fine bed. Immediately upon entering the room, Janlikorven noticed a fine bowl filled with gold trinkets sitting on the small table next to the bed. Janlikorven was shocked and stopped as if hit by lightning. He turned to the servant, pointed to the bowl and said. *"What is this?"*

The servant bowed and prostrated himself in front of Janlikorven.

"I am unsure sir. My master did not inform me of the gift."

"Gift?" Janlikorven responded.

"I will inquire for you if you wish," the servant answered in an apologetic voice.

Janlikorven had already walked over to the bowl and was fondling one of the gold pieces. He seemed almost mesmerized as

136

he scrutinized the bauble in his hand. Although Janlikorven was well taken care of by Xerxes, this amount of gold was over a year's compensation. At careful observation, it could be two or three years. Janlikorven did not respond to the servant but continued to stare at the gold. His well practiced composure was evaporating like a drop of water in the desert sun. His stare was interrupted by the servant raising his voice and asking, *"Sir, would you like me to inquire?"*

Janlikorven hesitated for a second then turned to the servant and declared, *"No, it is unnecessary."*

As the servant began leaving, Janlikorven turned to him again and said, *"Wine. Wine, too, my good man. Bring me some of your finest wine."*

The servant turned and bowed to the emissary as he left.

****

Back in his chamber, Demaratus smiled to himself as the servant entered his room after begging one of the guards to be allowed to speak with him. Demaratus already knew what the question was before the servant uttered the words. But Demaratus was a patient and theatrical man. He would allow the servant to make his request. The man entered, almost crawling to the King.

"My lord," he declared as he bowed even lower. *"Speak, I await your request."*

Demaratus said, again cherishing the moment. The servant continued with his enquiry. *"The emissary, my lord. He entered his chamber and found a bowl of gold at his bedside. He appeared confused by the gift. I asked him if he wanted me to inquire about its purpose and he denied. Should I return and explain the gift to him?"*

Demaratus stared at him as if he didn't understand the question. He leaned back in his chair as if thinking. He then slowly leaned forward and whispered to the servant, *"if he inquires again, tell the emissary that the gold is his reward for his loyalty to his King"*

He leaned back, hesitated and continued the sentence, *"To my master, Xerxes."*

The servant repeated his message to the King's satisfaction and left the room. Demaratus laughed softly when he was alone. The gold was a small price to pay for securing his future. He had always felt Janlikorven could be had for the right price, and now hearing his

138

response, Demaratus knew that his instincts were still good. What Janlikorven didn't realize was that the gold not only bought Demaratus a good report, but it bought him a spy within Xerxes' castle. Accepting the bribe locked Janlikorven to Demaratus. Demaratus knew that Janlikorven couldn't allow Xerxes to find out about the bribe, so the secrecy would be maintained. That is when he took the gold. His discipline and his singular devotion to the Great King would surely be tested. Either way, this situation pleased the Spartan turned Persian.

It was now time for Demaratus to read the message from the King of Kings. If his spy was correct, the King would entrust him with an army in the reconquest of the rebels in Canaan and Egypt.

Demaratus slowly opened the leather pouch. Leather of this quality was, in and of itself, a prized possession. He slowly read the papyrus scroll that it contained and he was initially stunned by its contents. It did not say that Xerxes would offer him an army as Demaratus was assured it would. What it read was,

"**Says Xerxes the King of Kings. Without haste, your presence is required in the grand ballroom at Susa. The**

meeting will occur the night of the new moon"

Demaratus swallowed hard. He immediately had to begin preparation for his journey to the Persian capital.

★ ★ ★ ★

PERSIA

CHAPTER V - PENISH

On the day of the insult, the King retreated from the after chamber within the great temple to a side room. He was immediately catered to by the female entourage that accompanied him to the ceremony. Their task was not an easy one. Xerxes was infuriated and the women would have to absorb his wrath. When a man with Xerxes' power was made to look foolish in front of others, this insult could become lethal to others. Anger was sometimes taken out on those who didn't have any part in its creation.

Upon entering the room Xerxes immediately shed his robe and threw down his jewelry. His rage was still in full bloom. He ranted and stomped around the room. His face was red and distorted. His white teeth gleamed from his darkened face. *"I am the King of Kings. This dog shit must pay for this insolence."*

He stalked around the room as his ranting continuing, *"I thought this man was a friend of my father. But today he spits on my father's memory. I will have his bones pulled out of his skin and hang the carcass upside down on the walls of the palace."*

A beautiful, young, dark-haired woman entered with wine and fruit. Her steps were hesitant as she approached the distraught ruler. She bowed low placing the food in front of her, visibly shaking as she awaited the King's approval. Imperceptibly she moaned as she heard the King cursing and stomping around the room. She hoped that she could lower herself to the point of not being seen, disappearing into the earth itself. It took all her strength to keep her eyes focused on the floor and not watch the tirade that was unfolding around her. She knew that if she made eye contact with the King it would humiliate him and refocus his rage onto her. She stayed as low as she could for what seemed like hours, but was in fact, only a few moments. By this time, the floor under her face was wet with her tears, and she felt the perspiration welling up across her chest and arms. She winced as her legs were becoming numb under her. Twice the King appeared to be moving towards her in his fury, only to brush her with his leg and continue to the other end of the room where he pounded the wall, breaking pottery and furniture.

Suddenly the King walked directly towards her, roughly placing his left hand on her back-putting pressure on her to remain in her position. It was as if he was tiring and using her to lean on. With his right hand he lifted the pitcher of wine and proceeded to the chaise. Xerxes threw himself into the chair and began guzzling from the bottle. The slave girl remained in her position, too scared to rise from her knees. Even though her eyes remained staring at the floor, she could sense the King's stare as he drank the wine. At that moment, a second and third slave girl entered the room with other delicacies. Without hesitation, Xerxes jumped from his chair and with haste moved quickly to meet these two young women. Xerxes seemed to transverse the distance across the room without his legs touching the floor. As the two women realized that their Lord was hurriedly approaching, they immediately dropped to their knees in deference. With each hand and in unison, the King lifted the woman up. He said nothing, but roughly pushed them backward gesturing them to leave the room. He forcibly shut the door after them and banged his fists into it.

Having heard the other woman entering the room, the slave girl felt the dread lifting from her. Their subsequent banishment from the room redoubled her trepidation. The slave girl, still cowering in the center of the room, began to shake noticeably. She was having increasing difficulty keeping her emotions under control and not letting the King know that she was crying. The incident at the door seemed to enrage Xerxes again and the loud voice and cursing was renewed.

★★★★

Penish was a bright and experienced army officer. He understood that his job was not to think or consider implications. His job was to carry out the King's orders. But Penish was not a stooge. He reasoned the complexities of his devotion. His order to remove the gold statue of Bel-Marduk from the Babylonian temple was complicated, in truth, but generally simple in concept.

Penish would bring enough men to assure success and the deed would be carried out in the middle of the night when the least amount of resistance would be expected. Before the King left the room, Penish had already planned how to accomplish this simple part of his mission. The difficult, and by far the most dangerous aspect of the King's orders, was capturing the wily priest.

Penish had lived in the holy city as part of the King's guard from the time Xerxes was a much younger man. Although his commission was to protect the young King, his hidden talent was establishing an undercover organization within Babylon. Penish also knew the deep nature of the King's rage. He would not accept failure. Penish had to return in two months' time with the priest's hands. Failing this, the King's rage would shift away from Ningizzida landing directly on his head. His long-devoted dedication to the King would not make up for one failure, especially one in which the young King's pride was at stake. More than almost anyone else, Penish knew the depth of this man's need for revenge. Capturing the crafty Ningizzida would be a monumental accomplishment. Penish knew that the walls in this city heard every rumor. He knew that the priest was already aware of his mission and had gone underground. The priest was very powerful and would be harbored by the local population. More than that, Ningizzida was uncanny in anticipating his enemies at every turn.

Penish had heard the rumors that the priest was able to read the future by reading smoke from holy candles. It gave the outlawed priest supposed awareness of the future, allowing him to know Penish's moves even before he himself did. The concept was ludicrous, but it still bothered the warrior. Penish would have to use a large percentage of his savings to bribe enough Babylonians to find where the priest was hiding. Even with Ningizzida's popularity, like all men, he could be bought. Penish also knew that he could not wait two months to locate the priest. By that time Ningizzida could be out of the Empire completely and never again be located. The task of finding the magus needed to start in earnest before he could slip away. Time was of the essence. Penish was sure that the priest's egocentricity would betray him. He did not believe that the priest would leave the Empire. Running so far would only show his fear, and Ningizzida would not admit such a weakness. *"No"*, Penish thought, this priest would stay within a few day's ride of Babylonia. He could not run too far from his worshippers. The further he got from this godly city, the more his power and influence would drain and the more vulnerable he would become.

Once the King left the room and gave him his charge, Penish began the process of finding the priest.   Penish also secretly disliked the old priest. He had no use for this religion. He relished the idea of making the old man beg for his life.   Penish wasn't afraid of Ningizzida's god. He believed in his sword and his wits.   He also didn't believe that this bent, old man could read the future. He would spit on him to test his power. Nobody had proven to him that any god was stronger than his sword.

****

Xerxes slowly walked across the room and stood over the slave girl who was still shaking in her horizontal position. He was sweating and breathing hard as if he just returned from a wrestling match. He reached down and grabbed the girl's long, flowing black hair.   His eyes were glassy as he stared at the girl's hair. Her head rose as Xerxes pulled her up to him. Her face was wide-eyed and fearful. Her makeup was melting off her face, although her dark brown eyes were still compelling. The girl stumbled to her feet as the King pulled her up by the hair. But as much as she wanted to, she dared not voice her protest. Xerxes looked past the slave but continued to walk to the lounge at the other side of the room. He did not release his grip on the girl's hair as he dragged her along with him. She stumbled to her knees, but Xerxes pulled her back up and she reluctantly followed him to the lounge. Having been raised as a courtesan, the young slave instinctively knew what the next half hour held for her. She would be violently taken, submitting to the King's needs, hoping to sexually douse the anger that currently controlled his psyche. If she could not, she would die this day. She prepared herself as the floor passed under her feet. Although she hadn't had previous contact with the young King, she had been told by other slaves that blood and pain were usually involved in his sexual pleasures. The rumors that she heard had made her cringe and now it was her turn. The young slave had nightmares about this day and her worst fears were coming to fruition. She had rationalized the other's pain by telling herself that to pleasure the King was the only important act a slave could accomplish. But now that it was her turn that logic didn't seem to make sense or help in relieving her fears.

The room was small but comfortable and Ningizzida sat contentedly around the small table. Across from him sat his longtime friend, Shamah-eriba. Both old men appeared comfortable as they sipped their wine. The third man in the room, Belshimanni, was much more nervous and overtly anxious. He circled the room walking in a loop. His stride suggested a purpose, yet within these confines there was nowhere to go. Belshimanni was a blow hard, and this situation was beyond his comfort zone. His clothes were wet with perspiration, still bloodied by the tongues, and his expression was one that centered on dread. He looked in desperation at Shamah-eriba almost begging for redemption. Shamah-eriba spoke to himself for many hours before attending this meeting. *"Should I sit down with a wanted man? I would become as wanted as he is."*

"Sit, my friend," Shamah-eriba exclaimed, *"Come. Join Ningizzida and myself for some of this excellent libation."*

Belshimanni quickly turned to his now friendly rival, opened his arms wide, and pleaded: *"What have we done Shamah-eriba, what have we done? In one day we have destroyed everything that generations of our ancestors took millennium to create. How can you be so calm?"*

He then made a swimming motion with his arms. It was quite dramatic but his face was not that of sarcasm. He was deadly serious, *"Please, Belshimanni, don't be so overdramatic."*

Shamah-eriba responded. He rose and walked slowly to his traditional family

149

rival. He continued: *"My friend, we have lost nothing. Ningizzida here has accepted all the danger. What he did today was bold and brazen. It took more courage than you or I will ever have in our lifetime."*

He turned and faced the priest, *"Did you see his face?"* he questioned, as a broad smile appeared on his face, *"The King of Kings was made red faced and bowed with our friend here slapping him until his eyes rolled. It was magnificent. He knocked the King out. One more strike and he might have killed the obnoxious child."*

Shamah-eriba laughed out loud although internally he shook with fear. He slapped his large hand on the table in front of him and continued. As he did, the priest wondered if he would eventually regret not killing the young King on the spot.

"Magnificent, magnificent!" Belshimanni was not convinced and responded in a hesitant fashion. *"We will now all feel the wrath of that young madman."*

Ningizzida turned to Belshimanni and confidently uttered: *"Maybe it should be the child King who will feel the wrath. He is no match for the gods. If we revolt, then his great Empire will disintegrate in front of his eyes. I had loyalty to his father, Darius, but there is none for this insufferable upstart."*

Ningizzida's eyes were wild with delight still feeling the afterglow of his triumph at the temple. At this moment in his life, he felt that he was at the height of his power, even though he knew he would have to hide from the King's revenge. It was a small price to pay for insulting this man in front of the elite of the city. Word would spread like the fire on a dry plain. Ningizzida knew that his name would go down in history. And when he escaped the King's vengeance, his legend would grow even further. However, as he basked in his glory, that gnawing feeling inside that he may have missed an opportunity raised its ugly head again. He had the King at his mercy. During one of his meditations after the event, the priest asked himself, **"should I have killed the young monarch?"** Although the moment had now passed, the priest still debated whether he would get another chance in the future. And if he did, he had to be wise enough to seize the moment.

Ningizzida's display in the temple, of insulting the King in front of the Babylonian royalty went against everything he preached to his young acolytes and to his broader congregation. One of his foremost lessons when instructing his young charges in how to secure a state of esteem in this world was never to allow the other person to know what you were thinking. Ningizzida had gained his prominence by never allowing even his trusted fellow priests to know his thoughts. He figured that what they didn't know they couldn't prepare for. This was especially true in the politics of Babylonia. Placing himself in harm's way by insulting the young King in public was allowing others to know his disdain, and worse, give them opportunity to betray him. It allowed others to read his thoughts. Ningizzida was usually so clever in this endeavor that he would purposely lead others to believe lies about his intentions if it allowed him to hide his true objective. He would often spread false rumors deliberately throwing others off course. Ningizzida also believed in the clout of rumors. **"A very powerful thing,"** he would say in private. Gossip and rumor could change the course of history. He knew that people believed what they heard even though they would have no evidence to support the stories. There was pure muscle in such events. Ningizzida also preached that if you allow people to get close to you, you could lead them by the nose like sheep that are raised in the mountains of the county. Sheep go willingly to the slaughter because they've been lured into the trust of their masters.

The second rule that Ningizzida broke in his behavior at the temple was that of deference. Ningizzida always allowed the former King, Darius, to feel superior to him. With Darius, Ningizzida bowed low, and asked for things with respect. Ningizzida would make Darius appear smarter than he was. He would ask questions that he knew the King had easy answers for. This created a tremendous amount of trust in Ningizzida from Darius. It also gave Ningizzida an undo amount of influence when Darius ruled the Empire. It was part of his strategy not to show the lord up. He practiced false praise and said it with conviction. When questioned about his behavior, he would say, ***"There could be only one sun in the sky.***" There were rumors when Darius died of poisoning, that Ningizzida and the Babylonian priests were involved in the death. It couldn't have been further from the truth, as Ningizzida feared the implications of the death. He knew the old King and knew how to manipulate him. His death meant that this young, headstrong, obnoxious man, Xerxes, would inherit the throne. Ningizzida's spies had told him that Darius was poisoned, but it was orchestrated by the Egyptian magi, not the Babylonians.

The priest's hesitation and dislike of the young King increased steadily over the past few years. Ningizzida knew

153

Xerxes immediately, as he helped raise the Vicar of Babylonia. In that time Ningizzida developed a deep ocean of contempt for the young prince. He resented Xerxes as much as he respected his father, Darius. Ningizzida was secretly behind the movement to make Artobazanes, Xerxes' half-brother, the new King following Darius' sudden death. Unfortunately for him, Xerxes triumphed in the power struggle. This was in truth, part of the underlying resentment that Ningizzida felt for the new King. He had thought that he had accumulated enough influence to affect the outcome of the ascension but he hadn't. He had misread the politics of Susa and it cost him. He took the disappointment of Xerxes triumph as his own failure and vowed vengeance against the new monarch.

And yet, even with all the internal discipline that he developed over his lifetime, Ningizzida allowed this young King to ignite this rage within, forcing him to drop all his defenses and long held strategies of control. He didn't know why he hadn't considered manipulating the young King as he had done with his father. No, for some reason, Xerxes aroused something in Ningizzida that he did not immediately understand. His resentment and contempt of the young monarch was remarkable, and because of it, the priest lost all perspective and judgment regarding the new King.

When Manishtusu, the priest whose status was just below the great Ningizzida, first realized the older man's blind anger for Xerxes, he decided to approach him about the problem. One evening after a large supper, Manishtusu sat down with his mentor and opened the conversation about many subjects. Finally, he swallowed deeply, saying *"Master, I have a concern."*

Ningizzida inherently knew that the issue was one that he would not like hearing about, *"I'm listening, Manishtusu"*

"Well, master, I have always been impressed with your balance regarding the ever-changing political world in which we live. But I am confused."

Ningizzida could feel the set up coming.

"Master, I have noticed that your feelings about the young King are, at times, unreasonably negative. It is surprising to me. I have seen you seduce men of power and influence. I have never been able to read your intention."

Manishtusu walked toward the priest. He raised his arm to emphasize his point.

"These men who you controlled were all influential, powerful men lord, and you handled them as easily as most men handle clearing stones and slugs from their garden. And this young King, he turns your insides. I can see it in your face. Just mentioning his name upsets you. I don't understand this, Master."

Ningizzida tensed as his muscles strained. His jaw clenched at the comments and he could feel bile rising in his throat. The priest turned with fire in his eyes. When Manishtusu saw his face, he felt fear like no other time in his life. *"Did I make a major life mistake?"* he asked himself in the seconds that followed. As he stared into those wide wild eyes, Manishtusu felt as though the man he knew had disappeared and was replaced by another worldly presence. He was truly terrified. The older priest just kept staring as if he was transmitting thoughts. In fact, Manishtusu clearly read his face, and what he felt unnerved him. Ningizzida reached his arm out to his acolyte and grabbed him around the collar of his robe. His face was still distorted in rage as he pulled the younger man towards him. Then, after what seemed like time everlasting, his lower lip began to shake. Manishtusu began noticing that the older man was beginning to sweat, and in a low, harsh, gravelly voice, that sounded like it came from beyond the grave, he began to declare. *"**He is not worthy of devotion**...... **he is not worthy of being a King. That child is now the head of a great Empire. His father was a great man. He is a bastard and a fraud. When his name crosses my thoughts I can feel the gods flinch.**"*

His grip tightened as he pulled the younger man closer.

*"**I will destroy him.**"*

His voice became lower and more penetrating. *"**I will destroy him**"*

And as he turned away, he thought to himself *"**or die in the process**"*.

The King was mentally and emotionally exhausted as he walked out of the room. He didn't seem to be lifting his legs but appeared to shuffle along the beautifully shined stone floor. It was unusual, but the King was half naked and appeared mesmerized. He was still inebriated as he staggered into the outer chamber. He was met immediately by a series of slaves who almost carried him back to his residence. When they lifted him up one of the slaves felt moisture on his hands. The slave initially thought that the King was sweating, but the liquid was sticky to the touch. The slave bent around the King to look at his hand and almost jumped out of his skin when he noticed his hands covered with blood. At first the slave screamed but recovered quickly. The other slaves froze at the sound. After their initial panic, the slaves began to realize that it wasn't the King's blood that covered the top half of his body. One of the slaves turned around and peaked into the chamber which the King had just left. He could almost make out the outline of the slave girl lying lifeless on the bed. He winced at the realization of what had just happened, but immediately put the death out of his mind. Slaves couldn't afford emotions and the slave girl wasn't worth the reaction. She had given her life to calm the King's rage. In their minds, a worthy and predestined sacrifice.

PERSIA

CHAPTER VI - THE WARRIOR QUEEN

She never hurried, guiding each step as she walked along the glazed brick floor. Parts of this palace was over three millennia old reaching back to the initial settlement of this area. It sat on the Mesopotamian plain near the Zagros Mountains. There were four great gateways that led to the temple. Each gateway was glazed in a bright color and faced in a different direction. Entering the first gateway, Artemisia was greeted by the recessed figure of a bull. Next to the colored bull was engraved a bigger than life relief of Darius, Xerxes' father. The bull was in place to ward off evil spirits and protect the inner sanctum.

The temple was built on the Apadana mound that overlooked the entire city. There was no question that royalty lived here, as every inch of the palace was adorned with ornamental rugs and beautifully carved and baked reliefs. Each relief was designed to tell different stories of Persian glory. Often, they were comprised of carvings of diverse foreign peoples carrying food to praise the King of Kings. Every nationality and race were represented in these stories. There were reliefs about peoples who were conquered by the Achaemenid Empire, and those peoples who were allied to the Empire. Other carvings showed troops surrounding ornamental animals.

The palace itself was built from the contributions of many allied and slaved peoples who went to great lengths to contribute to this palatial monument. The front of the inner chamber of the palace was adorned by great cedar trees imported by the Assyrians from a mountain that they called Lebanon. King Darius had imported the finest Egyptian goldsmiths to carve his image on the walls of the great meeting hall.

Beautifully colored brick was shaped into the images of lions and soldiers to protect the King's soul. The soldiers stood with their great spears flanking the King's chamber. These brick sculptors from the Elamite masters had been glazing reliefs for years. But their work in Susa stopped Artemisia in her tracks. She drifted into a daydream, hypnotized by the beauty of the designed brick. She could not remove her eyes from the sculptured lion that marked the entrance to the great chamber. Unlike free standing statues, this animal appeared moving even though it was inanimate and standing still. One could distinguish its burly limbs and its proud mane as it preyed upon its next meal. Artemisia imagined how its muscles bulged as it chased its quarry. As she stared she could almost feel it come to life and she almost had a sexual feeling as she stared at this creature's muscles. She stood in a trance imagining the chase. The majesty of the great beast took the Queen. The image excited the great Queen and she could feel the excitement pulse through her hips and legs.

The Warrior Queen was usually a stoic presence. There were only a few things that had the ability to raise Artemisia's blood pressure. A battle, especially a sea battle, in which the Queen faced overwhelming odds always excited her. The Queen had made her reputation pulling off "miracles" on the seas. The entire Aegean and Mediterranean basin knew of the exploits of the Queen from Halicarnassus. Her name, and those of her adopted brothers, the Phoenicians, worried every sea faring nation. In a fight, Queen Artemisia was a cold assassin. She was an uncanny military tactician. None of her captains ever questioned her decision; they had such faith in her judgment under pressure. The Queen was also a brilliant and almost compulsive military historian. For hours on end she studied the military strategy of her enemies. She prepared for every battle by understanding her opponents almost as well as they understood themselves. She was also well informed frequently sending out spies to scout the impending enemy.

Artemisia had been in this palace twice before, and each time she became transfixed at this very spot staring at this symbol of the Achaemenid dynasty. The Queen was drawn to this place like a moth to fire.

Eventually, Artemisia's trance was broken by her soldier escorts. But they broke the Queen's gaze with quiet interference. They had all learned that Artemisia was possessed with power that they only dreamed about, and they were very careful not to harshly disturb her meditations. When one of the guards moved, the Queen slowly turned her head and stared at the man for a few seconds. The message was given.

Artemisia was a stunningly statuesque woman. Her features were not girlish or soft but were striking nonetheless. Artemisia was known throughout the Empire as the Warrior Queen. She had long flowing black hair which she often wore in long, decorated braids. When she wore her hair loose, colors were often seen. Artemisia was a self-consumed woman. She was aggressive and had no equal in her battlefield strategy. She was certain in her decisions and seemed to be able to read the enemy's thoughts, some suggested, before they knew it themselves. Artemisia rarely showed outward emotion even when startled. She was always in control and others could not read her emotions or thoughts. Artemisia had few equals either in battle or in politics. But make no mistake, she was not a compromiser, she was a conqueror. Artemisia was also very loyal. When she decided how she was going to play a situation or align with an ally, she became a bulldog. It was known that Artemisia was devoted to the Achaemenid dynasty. Darius had supported her rise to power and the Queen would not forget such devotion. What people tended to forget about this elite warrior was her limited experience at negotiation. Because she could so easily read people

163

and situations, she was thought to be invaluable during discussion. Most didn't know that the Queen did not enjoy diplomacy. Her solution to most situations was aggression and decisiveness. She firmly believed "might makes right."

After being pulled from her trance, by being called by her Lieutenant, the Warrior Queen slowly turned, and without acknowledging him, began her slow walk towards the throne room. Artemisia looked back to give her silent regards to the animal that held her in a trance and then turned away, as if it never existed.

The room that Artemisia entered next was flanked by thirty-six cedar columns. At the top of the columns was a sculptured bull head. The beams appeared to rest on the bull's back, representing the strength that the dynasty held. At the center of the great hall stood the throne upon which the great Persian King sat. Artemisia knew that the throne would now be empty, as Xerxes was not yet back to Susa. Artemisia always took this path to briefly bask in the glory of this room. Behind the throne were two great doors which led to a large courtyard. Past the doors was a groomed path flanked by luscious and finely cared for gardens. But before the Warrior Queen would leave this area in favor of the beauty of the gardens, she pondered the throne and what its strength meant.

Artemisia was a fiercely loyal woman, but she could never be accused of humility. Her father, Lycydamis, was Dorian by nationality, and her mother was Greek. The Dorians had settled Halicarnassus generations before. They were a warlike people who took insult at even the smallest slight. It was rumored that Lycydamis had beheaded a rival for referring to his wife as fair-haired. He stood over the dead rival, spat on his body, and proudly pronounced his wife's hair as golden.

Artemisia's name was derived from Artemis, the god of the hunt. Her parents could not have chosen a more fitting description. By the time her father passed away, Artemisia was already a decorated and feared warrior. Upon his death she immediately assumed power with little resistance from any of her rivals whom she quickly eliminated.

Artemisia's city of birth, Halicarnassus, was a lush and rich province. A deep and sheltered harbor protected the island city. Halicarnassus was a multicultural city with a large and prosperous Greek population. Even though Artemisia's history of loyalty to the Persian King was uncontested, her Greek blood left lingering doubts in Xerxes' mind. Because even the great King couldn't read this woman's thoughts, he was never at ease around her. Artemisia knew this instinctively and found it to her advantage. There were few men who were comfortable in her presence.

Halicarnassus was famous throughout the Empire for its mercenaries. They were fierce fighters and excellent seamen. The Persians in general did not understand sea battles. They were strictly a land power. Artemisia, on the other hand, was comfortable in both venues, and this expertise made her an extremely important ally to Xerxes. It wasn't just her skill that attracted Xerxes to her, it was her fearlessness. There were many rumors and stories surrounding Artemisia's prowess in battle. She once sacrificed a portion of her army to entrap and destroy an enemy three times its size. When she retreated her enemy assumed she was defeated and walked into her ambush without persuasion. In truth, Artemisia rarely retreated. She believed in her own ability to out strategize her opponent and she faithfully trusted her instincts. Up until this point she hadn't been wrong. She believed that every part of life was a strategic game. It was continually changing and evolving. One could not afford mistakes as the fall from glory was always quicker than the ascent.

Artemisia had also been called "blood thirsty". She took pride in impaling enemies. She would report that their blood made her stronger. Some had seen her cover her body with the blood of a fallen victim.

As she walked past the throne Artemisia knew that the King would not be resting on it for the next few days. The King, she knew, was still in Babylonia preparing to return to the palace. The Queen wanted to arrive here before him to have time to prepare herself for the great meeting that was to occur three days after his return. Artemisia wanted to have already prepared a strategy to invade Canaan and Egypt. She knew that she would not be the only advisor to be presenting plans, but she wanted hers to be perfect. The Warrior Queen knew that her strongest adversary for the King's ear would be the general Mardonius.

Mardonius was Xerxes' first cousin and the highest-ranking soldier at Xerxes' ear. Artemisia also knew that Xerxes council of advisors in military affairs was made up of many different nationalities. The Phoenician Kings would be present, as would representatives of the Macedonians, Ionians, Cypriots, Cilicians, Lycians and the Aegean islanders. Xerxes required all the peoples living in the Empire to send representatives to the council. Every satrap or province would be represented at the meeting, some yielding significantly more power and influence than others, but all present.

Artemisia was no fool. She knew that Mardonius was also the chief commander of the Immortals. They were the cream of the Persian army: 10,000 men exceptionally trained. They were fed special food and even wore embroidered outfits into battle. One of Mardonius' chief lieutenants in the Immortals was almost as famous as he was. His name was Smerdomences, and his reputation of being the fiercest warrior in the Empire was generally accepted. Smerdomences was the only warrior whose reputation came close to Artemisia's. They were both extremely proud individuals who respected the other's achievements. At other council meetings Artemisia had contact with both Mardonius and Smerdomences. Although she respected Smerdomences, she disliked and resented Mardonius. Artemisia believed that Mardonius' success really came from Smerdomences' strategy. She saw Mardonius as taking the credit for another man's ability and it irritated her to no end. Even worse, Artemisia was not hesitant or shy to express her thoughts whenever the opportunity arose. Her impetuous mouth did not endear her to others. Artemisia had learned over the years to control her impulsivity. Control might be too strong a word, it was closer to regulate. She often used her sharp cutting tongue as a way of unnerving those she spoke with. It was also one of the ways she evaluated and manipulated those she was studying. The battle was not just won on the field. As with animals, a courageous show was important.

Unlike many of her rivals, Artemisia had the unquestioned loyalty of her entourage and troops. These people were loyal to her and nobody else. They followed her not their country, not their city, not their King, but they would follow her into the depths of hell. It allowed her to put her effort towards fighting the enemy and not have to focus behind at her troops. With this knowledge, she could look forward and not worry backwards.

As she entered her residence she called for her female courtier, Ekallatim. Although Artemisia was both statuesque and commanding, she was not feminine. Ekallatim was eighteen and had been in Artemisia's entourage for five years. Since she was old enough to bleed she was at the heels of her Queen. Unlike other children of the Mediterranean, Ekallatim was fair haired and blue eyed. There were many rumors throughout the Empire that Ekallatim was Artemisia's

lover.   For her part, Artemisia did
nothing to dispel these rumors.   In
truth, she was more attracted to
Ekallatim than she had been to any man.
Her skin was milky white and her long
flowing hair was silky to the touch.
Artemisia had to be hard in her life.
She lived and fought in a man's world and
had conquered every obstacle that stood
in her way. With Ekallatim, she could be
soft.   She would spend hours stroking her
soft skin and hair.   It would put her in
an almost meditative state.   Ekallatim
was Artemisia's means of escape.   When
Artemisia stared into Ekallatim's deep
blue eyes, many of her concerns melted
away, her muscles relaxed, and her hatred
waned.   It was an unchallenging and
totally one-sided relationship.

   Artemisia settled into her residential
hall.   The King had set aside a long
hallway in the palace for Artemisia and
her entourage.   Her guards took their
position protecting both the entrance and
the exit.   She had twenty-five soldiers
with her who were skilled in security.
They were all Phoenicians, and the
adopted brothers to the Warrior Queen.
This meeting was so important to
Artemisia that she brought with her two
members of her inner council, as well her
recorder, Herodotus.   Herodotus was
someone who Artemisia tolerated because
he was gifted as a historian.   But
Artemisia didn't trust Herodotus and paid

him little mind. He was there to observe
and document. He offered no strategy and
Artemisia expected none from him.

As she began to relax, feeling secure
that she could let down her guard, two of
her advisors entered with slaves carrying
food and drink.

Cassites was magus to the Queen. He
was a very conservative individual who
was originally from the Elam city of Kul-
I Farah. This city was separated from the
grand palace at Susa by the Zagros
Mountains. Cassites had traveled
extensively and had also lived in Bisitun
in the northern part of the province.
While there he had studied with a young
influential priest named Ningizzida.
Cassites had learned a great deal from
this teacher and eventually emigrated to
the western part of the Empire where he
met the Warrior Queen. He immediately
became enraptured by this woman and
became a loyal servant. While the
Queen's entourage stopped in the northern
city of Sippar on their way to Susa, he
had a clandestine meeting with his old
master. Ningizzida had contacted him
through a handmaiden and begged for
secrecy. Cassites could not refuse his
old master and snuck out of the
encampment in the middle of the night to
meet Ningizzida. Cassites had not told
his Queen about the shadowy meeting
because he had heard that Ningizzida was

a wanted man and he feared his sovereign would ask for him to betray the old priest. His fears were well founded because the Queen would have asked just that. Cassites also knew that if Artemisia knew about the secret she would have his head. So Cassites told nobody of his meeting. He also kept its contents secret, although some of the things that Ningizzida asked shook him to the bones.

Nabu-na'id, a eunuch whom the Queen freed during her conquest of Rhodes entered with Cassites. Rhodes was an island south of Halicarnassus which, for a brief time, rebelled against Xerxes' father, Darius. In the capital city of Lindos, the Rhodian King had a slave whom he tortured without mercy. The slave, Nabu-na'id, had been a member of the royalty until the King deflowered him. The King had taken Nabu-na'id's manhood because he was angry that Nabu-na'id had warned him against rebelling against the Persian King. Upon receiving his freedom from the Queen, the eunuch became immediately indebted to her, promising her his life.

The politics within the Queen's entourage was always fluid. Nabu-na'id didn't trust the magus and the feeling was mutual. They were both continually maneuvering for position in the Queen's favor. But Nabu-na'id finally had an advantage. He had a hunch and he quietly and carefully followed Cassites when the entourage was at Sippar. In truth he had followed Cassites at other times with no results. When he saw the rogue priest arrive for the meeting he could feel the excitement building in his body. This information was a special prize. Such an opportunity rarely came along and Nabu-na'id had to play it just right to take the most advantage of it. Of course, his initial instinct was to run to the Queen and expose the magus. He knew he might still take that approach, but he had to consider the various options before acting.

Both Cassites and Nabu-na'id were obviously confused as they sat before their sovereign. Cassites began first: *"My Queen, may I speak?"*

"You may," answered Artemisia, although she didn't remove her gaze from her food.

"My Queen, your vision is beyond my understanding." He bowed low and continued, *"I am shamed by my own stupidity and I am weak in your presence."*

With a disgusted look, the Queen shouted, *"Ask your question, Cassites, and stop the useless platitudes."*

The Queen continued to enjoy her meal. Artemisia instinctively knew her magus' fear, resulting in his trepidation to ask directly. Artemisia needed no compliments. They were useless for her. Cassites bowed again and continued. *"My Queen, we have traveled long distances with you to arrive at this place. It is truly magnificent. The halls and art of this edifice are as glorious as your presence."*

With this comment, the Queen stopped her chewing and looked at the priest with disdain. Cassites read the look and again continued. *"My Queen, I sit in your presence unsure of how I can help you. If you tell me why we have made this arduous journey I can offer you my council."*

Artemisia stood slowly and her black alligator leather boots almost sparkled in the light of the window. She shook her long hair and grabbed it throwing it to her back. With irritation, she commented almost sarcastically, *"We are here by the request of our King, Xerxes."*

Cassites already knew that information, as the answer was an avoidance of his question. *"My Queen, I will again ask. Why are we here?"*

Feigning anger, the Queen turned and faced Cassites. She knew what he wanted to know, but she was not yet ready to satisfy his itch. Artemisia responded. *"We will discuss our mission when it is time."*

She again looked intensely at Cassites.

"I am here Priest, because my King requested it. You are here, because I requested it."

With a sly smile she said, *"Does that answer the question?"*

She turned away and with a short wave of her arm dismissed the priest. Cassites understood the motion and quietly left the room. The Warrior Queen turned to Nabu-na'id. *"You have been quiet my friend, what are your thoughts?"*

Nabu-na'id bowed his head and pleaded. *"My Queen, I fear for your safety."*

"My safety?"

Artemisia questioned. *"Yes, my lord. I do not trust that priest."*

Artemisia smiled and returned to her seat. She answered, *"I know you have concerns, my friend. Believe me; my eyes stay open, even when I sleep."*

She went on, *"I do have a task for you. I would like you to listen to the walls. I need eyes in the castle that will make me aware of things that I do not know. There is something wrong here, but I don't know what it is."*

The Queen's face was deadly serious. *"Do you understand what I want?"*

"I do, my Queen," Nabu-na'id replied. *"I will not fail you."*

"I know you won't, Nabu-na'id, but you seem distracted. Is there something I should know?"

"Nothing, my Queen."

The Queen smiled, knowing at some level that Nabu-na'id was not truthful. She then waved her arm. As Nabu-na'id left, the Queen demanded to a slave, *"Send in Ekallatim."*

PERSIA

CHAPTER VII -
RETURNING HOME

After his embarrassment in Babylonia, Xerxes was happy to be home in Susa. Of all the six capitals, Susa was the most comfortable for him. Susa was the ancestral home of the Achaemenid and the Medes. Xerxes could relax now in preparation for the council meeting and the re-conquest of Canaan and Egypt. He was still reverberating from the events in Babylonia. The young King had many decisions to ponder over the next week. The council meeting was still two days away and Xerxes had to arrive at some conclusions before then. Although there would be debates among the various participants, the King was taught that even though he would listen, his mind had to be prepared for what needed to be done. This was not an egalitarian Empire. Xerxes had planned to use his Egyptian campaign as a testing ground for the bigger prizes - Athens and Greece. Egypt was merely an itch compared to the larger aching.

Even though there were many issues for the young monarch to deal with, he had to maintain his priorities. Xerxes had a slave whose only purpose was to remind him at various times during the day that he couldn't forget his vengeance for Athens. The slave mentioned the horrible defeat at Marathon and reminded the King of Kings that the Greeks erected a monument in Athens to celebrate their supremacy over the Persians. The King of Kings did not want his blood to stop boiling over the insult by the Greeks.

Egypt would serve many purposes for the Empire. Xerxes would be able to decide which of his generals and lesser Kings would take the lead in the Greek excursion. Egypt would be a testing ground. Xerxes knew that, and so did all his generals. But the test was also for the new King. Since his return home, the King had been besieged with presents and gifts from those seeking to gain favor before decisions were made. He had to speak with many envoys and members of the elite in Persian society.

The one issue that stuck in the King's side was that he couldn't rid his mouth of the bad taste that accompanied him home from Babylonia. That priest, the old crow Ningizzida who insulted him in front of the elite of Babylonia, still stuck in his throat. Xerxes wanted his blood. He could taste the longing. It was stronger and more palpable than any feeling that Xerxes had ever felt. He had conquered fear in his training, but humiliation and swallowing pride, was not a lesson he had learned.

Since Babylonia, other than the events with the slave girl, Xerxes had no taste for sexual release, an unusual lack of desire for this man. The events in Babylonia stripped the young King of his virility. Previously, Xerxes would often wake in the middle of the night hard as a rock needing satisfaction. But now he woke sweaty, dreaming intensely, all revenge-oriented nightmares. The gods were attempting to communicate with him. They were sending him a message. He spent two days sacrificing both animals and children of slaves attempting to satisfy his blood lust. So far, none of his attempts had achieved the desired results. Xerxes was internally distracted and self-consumed and his slaves all became fearful for their safety. There were rumors about an incident in Babylonia and the news was not lost on them. Whereas before Xerxes controlled himself with his slaves, but now he was explosive. Small mistakes would set him off into rages that suggested he was fighting for possession of his own psyche, by the evil internal god, Tiamat.

The great chamber that housed the throne was the recognized place to hold court. On this day the King walked slowly into his throne room. It was an unusually hot and dry day even for Susa. The first sense that one experienced when entering the room was the aromatic smell of olibanum. Xerxes favored this smell that was born from the flower of the Boswella tree. He identified with the plight of this tree. It could grow in the sparest of places, and somehow survived the desert, eventually giving forth it's fantastic bouquet. Xerxes bought frankincense from the Arab traders and decreed that the odor should always be in his nose.

The throne itself, although built with gold plated wood, was generally simple.

It was written, and part of tradition, that the throne could not outshine the King of Kings. For this occasion, Xerxes wore his favorite apple colored robe. Although he also favored purple, he felt that this day required red. Xerxes carried his diamond studded scepter in his right hand. His head was covered with a red cidaris that matched his long flowing robe. Standing next to the throne and present at every meeting that involved foreign dignitaries was the hazarapat. The hazarapat was one of the most powerful men in the Kingdom. He controlled both the royal stores and the royal bodyguard. Takhmaspada the Mede was the first in command under Xerxes' father, Darius. He retained the position of hazarapat under the young King, although Xerxes didn't trust him as much as his father did. The new King worried that Takhmaspada could stage a coup considering the amount of power he wielded. But also considering the suddenness of his rise to power, Xerxes could not replace the Mede. What he did do was demand that the Mede always stand to his right so he could observe his facial responses. Since his ascension, Xerxes had made clear to the hazarapat that he should consider his position more tenuous than it was with his father. The young King was lucky that the older hazarapat had no designs on more power than he already had. In their meeting, the hazarapat tried to assure the young

King that he had no hidden agendas, but doubt lingered. The King had already learned that reservation always lingered.

The cupbearer always followed the King into the throne room. Aspachana held this exalted position. His job was to carry the King's double sided sagaris. The ax was one of the young King's favorite fighting instruments. Aspachana also carried his bow, a weapon that the King practiced with daily. He could outshoot many of the immortal archers. Beyond the cupbearer stood the five general immortals who had earned their position by being fierce warriors. Under his robe, the young King carried his short sword on his right thigh.

Xerxes would spend a good part of this day speaking to those seeking favor and those that he had summoned to hear directions from their sovereign. As he entered the room he was confronted by a very familiar face. Sameron noticed him and almost leaped high enough to knock him over. The female lioness had grown up at the heels of this man and knew of him as a brother.

When an adolescent Xerxes went on a hunting trip. During that time, the lord found a young lion cub that had been abandoned by its pride. The young Prince adopted the beast and named it Sameron after an ancient Mesopotamian anti-god.

The King felt the same emotions about Sameron that the beast felt about him. Even though he stumbled backward under the lioness's strength, a smile finally spread across the King's face. The young King embraced the beast feeling more empathy and compassion for it then he did for most people. The lioness, probably sensing the need, stayed with her front paws over the man's shoulders for a few seconds. When the King met with dignitaries, Sameron lay by the feet of his throne acting as a tangible obstacle between all people and the supreme monarch. If someone ventured too close to Xerxes all Sameron had to do was raise her large ominous head and lick her beautiful canines causing even the bravest of men to gently back away. More importantly, her presence made the young King feel secure and back in control.

Mardonius was the commander of the Immortals. The Immortals were the Empires first line of defense. They were the selected of the elite. These 10,000 warriors were the boldest of all the fighters in Persia. It was a closed fraternity, as warriors from allied Satraps were not allowed into the units. On this day, Smerdonemces, Mardonius' second in command, was one of the first of the visitors to see the young King. He presented himself on the very night that Xerxes arrived. Because of his reputation, Smerdomences was given a respected place on the list of the people in line to see the King. When he entered the throne room he bent low placing his sword under his neck to show his subservience to the great King. Next, Smerdomences took out his stiletto and placed it on his neck. The gesture also indicated that he was giving his life to the King.

At the sight of Smerdomences, Xerxes smiled and rose to meet the great warrior. His introductory comments were an indication of the respect that he had for the cunning soldier. With an unusual exuberance rarely seen in the King, he rose in front of the bowed warrior, *"My friend, I am glad that you came to visit me."* Smerdomences understood the unusual greeting and its meaning. He exclaimed, *"Thank you my King, I am glad to see you in such good health. I pledge myself to your happiness."*

In a very curious move, Xerxes took Smerdomences into his confidence, expressing his inner thoughts. *"I am not happy, Smerdomences. Did you hear about the outrage in Babylonia?"* Smerdomences had heard of the occurrences during the Babylonian celebration. He would not admit such information to his King for fear that such knowledge would embarrass the young monarch.

"I have not, my King!" he said without hesitation. Xerxes' expression immediately changed to irritation as he responded to the warrior that stood in front of him. *"That priestly pig, Ningizzida, insulted the dynasty. He must be punished for his insolence. My relatives in heaven are all pleading with me to draw blood."* Smerdomences responded to the King's change in mood. *"Release me my King. Order me to Babylon and I will present the head of this infidel to you."*

The King withdrew, turning away from the great warrior. He stopped and responded, *"No, my friend. I appreciate the offer. Do you know the warrior, Penish?"* *"I do, my King. He is very competent."*

Xerxes again turned serious. He looked at Smerdomences and his mood was calmer. *"My task for you, Smerdomences, is also important. You have lived in Mardonius' shadow long enough. Your task is to assemble another battalion of Immortals. You will train those troops quickly and hone their skills with Egyptian blood. They will then become the vanguard of the attack on Greece."*

The King stopped and looked at the warrior, seeking to read his reaction to what was just said. He continued, *"Do you think you are up to this task, Smerdonemces?"* Smerdomences again bowed

185

his head and responded. *"I am, my King. Any task that you give me will be accomplished."* Smerdomences hesitated, but before he spoke, Xerxes again began talking. *I know what you are worried about my friend. I've already told Mardonius and he understands. He's not happy, but he understands. I also told him that you will choose four men for your top lieutenants. Again, Mardonius was not happy hearing that he would lose four more men."*

The King smiled. He liked rivalry between his army commanders. He believed that if there was this friendly competition they would perform better.

"My King, without thinking, Nergal, would be my first choice." The King replied, *"Good choice, Smerdonemces, good choice. You can make your other choices after some thought." "Thank you, my lord. You will not be disappointed."*

Smerdomences left with more life in his step than when he arrived. The King had broken the news to Mardonius and he was quite upset at the prospect of losing his first commander. He protested even more when the King told him that Smerdomences would be able to choose commanders. But when Xerxes outlined his rationale for the moves, Mardonius had to admit its necessity. Whether he agreed or not, Mardonius was not in position to

186

argue with the Monarch. The war against Greece would be a gargantuan undertaking and Xerxes was preparing to expand his elite regimens.

* * * *

Janlikorven lay prostrate in front of the great King. It took him over a week to ride home from providing the message to Demaratus. Xerxes had been expecting his report and Janlikorven had returned a few days later than the King had expected. Janlikorven's report and evaluation was crucial for the King's strategy. He was expecting to have Demaratus lead one of the battalions on the Egyptian campaign. He wanted to know the heart of this man, and Janlikorven's report would go a long way to helping him determine his worth. Unless Janlikorven presented a horrible review, Xerxes would test the ex-Spartan King.

Although his heart was bursting with excitement to hear the report, he sat stone-like in front of the envoy. He had employed this man's services many times before and was never disappointed in the information. Xerxes believed that he could look through any man and understand their inner purpose. He trusted Janlikorven. He had gained this trust through many circumstances in which Janlikorven was tested. Janlikorven had overcome and passed every test. The King had no way of knowing that this trusted envoy had been bought. His presentation would be tilted because of gold provided to him by Demaratus.

"My lord, my life has always been yours."

Xerxes retorted, *"Tell me, Janlikorven; tell me what you've seen."*

Janlikorven rose and smiled to his lord. *"My lord, I bring you only good news this day."*

"Tell me about the man, Janlikorven. What have you surmised?"

Janlikorven responded in a manner that suggested deliberation *"You've made a very wise choice my lord, in putting your faith in Demaratus. I believe he will serve you with honor and respect, even though he is not a Persian. Demaratus is devoted to your dynasty and the chance that you've given him to redeem his reputation."*

Xerxes sat back in his seat as his hand came to his chin. He seemed to be in thought as he listened to the glowing words that his envoy was expounding. One would think that this report would satisfy Xerxes but it seemed to make him uneasy. Janlikorven continued, *"I*

188

believe that Demaratus will serve you as well as any of your current commanders. He is a military man who also understands the politics of ruling peoples. He has something to prove. I only have two hesitations about this man."

The King's eyebrows rose. He was waiting for this part of the report. *"Yes?"*

Janlikorven continued his evaluation, *"Lord there are two issues that bother me. The first is that this man has never been in battle. He appears to understand the strategy of war, but I can't say about his reactions when leading men in the field. I am also concerned about his anger. He can taste revenge against the Greeks and this could interfere with his decisions."*

Xerxes rose to his feet and slowly walked toward the envoy. He placed both of his arms on his shoulders and thanked the small man. Janlikorven bowed and left the room. Xerxes stared at him as he left. The report was too positive for his comfort even with the obvious final criticisms. As he turned to return to his chair, he thought,

"I wouldn't have believed that Janlikorven could be bought. But now I know his true heart." His muscles

bristled and he felt his neck tighten at
this realization.

★★★★

PERSIA

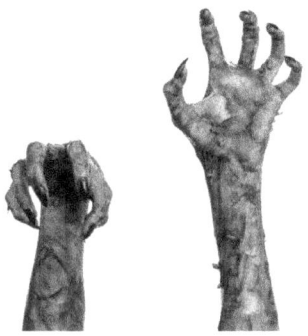

CHAPTER VIII - THE DREAM

He really couldn't see down the road. The path ahead was hazy and covered with fog. All he could see was white. Ningizzida knew that he had to keep walking but his steps were unsteady. Ningizzida also felt his feet hurting as the ground below his steps was uneven and the sharp objects made his legs shake.

Ningizzida heard the heavy breathing of an animal as he walked along this path. He cried out in fear, but nobody was there to hear his whimpering. His fear was palpable and his body began sweating profusely. As he strode, the ground seemed to be heating as if boiling water was under the rocks. He was walking into the underworld. There were no boundaries, nothing familiar, only the path before him and the fog permeating his soul. He tried stopping but knew that he couldn't. His legs began to spasm and he couldn't reach down to massage the cramping muscles.

The breathing of the animal grew louder as Ningizzida walked on. There were no other people around to help him in his journey. He knew that the animal was close and that he would soon reach it.

Suddenly the path turned and a hill stood in front of the Priest. Ningizzida was now on his knees looking up. To his surprise and horror what stood on the top of the hill was a gigantic bull. The animal was outraged and breathing heavily. Ningizzida saw the saliva dripping from his mouth and nostrils. With every breath the bull's nostrils expelled wet steam. Its eyes were glassy and red and were directly focused on the priest now lying in front of him. The animal looked at the priest and his large muscles were sweating as he began stepping toward Ningizzida. The priest could feel the ground begin to tremble as the great beast began to move closer.

Without warning, the ground began to shake violently and opened in the space between the priest and the animal. It was being ripped by a force greater than the gods themselves. Steam and fire rose from the newly opened hole. A black hand reached up and grabbed the bull by the horns dragging it into the ground. The animal protested with unholy roars and complaints but the hand continued to drag it to the unknown. The animal dug its legs into the ground and snorted mightily. Its eyes seemed to fall back into its skull as the hands continued to drag it into the depths. It struggled mightily, but the hands were persevering, slowly winning the battle. With every second the animal was drawn closer to the precipice.

And then, again to his surprise, the hands stopped pulling. Ningizzida knew they were waiting for his sign. Did he want them to continue the assault or should they allow the animal to live? Ningizzida held his hands to the heavens and began chanting that the end of the life of the bull had arrived. Take him, my father, take his soul, he screamed.

The hands, as if they were attached to Ningizzida's words, gave a final yank, and the bull disappeared into the unknown.

Ningizzida awoke sweating and covered with perspiration. He began shivering as the desert was as cold as the highest mountains in the Empire. He had been in the cave for five days and he knew that this isolation was beginning to cause the line between dreams and reality to dim. He had been smoking a special blend of hashish that was brought to him from friends within the city and was specifically earmarked for this meditative purpose. His days were spent in chanting, fasting, and reading the smoke. His only food over the past few days was two snakes that he caught on the first day of his forced isolation.

Ningizzida was now in hiding from the authorities. Before deciding on this religious isolation, he had been going from house to house and church basement to church basement to avoid detection. He knew that a price had been put on his capture and that close friends would be tempted by the reward. He needed to find the truth of his behavior and this isolation and meditation was the only way he knew to arrive at the answers.

Ningizzida leaned back on the sand by the wall of the cave. He wiped the sweat off his brow and covered himself with a blanket that he brought to fight the cold. As he contemplated the dream that he just awoke from he began to laugh. There was no interpretation for the dream

194

other than Ningizzida's triumph over the Persian King. Ningizzida himself held the King's fate in his hand. He was encouraged that the gods had given him such a clear message. Ignore the fear and the unknown. Continue the course that you have chosen and destroy the Archimedean dynasty.

The old priest also knew that Manishtusu would be arriving in the morning with food and drink. He had survived the five-day fast and had been given a clear message. Xerxes short reign was coming to an end and he would triumph.

Ningizzida arose from his prone position. His old bones ached, and his muscles were sore and painful. He was hungry and thirsty. As he proceeded to the mouth of the cave the sun's yellow haze was just rising over the mountains in the background. Ningizzida also took this as a positive omen. His friend and acolyte would be arriving soon and he was emboldened by his dreams and visions. The future was now in his grasp.

But as he stood the old priest became anxious. It was just an instinct. There was no apparent reason to have this trepidation. And as he stood in the time just before sunrise the old man found the connection that was eluding him and what created the tension. The vision he had was too simplistic. The gods never communicated in this fashion and the dream had been bothering the priest. That's why the smoke was puzzling him. The epiphany now hit him with a chill. The dream was not a message but a warning. He would be at the center of a controversy and worse, he now knew that he had created his own betrayal. But where would it come from? How could he protect himself from this attack? It all made sense, but the message was now very convoluted. He knew danger but not its direction. And worse, he didn't know whether to run, hide or stay still.

As he stood watching the sun rise and contemplating his next move, Ningizzida could see a few figures walking towards him. Although initially excited, he became confused why Manishtusu would be bringing others with him to the cave. As the men approached their features became clearer and none were familiar to the old priest. His confusion mounted and fear and anger began to arise within him. These men were strangers, and yet they approached with a purpose as if they knew where they were going. The five men were now only a few feet in front of the priest. The fear was now transformed to realization as the men in front of him were dressed in the Imperial uniforms of the Immortals.

The soldiers stopped and one man walked from the pack to a few feet in front of the priest. He looked deeply into the priest's eyes and whispered, *"Do you know who I am?"*

The priest didn't really look at the Immortal. His stare centered on his traitorous acolyte Manishtusu, who stood next to this soldier. For the moment it was as if nobody else existed except for the two religious men. The older man wanted to strike out or wail at the younger priest, but he stood stoically and just gazed, feeling the pain of betrayal in his guts. Ningizzida steadied himself and shook his head finally responding to the question. Without warning, the Immortal lashed out at the old man, striking him directly in the left eye, knocking him to the sand in front of the cave. Weakened by his fast, Ningizzida felt as though he had been hit by the mountain itself. Bleeding and bruised, his eye already swelling, Ningizzida could barely raise his head to look again at the man who had just knocked him down. Instead of looking at his attacker, Ningizzida stared again through his one good eye, at Manishtusu. Now the old priest's face asked why. The younger man just turned his head giving his master no direct answer.

While this silent communication played out, the Immortal leaned down over the

197

fallen priest and again asked, *"I asked, do you know old man, who I am?"*

Barely able to move, Ningizzida again shook his head indicating that he didn't know the answer.

"My name, old man, is Penish. Say it, old man, say my name."

Ningizzida was silent, but Penish kicked him violently in his ribs. *"I said, say Penish. I want to make sure you know the warrior that will bring you to your punishment."*

Ningizzida again used all his strength to turn away from Manishtusu and look at the Immortal. He spit out blood and sand from his mouth and screeched, *"Do you know that you've sealed your fate by this betrayal? You have attacked a prophet of the great God."*

The Immortal laughed. *"Am I to be afraid of your invisible God? Where is he when you need him, priest?"*

He kicked at the prone man once more, *"You are nothing but a defeated old man. Now I asked you ancient one, what is my name? Say it or I will continue to punish you."*

Reluctantly Ningizzida complied, *"Penish."* And again spit blood on the ground.

The soldier laughed.

Penish looked at the old man lying on the ground and bent down close to his ear. He started to whisper to the priest: *"Old man, I will bind you and take you to my King. Prepare yourself, old man, for my King will not just kill you, he will slowly drain the life from your bones. I hope that your god can protect you from pain you haven't yet felt in your long life. The day you insulted the great King you set the wheel in motion. And now you will feel the excruciating death of a traitor."*

Penish smiled then and gently patted the priest's face.

Penish rose from his crouch and ordered his men to pull the priest to his feet and tie his hands. He would bring his prize back to his King. He had completed his task and would bring the live goat to the slaughter.

* * * *

PERSIA

CHAPTER IX - NABU-NA'ID

Eunuchs held a special place within the palace. They were allowed a greater range of freedom than other men for obvious reasons. Remarkably, they also achieved favored status by their Kings. They were negotiators, confidants, and very specialized spies. It was reasoned that because of their ability to focus on non-sexual issues, they could achieve more than other men could. They did not have the hormonal distractions that other men had. Whether valid or not, it was the unwritten law of the land.

Xerxes himself learned from his father the importance of these men in the political workings of Empires. In court, Xerxes had two eunuchs that often gave him council. And it was not just chatter. The King paid close attention to what they said. His father had schooled him for many hours in the importance of advanced information. The oldest of the two palace eunuchs, Tiglath, was a sour and dysphoric old man. He was often pessimistic in his prognostations, predicting doom and gloom. Tiglath was a strange looking figure; he was bent and moved with his head almost resting on one shoulder. He walked very tentatively using a heavy walking stick. It was rumored that King Darius had the walking stick carved specifically for Tiglath because of the excellent service that he provided to the realm. He had once warned Darius of the possibility of a trap during a military excursion. His generals, to the one, laughed at the suggestion. Darius, trusting his instincts, listened to the deformed eunuch and subsequently avoided a massacre, as the enemy had planned an ambush which Tiglath somehow recognized. Three generals lost their heads the next morning. One could, with certainty assume, that when an issue arose Tiglath would outline the threat and the pitfalls.

Ummanaldash was the other trusted eunuch in court. He was a quiet, very private individual who was both observant and perceptive. He seemed to analyze everything often while it was happening.

He was meditative and only spoke when his point was informative. He was unflappable even in the face of extreme commotion. He was also a historian of sorts and was often found in the company of Herodotus, the keeper of stories that accompanied and chronicled the journeys of Artemisia.

The court eunuchs, because of their special position, moved in different circles than other men, and this stealthy ability made them irreplaceable to the nobility. The eunuchs throughout the Empire were familiar with and knew of each other. They often had had political dealings with each other. They had an underground society. In fact, they seemed to prefer working with their kind and only seemed to trust others of their kind. There was an unspoken respect between these diplomats. They were often summoned by their respective Kings to perform extraordinary and dangerous acts of diplomacy. Both Ummanaldash and Tiglath were no exceptions. Although Darius never let it be known, Tiglath was his most trusted advisor. Darius believed that if he knew the worst he could overcome anything.

Nabu-na'id was a neophyte in the world of intrigue and conspiracy. But his Queen was depending on his quick learning curve. He had been preparing and now was his time. He swallowed hard and went

forth into the palace to complete his
mission.

Nabu-na'id sat across from the tea
table with Ummanaldash. It took him some
time and money to secure a meeting, and
eventually he bordered on begging to
convince the elder Ummanaldash to meet
with him. The two men really didn't know
each other. Ummanaldash had been
relieved of his manly parts when he was
barely out of adolescence. In truth, he
really didn't remember being whole.
Ummanaldash had been chosen to be
castrated at a very early age. When he
turned 13 his graduation into manhood was
to lose his manhood. Nabu-na'id had a
late start in this business losing his
testicles when he was in his thirties.
The other eunuchs had heard the rumors of
Nabu-na'id's arrival in the palace and
were all curious about this new entry
into the "brotherhood". They heard that,
as a nobleman of Rhodes when it was
conquered by its enemies, he was hung
upside-down with the other nobility till
blood dripped from his eyes. His
testicles and penis were not cut off but
burned slowly. The pain of such a
torture was supposed to be excruciating
as the flame was held above the scrotum
so that the destruction was a gradual
roasting. This killed most of the others
who hung in the town square. In fact,
Nabu-na'id was minutes from his own death
when Artemisia swept into the city square

and within a short period had slaughtered the invaders. By tradition, Nabu-na'id became the Warrior Queen's slave for life.

Ummanaldash on the other hand, was stripped of his manhood at a very early age. He was born to be a slave and was educated for this position that he would hold throughout his life. What this meant was that he was expected to become, and was taught to be, a practiced diplomat and manipulator. But, Nabu-na'id interested him. He was the "new kid" on the block and Ummanaldash was bored with his other duties. His deductive reasoning had presumed that Nabu-na'id had a purpose for being here. He knew that Nabu was indebted to Queen Artemisia for saving his life, and he knew the Queen was aggressive, self-centered and self-promoting. A powerful figure, Ummanaldash was so curious about Artemisia's purpose that he couldn't stand it. He wanted to know what Nabu-na'id wanted, but he couldn't just come out and ask. He wanted Nabu to feel as though he was learning something that Ummanaldash didn't want to reveal. Then he knew that Nabu would believe whatever he "accidently" revealed. He had to act bored, almost distant and aloof, even though his mind was on fire with interest. It was a challenge that Ummanaldash had rarely faced. Usually he was dealing with experienced, perceptive

diplomats. But here was a novice, a
political virgin needing to learn his
trade amid the fire. He didn't know if
this man, Nabu, was up to the task but he
knew that he could lead him wherever he
wanted to take him. It would almost be
too easy of a task, but he would enjoy it
none-the-less.

Nabu-na'id looked at the man sitting
across the table trying very hard to read
this older man's face. He watched this
man's wrinkled eyes, trying to understand
what the lines meant. Could he determine
this man's emotions by understanding how
these lines changed expression? Nabu also
paid attention to eyebrows and lips. He
believed that minor changes in expression
revealed the real underlying feeling.
Could he peer into this face and be able
to determine whether the truth was being
told or if he was being led purposely to
a dead end? For some reason he wanted to
trust Ummanaldash, but Nabu-na'id really
wasn't sure why he felt this way. Was
this feeling really an accurate reading,
or was it just hope and expectation. He
didn't realize that he was betraying his
hidden feelings by his squirming and the
shortness of his breath. He knew very
well about blind faith. He saw it while
he was King in Rhodes. But even when he
was King, Nabu-na'id had difficulty with
trust. Early in his reign he tended to
implicitly trust some of those under him
which led to his study of faces. When he

was burned a few times by betrayal, he then developed an almost suspicious lack of trust. He finally uttered: *"I have come a long way to meet you Ummanaldash. Your reputation is that of a master diplomat. Your name is spoken of throughout the Empire with great respect."*

Ummanaldash loved compliments. Although sharp and instinctive, he was also a very vain individual. He wore more facial makeup than many of the King's courtesans. He sat perfectly still as Nabu sung his praise. He wanted to appear uninterested, suggesting that he was above this tribute, but a quick turn of his eyebrows gave him away. This man could offer him nothing so he kept his gaze slightly turned away from Nabu, yet his focus hung on every word and verbal innuendo. Nabu continued his remarks. *"This palace is magnificent, Ummanaldash. Have you lived here all of your life?"*

Again, Ummanaldash feigned lack of interest. Nabu desperately tried to establish communication. He didn't quite know what was going on, so he figured he should just continue to bait the hook. His Queen had given him a task and he had to come through for her. Ummanaldash on the other hand, was enjoying the suffering that Nabu was experiencing. *"Please show me around. I would love to hear the secrets of this wonderful building. I am an amateur historian and would relish hearing stories and rumors surrounding this magnificent structure."*

Ummanaldash stood up to leave the table. He looked back to Nabu and as he was leaving he declared, *"I don't know why I would waste my time with the likes of you. But you are so helpless I feel you would die of stupidity without my help. Tomorrow, find the place where the red light of the lion touches the earth. I will be there when the sun is at its highest point. I will wait only a short time so do not be lazy. If you are smart enough for such a minor task I will show you some of the hidden treasures that this fortress holds."*

* * * *

The pit was cold and hard. His bones ached. The space was barely large enough for him to sit, as even his bent legs touched the other wall. It was sparse and only hay covered the floor. What made matters worse were the heavy chains that weighed on his body. His face still held the dried blood from his capture. He was not allowed to wash or change clothes. His robes were wet from his own urine and he smelled from feces. Even a trusted friend would not recognize the old priest. He had been in this hole for nearly a week, but Ningizzida only had a vague sense of time. It was eternally dark inside so his frame of reference was gone. He could, at times during the day, make out the bars that covered this cavity in the earth in which he lived. His mind was racked with constant, pounding pain. It was difficult to tell the difference between sleep and unconsciousness. He was using all his meditative skills to try to separate his thoughts from the pain that was burning in his side and back.

Ningizzida's thoughts were becoming loose and disjointed. He was seeing his god, Marduk, and communicating with past spirits. Ningizzida's mind was expanding and running like a spinning top. Its direction was random and nomadic, shifting between the scriptures of the Enuma Elish and the Apsu. In between these drifting thoughts, Ningizzida found himself fighting with his old enemy Tiamat. But unlike previous encounters, Ningizzida had lost some of his will for success. He was finding that more of his thoughts were beyond his control and more and more time was spent in fear.

During those rare times of lucidity, Ningizzida knew that his physical body was in danger. The pain appeared to be spreading and he instinctively knew that his end of days was approaching. His bowels bled when he excreted and the pain burned for long periods. He knew he needed treatment, and yet at times he prayed for the peace of infinity. He was losing the battle, both for internal control and for life itself. Tiamat was on the verge of conquering one of his most difficult and intransient opponents.

Ningizzida's mouth was as dry as the desert. He doubted that he could speak without ripping his throat in two. He was only given two small glasses of water a day. Although it tasted like nectar it also hurt more and more to swallow. He could no longer eat solid food and only corn meal was palpable. His only frame of reference was his guard standing over him and urinating onto his head. To his surprise, Ningizzida looked forward to the event as the warm liquid not only felt good on his body. But the event was structuring and allowed him some brief focus.

Yet still, Ningizzida had not been brought before the great King. Xerxes reveled in his capture. Unbeknownst to the priest, the great King spent time every day standing near the entrance to the dungeons imagining his enemy's pain. He could sense the priest's life dripping away. Every drop of pain brought pleasure to the King. He ordered that the priest should not be killed, but that his life needed to be held close to death. Torture was more enjoyable than death. Xerxes also placed a slave at the top of the pit. He wanted to be continually apprised of the old priest's conditions. He relished in the stories of pain and suffering. He found himself getting hard listening to the stories. Since the priest's capture, the King had regained his virility. To his dismay the old priest was mostly silent alternating between shivering, moaning, and sweating. Xerxes had prayed that during one of his journeys to the pit he would hear the old man yell out in agony. Alas, it never came, and Xerxes cursed silently before he would walk away. He wanted to extend the delight of the priest's capture. Since the capture of the old priest, the King had slept well. His dreams were calm and comforting. Xerxes didn't want to torture the old man too much but wanted life to slowly drain from him. Physicians were put into place to continue to monitor the old man's health so that he couldn't slip away without Xerxes being able to strike the final blow. He wanted the old priest to curse him with his final breath. He wanted to look deep into his dying eyes and pull his life from him. This was a delicate game of cat and mouse. Xerxes was trying to time the old man's death. The slaves and physicians all knew that if the priest died there would be hell to pay with the King of Kings.

When the word was spread to the King that Penish was bringing Ningizzida home to Susa in chains, Xerxes felt light

210

headed. He saw the priest's capture as a positive sign from the gods. The King was especially indebted towards Penish. He was told by his other advisors how difficult a task he had given his old friend. The King had seen Penish perform other miracles and he had always known in his heart of hearts that he would be successful.

When Penish entered the throne room followed by the priest in chains, Xerxes did not make an outward expression of emotion. He sat stoically watching the men approach him. The King did not show his initial gratitude towards Penish and his great capture. He made sure to have four years' worth of gold sent to his home to ensure Penish knew how grateful he truly was. He also gave him three prized bulls and a young stallion from the royal herd. The money was welcomed, for Penish had spent his life savings paying for information to locate the renegade priest. Penish had known that his professional existence, and life itself, depended on his ability to locate the elderly cleric. The young King did not handle disappointment well, but Penish wasn't as self-consumed to always anticipate success.

In this pursuit, Penish had spent a fair amount of his money chasing shadows. He learned quickly that he just couldn't throw silver at people and receive accurate information. He spent many nights cursing at the pig hearted Babylonians, as they led him into many blind alleys in his search for the renegade priest. It wasn't until Penish sent soldiers, arresting, and punishing those who led him astray, that his luck seemed to change. He became so angry at one priest who had promised that he knew the hiding place of Ningizzida that he burned the church down after cutting the priest's tongue and eyes out. He also killed half of the parishioners. It wasn't until after this tirade that word spread about the seriousness of his intentions and the wrath of his anger.

It was on a cold evening that Penish had found out that Ningizzida's second in command didn't always have positive thoughts about his master. He then knew that if anybody had information about Ningizzida, it was this man.

Penish had his subordinates drag Manishtusu into his chambers. It was during the evening service when the temple was completely full of parishioners. He wanted as many witnesses as possible. The congregation had just begun a vigil to pray for Ningizzida when the soldiers burst through the temple doorway. They paraded down the middle of the church brandishing their weapons in case any of the people decided to defy their intentions. None of the people would have challenged their authority. However, the aggression from the soldiers was a secondary message to the populace. The sergeant triumphantly walked up to the pulpit and grabbed the young priest by his robe. Without saying a word, he dragged the priest out of the church. Manishtusu lost his footing and was dragged through the streets and thrown onto a cart with his arms tied. His stunned congregation watched as their leader was forcefully taken away by the soldiers.

The soldiers threw Manishtusu on the floor in front of Penish. He gestured for them to leave as the priest lay on the ground. Penish followed the soldiers to the door and made sure they were gone. He ordered the slave outside of the door that he didn't want to be disturbed. He turned and looked at the prone priest and smiled. He ambled over to the monk and untied his hands. Manishtusu then crawled to the bench in the corner of the room. The priest, still shaken from his ordeal, slowly rose from the floor. He wobbled as he tried to gain his composure.

Penish rose, took his sword out, and wiped it slowly with a cloth. He then took the large rag and threw it at Manishtusu. ***"Wipe your face,"*** he demanded. ***'You have blood on your face."***

213

While he was being dragged out of the temple he slipped a few times, once banging his head on a stool located by the door. His face was swollen as if he had been in a fight. **"Why did you do this to me?"** Manishtusu protested in anger.

"What did you want me to do?" Penish retorted, appearing as if he were bored by the conversation. Manishtusu just threw down the towel in disgust. He continued. **"Your crowd had to be convinced. When we detain that snake of a priest, I don't want anyone to connect you to the arrest."**

Penish began laughing, **"Don't worry Manishtusu, you're safe. Nobody will know about your betrayal."** Manishtusu didn't move as Penish spoke. Penish rose again and removed a pouch from his vest. He threw the pouch on the floor in front of the Priest. **"Consider this a donation to your cause."**

Manishtusu didn't protest, he reached down and picked the pouch up.

"Now," Penish ordered, **"I want the snake. Tell me what rock he is hiding under."**

****

Nabu stood in the great hall. As it was truly spectacular and welcoming, it was unusual that the great hall was abandoned. Great marble columns with an inlaid floor of painted brick and ceramic decorations were everywhere. As he stood surrounded by this structural marvel waiting for Ummanaldash, Nabu couldn't decide which of the intricate ceramic designs to stare at. He had thought that he had seen wealth in Rhodes and then again when he briefly saw Babylonia. He had heard about the wealth of the Greeks. But this, this was beyond belief.

Although it began as a rouse to engage Ummanaldash, Nabu was now excited about being shown around this magnificent temple. Nabu was staring at an inlaid brick picture of a lion killing a golden-hooved, white bull when Ummanaldash tapped him on his shoulder. Nabu almost jumped out of his skin at the sudden appearance.

"It is impressive, isn't it?" Ummanaldash proudly admitted.

Nabu quickly recovered and proudly responded, *"It is the most unbelievable inlay that I have ever seen."*

Ummanaldash turned to the Queen's eunuch and handed him a cup of wine. *"For you, my friend, It comes from the special wine cellars of the palace. It is date* wine. I realized that I misjudged you yesterday and I brought this special libation as a peace offering."

Nabu took the cup.

"*Go ahead,*" Ummanaldash urged. "*There are very few men in this world who have had the opportunity to drink from the King's special date wine collection.*"

Nabu slowly brought the cup to his lips. The smell was very strong and seductive. He drank the heavy liquid slowly as it burned going down. But this was not a painful burning, but more of an awakening.

After a time of silent staring, the two began walking and Ummanaldash continued talking. "*This site has been the home of a temple since ancient times. It is called the Hadish palace. It is a sacred place, protected by the gods. We gain our strength from this soil.*"

"*I am without words,*" Nabu commented.

"*This temple was constructed by people from the entire Empire to honor the King of Kings. The cedar was brought by the Assyrians from a mountain called Lebanon. The Babylonians brought it to Susa. They say that north of the black place is the most beautiful wood on earth. It is called teakwood,*" Ummanaldash pointed upward, *"That wood you see adorning the ceiling columns came from Gandea. The stone to carve the columns was brought from Sogdiana."*

Ummanaldash continued to speak and point as the two eunuchs walked down a long corridor. *"The beautiful turquoise that is inlaid along the ceiling came from Chorasmia, the silver and copper for the sculptures came from Egypt. These beautiful stone pillars were brought, already carved from Abiradust. They say it took 2000 slaves to accomplish the task. The story is that at one point, when the pillars were stuck, slaves offered to use their blood to grease the wood blocks. That is why the pillars have a reddish tint. Yes, my friend, this temple is truly a place that belongs to the vast Persian Empire."*

The two men were entering the central court of the palace when Nabu stopped in his tracks and his mouth dropped open. No sound escaped, but he stood dumbfounded in awe at what he saw. In the center of the great court stood the majestic Ahura-Mazda Sun Disc. The disc was as wide as a man is tall. It stood in the exact center of the court which was at the exact center of the temple itself. There were only rumors about this disc outside of Susa. Some of the stories held that the Sun Disc was an oracle that could tell the future. Nabu-

217

na'id had heard of the disc, but for as many stories that foretold its unique attributes, there were just as many proclaiming it was a myth. This was no legend; here it stood in its entire splendor.

Nabu appeared to be afraid to approach the object as he stood fixated with a frozen stare on his face. The disc was known throughout the Empire but very few men had seen it. On the sides of the structure were two sphinxes with the bodies of lions crowned with triple horned helmets facing each other. The faces of the two beasts were reversed to reveal their prominent eyes staring outward towards the horizon. These creatures wore their menacing looks to prevent evil from entering the Empire. They were guarding the Empire from the evil gods that sought to destroy it.

In the center of the disc was the stylized figure of a bird called "the spread eagle". Even though the figure had wide wings, the center of the image was a man. His hand was pointing skyward and at its center was a beautifully decorated sphere.

Ummanaldash broke the silence and asked *"You are impressed, my friend?"*

Nabu nodded his head and Ummanaldash continued: *"Do you know the meaning of this symbol?"*

Pointing to the spread eagle:

"I do not," Nabu responded.

"It is the symbol of our god." Ummanaldash pointed to the side wings of the figure. *"Notice that each of the side wings has three prominent rows of feathers."*

Each line of feathers was a different shade of blue. *"Each line of feathers represents a different expectation of a Persian. The top row makes us realize that we must have good reflection. The second row reminds us to speak good words, and the third row reminds us to act with good deeds."*

Nabu was again fixated but this time listening to the description. Ummanaldash proudly continued his religious lesson: *"The circular symbol in the center of the man represents our human spirit. Our god teaches that the spirit lives before we are born and continues after we die. The purpose of a Persian's life is to live well enough to attain union with our God, Ahura-Mazda, the wise lord. The circular design is a representation of our god telling us that*

219

our spirit is immortal, having no beginning and no end."

"Why is the man pointing upward towards the sky?" Nabu- na'id inquired.

"The man reaching up tells us that life is always a struggle to live."

Nabu turned to his senior, and asked, "Now that you've told me about your god, tell me, Ummanaldash, about your King. I have never met him and I've heard such wonderful stories."

The preliminaries were over, and the game was on.

"Have patience, my friend," Ummanaldash demanded. "Before we leave this area you need to know that there is much more to this disc than you realize. Nabu, do you see the sun reflecting off the sides of the disc?"

Nabu stared at the glimmering light. There were many different squares of reflection.

"Watch the light, my friend. Notice the different colors as they reach your eyes."

Nabu had not noticed the varying colors before. The reflection seemed to differentiate before his eyes and he appeared to be compelled to watch it. His strength of will seemed to leave his body as he was engulfed by the light as it continued to change.

"Here, my friend, as you watch the colors change, have another glass of date wine."

Nabu automatically reached out. The older eunuch placed another cup in his hand. Ummanaldash helped the younger man raise the cup to his lips. He then slowly tilted the cup so that the liquid flowed down Nabu's throat. Throughout this process, Nabu continued to stare at the colors.

"Good," Ummanaldash exclaimed. *"Good."*

After a minute, Ummanaldash gently pushed on Nabu's shoulders, saying, *"Sit, my friend, I can see you're tired."*

Nabu slowly sank to the floor, his eyes growing heavier by the second. Before he could blink he had lost consciousness.

Ummanaldash stood over him and began laughing. He waved his arms and slaves appeared seemingly appearing from the walls. He pointed to Nabu lying on the ground. *"Take this man to my chamber."*

As the slaves lifted Nabu off the ground, Ummanaldash spoke to his unconscious body. *"So, you decided to be a spy, did you? Well now the tables have turned and you will reveal all of your Queen's secrets to me!"*

PERSIA

CHAPTER X – CARTHAGE

Herodotus the historian, hurried into the Queen's chamber, only to be stopped in his tracks by her Phoenician guards. The Warrior Queen preferred Phoenicians as her close associates because of their knowledge and expertise about the sea. She considered them her brothers and they had always been faithful allies to Artemisia. Although an accomplished tactician in all forms of warfare, Artemisia was most at home on the sea. She trusted the Phoenicians. They were decedents of the Canaanites. Although they were expert traders, their seafaring knowledge was legendary. Besides the Warrior Queen herself, only the Phoenicians knew the tricks of maneuvering vessels in the dark of night. It was said that Phoenician sailors could read the stars even in a starless sky. In truth, Artemisia was also attracted to their fashion and colors. The Phoenicians had mastered the murex shellfish. They transformed shellfish with a secret formula, into the most beautiful color of purple imaginable. The process to get the color from the shellfish was expensive and difficult. Artemisia had traveled to Tyre where the dye was made and decided to use this color in her flag. She also had her garments colored with the murex. She considered the color lucky and only wore her purple garments when she was preparing for war. She also sometimes wore the color in her hair.

The Phoenicians were also on Xerxes' counsel and were one of the peoples allied with the Persian King. They were travelers. They understood the Egyptians, the Greeks, the Balcaric traders and the Iberians. This experience made them valuable allies. It was the Phoenician informants that told Artemisia about the unexpected conquest of Rhodes, allowing her to counterattack. The Phoenician Kings also respected and trusted the Warrior Queen. She had been trading with them since she was a child and she could speak their language fluently and write their forms. Besides the Greeks and Egyptians, Artemisia was one of the few outlanders who could write Phoenician. She knew their secrets and they knew hers. It was a mutual trust.

The Phoenicians were also very important allies to the Persian King. The Persians were land fighters. They had few people who understood warfare on the seas. The Phoenicians were the great navigators and seamen. It was told that the Phoenicians had learned the secrets of the ocean directly from Poseidon himself. In this way Artemisia and the Phoenicians spoke the same language. She had learned the delicate art of navigation from her Phoenician friends. It was a secret that few knew. The Phoenician navigators protected their seafaring secrets with their lives. Most importantly, the Phoenicians also spoke a secret and non-verbal language that few even knew existed. Their gestures meant many things. In a crowded room they could "talk" with their comrades without others knowing they were communicating. Raising their arm or hand in a certain manner indicated much. At diplomatic sessions, the Phoenicians always had the upper hand because of their hidden words. Artemisia had learned this hidden language as a young child. It was more natural for her than her words.

What made Artemisia such a special diplomat was her ability to read others. If you became purgerous in front of the Warrior Queen, she would pick up the change in heart. To lie with Artemisia in the room was a dangerous game.

As much as Artemisia trusted her brother Phoenicians, her recorder and historian, Herodotus, did not have the same faith in them. Whenever he had the Queen's ear he railed on what he called "the barbarians". It bothered him that he had to travel with the Phoenician thugs. The Queen enjoyed this conflict. She liked the idea that the historian could balance her thoughts about the Phoenicians.

The Phoenician guards enjoyed putting their hands-on Herodotus because they knew his thoughts about them. Whereas the Phoenicians were tall, strong and athletic, Herodotus was short, flabby and sedentary. In this instance, one of the Queen's guards stopped the historian by placing a big hand directly in the center of his chest. The historian looked surprised at the reaction of the guard. The Persian looked him right in the eye and sarcastically said, **"This barbarian forbids your entrance."**

A smile came over the big man's face.

"Let me go," Herodotus protested.

"I must see the Queen."

"You must wait until my sister is ready to speak with the likes of you."

As the Queen referred to the Phoenicians as her brothers, they returned the compliment for her.

"But the information I have is important to the Queen."

"You always talk too much," the guard responded. By now, Herodotus' enthusiasm was calming. The guard put him down and the historian adjusted his tunic to regain some respect. As his mind began to catch up with his body, he approached the guard and tried a different tact, saying, *"Your sister will be angry with you for not allowing me entrance. When she hears what I must say, you will be diminished in her eyes."*

With that thought, the Phoenician guard hesitated, but pointed to a bench, *"sit, historian."* He went back into his guardian stance but after a few minutes decided to inform the Queen that she had a visitor. Herodotus had to wait an hour before the Queen would allow him entrance to her chamber.

As Herodotus was ushered into the chamber by a slave he was stopped in his tracks by what he saw. The Queen was lying half naked on her bed. Herodotus' mouth immediately became dry and his tongue almost began hanging between his lips. She was truly magnificent. He realized that he had never pictured her as a woman before. Her long legs and shapely hips were so compelling that he had difficulty averting his eyes. Just then something moved just outside of his vision to the left. With some effort, Herodotus looked to the left. He was stunned. There stood Ekallatim, completely naked. Whereas Artemisia was tall, slim and dark, Ekallatim was petite, with flowing blond hair. As she walked into the adjoining room, Herodotus was fixated on her hips enjoying watching her leave.

While watching the show, the Queen began to laugh out loud. Her amusement rose as the historian began to stutter in trying to regain his composure.

"So, my historian," the Queen said in a chuckling voice. *"Do you see anything to write about?"*

"W-what, my Queen?" Herodotus again began to stutter.

"I asked," the Queen questioned, *"Whether what you see in this palace is impressive enough to write about."*

The historian fell to one knee finally realizing that he was in the presence of his Queen. *"My Queen, I have important news."*

The Queen immediately became serious. *"I'm listening."* Herodotus remained on one knee as he spoke. *"I was walking through the great gardens at the rear of the chambers. There was a procession moving through the gardens heading to the King's chambers. Then I recognized the man at the center of the group."* *"I continue to listen, yet have heard nothing,"* the Queen responded in a boring, detached tone, now sitting up on the side of her bed.

"His name is Hanno. Do you know one of your brothers?"

His sarcastic tone was evident. The Queen jumped out of her bed and moved to the historian. She was now obviously incensed. *"Tell me, historian, do you value your life?"*

Herodotus seemed frozen.

"I said, historian, your life is in a very delicate place right now. Be

careful that the string that holds it together isn't cut."

Herodotus dropped again to one knee in deference. *"I'm sorry for my disrespect, my Queen."*

Artemisia turned and walked back to the bed sitting down. There was quiet for a few minutes as Artemisia allowed Herodotus to absorb her irritation. She was tired with the sarcasm and she was clear in her message. Finally, the Queen broke the silence with a leer. *"Well, historian, tell me about this man, and why do you think he's here."*

"He is from Carthage, my Queen."

Artemisia thought and then asked, *"Is he here for the council meeting?"*

Herodotus shook his head. *"I don't know. my Queen. I don't know."*

"How do you know this man, historian?"

"I know of him not, my Queen. I have heard rumors about his exploits."

"I thought that you were a recorder of truth, not a spreader of fertilizer and rumors!"

Herodotus ignored the criticism and continued his story. *"It is said, my*

Queen, that Hanno is one of the greatest explorers of the world. He has sailed from Tripolitania to Benin in the southern wild place. Hanno wears a black coat made of thick fur. Such a garment is not seen in the world. It is how I recognized him, lord."

The Queen's interest was piqued as Herodotus continued. "It is told that on one of his journeys to the undiscovered place, Hanno took a landing party to the inland of the southern lands. Vast forests spread for as far as the eye can see. They were dense with many unknown animals and plants. It is said that he took Nubian scouts that showed him wonders beyond belief."

The Queen stood and with a wave of her hand urged the historian to continue, now apparently interested in the tale. "Hanno, it is said, found a strange race of savage men. They were covered in hair, had large teeth, and walked on their hands and legs. These people were such savages that they spoke no language, only communicating with grunts and growls. I am told that they banged their chests with fierce fury when angered."

Artemisia interrupted the story and waved her hand. "This is impossible, historian. You listen to children's tales of monsters."

"It *is* no children's tale, my Queen, for I have seen the robe."

The Queen bellowed, "It **has been years** since I have heard children's tales historian. So, this once, I will allow you to continue."

Being an accomplished story teller, Herodotus was in his glory relating this information to Artemisia. His voice was animated and vigorous as he continued. "**Hanno and his men captured some of the men of this barbaric tribe to use as slaves. It was told that they had the strength of five men. He had to kill them because they were too savage, even for slaves. His men also captured females and tried to domesticate them. They took the females back to the boats and left the coast. While at sea, it became clear that the females could not be mated or trained. While attempting to mate one of the females, one of Hanno's men had his face bitten off. The females were killed and skinned. Hanno made jackets out of their hide and he proudly wears them on his journeys.**"

Although intrigued by the strange story, Artemisia feigned indifference saying, "**why should any of this interest me, historian?**"

Herodotus, stood and wiped his forehead of sweat. He slowly moved towards the Queen. He now lowered his voice and slowed his cadence. **"The Carthegians are great sailors. Being cousins to the Phoenicians they possess vast knowledge of the seas. If they come to speak with Xerxes they will probably offer an alliance."**

The Queen squatted. She began playing with a string that lay on the ground in front of the historian. She continued to look at the ground as she spoke in lowered tones. **"Are you suggesting, historian, that I should fear the Carthegians?"**

Herodotus remained silent.

"For if that is your guidance, then your opinion is worse than I had thought. I obviously have given you much too much credit, historian."

Again Herodotus remained quiet and his eyes widened. The sweat continued to pour down the side of his face.

"No matter how skillful this Hanno is, his strength cannot match that of my brothers."

She looked at the historian. **"I control the seas. The Gods have decreed it. Now leave me with your children's tales about woman who eat men's faces."**

****

Hanno entered the throne room surrounded by his entourage. They walked slowly to the throne where the King of Kings sat. Xerxes watched the group approach with no expression on his face. When he was about ten feet from the King, Hanno lifted his arm. His men abruptly stopped and they all bowed deeply. Hanno went down on both knees. He almost disappeared under his thick black robe. Hanno was a chiseled young man obviously very confident, as he held himself with honor and conviction. In many ways, he reminded the King of himself.

The King spoke, *"What do you have for me, trader?"*

Hanno rose and brought out a vial of water and a pouch filled with dirt.

"My father, Hamilcar, hopes that this finds the great Xerxes well and prosperous."

Earth and water were the signs of submission to the Persian King. The King lifted his hand to his forehead and asked, *"What is your father's plan?"*

Hanno smiled and responded with assurance, *"My father is hiring 30,000 Iberians to support our navy."*

The King smiled and nodded. Hanno continued, *"We will support you, my King. While you attack Athens, my father and I will defend your flank by conquering Sicily. We will destroy the Greeks from the west leaving them no place to withdraw to when you crush their cities."*

The King nodded again. They would trap the Greeks in a pinching action. They could not escape. Xerxes leaned back and briefly closed his eyes. He imagined the bloodletting. The King was cognizant of the history. After the Greeks helped the Ionians revolt against the Persian Empire, Xerxes' father, Darius, was incensed at the Greeks. He sent envoys to Sparta and Athens demanding that the Greeks succumb to Persian dominance. The Spartans threw the Persian emissaries into a deep pit and left them to die.

In hearing this news, Darius was beside himself. He threw a two-day temper outburst sacrificing twenty-five slaves to his anger. He then sent a large army to punish the Greeks. The battle at Marathon resulted in the most embarrassing loss that the Persians had ever experienced. Darius had sent 60,000 warriors to punish the Greeks. The Athenians and their allies, the Plataeans, could only field 20,000 Hoplites. The Athenians had asked Sparta for support, but the Spartans were engaged in ceremony and did not send a contingent. The Athenians, even without the Spartans, routed the Persians. Xerxes' slave would utter the name Miltiades every day, reminding him of the Greek general that surprised the Persians by attacking the superior force. To add salt to the wound, the Athenians built a temple on the Acropolis to honor the victory. Xerxes dreamed of the day that the Parthenon, the building that represented this horrific victory, the building that the Greeks erected to disgrace his family and people, would burn. He smiled again at his vindictive thoughts.

The Bedo were nomadic people, roaming the deserts and high mountains throughout the middle east and Asia minor. They frequently spent time at specific oases and knew the routes to and from their special places like knowing the lines on their hands. They wore flowing hooded robes that they called jalabiyya. Although they were used to living within their small roaming tribes, these people were generally friendly and hospitable.

Jamak-el-sid was the leader of this small group of Bedo. They were a hardy people who were genetically used to surviving on little and asking for less. It was the third day of one of the worst sand storms that the families could remember. For the first two days, the families stubbornly continued their trek towards their next stopping place. However, navigating in a sand storm as ferocious as this one had become next to impossible. It would not be unusual in such a storm to walk in a circle as bearing was completely lost.

Jamak-el-Sid had made the executive decision to slow the pace. It was against his better judgment, but people were losing strength fighting the wind and sand. More importantly the animals were showing signs of obvious weakness. The mountains they were heading to were still nowhere in sight, although Jamak-el-Sid wouldn't have been able to see them even if he were standing at their base.

That night Jamak met with two of the other highly respected men of the families and they decided as a group to rest as much as they traveled, at least until the storm subsided. Such a storm although rare, could last a week or more. The men appeared beaten by the weather and Jamak-el-Sid felt a general dysphoria at their short-term prospects. The family's health and prosperity was his responsibility and he took its success or failure very seriously. In such conditions, the tents were placed almost next to one another so families could commiserate. Much time would be spent in prayer, pleading with the desert God to free them from their burden.

These past few nights the prayers appeared to go unanswered and Jamak felt uneasy at the Gods sudden wrath. Without warning, the cries of one of the lookouts broke the constant droning of the sand hitting the tents. The child letting out the warning cry was a youngster of renown within the families. No other child of just ten years could stand watch with the skill of this youngster. His name was Gouad, and his cries in the night aroused every member of the families. Jamak knew that if Gouad was issuing a warning, attention better be given.

Jamak's curtain flew open, and Gouad entered out of breath. *"Hukhshthra, two men, strangers, have entered our space. They wait outside to be given entrance to our tents. They asked who our leader was and I brought them to your tent."*

The boy was obviously overly excited and his voice was fast and unsteady. Jamak always straightened his back when anybody referred to him as Hukhshthra. The term meant "good and wise ruler" and was used as the ultimate praise and respect.

"It's all right, Gouad," Jamak commented, placing his hand on the boy's shoulder to calm his blood.
"They are probably travelers who have lost their way like we have. They are

238

most likely looking for a place to stay until they can continue their journey."

"I don't think so," Gouad added his opinion. *"They are different. They are not travelers."*

"How do you know, Gouad?"

"They are hard men. Should I allow them in?"

"Yes, of course, Gouad. They need shelter. God himself couldn't be without shelter this night."

With haste, Gouad left the tent and ushered the two men in front of the leader of the families. They were as Gouad had reported, not travelers. Their faces were stern and athletic. There was an ominous sense about them. Their eyes searched the tent when they threw back the entrance. As they entered the tent they walked up to Jamak and bowed **"Hukhshthra, we bid you welcome to our land."**

One of the men raised his head, the other still bent in submission. He continued to speak: *"My name is Paro-Dasma. This is my friend and brother Fiz-nel. We welcome you Jamak and your families to our land."*

Jamak's face became serious. This was an unexpected introduction. He looked directly at Paro-Dasma and enquired. *"How do you know my name?"*

The man smiled and bowed again. *"These mountains that you are entering are our lands. We welcome you and offer you hospitality. My brothers and I have watched you and your families pass us for many years. We know of you, Hukhshthra. You give us great honor with your..."* The man hesitated for a second, *"unexpected visit. My brother and I are sent here to offer you and your elders to join my master for supper this evening. We will lead your families into our enclosure."*

Jamak straightened his back again. There was something about this man that exuded danger and yet the leader of the families could not refuse such an offer. It would be disrespectful and considered an insult. Jamak bowed his head in acceptance of the invitation. The two men rose and began backing their way out of the tent. They stopped at the entrance and pointed to Gouad. Paro-Dasma spoke again: *"This child is special. He saw us approach before we saw him. That is highly unlikely even for a trained scout. He is Huarechaeshman and has eyes like the sun. You should be proud, Jamak. He has a rare gift."*

The two men left as silently as they arrived.

After about fifteen minutes, one of the elders of the families, Fiz-nel, entered Jamak's tent. He looked as if he had seen a ghost. *"Jamak, we must speak."*

"Calm yourself, Fiz-nel, I await your wisdom."

"Jamak, did you notice the tattoos on the necks of our visitors?"

"I did not, Fiz-nel."

Jamak noticed that his friend almost began shaking as he was questioning his observations about the two visitors that had left not a few moments prior.

"When they flung back their hoods, there was a black blade tattooed on the sides of their necks. Do you know what that means, Jamak?"

"I continue to listen, Fiz-nel."

"Those men whom you have agreed to lead us to, are brothers of the Sand Dancers!"

Jamak shot into a standing position as if an incendiary devise had erupted under him.

His voice quivered, *"What? Are you sure?"*

"I am, Jamak, I am."

It took Jamak a few minutes to wait for the anxiety that ran through his blood to lessen. But when it did he said, *"If we really have stumbled onto one of the hiding places of the Sand Dancers we could all be dead by this evening. But if they had wanted us dead, these men could have butchered us without us knowing. Why did they not, Fiz-nel?"*

The elder shook his head not having an answer for his leader.

"We have agreed to join them this evening. Say a prayer, Fiz-nel, that our lives will be spared. Whatever you do, prepare yourself. When we join them for supper any sign of fear or weakness on our part will undermine our position. So be strong, Fiz-nel, our families will be dependent upon it."

****

Nabu-na'id was called in front of the Queen. Ever since hearing about the Carthaginian arriving in Susa, Artemisia was anxiously nervous. She paced around the courtyard mumbling to herself, although she wasn't sure what she was concerned about. Slaves walked by her as she walked through the gardens. They bowed to the Warrior Queen but she continued her circular excursion as if they didn't exist. Other thoughts were distracted by her need to know. Artemisia didn't like being excluded from decision making. It had been days since Xerxes returned to Susa and he had not yet called for her. Whereas others might feel as though they had lost favor with the monarch, Artemisia was irritated by not getting the attention that she felt she rightly deserved. If the King was planning a military adventure then he needed the Warrior Queen at his side.

Nabu had waited in the Queen's quarters but the Queen was nowhere in sight. He decided to track her down; he knew that she didn't like to wait when she summoned somebody to her council. He heard from one of her slaves that she was in the gardens and not in a positive mood. The slaves couldn't prepare Nabu regarding what was troubling their Queen, but they were usually accurate purveyors of the moods of the monarch.

When the Queen noticed Nabu entering the gardens, she was standing more than 100 yards away. Upon noticing the eunuch in the distance, the Queen bellowed across the expanse calling her slave. Nabu hurried to his Queen. When he approached her his excitement was noticeable. Nabu dropped to the ground, pleading, *"My Queen, I am your loyal slave."*

"What have you learned?" Artemisia replied, tapping her foot as if crushing a bug underneath.

"I've learned much, my Queen. I learned why the Carthaginian has visited Susa."

Artemisia's eyes widened with surprise. *"Really,"* she said almost mockingly.

The Warrior Queen suddenly turned away from her trusted eunuch and asked, *"You mean you learned more than what was in Ummanaldash's bed?"*

Nabu-na'id blushed a crimson red. When he woke up from his drug induced stupor he was naked in Ummanaldash's bed. The older man was smiling looking down at Nabu. When he noticed that Nabu was awake, *"So, did you find enlightenment in your journey?"*

He began to laugh. Nabu was frozen and he pulled the blanket over his body. As he did he realized he was wet especially on his back and thighs. He remembered nothing of what had happened but just stared up at the older man.

"Yes, yes, Nabu-na'id, I think you did find enlightenment. And since you have arrived at that holy state, I will tell you some of the secrets you wish for."

Ummanaldash had sat next to Nabu on the bed and was ran his long sharp nails down his face.

Artemisia spoke again breaking Nabu's brief historical journey. *"Yes, yes. Nabu, I know about your initiation into the world of the nowhere people. I should warn you that your dreams will be disturbed for at least one full moon. Don't let it trouble you dear. It had to happen for you to become a worthy diplomat."*

But now Artemisia bent to a crouch in front of her eunuch. In a lowered voice she whispered, *"I also know you don't remember anything that happened. The truth will return to you in your dreams."*

She rose quickly and looked at his questioning face. *"As much as I love you, Nabu, I cannot tell you about the ritual. Part of your growth into that nowhere society is the slow remembrance of the initiation ceremony. I am told that with the knowledge come hidden wisdoms."*

Nabu was still shocked. He couldn't tell if the upcoming awareness scared him more than Artemisia's knowledge of what happened.

"Now," she insisted, *"tell me what that whore, Ummanaldash, told you"*

"I have also learned the purpose of the council meeting, My Queen."

Artemisia leaned down and smiled at the eunuch. *"But before you start, eunuch,"*

Artemisia pronounced, *"tell me if you trust the words that Ummanaldash said"*

****

Jamak and Fiz-nel prepared themselves for their supper rendezvous with the master of the Sand Dancers. Their peoples and their animals were led into a blind valley into semi hidden caves. The families were left on the side of the valley entrance and only the two elder men of the tribe could follow in. Hoods were placed over their heads and they were led in circular patterns over varying terrains. It took over two hours for the procession to reach its final destination. Both men were terrified by this time, and when the hoods were removed, Fiz-nel seemed near fainting.

When their hoods were removed and their eyes cleared they were standing in

246

a limestone cave with many small openings toward the sky. The place had obviously been carved from an ancient river that flowed through this land for what must have been thousands of years. The walls were varying shades of tan, red and gray, and smooth as glass. The walls were curved, probably matching the flow of the water. It was an enchanting place.

The two elders of the people were asked to sit. They were given drinks, as well as small pieces of cooked lamb that had been smothered in a honey sauce. There was a strange eeriness about this place as a flutist played a temperate meditative rhythm in the background. The sound was carried by the limestone walls and echoed back behind the two sitting men.

Before long Paro-Dasma appeared. He sat next to the men and explained that their master, Delir-el- Bar, would be joining them shortly.

Paro-Dasma looked at Jamak and asked: *"Hukhshthra, do you know who we are?"*

Jamak nodded his head in affirmation, *"You are a great legend."*

Paro-Dasma smiled and bowed his head. He looked at Jamak. *"Mistakenly, you and your families have entered the world of the Sand Dancers. You are the first* outsiders to see this place in many generations. *Those who have seen it before you have not left with their eyes."*

Both elders swallowed hard at the thought. *"My master, Delir-el-Bar, is actually a very fair man."*

With those words another figure appeared from the limestone walls. He had obviously been standing in an enclave unseen to the two elders. He had been watching and measuring the two men. Delir-el-Bar entered the small circle where they sat and bowed to the two elders. He sat near, continuing to have his head bent as he spoke. *"I am honored, Hukhshthra, to be in your presence."*

He lifted his face revealing a man with only one useful eye. Two great scars ran across the center of his face. His neck was heavily tattooed with many symbols. The two elders reacted to this somewhat grotesque figure. Delir-el Bar just smiled. *"Yes, I do know that it is shocking when someone first sees my face. But please, enjoy the food we placed in front of you."*

Delir-el-Bar clapped his hands and ordered special tea to be brought. After a time of silence while all four men ate, Delir-el-Bar said, *"You are probably both wondering if you will leave here alive."*

248

After a pause he continued. *"The answer to the question is still in the wind."*

Silence ensued. *"I know that your families were brought here by the desert storm. I know it was not your intention to spy. But your life and the lives of your families create a dilemma for me. There were some among us who argued that you and your families should be taken during the night with little attention paid. The women would be enslaved and the strong boys taught our ways. But the gods must have had a purpose to your visit, so, I offer this compromise to you, Hukhshthra."*

Jamak was frozen.

"One of you will be sacrificed this evening. Our gods must be appeased. The other will swear an allegiance to us, knowing that to even hint at this visit will mean the death of all in the families. You will provide three of the most attractive women of the families to become courtesans, and the boy, Huarechaeshman, will stay and be trained in our ways."

This was not an open discussion. Delir-el-Bar rose and left the area. As Jamak watched him leave, Paro-Dasma leaned over, grabbed Fiz-nel and quickly ended his life, by cutting his throat. Jamak almost fainted.

PERSIA

CHAPTER XI – ENGINEERS

The great King sat on his throne in all of his splendor. It had taken almost two hours for slaves to apply his makeup. Xerxes was very particular how his face appeared to others, especially his eyes. Their shade was central to his look. His teacher, Hamath the teacher, had schooled him for many long hours about how the eyes were held, or the "eyes of a King". The color had to be darker than his brown skin. As a young man, he would practice the stare for hours. Hamath wanted the opponent intimidated before the battle began. Hamath was a visionary and an expert in the use of power and intimidation.

For this occasion, The King wore a blue robe of fine sheep skin. Blue symbolized friendship and was worn when delegations from outer satraps or foreign countries were expected to present to the King. The robe was stylish in its stitching with detailed white symbols lining the sleeves. The texture of the garment was soft and smooth. It offered free range of motion as the King could wield a sword or a knife with ease.

Xerxes was alone in the vast chamber, an oddity, but one which he enjoyed even in its rarity. It was like a fine wine to him, a period that he could not waste because of its infrequency. He walked over to the large window and watched the sun rising over the plains. It was early in the day but the King was already anticipating the agenda. The council meeting was fast approaching and many of the preparations had not yet begun. Xerxes was feeling energized by the anticipation of crushing the Egyptians. His body was tense and he could feel his stomach muscles tighten as he thought about the upcoming campaign. Xerxes knew that he had no choice but to humble the Egyptians. He blamed them for his father's death. Although no direct proof existed, Xerxes was convinced in his own mind that somehow the Egyptian Magi were responsible for Darius' death. This revenge was not his only incentive. He had political motivation as well. Being a new King, he could not allow such an important satrap as Egypt to flaunt their opposition to the Empire so openly. If he allowed the Egyptians to so easily rebel, then how far behind could the Babylonians be? It would make him look like a cheap imitation of his father and he could not afford to have enemies consider the possibility that Persia was now hollow. No, Egypt had to be crushed. And the campaign would allow him to evaluate his generals and allied Kings to determine how they responded when he carried the fight to the Greeks. The King had spent the last few days reviewing and modifying these issues in his mind. He knew he had no choice but to invade Greece, but there were many challenges that stood in the way of success.

Calah, the King's personal attendant entered with a hot drink. Xerxes saw him out of the corner of his eye but he continued to stare at the horizon. Xerxes had uncanny peripheral vision. Hamath called him the, "eagle", for his ability to anticipate and notice the slightest of movements. Such an advantage was crucial during his training as a warrior. The eagle could see two men approaching from different directions and be able to strike at the weakest, while keeping a wandering eye on the other.

Calah knew that there were only certain times when he could interrupt the King when he was not looking at him. Calah was one of those silent advisors that Xerxes had. Very few people knew that Calah had the King's ear, and even though Xerxes often outwardly ignored his servant, he would end up paying attention. He often took credit for many things that Calah had whispered quietly into his ear. Calah was convinced that if the King had allowed him to go with him to Babylon, as he argued before he left, that the issue with the old priest would have never happened and history would be written differently.

Calah was a small, thin man. He often kept his hands together on his stomach as he spoke and listened. Calah was a perfectionist. He covered every option; every minute detail gained his attention. He walked with short quick steps as if he couldn't bend his knees. His behavior and demeanor infuriated most other people, but the King knew what his inclination was and he didn't have to pay such close attention. Calah always did his homework. Xerxes thought that he would have made a great general if circumstances were different.

Calah always wore the same robe. He never changed color, never changed design. If nothing else, he was consistent. He considered himself more than a servant. He thought of himself as an advisor and frequently made glib comments about visitors or delegations to the King. For some reason the King never became offended at Calah's intrusions. Even though acting indifferently, Xerxes usually remembered the intonations.

Calah waited patiently watching the King stare out the window. Surprisingly, and catching Calah off guard, the King commented, **"The air is heavy with intrigue."**

His stare didn't change, but he continued, **"There are many decisions to be made, my friend. The destiny of the Empire waits in the balance."**

Calah was astonished that the King was so frank. He was speechless. Xerxes continued, **"Egypt will fall easily."**

"You hesitate, my Prince,"

Calah injected, attempting to read the King's expression. **"Circumstances and relationships are changing, Calah,"** the King replied. Xerxes slowly moved away from the window but didn't turn to his trusted servant. He walked slowly back to his throne still obviously in thought. To Calah's surprise, the King began to converse, **"Today is a crucial day, my friend. Things will be set in motion."**

Calah knew that he could not ask for clarification. He stood silently with his hands crossed at his waist and listened. *"When the day begins many things will be promised. There are many people out there who offer much and pledge their allegiance to Persia. Calah, when I was a boy one of my teachers told me the story of a red fox. The fox was a shrewd hunter. The fox hunted many animals that are faster and smarter than he. But the fox was an experienced enemy. He only fought as a last option. If he could, he would steal food saving energy. He would search for the sick, weak, and old, and target them as victims first. The fox did not let pride or revenge stand in his way of a conquest. The fox's pups did not ask its mother where the meal came from, they just ate."*

Xerxes turned toward Calah and began a slow walk back to the servant. *"Remember this, Calah,"* and Xerxes lifted his hand and raised a finger to the sky. He looked serious as he continued to make his points. *"You have taught me, my friend, to evaluate and make plans for every possibility. Like the water that runs to the sea, it takes the route that offers the least resistance. I warn you, do not believe all that you see and hear."*

There was a lull and Calah instinctively knew that the King was ready to start his day. He slowly walked to the throne where Xerxes now sat. The King had begun switching his position in the chair away from a relaxed position to the more stoic exterior.

"My King, the brothers from Thessaly are here to pledge their support." Calah expressed with a little bit of sarcasm. Xerxes straightened himself in his seat and told Calah to usher them in.

****

There were two guards standing at the entrance of the hallway. They were both tired, having been standing in their position for almost five hours. Their replacements were unusually late and the two leaned against the brick wall trying to save their strength. They both silently cursed the lack of punctuality of their replacements. Both were experienced guards and had learned the art of dozing while standing erect.

The guard closest to the long dark hallway that led to the dungeon area heard something to his right, and out of the corner of his eye, saw some movement. Although he was half asleep, the movement startled him. Turning to his right he saw the other guard's legs begin to buckle. His automatic thought was that he had fallen asleep while standing and had lost his balance. His mood quickly changed as he saw blood spurting out of the man's neck. He felt wetness on his face as the spurting liquid reached him. The awareness of what was happening was fleeting as pain shot up from his legs. Before he could scream, his face was being covered with a heavy bag. The pain was all consuming, although his mind quickly blackened, as death quickly overcame him. Both legs had been separated from his body just below the knees. His wound was so efficient that the period between the contact of the sword and his death was a matter of seconds. Both eliminations happened quickly and efficiently. Other than the two bodies hitting the floor there was no sound accompanying the event.

The three assassins stepped over the two bodies without a second thought. The largest stayed behind at the hall entrance as his two accomplices proceeded down the darkened hallway. The man moved the two bodies out of sight and stood guard at the entrance. The two other men proceeded down another brief set of steps and entered the dungeon area. They continued to the end of the large room in which there were four caged areas buried in the ground. They identified the hole that housed the priest and unlocked the top of the cage. They both fell to their knees and covered their faces to pray.

These men were not murderers, they were there doing God's work. They were there because they were followers of the Sheshgallu.

Before they lifted him out of the hole they had to pay homage to the god that allowed them to be successful in this rescue attempt. Peering into the dark hole they saw a man who had already stepped with one foot into the house of death. His weight was down to just over one hundred pounds and he appeared lifeless as one of the rescuers lifted him out of the hole. When they felt the faint breath coming from his nose again they paused to thank the gods for their success.

* * * *

Thorax of Larissa was an effeminate looking man. He shuffled into the throne room followed by his two brothers, Eurphalus and Thrasgadaeus. The three brothers were members of the powerful Aleuadae family of Thessaly. Thessaly was a northern Greek province that had been ruled by the Aleuadae for generations. Due to the circumstances they had lost their position of prominence and were here in Susa to petition the Persian King. The three men approached the King but were stopped in their tracks by the King's guards who crossed their great swords in front of

Thorax.   Realizing his mistake, the Thessalion immediately dropped to one knee and bowed his head.

Calah noticed the faintest facial movement on the King's face signaling to him that he was amused by the ceremonial mistake.   There was silence for a few moments and Thorax raised his head and began to speak.   Before the first word left his lips, the King raised his hand and silenced the brother.   Xerxes stood up and walked slowly to the man who was now standing but obviously scared.   As he stood next to the two guards with Calah walking slowly up to him from behind, the King took two steps towards Thorax and stopped. Xerxes looked at Calah and the servant stepped between the two men. Calah looked at Thorax and asked, **"do you have a reason to insult the Persian King?"**

Thorax again seemed confused and anxious.   His mouth slowly opened but no words came out. Calah began to speak, **"the Persian King is not used to such treatment, especially from a Greek."**

Xerxes stood as still as a statue, but fire appeared in his eyes and his hand was firmly resting on his scabbard. Calah moved closer to Thorax and in a lower voice murmured, **"Thessalian, the Persian King the great Xerxes, should rightly** take out his sword and slay your brothers and yourself for your insolence."

Calah turned around, his back now to the Thessalions and gave a quick smile then turned back to the Thessalion brother. "I would advise that you present your gift to appease the King's anger. Then wait until the King responds before you speak."

Thorax of Larissa turned to his right and summoned his slaves to bring forward a wooden chest. It was placed in front of Xerxes and one of the slaves opened it, revealing that it was full of both gold and brightly colored diamonds. Although pleased with the offering, Xerxes again showed little response or emotion. Thorax bowed again. Finally, Xerxes looked at Thorax and spoke: "I am pleased with the offering that you bring. I am curious what you ask Persia to do in return."

Thorax looked briefly at Calah who nodded his head in affirmation and then hesitantly answered the King's question. "The whole world knows of the mighty King of Persia, of his magnificence and generosity. As you know, my brothers and I are the rightful rulers of Thessaly. We offer the King guidance when he enters Greece in his quest to punish the Athenians. Our brothers can offer the King valuable information about the strength of the Athenians and their allies. We will begin to gather this information and present it to the King to make his conquest easier."

Calah spoke for the King, "Are you men visionaries?" "What?" Thorax asked. "Visionaries? Can you see the future?" Again shaken, Thorax spoke in quivering speech. "My brothers and I are not visionaries." He bowed his head almost as if in defeat. Calah, raising his voice and his arms yelled, "Then how do you know that Persia will attack Greece?"

Thorax, now completely off balance, again bowed his head.

"I am sorry, Lord, I did not wish to insult."

Although enjoying the interchange, The King of Kings began to speak. "And what do you ask of Persia in return for this......... surveillance?"

This time, Thorax's older brother, Eurphalus, spoke. "We ask only, great King, that after you conquer the dogs of Athens, that you return my family to their rightful position."

Xerxes almost unperceptively nodded his head in affirmation.

Eurphalus spoke again. *"Oh, great King, as a gift for you to celebrate our alliance I have brought with us Onomakritos."*

The King raised his eyebrows, *"Onomakritos, my King, is a seer – he can read the future. He is famous throughout Greece for his insight and prognostations. I can send him to your chamber if you like and he will answer your most urgent questions."*

The King turned to Calah and brought his hand to his forehead indicating his uncertainty. Calah turned to the Thessalian and spoke. *"With all respect, I was under the belief that only the Oracle at Delphi could read the future."*

Eurphalus turned to the King and responded to Calah's remark, *"This is true my lord. The Oracle at Delphi is the most respected seer in the known world. Its powers are great."*

Calah intervened again: *"There are many who claim to see into the unknown mystery of what is to come. Babylonian priests claim to be able to read holy smoke and foretell events. We have heard of an oracle in Greece that reads Zeus' thoughts by the rustle of certain trees. Egyptian priests read the falling of rocks from their hand."*

Calah stopped for a moment and unfolded his hands before speaking again, *"So, tell me, Eurphalus, would you place your future and your family's future in the hands of this Onomakritos?"*

Before Eurphalus could answer, Calah walked up very close to him. He looked the Greek in the eyes with his face barely two inches from the Thessalion. Calah bent his head slightly before he began responding, *"For you see, our new ally, if Onomakritos is wrong and leads the King of Persia down a dark and blind path, then when our army marches through Greece, the King will remember Onomakritos's lying words. He will revisit your city of Larissa and its inhabitants will become fertilizer for the ants."*

Calah turned away from the Thessalion and faced Xerxes with a slight smile. He continued to talk with his back to Eurphalus. *"So, Eurphalus- it is now up to you whether you send this seer to the King's chambers."*

The Thessalians, looking shocked, bowed and backed out of the room.

****

Asanaladace was the chief engineer for the Kingdom. He was a heavy-set man with knowing eyes and many wrinkles on his forehead. When he thought, he crunched his face, almost looking in pain. His years showed readily during these periods. Asanaladace had very dark skin that resembled well-worn leather. His hair was nearly white. He wore it long and braided down his back. Asanaladace also proudly wore the King's opal around his neck. It was a gift given to him by Xerxes' father, Darius, for the magnificent temple designs that he prepared. Every new structure ordered by the King required Asanaladace's approval. He was very particular in his architecture. The beautiful reliefs of Susa were all approved and many designed by Asanaladace.

In his early years, Asanaladace had studied in both Egypt and Phoenicia. He was captivated by the great Egyptian architectural and structural feats. He spent three years as a guest of the Pharaoh and accompanied the great Egyptian builders on many of their adventures. The Egyptians were the first to use post and lintel construction in which thick walls support huge stone roofs. The outside walls also sloped away from the building. Asanaladace then spent time in Giza studying the pyramids of Khufu, Khafre and Menkaure. He then traveled north to the temple complex of Karnar where the most beautiful temples to Amon-Re and Amenhotep stood. But in this entire splendor, Asanaladace spent the most time studying the techniques of the great Egyptian genius Imhotep.

Asanaladace had a special attraction to the great Imhotep. He considered him the smartest man that had ever lived. He was not only a superior architect but was also a physician and a philosopher. After his death, he was deified. This made him a special intercessor for the living. Asanaladace believed that Imhotep communicated with him. He had a spiritual experience while visiting the great man's grave in Saqqara while studying in Egypt. While there, he sacrificed a mummified ibis in deference to the great soul. That evening, Asanaladace had a vision that Imhotep answered his prayers, promising to make him the greatest architect since his passing. Since that time Asanaladace never questioned his ability. He prayed faithfully to his patron saint whenever a new challenge was placed at his door.

Asanaladace was also taken by the wall sculptures which pictured the great Egyptian victories and their conquest of the Nubians and Ethiopians in the land of Kush. The raised bricks with the scarabs, solar discs and the vultures inspired some of his work back in Susa.

After leaving Egypt very regretfully, Asanaladace went to Canaan. He studied the work of Hiram, the architect who built the great temple of the Judaic King Solomon. He next traveled to Hiram's home in Tyre to see the temple he erected to the god, Melqart. In all instances Hiram had two spectacular pillars that marked the entrance to the temples he created. For the Judaic people, there was one pillar of gold and one of silver. The gold pillar at the entrance of Solomon's temple represented strength and the clouds. The silver pillar represented the earth and fire. Together the Hebrews believed they represented the one true God. In Canaan, Asanaladace had personally supervised the cutting and sculpting of the great Lebanese timbers that were evident throughout the temple at Susa. He brought back many designs from the great cities of the desert.

But on this day, Asanaladace was not called in front of the King of Kings to expound on his life experiences. The King was going to propose two projects that would test even Asanaladace's creativity and knowledge. He would require Imhotep's interference for both.

"Asanaladace, my friend, thank you for coming to my chamber so quickly."

The great King began walking toward his engineer.

Asanaladace smiled and bowed his head in deference. It was obvious that he respected the sovereign but was not overwhelmed by his presence. *"My King, I am here at your command,"*

"Asanaladace, you have skills that others only dream about. I need your expertise."

Asanaladace bowed his head again at the compliment. After a second of silence he responded to Xerxes. *"My King, whatever task you decide for my eyes and hands, I will put all of my strength into its successful conclusion."*

The King smiled and stood up. He responded to his chief engineer. *"You might taper your enthusiasm when you hear of my ideas."*

Xerxes again hesitated, lifting his arm to his chin. He turned slowly to the engineer and then walked over to him placing his arm around his shoulder. Asanaladace could smell the sweet perfume that the great King wore. The two walked slowly toward the gardens behind the great throne room. The sun hit them both at the same time and they both raised their hands to their eyes and squinted. Finally, the King of Kings admitted: *"I know you are a great engineer and architect, my friend. We Persians have learned much in our domination. One of the true lessons is that history predicts the future. Stay close and understand* the past to conquer the future. Do you understand history?"

Asanaladace quickly responded, *"In what way, my King?"*

"Do you know the importance of the Athos Peninsula?"

As Asanaladace stared into the King's eyes, he could feel Xerxes' muscles tighten. He could almost feel the tension emanate from the King's body as he brought up the devastating battle of Marathon. The Persian fleet was caught in the straits of the Athos Peninsula, a historically dangerous body of water to navigate. A great storm met them in the straits and destroyed half of Darius' fleet. This partial destruction of the Persian fleet was one of the events that led directly to the horrible defeat at Marathon.

After contemplating the question, Asanaladace nodded his head in affirmation. The King continued with his explanation. *"If I decide to take the Persian Army to Greece to regain our glory, I do not want my Navy getting caught in the same trap that doomed my father's expedition. Our fleet must be able to support my troops when they reach Greece. To guarantee our success I cannot afford to have my fleet compromised in that strait."*

Asanaladace looked confused and responded to the King's inquiry *'I appreciate this problem, my King, but I cannot understand how I can help with this."*

"You, alone, can save my fleet, Asanaladace."

Asanaladace looked confused. He muttered, *"I cannot sail ships, my lord."*

Xerxes laughed at the comment. *"I know, Asanaladace, I know. But I don't need you to sail. I need your expertise to dig."*

"Dig, My lord?"

The two men had stopped. The engineer, at least a head shorter than the great King, looked up into his eyes with a questioning stare. He asked again, *"Dig, my lord?"*

Not believing what he had heard only a few seconds before. The King smiled and explained in detail. *"I will give you Phoenician and Egyptian engineers. I will also provide you with as many slaves as you require. I want you to dig a canal big enough for two ships abreast to pass through. I want a canal so my ships can avoid these dangerous straits."*

The King stopped for a moment and turned to his engineer. Asanaladace looked to be in his own creative trance as the King spoke after him *"Engineer, remember these numbers. I am told the canal will need to be one and a quarter mile long. The center of it needs to rise to over 50 feet. And allow two ships to go through, it will need to be at least 100 feet wide."*

Asanaladace understood the problem and began considering the possibilities. He turned away from the great King and began walking down one of the garden paths. Asanaladace began moving his arms and hands as his mind continued to ponder the enormity of the task that the King had just placed in his lap. The King watched in amazement as the engineer walked away as if nothing else existed in the world except for the problem of digging such an enormous canal. Xerxes walked after the engineer catching up with him and placing his hand on Asanaladace's back.

The engineer then stopped short as if struck by lightning. He turned to the King with a smile. *"My lord, I can solve this problem."*

The King smiled but turned the engineer around to face him. *"I want you to understand the importance of this project, Asanaladace. I want the world to understand that this Empire can do anything. I want the Greeks to tremble when they hear the name Xerxes. Right now, Asanaladace, these Greeks sit in their cities and call us barbarians. They defeated our armies at Marathon and now they look down at us thinking we are easily beaten. Asanaladace, I want them to see that the Persians can row their boats over any land! No land is big enough to stop the Persian tide."*

The King smiled again, now placing both his hands on the engineer's shoulder as Asanaladace smiled. *"I know you can complete this, Asanaladace. But that is not the only miracle I will ask of you this day."*

Although still smiling the engineer's face now looked perplexed and concerned, not imagining another task harder than the first miracle.

Xerxes started laughing as he reacted to his engineer's puzzled look. He slapped him on the shoulder in a very unusual display of affection. He turned quickly and almost took a dance step leaping away from Asanaladace. The King landed gracefully and exclaimed, *"I never thought I would see the day! The great Asanaladace looking shocked and surprised. My father used to tell me stories of your greatness. He always ended them looking me straight in the eye and saying there was no greater magician*

than the great Asanaladace. The canal
is one thing, my friend. But for this
next task, I will require your greatest
magic."

The King became more serious. He
began walking around a large flower bed
that bordered the path on which they
stood.

"My father, the great Darius,
believed,"

And he raised his hand towards the
sky, and raised his voice, "that eminent
Asanaladace could solve any riddle, make
simple every puzzle, and with his
thoughts make the sky clear of clouds."

He now moved closer to the engineer.
He looked up to the heavens and yelled,
"Magic, magic in your hands,
Asanaladace."

Xerxes reached over to the engineer
and grabbed his shoulders.

"My Kingdom, Asanaladace. My Kingdom
is in your magic hands."

This display stunned the great
engineer. He had no words to respond as
his mouth was as dry as the desert sands.
The King now put his arm around the
shoulder of the older man. He said in a
murmur, "My friend, my ultimate victory

273

over the Athenian pigs will not ride on the alliances that I make with puny and worthless peoples. The Persian Empire will endure long after their bones have been ground to dust. My victory will not depend on the spies that I have in place or the desires of my generals. My victory, and the honor of the Empire, lay in the hands of the magic man."

The great engineer and architect again looked surprised. The King of Kings spoke again. *"The magic I need from you involves a bridge."*

"A bridge, my lord?"

The King smiled. *"Have you ever visited Abydos, my friend?"*

Asanaladace nodded his head in affirmation.

"I've already asked you to build me a canal, to allow my ships to reinforce and support my armies as they trample the worthless Greeks. But my plans are to take the largest army ever assembled to trample and burn Athens."

Now he was completely focused and serious. His face became tense and he spoke with intensity. Xerxes almost sounded angry in his question. *"Have you studied the work of Mandarocles?"*

274

"*My lord, do you mean the Ionian who built the bridges to help your father, Darius?*"

The King grinned. He shook his head in affirmation. Xerxes continued. "*I must take the greatest army ever created across the Hellespont not around the body of water. It will save me months of transport. I need your magic hands to craft me a bridge to allow my army to transport across the waterway.*"

Asanaladace thought for a moment. He turned his back on the young King again and then spoke. "*You are correct, lord, that the distance between Abydos and Sestos on the other bank is only 1500 meters. But that strait is infamous for its treachery. I have studied the terrain and the waters before. The currents are strong and very unpredictable. It is turbulent and worse, violent winds arise from the heavens with no warnings. It is said that the gods fart and piss in these waters!*"

The King laughed but confirmed these dangers. "*I know these facts my friend. Therefore, I've called on the greatest architect of all time to plan this project. I need your magic hands and your creative mind to solve my problem.*"

Xerxes then bowed his head with a forlorn expression. "*I fear, my friend,*

275

that if you cannot solve my dilemma we will not be able to fulfill our destiny. The future of the Empire rests in your hands, my friend. You see, when the bridge is complete the Greeks will see that the Persians can row their boats across land and walk their armies over any water. Nothing besides the gods themselves can stop us from fulfilling our purpose. And your name, Asanaladace, it will go down in history with the greatest of all architects. It will be written that Asanaladace the great Persian visionary, eclipsed the Egyptian Imhotep. It will be rumored that Imhotep lives within your soul."

Asanaladace smiled inside at the thought, bowed and slowly withdrew.

"Wait," Xerxes demanded, as the engineer was leaving. The King made a summoning gesture with his hands. Two slaves entered carrying two boxes. He pointed to the boxes. *"As well, these are for you."*

"What are they?" Asanaladace questioned.

"They are for you, they are for your sacrifice,"
Xerxes said with a very serious expression and as he continued Asanaladace looked questioningly at him. *"Sacrifice, lord?"*

276

"Imhotep, Asanaladace. Your patron. For Imhotep. We now require his assistance. Build a temple to your hero, Asanaladace. Imhotep understood the grandeur of dynasty. And when this is over, even his memory will bow to your greatness. Long after our bones have turned to dust the stories about the great Asanaladace and his engineering wonders will be passed on from generation to generation. Others will sacrifice at your grave, my friend, and pray to their gods for the visionary skills that you possess."

* * * *

PERSIA

CHAPTER XII - MARATHON

Since arriving at Susa, Artemisia had been in a foul mood. It made it very rough on her entourage, as she ranted throughout the day and much of the night. The Warrior Queen was insulted and put off by the King of Kings. Xerxes had summoned the presence of many of the patron Kingdoms that had come to Susa in preparation for the great council meeting, delegations that held only minor pieces of the great puzzle. But Artemisia had not heard a word. Not a greeting, not a request for advice, nothing. She had attempted various means of communication with the King from the direct to the circuitous. There was no reply to any of the inquiries. At some points her Phoenician guards restrained her from bursting into the throne room and confronting the young Monarch amid a meeting with a minor King. During one rant the Queen threw things at anything that moved. She cursed and ranted in three different languages. Her guards and slaves took the most abuse there was blood letting (on almost an hourly basis).

Being the unique strategist that she was in her calm states, Artemisia reasoned that the King of Persia would have to depend on a strong navy to threaten the Greeks. Her reasoning didn't just center on the ability to reinforce the ground troops, but all of her advanced information suggested that the Greeks were investing heavily in a navy anticipating the Persian invasion. If the King was not able to match the Greek navy, the army and subsequent invasion would falter.

Nobody could sail like she and her Phoenician brothers. Artemisia had boasted that she could even attack any enemy at night with no moon, slaughtering them before they were prepared to defend themselves. She believed she could not be defeated in the open seas and most knew it wasn't an empty boast. Artemisia was vicious and next to invincible during battle.

But here she was, traveling all this distance through this god-forsaken territory, vast barren desert, and ugly mountains. This was all to show her support for the Persian King and she was being ignored. It was beyond her grasp. She had heard contradictory rumors from every corner of the palace. Although she claimed to not believe gossip, her behavioral and emotional reactions betrayed her true concerns.

The Warrior Queen had heard that the King was lining up allies for his eventual attack on the Greek peninsula. She heard from her Phoenician brethren that the greatest engineer throughout the Empire had been summoned to create the infrastructure which would bring success to his invasion. She even heard that Demaratus was in the palace to meet with the monarch, possibly becoming the general that would lead the troops into battle. While she sat, a Greek traitor was being groomed for the invasion! Had the young King lost his mind? Was he succumbing to lust or madness?

Artemisia hated the Greek defector, Demaratus. She believed that the ex-Spartan, could very well be a Hellenistic spy, planted in the Empire to give warning to his birth brothers. Other than her gut feeling the Queen had no evidence for such a conclusion. If she had hard evidence of this betrayal she would slit his body down the middle. She had sent spies into his territories to attempt to ascertain his true loyalties. How could the King trust a man who was betraying his own country? A snake doesn't ever become a cat, it remains a snake. Its poisonous head must be cut off and buried in the sand.

Artemisia had met Demaratus twice before. The first meeting was a nondescript encounter when Demaratus had just entered the Persian territory and was traveling to Susa to meet the King. She gave him no mind at the time. He was another turncoat running from his treacherous ways. When the Queen heard that Xerxes had given him a group of cities in the Empire to rule as King, she was flabbergasted. The most memorable encounter with Demaratus was when she traveled through his territories after the Persian King had granted him certain satraps to reestablish his credibility. All the countries and cities in the Empire were transformed into satraps or provinces of the greater whole, each ruled by the loyal King or tribal leader.

Artemisia had purposely traveled to Demaratus' capital to see for herself why the King had honored treason. After arriving at Demaratus' court, Artemisia claimed that the Persian King had sent her to explore the northern territories and to decide the level of support they offered. The border territories of the Empire always offered instability. The Warrior Queen spent two days in the small palace that Demaratus had established as his capital. Her people had infiltrated the city and had reported to her that the local people were surprisingly in favor of the transplanted Greek.

In truth the Spartan worried the Queen. She had heard the rumors about the ferocity of the Spartan warriors, although she believed that the gossips were overblown and exaggerated. She had trouble giving credence to these stories considering that one of their Kings would abandon his people in favor of the enemy. Although she understood the concept of such treachery, the Queen would personally consider ending her life before abandoning her allies. She understood that somebody could be forced to betray loyalty out of fear. But in her life, the Warrior Queen had no frame of reference for such a depth of apprehension. Her life was less important than her loyalty.

In their meeting the Queen could not ascertain any precise leaning from this stoic man which only increased her anxiety. She left the city more confused than when she arrived. Artemisia's concerns always returned to whom she could trust in a battle. Part of her strength of purpose arose from her knowledge that her brother Phoenicians sailed beside her and she could turn her head and see them. She counted on them to defend her flank and they had never let her down. It was rumored to her that the Greeks were strange animals, making excuses for their weaknesses by blaming it on one of their many gods.

Without the assurance of loyalty, war became tenuous. The Phoenicians were also adept at taking advantage of the opportunities that always arose during battle. They were an adventuresome people and were always willing to take what others would characterize as "unreasonable risks". In her heart she knew that this man, this Greek, this ex-Spartan traitor, couldn't be trusted. If he turned on his own people, the Queen concluded that he could turn on anyone, and would for the right price.

On the fifth day of her stay in Susa, the Queen's servants entered her room to perform her daily routine and found her missing. They came rushing out of the bedroom and in a panic aroused the half-sleeping Phoenician guards. They initially searched every room of the suite that was assigned to the Warrior Queen with no luck. They expanded their search to the larger palace and were joined by the King's own guards. But again, the search proved futile. Artemisia had vanished.

* * * *

Onomakritos was a very strange looking small heavy set man. His face was pockmarked and his hair long and disheveled. He also had a heavy beard, which in conjunction with his other attributes made him appear a wild man. His beard was braided with colorful twine. What was worse for Xerxes, was that the man smelled horribly and the King was immediately repulsed when he entered the room. Although Xerxes usually believed in oracles and soothsayers, this man created skepticism and mistrust by his general demeanor and appearance. It was unusual that the King showed his displeasure on his face. However, the moment Onomakritos walked into the King's quarters Xerxes was put off. Calah immediately picked up on the King's uneasiness and he himself felt off balance by the King's expression. It was such a strange reaction that the servant was unsure how to respond. He didn't know whether to throw the oracle out or to let him continue. He hesitated.

Also noticing the King's uneasiness, Sameron became jittery. The lioness sensed the King's and Calah's unusual reaction and she rose from her position and began showing her teeth. After the brief display of defensiveness, the lioness turned and looked at her master for leadership. Xerxes, now more composed, signaled the oracle to walk forward. The lioness returned to her prone position convinced that all was ok.

Onomakritos, sensing the uneasiness of the two men and the reaction of the animal in the room, completely misinterpreted the reaction. His sense was that the King was impressed by his charisma. The lioness' reaction suggested to him that he was exuding power and dominance. He stood tall and threw out his chest as he approached the young monarch. Then the false oracle made his greatest mistake. When approaching the King he didn't show enough deference to the Persian Man-God. This mistake sealed his fate.

Xerxes rose off his throne and raised his sword into the air. The Greek finally realized the perilous nature of his position. He fell to his knees making a banging sound generated by the force of this purposeful drop. The King stood in his position and pointed his sword at the prone man. He began sneering, *"I've been told you can read the future."* He took a step forward, again pointing at the Greek, *"I've been told by those who I don't trust that you can be believed."*

The bulbous man shocked by the insult against the Thessalonians lifted his head, there were beads of sweat appearing on his forehead. The King pressed his advantage over the man continuing to move closer to him with his voice rising.

"You don't appear to be a rod that leads to the gods. You seem like a pig that leads to shit. You seem closer to mud than to the sky."

Xerxes was now directly in front of the man. He bent down placing his face within an inch of the other man's nose. *"Tell me oracle, tell me what you see in my future."* Onomakritos tried to smile but his lips quivered. The King placed his sword under the man's chin forcing him to his feet. The man's face and neck were now red and the sweat was pouring down his face. A small amount of blood was beginning to drip from his throat where the sword was spearing his neck. Onomakritos cleared his throat and in a hesitating manner answered the King's inquiry, *"Lord, I see great things- a great conquest in your future."* The King smiled. The sword dug slowly into the Greek's neck and he gasped. He turned his hand slightly and whispered, ***Tell me, oracle, would you tell me the truth with a sword in your neck if you saw my defeat?"***

Onomakritos stood silent, unsure of how to answer the obviously angry Monarch. Xerxes smiled at the man's frozen demeanor. Time seemed to stand still as the young King stood with his sword underneath the fake oracle's chin. And then, with a short flick of his wrist, Onomakritos' head was liberated from his body. Calah jumped at the surprise move by the King. Xerxes sneered as the head fell away and the blood encased the body. Upon decapitation, Onomakritos' body fell, shook a few times, then remained still. Leaning down over the severed head the King laughed, ***"tell me oracle, did you see that coming?"***

He raised his head and began to laugh. In the background Sameron roared her approval and began licking the spilt blood on the floor.

* * * *

Demaratus was energized by his anticipated meeting with the great King. He received what he had hoped for, and prayed to his gods for, when he met with Xerxes. Although he ruled a large satrap in the Persian Empire, Demaratus'

287

ultimate goal was to return to his native Sparta and reassert his born right to rule. In truth, his desires stretched beyond his glorious Sparta. Demaratus wanted to spread his rule over the entire Hellenic peninsula. He believed in his silent that it was his true destiny. The formula for Demaratus was simple: gain the confidence of this Persian monarch and prove that his ability to lead troops was beyond anything the King knew. Egypt would be his proving ground. His true nature for bravery and combative strategy would be revealed. With his newfound status within this massive Empire, he would be part of the lead armies in conquering Greece. Once the Greek cities were in flames he, Demaratus, would be placed in power by the King. He would rebuild his city, his beloved Sparta in his image. Once he centralized his power he could become an important ally to the grand Persian Monarch. They could form an alliance that could last a thousand years. He believed that his future was already written.

Demaratus had already begun his silent preparations for the invasion and conquest of Greece. Prior to that he would have to prove his worth in Egypt. Demaratus knew that other Persian generals would also have positions of importance in silencing the Egyptian rebels. They were Persian and he was Spartan, so his ability would have to outshine all his rivals. After all, he came from the greatest fighters the world had ever known.

Demaratus had a thin line to walk in his meeting with the King. He wanted Xerxes to know and accept that the Greeks were superior warriors, but he didn't want to slight the King or insult the Persian fighters. Xerxes himself gave him the opening. *"Tell me, Demaratus, why do you think the forces of my father were defeated at Marathon?"*

"I think, my King, there were many reasons that led to the defeat."

"Tell me, Demaratus. I ask you for your most truthful evaluation. Have no fear, my friend. Have you studied Marathon?"

The King's face had grown more serious when he focused on the question.

"I have studied it, my lord."

"Well tell me, my Spartan friend what the mistakes were."

The King rose. Demaratus quickly evaluated the King's tone and did not believe Xerxes to be sarcastic in his question. He stared at the King's face reviewing his inflections and reaching the conclusion that he wanted a candid answer to the question. *"My King, there were mistakes and circumstances that both contributed to the horrible result."*

"Continue," urged the young King. Demaratus knew he was taking a chance if he chose the naked truth. He believed that he needed to push his luck. Demaratus had impulsively decided to put all his eggs in one basket. He knew of the King's volatile temper and realized that if he bet wrongly, this could be his last hour of life. *"Well, my Prince, first, the Persian generals were overly ambitious. If I understand what happened, the force landed on the Marathon plain, on the Schonia beach. They were a formidable force, my King. It was enough strength to defeat any Greek army. Then they made their first mistake. They decided to put faith in a group of Greek traitors, the Alcmaeonidaes, who promised them the keys to Athens when they arrived at the city. The Athenians and their allies, presenting a much inferior force, arrived at the beach to stop the advance of the Persian troops. Had the Persian general immediately attacked the inferior force he would have quickly and easily, in my humble opinion, ruled the day. And, the Greek peninsula would be a Persian satrap this day."*

Xerxes had a serious expression as he intently listened to the Spartan King.

Demaratus became more animated as he spoke, moving closer to the great King. *"But, my lord, that is not what happened. The Persian generals hesitated, placing their fate in treachery and not in their own strength. Then, great King, they made their second crucial mistake. The Persian general, Datis, decided to split the force. He took his fleet and the bulk of his troops and left during the night for Athens. He believed that the remaining troops would easily defeat the Greeks. He supposed that he would arrive at Athens and then be ushered into the city by the treacherous Greek malcontents."*

Demaratus hesitated and turned to the door. He then spun around and faced the King. Demaratus was wide eyed and almost ranting. He was now caught up in his own excitement. He felt the sweat pouring down his back and sides. He was fully engaged in his show and chose not to think about his behavior, for if he had, he might have withdrawn from this course of action.

"My Lord, the cavalry. Datis took his advantage, his cavalry, back onto the boats and left the battlefield in the hope of advancing on Athens. It would take him more than twelve hours to reach the beach outside of Athens, then an additional day to disembark and prepare to attack. The Greek general, Miltiades,

knew of the Greek treachery, and watched as Datis left with his mounted troops. He took all his cavalry and his archers. In fact, I believe that Miltiades was behind the deceit, convincing his enemy to split his forces so he could overcome them. The trap had been set and the mouse Datis, took the cheese. It is told, great King, that Miltiades danced when he watched the ships leave the beach at Marathon and head south. Miltiades knew that his window of advantage was open and he decided to attack the great force during this time of opportunity."

When the name Miltiades was spoken, the great King felt the rush of anger run down his back and his hatred of this man, Miltiades, and everything he stood for, rushed through his body. The King considered him an evil sorcerer whose brilliance arose from a pact that he made with the great Lie. Xerxes was convinced that his god was commissioning him to return the world to its proper equilibrium, back to Truth. Demaratus, realizing that the King was becoming anxious at the reality of what he was saying, decided to throw caution to the wind and continue his critical assault on the Persian military machine. Like Miltiades, he decided to strike now having noticed an opening. *"Great King, the next mistake was made at this point. The Persian general, Artaphernes, the man who was left in charge of the Persian army on the Marathon plain, realizing that the Greeks were preparing to attack, placed his most disciplined and strongest troops in the center of the defense line. He manned the flanks with the inferior regiments. This, my King, was the usual Persian battle strategy and the Greeks had studied and anticipated this formation."*

Xerxes rose again, but this time in obvious anger. He reached for his sword but left it in its place. Demaratus had hoped that he hadn't gone too far in his exactness. He decided to continue even though he could see fire brewing in the young King's face. He needed this man to believe in him and he would flog him with reality until he acknowledged that he needed the Spartan. He wanted Xerxes to know that he understood the Greek mind and that he, Demaratus, was his only hope to defeat the hoplites in open battle. This gamble was designed to prove to the King the worth of the Spartan King.

The hoplites were the warrior class of Athens. They came from the upper classes and spent their lives in the service of others, whoever could afford their services. The word hoplites came from the Greek word Hoplon, meaning large shield. The hoplites would band together in a closely-knit formation which was called the phalanx. They would then attack with the protection of this impermeable shell.

"The Greeks, my King, purposely left the center of their line weak, hoping that the Persian infantry would break through. They were luring Artaphernes, the remaining Persian general, into the trap. With their strongest troops attacking the Persian flank, Miltiades created a pincer movement leading the Persian general into a trap."

Demaratus then moved toward Xerxes and started to shake his hand in front of the King. *"And then my lord, the most dazzling part of the Greek strategy came into play. After they defeated the Persian flanks, rather than continue their attack against the reserves, the Greeks retreated along the flanks and attacked the Persian troops that had broken through the attack line. This lead to a great and hurried retreat by Artaphernes. And the Persians had mistakenly positioned themselves with the great Marathon marsh at their rear so they had no place to go except to retreat into the Panaghia Mesosporitissa swamp. The trap was complete. Most of the Persian elite troops drowned in the quicksand of the marsh."*

Xerxes was now verging on uncontrollable rage. Hearing the truth in this manner seemed to drive him into frenzy. He jumped up and released his sword against the nearest wall. His breathing became irregular and he almost lost consciousness. He was now slashing his weapon rapidly into the wall. The room was quiet except for the King's rant. Everyone stared at the King's tirade. But as quickly as his anger peaked it subsided. He stared with what appeared like hate in his eyes at the now soaked Spartan. But in truth, Xerxes was not angry at the Greek. He was impressed by his presentation. The King, having regained his composure, took a few deep breaths and began to speak. *"Like your Miltiades, you are a gambler, Demaratus"*

The Greek stood in silence breathing hard with his head bowed. The monarch continued. *"Yes, a gambler. You decided to throw your fate to the winds."* The King now stepped forward toward the Greek. His sword was still in the ready and Calah did not know if another man would die tonight. He pointed the sword at Demaratus. *"I like strong decisive men. This man, Miltiades, I hate with every bone in my body. And yet, I respect him as well. Odd, isn't it? My blood and my ancestor's blood boil from this insult."*

The great King was now only a foot from the Spartan. His anger rose and in a very low, threatening voice whispered, *"I was told that of the ten thousand men that took the battle field at Marathon, sixty-five hundred were left dead on the field and over two thousand drowned in the swamp."*

His head now turned to the side and with a sneer said, **"And all told, only one hundred and ninety-two Greeks perished.** *Even the renowned Sakr ax men were routed by the Greeks."*

The King turned, and for what had seemed like an eternity finally breathed. He swung around and returned to the throne. **"One more question before you leave, Demaratus."**

"My lord!"

"Tell me what the phalanx is and how to defeat it."

The King returned to his room and was concerned about these stories of the Greek hoplites. He had asked a slave for a man to be brought to him. Jyylim entered the King's chamber and prostrated himself on the floor. Xerxes was not in a hurry to speak with the spy. He stared at the man as he lay in front of him. He had confidence in this man, but he was concerned about the chances of success. He had already spoken to Calah about the possibility of involving the infamous assassins called the Sand Dancers in this episode. He had called Jyylim because he wanted a backup plan. Although the Sand Dancers were incredibly successful in carrying out their assassinations, Xerxes wanted one of his own men involved. Besides, he personally had defeated these practiced assassins.

Xerxes had heard the rumors. These Greeks were being led by a group of men. He didn't quite understand how such a system could exist, but he was convinced by his advisors that just such a government ran the city of Athens. It stupefied the great King. He had also heard that this government was led by some sort of miracle worker named Themistocles. His spies had told of his great influence across the Greek peninsula, but he was not a soldier, not even a warrior. It was told he performed as a soldier at Marathon but didn't have a significant involvement. He had also heard that this man would be one of the leaders of the Greek resistance to the Persian advance.

"How could this be?" the King bellowed when he first heard this report. *"How could a man who was not trained in the martial arts hope to successfully defend his country against the great Persian army? Was he some sort of witch?"*

Finally, the great King asked for the spy who was still prone in front of him to rise. Jyylim slowly stood up to face his monarch. Few things scared the spy. Even death was not of consequence to this man. Others had commented that Jyylim was happiest when death was tapping him on the shoulder. But the King of Kings was another story. Jyylim's legs imperceptivity shook facing the Man-God. He believed that this man not only controlled his life but also controlled the afterlife. Eternity was a long time.

Xerxes paced the floor as if the he was alone in the room. Finally, after what seemed like perpetuity, he turned his head to the window and spoke, *"Do you know why I summoned you here?"*

"It is a great honor for me to stand here, my lord."

Xerxes seemed to grunt at the response. He turned and continued, *"You have served the Empire well, Jyylim."*

"Thank you, lord. My life is yours."

"Is it, or does it belong to Artemisia?"

Jyylim thought for a moment then replied, *"It is true lord that I am Phoenician. I belong to her and she belongs to you!"*

The great King did not respond again to the comments. He just stared through the man. Finally, he began walking slowly toward Jyylim. When he came close enough to smell the man he looked deeply into his eyes and said, *"Can I trust you, Phoenician?"*

Jyylim hesitated. *"Lord, I am not a political man. My honor is my loyalty. I will carry out any duty you have for me."*

Xerxes spoke, *"There is rumor that one of my generals is going to betray the Empire."*

Jyylim swallowed hard. The King continued. *"A boat waits for you, Jyylim. It will take you to Greece, where you will continue to a town named Pallene. Your mission is very important, Jyylim, as after you meet with a Greek in Pallene you will go to Athens. There you will kill a man named Themistocles."*

Jyylim bowed. *"Consider both of my missions accomplished, lord."*

As he began to back out of the room, Xerxes spoke again. *"You will now go and speak with my advisor Hamath. He will go into detail about what you are to say at your meeting. Listen to him closely, spy, for his words are very important."*

Jyylim bowed as he left.

PERSIA

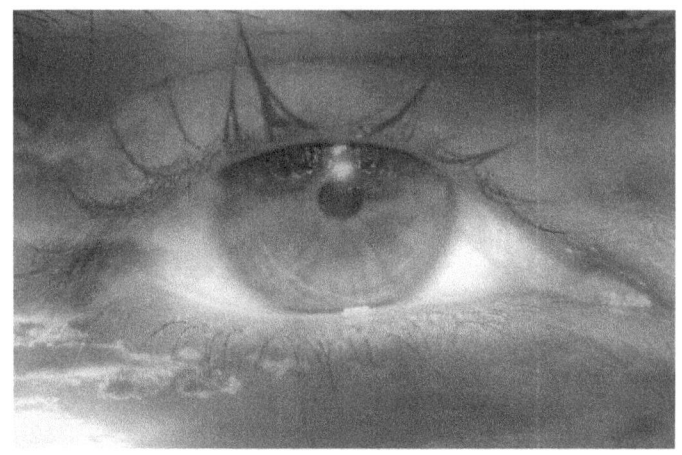

CHAPTER XIII - THE TEMPORAL RELEASE

Her temper was infamous. The Warrior
Queen knew that when she became this
engrossed in her angry rants she needed
to distance herself from others. In the
past, her anger had led to the demise of
many slaves. Although she never showed
it outwardly, the great Queen wrestled
with her guilt after such outbursts. She
could not express her guilty feelings for
fear that they would be interpreted as
weakness. These angry eruptions masked a

continual underlying turmoil. Artemisia's reputation was based, to a degree, on aggression and ruthlessness. The Queen was not as unflappable as her reputation suggested. Early in her lifetime Artemisia learned to turn her fear and frustration towards motivation during war and battles. **"Carry your pain with you to use when you are in danger,"** was the advice she was given. Unfortunately, she could only disguise her feelings for brief periods of time before her disappointment in some event would detonate the volatile mixture that curdled within her. Living near the Warrior Queen was akin to living on a geological fault. Eventually the ground would shake and usually people died. To safely release this pent-up aggravation, Artemisia had to isolate herself or else her fear would explode to the surface like a spewing volcano. Discharging anger and rage outward, her behavior would serve to refuel the guilt that was being released by the outburst. It was truly a vicious cycle which kept the Queen on edge. Others saw her as powerful and stoic. Yet inside that unnerving outward posture, was a boiling cauldron of undifferentiated and primeval emotion. At these times, her only escape from the stomach wrenching emotional bile that overcame her equilibrium was to withdraw from others, escaping into her own self-imposed exile. This solitude led to her healing. Often during these retreats, the great Warrior Queen would curl up in a ball and cry for hours. Her personality would contract into turmoil before it regained its structure. At other times she would speak to the heavens as her ancestors were the only souls that she trusted enough to reveal her true thoughts.

This rant was ignited by her insecurity. She needed the great King to want and trust her. Artemisia wanted to be the integral part of the attack on Egypt then on Greece. The large Persian fleet that she anticipated being assembled to support the ground troops attacking the Greek Peninsula should be headed by either herself or one of her brother Phoenicians. Since the young King appeared to be ignoring her presence since arriving at Susa something primal in her soul was crying out in protest. While in this state Artemisia was not only inconsolable but irrational as well. The decompensation was so complete that the Queen would drift into hallucinations in her stupor.

She had now been missing for almost eight hours. The Queen had found a small room near the dungeons in which to escape. She covered her face with cloth to keep her whimpering silent to anyone passing. The room was small and quite damp. It was somewhat remarkable that she hadn't been discovered in her hideout. Unbeknownst to her, guards had passed at two different times during the hours, but they were distracted by their own chatter and didn't notice the Queen. But she was now recovering. She could feel the strength returning to body and mind. As she stood in the room her legs were initially wobbly, but they quickly strengthened. She stretched her muscles and felt completely in control of her thoughts. She stepped out of the room and was immediately confronted by two Persian guards. *"Well, what have we here?"*

One of the sentinels smiled as he spoke to his fellow guard. The other sentinel turned to him and responded, *"I've not seen this one before, but she looks as though she could make our evening one worth remembering."* The two men laughed as they made eye contact with each other confirming what they both thought. They obviously didn't recognize the tigress that stood before them. Neither realized how close their life was to ending. The Queen, being dressed in scant and disheveled clothes and not carrying any weaponry smiled as she watched the men exchange knowing glances. She leaned back against the wall outside of the room she had just exited and made no effort to protest. The sentinel on the right instinctively pulled out his sword and faced this exceptionally beautiful woman. *"Well my, beauty, it is your lucky night, as you will be able to satisfy two of the King's elite sentinels."*

The Queen's eyes widened as she smiled at the large man. It had been a while since she had felt the hardness of a man and she could feel herself moisten at the prospect. The Queen walked slowly to the large man who must have stood at least six feet tall. It was unusual to see such a large man in this part of the Kingdom. She put her hand on the man's chest as he lowered his sword to his side. The Queen smiled and asked, *"What is your name sentinel, and why are you deserving of my thighs?"*

The young man, taken aback by the woman's forwardness stuttered and said, *"Ebabbara, Ebabbara is my name."*

The Queen, now with both hands on the man's shoulders, rubbed up and down his front. She lowered her hand below his waist and cupped his manhood. *"Well, Ebabbara,"* she said smiling, *"Tell your friend to give us some privacy."*

Regaining his composure, Ebabbara looked at the woman in front of him and exclaimed, *"my friend will join us, my fine wench."*

The Queen looked at the other smiling sentinel. He was a much less impressive individual than Ebabbara. She stepped towards the other man, still smiling. *"What is your name, little one?"*

Ebabbara chuckled at the comment. The smaller man, obviously put off by the comment, decided to become a little more aggressive.

"What is your name, Bitch?"

The Queen smirked and put her hands on the smaller man's chest, making circular movements. Without warning the Queen lifted her knee making immediate contact with the smaller man's groin. As he began to fall, Artemisia grabbed his sword, and in a fluid motion, placed it under Ebabbara's chin. With the smaller man groaning on the floor the Queen now looked directly at the tall sentinel. *"You now have a choice, Ebabbara. You will either quench my bodily thirst in the room behind us, or I will slice you as a roasted pig. Either will satisfy me.'*

Ebabbara, his face now blood red, seemed to shrink in his boots. He walked towards the room. Artemisia gave another look at the man prone on the floor. She pointed the sword at him as she followed Ebabbara. *"If I see your face again today, you will not see the sun rise tomorrow."*

****

Nobody wanted to tell the King. It had been two days since the old priest escaped from the palace. When he was told about the bloody escape Calah decided to wait until he gained enough courage to tell the young King. He had an opportunity before Xerxes spoke with Demaratus but decided not to mention it. Calah knew that Xerxes was looking forward to his meeting with the Spartan King. Even though he thought he knew the King well, Calah couldn't predict how he would react to the disturbing news. The meeting was now over with Demaratus. Calah knew that if the King threw one of his famous temper tantrums, the bearer of the news was in a very precarious position.

Xerxes had retired to his sleeping chamber. The burden of the Persian Empire was beginning to weigh on the young monarch and his shoulders slumped. He looked tired Calah thought as he entered the large chamber. The King was now half lying on a long couch as his attendant entered the large space. But even though tired, the King didn't lose his visual perceptiveness. **"You look concerned, Calah. You must have bad news for me."**

The attendant was shocked by the insight that the King showed. He had reasoned to himself that since Xerxes was so self-consumed he rarely noticed the moods of others. However, the more time he spent with this young man, the more he realized that the King understood the subtleties of human interaction. In many ways he was perceptive beyond his years.

"My King, I do have bad news for you. I'm sorry that your ears have to hear what I have to say."

The King held his hand up, stopping Calah in mid thought. *"Calah, please, don't speak."*

Calah bowed in deference. The King gave a half smile. He slowly put a piece of apple in a bowl of honey and took a bite. *"I already know all the bad news that covers my beautiful palace."*

Calah remained silent. The King continued, *"The escape of that dung heap of a priest has shaken my faith. I know he had help and I know there are those within this palace who plot against me."*

His speech was slow and measured. He was not angry, not out of control emotionally, but very calm and intense. He motioned for Calah to rise, *"No, my friend. You see, I know many things that people think I don't."*

He smiled slowly at the servant. *"For all the deception and deceit that exists in this Kingdom, I still possess the Persian ears. The walls in this building are mine as are the ceilings and floors. The very air that runs through this room also runs through my mind. When a fly dies in this palace I can feel the loss. My ancestors walk with me along my path. They protect and watch my journey."*

The King leaned back again reaching for a piece of apple and honey. There was silence as he slowly ate the fruit. He looked again at Calah who stood in a motionless void of purpose and speech, in shock by the lecture he had just received. *"My ears will reveal the traitors to me. And when I find them, Calah, I will cut off their testicles and feed their bowels to the snakes."*

His face turned dour as he continued. *"But, my friend, the escape of the renegade priest has brought up some uncertainty in my stomach. I am confused. I need the Egyptian."*

The King hesitated as Calah made no movement. Xerxes was not speaking of the upcoming campaign to return the rebellious province of Egypt to the Persian womb. Calah knew what the Egyptian meant, and it scared him. When Xerxes' father Darius was Pharaoh of the Egyptian realm, he married a sorceress.

Her name was Hor of Sebennytos. Her power was known through the deltas and rivers of the dark Continent. Hor, it was rumored, could communicate with the dead. It was told, that in her hypnotic state she could write letters using her symbolic script to those who have crossed over to the underworld. The spirits would then answer the requests of the writer by communicating with her through dreams. Darius would take part in the ancient death rituals of the Egyptian cult, as any true Pharaoh was expected to do. When he married Hor, she returned with him to his beloved Susa. Hor, to Darius' surprise, refused to enter the great palace. Instead she took up residence in the mountains outside of the castle. Darius would visit her in times of stress and she would read his dreams, helping him make decisions by foretelling the future. Xerxes knew that his father trusted this woman even though he had only met her a very few times in his life. Xerxes saw her as his mother and treated her as such.

Xerxes read the hesitation of his servant, *"I sense in you a disappointment at my request."*

Calah responded with a reassurance and directness that surprised him. *"No, my King. I could not be disappointed in the man-God. I am uncertain about this decision. This woman is a witch. There* are those who believe that she is demonic. *That writing that she does, my Prince, that hieratic scripture that she reads. You know, my lord, that there is little that scares me, but this woman. When I am in her presence my blood turns to water. And if I may, my lord, how do we know that that the evil presence that freed the priest does not derive from her?"*

Xerxes rose slightly and held his hand up *"Careful, Calah. Be aware of whom you speak. Hor is my mother, my father's wife. I will ignore these last comments, for if I thought you were serious, I could consider it sedition and I would have your head."*

Xerxes shook his hand in disgust at his servant's skepticism. There was silence as the King sprang from his couch. He paced the floor a few times then turned again to Calah. *"I will go see the Egyptian. Find where she resides and prepare my servants. Change all my meetings for two days. I need her advice."*

Calah bowed in reverence to his monarch. He backed himself towards the doorway. *"My King, is there a specific reason I should present as the cause that the meetings with the delegations will be delayed?"*

The King, still in thought, turned away and walked to the wall. Calah pressed the issue. *"My lord, another issue has arisen in the palace. The Warrior Queen is restless. I heard she is concerned that you have not yet called her into your council. She has disappeared."*

A laugh came from the other side of the room as Xerxes' head started to bounce from his humor. He turned to his servant with a smile on his face. *"An anxious, concerned woman. The best kind, Calah."*

"Lord?"

Xerxes immediately turned more serious. *"The more she anticipates, the sweeter the reward. Don't worry about the Queen. She will survive the wait, I like to see her irritated. As for the delegations, tell them anything, Calah. Most don't deserve a reason. "*

Then he stopped before Calah finally exited the room. *"Wait, Calah. Tell them anything, except the truth."*

E ven before the King was informed of the escape, Penish knew of the tragedy. With his high position in the palace security, Janlikorven personally went to the dungeon to evaluate how this calamity took place.

He needed to discover how the three men infiltrated the palace and could go undetected to the prison area. Although Penish's security position was not related to the prison area itself, he took this escape very personally. He had originally captured the rogue priest and returned him to Susa. He felt that he personally let his King down. It took Penish only half a day to punish some of the palace guards who slept while the men entered the palace area. He breached protocol and ranks, and punished a senior officer for not disciplining his men enough. The man's penalty was for him to be separated from his arms. Penish, being an excellent swordsman, turned away from the man, and as the screams were leaving his mouth, quickly bent down and with a single sweep cut the man's legs off. His anger continued to erupt, and as the man writhed in pain, he continued shredding body parts.

With the man lying in pieces in front of him, and his men staring in disbelief, Penish turned quickly to the second in command, Enki. He grabbed the man by his throat and pulled him by the collar towards him. He was wide eyed and wild. *"I give you three hours, Enki. I want you to choose three men and prepare horses and provisions. We will follow, find this runaway dog, and return the priest to the palace. I want you to locate the tracker, Sippar, and bring him* with you. *He is the only man I know who can accurately track through both desert and mountain."*

He shook Enki back and forth and proclaimed, **"We will find the Priest. If I must drag him back in pieces I will. I swear it to you this day!!"**

Two hours later, Penish met with Sippar in preparation for their journey to recapture the rogue priest. Penish had recovered his composure by this time. He towered over the shorter Sippar as they met in the stables preparing the horses for the journey.

"Tell me, Sippar, can you find this man?"

Sippar was a hardened individual. He had lived a difficult life. His skill at tracking came from being forced to live in the desert and having to survive directly off the land. Because of his past, the man was not threatened by the larger Penish. He looked at him when he asked the ludicrous question. With a sardonic look the trapper proudly admitted, **"I can find anybody. I can smell people."**

"Do you know of the priest?" Penish asked.

"I know of him," The tracker responded.

"He is from Babylon."

He hesitated and turned away from Penish. As he turned Sippar concluded, *"But he won't be returning to that ancient city. He needs to heal."*

"There are many places to hide in the Zagros Mountains," Penish rebuked.

"No," the tracker interrupted. *"He will not go to the mountains. They are too barren. He is an old man and needs some comfort. He will not go south to the great sea. His power doesn't extend south. No,"* the tracker continued as he rubbed his beard, *"No, he will go north towards Assyria. It was his home before the great walled city of Babylonia. We will find the priest in the north."*

"How can you be so sure?" Penish asked with a skeptical sneer.

"I understand my business and I understand snakes," the tracker said as he began to walk towards the horses. He lifted himself on the horse and prepared to leave.

"I think he is going to the Zagros, to the mountains," Penish concluded.

.

The tracker stopped his horse. He turned in his saddle and said with a smile, *"Then you go east to the mountains. Take your men and give the snakes my regards. I will go north and follow the Choaspes River until it runs into the Diyala. We will find the Priest in the north."*

The tracker smiled to him and began to ride away.

****

PERSIA

CHAPTER XIV - THE RITUAL OF KALU

The others were surprised at the remarkable recovery skills of the old man. After his rescue from Susa, the old priest was taken almost 400 miles west - northwest of the capital. He was not taken back to Babylonia, for although his power base was still strong within those walls, every precaution was being made to disguise his whereabouts. For the first week of the journey the old priest drifted between consciousness and stupor with his rescuers fearing for his life on many occasions. The men were heartened when they finally crossed the lower Zab River and entered the province of Assyria. Their destination, the city of Ashur, lay just beyond the river's fulcrum where the Zab ran into the mighty Tigris. Remarkably, the small caravan encountered little resistance in their journey from Susa. Their expectation was that they would spend a majority of their journey dodging the Persian pursuers. This fear never materialized. At one point, to avoid detection, they decided to take a circuitous route, traveling north to Kermanshah to confuse their pursuers. To their surprise and delight no Persian pursuer appeared. The rescuers had prepared their escape well, storing fresh horses and supplies in Kermanshah to hasten their retreat. Their spies and co-conspirators spread throughout the region offered confirmation of their successful escape.

While resting in a safe house in northern Kermanshah, the old priest became delirious. He began to repeat the creation story word for word from the seven tablets of the Enuma Elish. He followed this by writing a letter to his god, Marduk, using the old language of Akkadian. Akkadian was a Babylonian dialect that was rarely used anymore. His rescuers were shocked and awe struck by the performance which lasted almost three hours. Between outbursts

Ningizzida would shake, sweat profusely, and place curses on all Persian royalty. This pattern seemed to repeat itself in a cyclic fashion. With every repetition, another layer of strength returned to Ningizzida. It was as if his mind and body were healing themselves by their tirades and prayer.

His moments of lucidity were rare on the harsh journey to Ashur, but when they came, the men who rescued him were held in religious rapture by his words laden with symbolic religious fervor.

By the second day, the small entourage moved from their original location to a second "safe house". Although there was no apparent threat to their discovery, the rescuers had decided that safety should be paramount.

Jehoash was the chief Babylonian warrior that led the rescue of the renegade priest from the Susa dungeon. Jehoash's family had been one of the wealthiest trading clans of the Babylonia high class when the Persians first conquered the area almost three generations before his birth. Jehoash's family gradually lost their influence and their resentment compounded over time. Jehoash was one of a large underground organization whose sole purpose was to rid their land of the unwanted Persians. They saw the old priest as their messiah.

318

His power, combined with their organization, could ignite a groundswell of popular revolt against the Persian usurpers. It could reinstate Babylonia back in the hands of its rightful people.

After their transfer to the new hiding place, Jehoash ordered the others out of the room and spoke alone with Ningizzida. Ningizzida was now almost fully aware even though his body would take many months to fully recover. Ningizzida was huddled in a corner of the room covered with white robes. When Jehoash approached his first thought was that this old man was so frail, how could his power be so great? His visual image didn't fit the stories that he had heard. When he entered the Persian prison, he had expected to see a Herculean individual chained to a wall, not an old prune soaked in urine and feces cowering in a hole in the ground. Over the past few days he had worked hard to readjust his attitude. This man held the future of his beloved city, in fact his whole archetypal civilization in his hands. He could be the only one to lead a revolt. Jehoash knelt before the man sitting across from him. He really didn't know how to address this man with the proper respect. Ningizzida had his eyes closed so Jehoash sat quietly trying not to disturb him.

After a time, the old priest opened his eyes to see the young man. The Sheshgallu spoke first. His voice was barely audible and it sounded as if his mouth was filled with gravel. He spoke in a slow, labored fashion.

"What is your name?"

His words were interrupted by a coughing spasm. Jehoash waited for the old man to regain his breath. Then he answered. *"My name is Jehoash, master."*

The old man's eyes opened wide and a smile covered his wrinkled face, *"Jehoash, I am proud to know you. You and your men saved my life"*

Jehoash bowed his head, accepting the compliment from the great man. Ningizzida looked at the young man and asked, *"tell me, Jehoash, why did you save me?"*

Surprised by the question Jehoash hesitated before responding, *"Since I was a young child, I heard of the great Ningizzida. Nobody in our entire land had the courage to stand up to the Persian King except for you, master. Even now, the manner in which you insulted the young King at the ceremony has become legend. The people have written songs about you and dedicated prayers to your salvation."*

Jehoash became emotional, stopped for a pause and then continued. "*I love Babylonia, master. I love it more than my life itself. The Persians have stripped us of our heritage. They act and talk as if we are equals to them, but we are not. We will not be until we are a free city again. Babylonia was the greatest city in the world. Great monuments, beautiful gardens, the world was jealous of our home. And then the Medes came and stripped us of our dignity. As long as I am alive, I will fight for Babylonian glory. Some of my friends think that splendor is fighting with the Persians, doing their dirty work. I will not die for Susa. To me, that is only glorified slavery. The Persians care not what happens to us. They would sacrifice us at their holy temples if they thought it would bring them salvation.*"

As the old priest looked on the young man again hesitated. His face turned bright red with rage as he continued. He banged his fist to the ground. "*I am sorry, master, but my anger for these shit eating insects overcomes my common sense at times. What makes me the angriest, is how they pretend to pay homage to our god, Marduk. That Persian slut doesn't believe in our god. He just participates in the ceremony because he thinks it is the right thing to do. He walks around like a stuffed bird parading* up and down our city. He even declared Babylonia to be one of the Persian capitals. But underneath all that show and pomp, we Babylonians are second class citizens to the Persian tyrant."

Tears came to the young man's eyes. "When I heard what you did at the ceremony I knew that our people had only one road, one direction. I believe you were sent to us by God to lead us to our destiny."

Ningizzida held up his hand, "Jehoash, you have not answered my question. Why did you rescue me in Susa?" briefly interfering with the young man's tirade.

Jehoash swallowed deeply, sweat dripping from his red face, his cheeks still wet with tears and his long black hair flowing out in all directions. There was spittle on his beard from his ranting. He was now more fearful than he was when participating in his dramatic rescue of the priest.

"Master, you are our hope. You are the only man in our city that is loved and admired and has the strength to stand up to the Medes."

Ningizzida again held up his hand. "Will you die for such a cause, Jehoash?"

"Without hesitation," the young man immediately replied. *"Without hesitation, master,"* he repeated, and bowed his head in reverence.

Ningizzida, using all his strength, lifted himself from his mat and although shaking, stood upright for the first time since leaving Susa. He motioned Jehoash to also rise and the young man complied. Ningizzida stood close to the young man's face.

Ningizzida stared at the young man. With hesitating steps, he walked to his belongings and took out a vile of liquid. The priest asked for wine and emptied the vile into the glass. He asked the young man to drink the potion. The priest sat and asked his new acolyte to sit across from him. There was a long period of silence until Ningizzida asked, *"Tell me, Jehoash, when you entered the Persian dungeon, what did you see?"*

"What did I see?"

"Yes, Jehoash, what did you see?"

The young man thought about the unusual question. He was quickly becoming dizzy and somewhat chaotic from the drink. Jehoash wanted to give the right answer, but he didn't know what the correct answer was, so he related, *"Master, I saw you in a deep hole in the* ground. *You were covered with urine and feces.*"

Ningizzida smiled. He responded to Jehoash's answer. "*No, Jehoash, that's not what you saw.*"

Ningizzida smiled again. The young man was now having trouble keeping himself upright.

"*If you will be walking on this very dangerous path with me, you must be able to see the truth. Now close your eyes and free your thoughts. Imagine where you were and use all your power to think. Now imagine walking into the dungeon.*"

Jehoash had always been uncomfortable with his eyes closed but he didn't want to fail this godly man. He hesitated but shut his eyes. He now realized he was not completely in control of himself. Jehoash felt his body drifting. He could see waves as reality began drifting away. At first Hesitant to close his eyes, now the young man couldn't open them. The only sound he could hear was that of the old priest. "*Think carefully, Jehoash. Can you see the river in front of you? Watch the water, Jehoash. You are floating with it, Jehoash. You are not scared, but completely relaxed. Now Jehoash, you are entering the dungeon. Can you see the chains on the walls?*"

The young man nodded his head up and down in affirmation, *"Do you see the light emanating from the ceiling?"*

Jehoash affirmed the vision.

"Watch the light, Jehoash. It is brilliant and you must shade your eyes from its brightness. Follow it from the ceiling Jehoash. Do you see it coming down and funneling into the darkened pit?"

"Do you see it, Jehoash?" The priest's voice now excited and intense. *"Follow the light Jehoash, where does it go?"*

"The light goes into the pit. It is very bright master."

"Watch the light Jehoash, keep your eyes focused on the divine glow."

"The pit, Jehoash, do you see who is rising out of the pit? Do you see me, Jehoash? The light, Jehoash, the light is lifting me out of the pit! Do you see it, Jehoash?"

"I can see it, master. I can see you. You are floating up from the pit. The light is carrying you up. I can see it, master, I can see it."

"Good, Jehoash, good. God is now letting you see the truth. He allowed

you to see the truth. You are blessed, Jehoash."

Ningizzida continued, *"Look around in your mind, Jehoash. Do you see the chains?"*

"I do, master."

"Good, do you see the rats?"

"I do, Master!"

"Good. Do you see me rising?"

"I do, Master! I can see you!"

Ningizzida beamed. *"What am I wearing, Jehoash?"*

"You are wearing a gold and white gown, Master."

"Yes, Jehoash, I was. What am I doing, Jehoash?"

"You are shedding your chains, Master."

"Good, Jehoash, Good. Look at the light from above melting the chains."

The old Priest continued to talk. As he spoke, his voice gained clarity according to Jehoash's ears. His voice became clearer with each word.

Remarkably, the images in his mind simplified, fitting the words he was hearing almost exactly. *"Do you see the light, Jehoash?"*

"The light, Master?"

"Yes, Jehoash, look closely, look for the light."

The young man was quiet for a few minutes.

"I can see the light again, Master."

"Describe it, Jehoash, describe it fully to me."

"It's in the black and dark room and a bright light is hovering like a hunting falcon over your head. It is so strange to see it for it does not illuminate the rest of the room as it should. It just gives light to your body."

"Wonderful, Jehoash, wonderful. Keep talking. God is listening, Jehoash."

"As the light shines, the chains binding you appear to be melting away. And strangely, the smell of the room is gone. Light seems to encompass your body, Ningizzida. It's remarkable. Oh no, gone."

"Open your eyes, Jehoash."

Jehoash opened his eyes, and Ningizzida put his hand on his shoulder, gently pushing him down onto a knee. He continued to speak. *"Calm yourself, my son. Your images were truly inspirational. You can see where others are blind. It is a gift my son, a gift."*

The young man smiled as he bowed his head.

"The ability to see the truth is given to you by God, Jehoash. Do you know that? God has chosen you for this task. He has made you one of his messengers. You are blessed, Jehoash. I am truly lucky to have found you, as you will stand by my side as we rid our beloved city of the Persian sickness. Jehoash, when I was in the pit God visited me and foretold of your coming."

The young man nodded his head in affirmation.

"Tonight, Jehoash, think on this image that was God inspired. In the morning you will return to me with two candles. There is a temple in this city run by Erib-biti priests. Do you know of it, Jehoash?"

"No master, I do not."

"Find the temple, Jehoash. The Erib-biti sect is one of the most powerful of the different cults of our priesthood."

Jehoash responded, "my lord, I am uneducated in such things, but I will locate the temple."

"Good, Jehoash, good. Give the two candles to the priest in the temple and tell him that you were sent by the supreme master, Baldigul-el."

Jehoash looked puzzled.

"Repeat the name, Jehoash,"

"Baldigul-el."

"Good, Jehoash, good."

"Don't worry, Jehoash. They will understand what you are saying. Tell them that you are giving them these candles so they can bless them. Explain that we will be performing the ceremony of Kalu- the ridding of the evil this evening. During the ceremony, Jehoash, you will be transformed. You will be molded by God into one of his warriors. Be prepared, Jehoash, for the ceremony is painful and it will press you to your earthly limits. Think on this, Jehoash, for once performed there is no turning back. Your status as a warrior of god will be cemented. It will require great *sacrifice to remain on the true path. Once you achieve this the world will look different to you, Jehoash, so tonight you must decide if this is your fate. You will have to follow the will of God without question. What you will be required to do on earth will only be rewarded when you to stand face to face with the true god, Marduk."*

Jehoash seemed excited. He blurted out, *"I am ready, Master, I am ready for the ritual."*

"No, Jehoash, you are not. You must consider it tonight. It cannot be a rash decision. The Erib-biti priest will give you things that will help in our ceremony. It is very important that you bring them all to me. They will give you certain plants and certain covers. They will provide you a flask with a potion that has wondrous powers. You must guard these things carefully, for they must be returned to me exactly like the Erib-biti give them to you."

"I understand, master."

"Good, Jehoash, good. Now leave me and go to your quarters and prepare your thoughts. The other men, see if they understand the vision in the prison. If they hadn't had the revelation, then you know how to handle it."

Artemisia returned to her quarters. She was now more controlled and it was immediately apparent that her equilibrium had returned. As she entered her chambers her servants all immediately fell to the floor in apparent ecstasy. The Queen looked different to them but none of them could put their finger on the change. Artemisia ordered food as she was famished from her ordeal. She ate as if she had never seen food before. After her meal she sent her servants out and called for Ekallatim. The girl immediately emerged from the shadows and the Queen spent the next few hours in massage and pleasure with her favorite possession. The joy that Ekallatim gave the warrior Queen was unmatched as she understood her very essence.

Ekallatim understood the sensitivities between the Queen's legs. The time Artemisia spent with Ebabbara was only a passing diversion from her accepted practice. Although Ekallatim could sense a transitory shift in her sovereign, it was not new to her and she had known it before. It offered her no concern as she knew that Artemisia would always return to her true nature. When the Queen combed her long blond hair and stroked her smooth hips it comforted Ekallatim as she felt the warmth return to her legs. Although the servants had told her that Nabu-na'id waited with important news, the Queen gestured them away, demanding that he wait until she was ready to see him. Such an action also provided Ekallatim with assurance of her position in the Queen's heart, and Artemisia did it with purpose, even though she was burning to hear what Nabu had to relate. She was also told that one of her Phoenician spies had some interesting information to share with her.

The sun was setting over the vast desert as Artemisia decided it was time to think again. She gave Ekallatim a pouch with silver and gold and ordered her to give it to a Persian guard named Ebabbara. Ekallatim was surprised at the task but the Queen responded to her hesitation by reminding her that, **"Even though I sometimes pet the dogs they will never replace the silky tongue of my cat."**

Ekallatim smiled widely and knew that she would enjoy paying this guard for his services to the Queen. She even thought of trying the feast herself. It was an intriguing consideration.

After Ekallatim left the Queen's presence by the back-entrance, Artemisia ordered her servants to fetch the Phoenician spy, Jyylim. Jyylim had been in her service for years. Even though he was a below average sailor he had a skill for gossip. His information was generally reliable although sometimes the specifics of it were not dependable. Jyylim only had a partial tongue. He spoke with both his hands and his voice. Once one understood what his gestures meant, he was remarkably easy to understand. He used certain grunts to make points when he wanted to emphasize a situation.

Jyylim had three absorbing pieces of information for the Warrior Queen. The first was that the King was not seeing any more envoys until the council meeting in three days. He followed this up by insisting that the King had left Susa and was headed to the mountains. Jyylim had no reason to back up this information but he believed it to be factual. *"My Queen, I was recently called before the great King."*

"I heard this, Jyylim!"

"My Queen, the King asked me to go on a mission to Greece."

"Yes, Jyylim, and what did he ask you to do in Greece?"

Jyylim bowed and resolved, *"I will tell you all, my Queen."*

Artemisia was shocked by this presentation. What was this young King thinking? Had he turned his back against

her and her Phoenician brothers in favor
of the ex-Spartan King and his
incompetent mystics? She could feel the
anger build within her but she managed to
restrain herself. She knew she needed to
understand the King's reasoning and not
assume that he had turned his back on
her. She was hoping that Nabu-na'id
could clarify what she had just learned.
She immediately sent for her eunuch when
Jyylim left.

Nabu-na'id had been waiting patiently
for hours. He felt irritated when he
noticed that Jyylim had been summoned
before him; however, he dismissed the
event as inconsequential. He entered the
Queen's chamber and dropped to his knees.
*"I have missed you, my Queen. I thank
the gods that you returned to us safely."*

Artemisia was quiet and gestured for
him to continue.

*"I have learned some interesting bits
of information."*

The Queen gestured for him to stand
and continue.

*"First, my Queen, the King's engineer,
Asanaladace, has been given orders to
prepare plans for a crossing of the
Hellespont. Clearly, Xerxes is planning
to invade Greece."*

Nabu had some disturbing news for the Queen and hesitated to deliver it. The Queen sensed his reluctance and urged him to continue. *"Well, my Queen, I am really not sure whether what I am about to tell you is factual or not. Due to the nature of the information, I am hesitant to relay it."*

"Go on, eunuch, the Queen demanded."

Nabu-na'id bowed to one knee and lowered his head. He feared the Queen's reaction at the next piece of information.

"Well, lord," he went on, *"My sources tell me that you will not be invited to the council meeting."*

Artemisia jumped out of her chair and drew her knife. She leaped across the room and held the knife under Nabu's throat. *"Be careful eunuch, for the next words that you utter could be your last. You have already lost an essential element of your body. Are you prepared for me to remove your tongue?"*

Nabu-na'id was visibly shaken by the Queen's attack. He hadn't considered such an intense reaction to the news. He attempted to speak but the monarch had him by the throat and he could barely breathe. He finally gained enough breath. *"My Queen, my life has always been yours for the taKing. You gave me back my life and I give it back to you with joy. My Queen, before you sullen yourself with my blood, I want to tell you that there is a positive side to this information. My source indicates that the King has not lost confidence in you and your brothers."*

Artemisia threw the eunuch to the ground.

"Be gone from my sight, eunuch. Cherish your tongue tonight when you eat for this might be the last day that you own it."

Nabu-na'id almost crawled out the room. Artemisia felt defeated. She couldn't understand why the King had forsaken her. What she wanted to do was follow him to the mountains and remove the spine from his back with her blade. The Queen threw herself down on her bed and began to sulk.

An hour later a servant girl begged entrance to her chambers. Still in a foul mood, the Queen barked at the young woman when she came into the room. *"Why do you disturb me?"* The girl almost wet herself at the Queen's reaction to her entrance. *"My Queen, there is a messenger from the King to see you."*

"What?" Artemisia said as she rose from her prone position. She thought for a moment, "*that spineless snake now wants something from me. I will send his courier away to show that pig my anger.*" She paced for a few seconds, regained her composure, and then said, "*give me a few minutes and then escort him in.*"

∗∗∗∗

It was almost noon before Jehoash returned to the old priest. He had found the temple with little trouble but the priests questioned him about his relationship with Baldigul-el. The priests were hesitant to acknowledge what Jehoash was asking for. Baldigul-el had passed away and when Jehoash indicated that he had sent him for the ritual instruments they began questioning his sincerity. The priests had become paranoid about outsiders questioning their rituals. Jehoash was unrelenting in his quest and he recognized that he couldn't admit to anybody that Ningizzida was in their city. Eventually the priest succumbed to his insistence but not without reluctance. They took the candles and disappeared behind a large pulpit. It took over an hour but eventually one of the priests returned with a large box. They explained that everything that he needed was enclosed in the box.

The man, who Jehoash concluded was the high priest of the temple, stood holding the box. *"Before I give this to you, I must ask a few questions."*

Jehoash stood in silence as he listened. The old priest began speaking. *"You have told me your name is Jehoash so I will tell you mine. It is Yannul. It means "the inquisitor" in an ancient language. I have heard a strange story, Jehoash. It is being told that the great priest, Ningizzida, has escaped from the clutches of the Persian King."*

Jehoash tried not to give any facial response to the statement. Yannul continued. *"We hear that the Persian King has sent his minions out to recapture the priest but stupidly sent them in the wrong direction. Some have even wondered whether this priest has taken refuge in our city. Of course, Jehoash, you and I don't believe in rumors. It is curious, however, that a man shows up at our temple asking to have candles blessed for a ritual that few living men know about."*

Still Jehoash stood silent. The priest handed the box to Jehoash and the younger man bowed. Yannul continued. *"The funny thing is Jehoash, at this temple, Ningizzida is considered godly. Before you leave I have another bag for you. It has food and drink for you and your compatriots, whoever they are."*

Before he left the priest bowed to Jehoash. He inquired why the priest was giving him such a respectful salutation. The priest asked if Jehoash understood the purpose of the Kalu ritual. When he replied that he did understand, the priest explained that few men are offered the opportunity for such an honor. Jehoash smiled again and bowed back to Yannul.

Returning to Ningizzida, Jehoash felt as if there was a space between his shoes and the desert sand as he hurried along. And yet there was also a tinge of fear knowing that the ritual involved pain and transformation. Even though he knew he was committed to the old priest, such a transformative spiritual rebirth was unsettling.

Jehoash was surprised to find that Ningizzida was no longer in the residence where they were staying. When he inquired to his host, he was told the priest had gone to a friend's house and that Jehoash was to meet him there when he arrived. Jehoash immediately left with his box and found the new resting place of his mentor. The people who greeted the young warrior were also quite old. They offered Jehoash some unusual herbal tea while he waited for Ningizzida. The woman, whose name was Wilfer, explained to him that they had known Ningizzida when he was a young man. He had practiced in this primeval city until he moved on to bigger and better places. These people became very close with the young Priest, and he spent many hours explaining life to them. Wilfer also brought Jehoash an exceptional lamb stew that she told him would give him strength for his upcoming ordeal. She continued to press the tea, filling his cup whenever he drank a portion. When he began holding up his hand to refuse more, Wilfer begged him to continue to drink using the excuse that it was important for his wellbeing.

After about an hour, Jehoash began becoming anxious wondering where the Priest was and what the delay was. He began pressing Wilfer for answers, but she only smiled, stroked his hair and told him to be patient. After another long period of time, Wilfer's husband, Job, entered the kitchen eating area. Job was different looking to Jehoash. His head was shaved and he sported a long white beard. He was a small man but possessed the air of authority. His eyes were as black as coal and it made him look imposing even though he was short in stature. The other aspect of this kitchen which made Jehoash uneasy was the presence of certain symbols that hung on the wall. They were foreign to him and he had difficulty averting his eyes. Job noticed his distraction, smiled, and explained that he and Wilfer were followers of the Hebrew god.

"Is Ningizzida a Hebrew?"

Jehoash blurted out without thinking. Wilfer and Job both looked at each other, laughed, and shook their heads. *"Ningizzida is a great, spiritual leader, but he is not Hebrew."*

Jehoash felt immediate relief for he had heard stories of the Hebrew god. He had heard that the Hebrew God demanded sole obedience. After he thought for a while Jehoash asked, *"Why has Ningizzida come to your house to perform this ancient Babylonian ceremony?"*

"For generations," Job replied, *"The Hebrews and the Babylonians were brothers. Some of our ceremonies are very similar. The ritual that you are about to undergo will occur in a special hut behind the house in which the revered priest now sits. Ningizzida is in the hut preparing it for the ceremony."*

Jehoash became anxious. Was he about to endure a Hebrew ceremony? He had also heard that in one of the Hebrew ceremonies a man's penis was sacrificed to their god. The thought brought severe pains to the young man as he unconsciously reached down to place his hand on his genitals. Jehoash's parents feared the Hebrews. Although the Jews were part of Babylonian society, they were always seen as separate, different from them but accepted as a necessary evil. Jehoash had only been face to face with only a handful of Jews in his life. And now he had eaten their food. His stomach turned at the thought. Without warning, Job interrupted his thoughts and declared that it was time for him to join his master.

Job escorted Jehoash out to the back of the house where about twenty yards behind the structure, he saw a small, flat hut that looked more like a gigantic turtle than a structure. As they approached, Jehoash couldn't immediately identify an opening from which to enter. Job led him to a place and explained that he had to strip his outer clothes off and crawl through a little hole. Again, Jehoash reached down to protect his genitals. Job had pulled back a small curtain that revealed the cave like opening.

Jehoash bent and began to crawl through the small opening. He immediately felt the rush of warm air. As he crawled, his thoughts began to wander.

"What am I doing? I thought I had a clear vision of what was happening but I've lost control of my future. I am following this holy man and have

committed my future to this path. I thought I was prepared for sacrifice but where am I? What am I doing in this place?"

Jehoash stopped for a minute breathing hard. He now felt unsure. This was not a game; this was a commitment with his very life hanging in the balance. Jehoash realized he had stopped moving forward. He was scared and he was becoming incontinent. Jehoash swallowed hard and continued to move.

Suddenly Jehoash entered an open area where the heat was even greater than in the tunnel. It was dark in the space. Jehoash could feel the steam entering his nostrils and lungs. His forehead began burning. A light appeared in the corner of the space and Jehoash immediately identified Ningizzida sitting quietly in the corner. Jehoash was now sweating profusely. His chest was heaving and his heart was pounding through his chest. He was worried and scared.

The old priest was sitting quietly and Jehoash pushed the box towards him and waited. Ningizzida was quietly chanting. It was an eerie sight; the old man, sitting and chanting in the mist of the steam with a translucent light flickering in the background. Jehoash was transfixed. As the old Priest chanted, Jehoash began feeling a little light headed. His heart began to flutter, and he began worrying that he would faint. He closed his eyes for what seemed like only seconds trying to reorient himself. He immediately felt the sting of a leather belt that slashed across his back. He was now in a daze and the pain almost felt pleasant. Jehoash looked towards the priest but he continued to chant. Jehoash could feel the blood that oozed out of the wounds on his back. Before he knew it the whip struck again and Jehoash found himself lying face down. The whip stung again and Jehoash had no strength to resist the onslaught.

Jehoash was having increasing trouble focusing his eyes. Colors seemed to radiate from the walls as his sense of reality shifted. Spots began appearing in his vision and flashes of light passed by his face. Lying in pain, in a semiconscious state, he could smell the aroma of burning herbs. He now felt the closeness of the old priest. The Sheshgallu grabbed his long, sweat-soaked hair and tugged his head backwards. The priest began chanting loudly. Jehoash's eyes were now wide in pain and confusion. And he instinctively began chanting the same words that his mentor was saying. He didn't know what they meant but the chanting went on. It was rhythmic in its eloquence. And when certain beats arose, the belt reappeared to bring more blood to the surface on Jehoash's back. For what seemed like hours the hot water poured over the stones and steam filled the room. It became heavier and heavier, at times making it difficult even to breath. Occasionally the priest would raise his head and offer him a foul-tasting drink. The stones were soaked in special herbs and the chanting seemed to get louder and louder. At some point Jehoash began hallucinating. He saw colors and forms floating over the ceiling of the hut mixing with the steam and reappearing in varying shapes. He began anticipating the lash, almost wishing that the frequency would increase. It was his only hold on reality. He would recall later that the priest took out a dense liquid from a flask and began lightly rubbing it on his wounded back. He lifted his head and gave a small smile at the soothing feeling and then everything spun very quickly and Jehoash lost consciousness.

Later that night Jehoash opened his eyes to see Wilfer standing above him.

"Am I still alive?" he heard himself ask. Wilfer smiled at him as he sat up in his bed. When he was partially erect he suddenly located the pain that emanated from his back. He winced as the full extent of his wounds became apparent. Wilfer, noticing his tenderness, produced a flask of warm oil. She began to open

it and Jehoash enquired, *"What is that? I am thirsty!"*

Wilfer chuckled saying, *"No, this is not for your mouth, but for your wounds."*

"What is it?" Jehoash curiously asked.

"It is called Abramelin Oil. It is made of myrrh, anon, calamus, carrion, and phalleform. It will heal your wounds"

Jehoash smiled and instinctively turned his body to reveal the reddened slashes that covered his back.

"You should be proud of yourself!"

Wilfer added as she gently applied the heavy liquid to the young man's skin.

"I'm just happy that the gods saw me fit enough not to take my useless life."

Wilfer laughed again. In her years she had seen this ceremony take the lives of many strong young men. She had wondered to herself if the purpose of the rite wasn't just human sacrifice. Her thoughts were interrupted by Jehoash's words.

"I am still tired, Wilfer. Sleep is coming again."

When Jehoash woke again the Sheshgallu sat opposite him. When his eyes focused he said, *"Master."* The priest smiled at Jehoash. *"How do you feel?"*

"I survived, Master."

"Good, Nin-nibru, good."

"What did you call me, master?"

"You are no longer Jehoash," Ningizzida said, his tone turning more serious. *"You are Nin-nibru and you are very much alive."*

"Nin-nibru?" Jehoash inquired.

"Who is Nin-nibru?"

"You are," Ningizzida said smiling at the young man. *"Last night Jehoash died and was reborn as Nin-nibru. You are now a new individual, able to begin your life anew."*

"Nin-nibru?" Jehoash queried again.

"A fine name for the man who will lead the new Babylonia back to its glory."

"But I am just your servant, master."

"Yes, you are. And we are both on a pre-designed path." Ningizzida answered. *"But how you are now a warrior working to*

347

free your land of the Medes. It is your path, Nin-nibru. You cannot avoid it. You will follow the path and bring to us a new, reborn, Babylonia."

Nin-nibru smiled and fell back into a deep sleep.

＊＊＊＊

The Queen had spent the last twenty minutes fixing herself. She wanted to be impressive in front of the envoy sent from the King of Kings. After all her disappointment she had hoped that her defining moment was finally arriving.

The envoy was eloquently dressed in a bright red robe. His tunic was covered with brightly colored sequins. He was unquestionably more stylish than the Warrior Queen and she winced at the thought of being out dressed by a courier, even if it was a royal one. However, she was excited and spent a fair amount of her psychic energy controlling her reactions.

Upon entering, the courier prostrated himself in front of Artemisia. The Queen stood from her chair and motioned for the man to rise. He didn't move or heed her request. She took a step forward and said, *"Please rise."* Again, the courier was motionless on the floor. The Queen, now frustrated, didn't know how to reply.

"What is your name?" Without moving, the courier responded, *"My name is unimportant, my Queen."* *"Unimportant?"* *"I am also unimportant, my Queen."*

Artemisia started to pace slowly in front of the man, her hard-soled boots making the only noise in the room.

"My Queen, I was told by my master, the great King of Persia, to remain on the floor by your feet."

She stopped her pace and stared at the man, her dark brown eyes blazing with disbelief. She unconsciously was palming her stiletto, an act which betrayed her nervousness. The courier continued. *"My master said that he has offended your honor and he offers my life as payment. I am not to rise until your honor is satisfied, my Queen. If you wish, I will cut my own throat to appease your anger."*

Although intrigued by the thought, Artemisia said nothing but continued to glare at the man. Suddenly her eyes began to flare as she bounded towards the man. Her blade was now in her hand and she placed it by the courier's throat. In a lower voice the Queen hissed, *"Does you master believe that my honor can be satisfied by the likes of you?"*

She threw his head down and stood up. *"I agree that your life is insignificant.*

So my King is giving me an insignificant present. Now rise and return to your master and tell him I am insulted by this worthless sacrifice."

The courier was obviously stunned by the Queen's reaction. He remained prone in front of her. *"Did you not hear me, you useless dog?"* The courier was now sweating. *"My Lady, I cannot return to my King with that information."* He raised his head. *"Please lord, end my life now."* The Queen returned to her chair. *"I will consider your life in a while. Now rise worthless one."* The courier, now flushed with fear, rose from his position. *"I am at your beckon, my Queen."* *"I wish no revenge of the flesh. Tell your King upon your return that my mood has softened by his gift. Now courier, tell me your message before my anger peaks again and you surely will lose your life."*

The man straightened himself and rearranged his wardrobe, pulling down his velvet vest. *"Xerxes, the Great King of the known world, has a detailed and important message for you my Queen. First, I must ask that before I reveal his thoughts to you that you dismiss your servants. The room must be emptied of all other ears before I proceed."*

The Queen, ever vigilant, placed her right hand on her sword as she motioned

350

for the others to leave the dwelling. They all hurried to the exit. The Warrior Queen now stood alone with the King's unnamed courier. *"The great King of the Persian Expanse again wishes to apologize to you for not acknowledging your presence at his great Palace. He would like to assure you that it was not a slight but a purposeful maneuver on his part.*

The King wanted to give credibility to others and have them believe that the great Warrior Queen was no longer in his favor. There was a purpose in this deception that I am here to explain. The King had hoped to explain this to you in person but a need arose for him to leave the capital. He will return in three days for the council meeting at which time he will raise an army to punish the Egyptian magi who have fostered rebellion from his loyal subjects. The great King does not want you involved in the Egyptian campaign for while it occurs, you will have a more important mission, more essential to Persia than any minor military campaign."

The Great Queen was clearly interested as her face betrayed her blooming intoxication. She looked at the courier and responded to his silence. *"Courier with no name, so far your message matches your status. It appears to me just plain hot air."*

351

The Courier straightened his posture and continued. *"My Queen, please excuse my stupidity. I didn't mean to lose my voice for so long. The mission that the King has for you is to negotiate the surrender of the Greeks."*

The Queen looked surprised at this suggestion. She blurted out, *"Negotiate? Why would I want to negotiate with the Greeks? I want to bury the Greeks in their own blood, burn their useless temples, not negotiate. Talk is useless, people respond to fire and rage."*

The courier seemed to want to smile, but he didn't. He did answer her comment *"The Great King anticipated your objection, my Queen. He wanted you to understand that you were the only one that he could trust with such an important undertaking. You will travel to Greece to the great Oracle at Delphi. Once there, you will consult the Greek God. Xerxes will provide you with a list of secret questions you are to present to the god of the Oracle for his reflection."*

The Queen appeared interested at the prospect. She had only set eyes on the Greek shoreline from a distance but had never really stepped onto Greek soil. She had also heard of the great Oracle. She had heard that the god, Apollo, spoke through the priestess there.

352

The courier continued with his message. *"The consultation of the god is only part of your mission. You will secretly meet with representatives of the Athenian council. There is a possibility that given the correct incentive they will voluntarily bow to the Persian King. It is in their best interest. The King has had some underground correspondence that suggests to him that the Greeks are not interested in fighting this great Empire."*

The Queen was now starting to embrace the concept that she would not be part of the Egyptian victory. She looked seriously at the courier and asked, *"Is there more, courier with no name?"*

He bowed again: *"There is, my Queen - the most important part of the mission in Greece. The Persian King has many spies who are evaluating the Greek strength to resist our armies and navy. Your last assignment is to rendezvous with these individuals and receive their reports of the Greek strength."*

Abruptly the courier stopped his report. For the first time he looked at the Queen. His face distorted as he spoke: *"I have reported to you word for word, what my King has desired me to present to you. My purpose in life is now ended."*

The man bowed again to the Warrior Queen. He began to back off. As he moved, to the Queen's surprise, he produced a large knife that was hidden under his robe. The Queen, reacting unconsciously, started to draw her sword at the sight of the blade. The courier did not approach the Queen but continued to move backwards. Halfway to the door he fell to his knees. The courier looked to the heavens and began to chant some unknown incantations. His eyes were now not worldly but blank and vacant. He looked directly at the Queen without seeing her at all. Although his voice was deep and slow he started to talk. *"My King,"*

He now switched his gaze to the heavens, as if pleading with God. *"My life has always been yours. I have presented your message and now it is time for my life to end. My purpose has been served. There will be no witnesses to this message. It will remain between you, my Lord, and the Warrior Queen."*

In one motion he swung the knife, cutting a deep slash in his neck. His head, although still connected to his back, seemed to flop to one side of his body. The blood flew from him, reaching a full man's length from his body. The Queen watched in amazement as his eyes

354

went blank and his body gradually fell forward as if in slow motion.

＊＊＊＊

The day was warm and even though it was early one could tell that the sun would be stifling when it finally reached its pinnacle. It had been two days since the young man who was formally known as Jehoash was transformed in the sacred ritual to Nin-Nibru. Miraculously his back was almost healed as his wounds had scabbed over. The oil that Wilfer applied twice daily was having its desired effect.

Suddenly, Job entered the room and approached the newly named Nin-Nibru. *"Are you ready, my friend?"*

"Ready for what?"

Nin-Nibru asked surprised by the question,

"The great priest awaits your awakening. Ningizzida wants you to join him as soon as you are strong enough."

Nin-Nibru tried not to hurry but his heart beat as if it were going to explode out of his chest. He walked quickly to the rear entrance. Nin-Nibru swallowed hard and tried controlling his breathing as he walked across the back of the house.   He was trying hard to feel reborn, but he had always survived by his forwardness and ability to throw caution to the wind. His decision to go Susa and rescue the great priest happened without deep thought.   Nin-Nibru was overcome with passion and decided that the Priest was the only way to save his beloved city and his heritage. Now what did it mean to be reborn? He would have to change his temperament.   Nin-Nibru had never been governed by anything except his own emotion and his impetuous decisiveness.

When he entered the room, the old priest was in a contemplative state. Nin-Nibru sat in front of the master and patiently waited for him to come out of his trance. While he waited his mind drifted into many different areas. He knew that he needed to learn to train his mind. Although he was strong, decisive and fearless, Nin-Nibru lacked discipline. He inherently knew that he would need to change his approach if he was to help the priest expel the Medes from Babylonia. And what's more, he knew that the Sheshgallu knew it as well. He was ready for his metamorphosis.

After a good while that seemed close to forever for Nin-Nibru, the old priest opened his eyes. He smiled as he saw the young man sitting quietly in front of him. *"This is difficult for you, is it not?"* Ningizzida probed.

356

"What is, my Lord?" *"Being patient.*
Your mind is like a wild horse. It needs
to be trained," **Ningizzida** explained.
The young man just nodded his head in
affirmation, as the priest laughed
silently to himself, recognizing similar
traits that he himself had to overcome as
a young man. But the restoration of a
free Babylonia was something that
required planning and stealth. It was a
dangerous game that the priest was
beginning to play. The Medes were
treacherous men. Ningizzida knew them
well and feared and hated them with equal
passion. To defeat these Persians and
vanquish them from the great city they
would need fate to lean heavily on their
side. Ningizzida knew that the Egyptian
revolt provided a small window in which
to operate, but that the real opportunity
lay in a war with Greece. He also was
aware of the burning hatred that the King
held for the Greeks. Anger was
motivating but only made men blind,
Ningizzida remembered hearing as an
acolyte. His plan was simple. While
the Persians were in Egypt regaining
control of the rebellious province,
Ningizzida's plan was to seize that
opportunity to vanquish the Medes from
Babylonia. The Sheshgallu and his
followers would have to convince the
people of the importance of this mission
to arouse groundswell support. He would
use a combination of religious and

righteous fervor and manipulation to convince the masses of their need. Ningizzida knew that expelling the Medes would be the easy part of this process. He had no doubt that the Persians would easily retake Egypt from the renegade magi priests that had seized control. The Egyptians had forgotten that the complicated aspect of gaining power was maintaining it. Ningizzida knew that they had played the wrong card in their reasoning. He felt that the Egyptians had mistakenly believed that the Persian King would ignore them in favor of his hatred of the Greeks. Their logic was that Xerxes would choose to ignore their revolt and instead focus his vast army on Athens. They were wrong, as Xerxes could not afford to let their rebellion stand. It would be like accepting someone spitting in his face.

This led to the Shesgallu's dilemma. How could Babylonia achieve a different fate than the Egyptians? The wily priest's plan was simple. In the process of killing the installed governor who the Persians planted in his city, he would create information that implicated the Persian governor in a plot to overthrow the young King. The Babylonians could then plead that killing the Persian governor was, in fact, in support of the great King, not in rebellion against him. *"Create the illusion and they will want to believe"*, his teacher once professed

358

to him.   Ningizzida knew that Xerxes
would never accept him in any kind of
government for Babylonia considering his
insult to the monarch at the religious
ceremony. He knew that he would have to
"die" in the King's eyes.   That is why
the priest needed Nin-Nibru so much.   He
would have to be his eyes and ears in the
government and be able to, by proxy, let
Ningizzida rule the province.   He
believed that the Babylonians would be
able to convince the King of their
loyalty, thus leaving their holy city in
their hands rather than in the hands of
some Mede governor.   Ningizzida
understood that it wasn't total freedom,
but it was the best that they could hope
for now.   Eventually, when the Persians
decided to invade Greece, Ningizzida
would be able to cement his power base
and rid Babylonia of the Medes forever.
A new birth for his beloved Babylonia and
a new leader of the civilized world, the
Sheshgallu.

    Ningizzida's plan centered on three
things: first he had to ferment the
revolution among the people of the great
city. Without their support and loyalty
there was no hope for success. The people
who had lived under the Persian laws and
the inconsistency of their application
had to band together under the common
banner of freedom. Ningizzida had to set
a fire under the disenchantment that he
believed was harboring just below the

surface. Second, he had to train his acolyte with the skills to influence the new government. Ningizzida did not want Nin-Nibru to govern. He reckoned that such a move would endanger the entire process. Nin-Nibru might be too easily traced back to him. He would use one of his old friends from the city to serve as a "figure head". They would all be easy to manipulate, and if God wasn't willing and the revolt failed, then they could take the fall for the uprising. The third part of his plan was the most deceptive. The young King of Persia had to be convinced that the revolution was in his best interest and not one that was designed to circumvent Persian rule. This would be the trickiest part of Ningizzida's plan, but with God's help, this could also be accomplished.

"Master, I am here for your convenience. You will lead me and the people and we will gratefully follow."

Ningizzida appeared to be distant as he responded to the young man's salutation. He finally became serious, *"Nin-Nibru, have you ever spent time in the desert?"*

The young man nodded his head in affirmation.

"Tell me about your experience," the old priest asked, *"What did you learn from your stay?"*

Nin-Nibru thought for a second, *"I learned that hunger and thirst began to control my mind. After a time I was having trouble separating my dreams and wants from what was really in front of me."*

"Did you see water, my student?"

"I did, master!"

"Did you taste it?"

"I did, master! I could taste the water even though there was none. The longer I stayed in the desert the more I believed that I could find water. At one point, I could see a small pond. Of course, there was no pond, as the water just materialized in my mind because of my desire."

"You needed water and you imagined water! Now think, Nin-Nibru, what does this story tell you about Babylon and the Persians?"

Nin-Nibru thought deeply. He struggled with the lesson. The two men sat opposite each other for some time as the young man pondered the message. Finally, Nin-Nibru answered. **"Master, the** desert represents the Persian plague. The people thirsty for freedoms are willing to believe that they can taste it. They will believe anything to satisfy their thirst."

The Priest nodded his head. "*Good, Nin-Nibru, good. The people are both hungry and thirsty. They will believe anything or anyone who can lead them to their true destiny. We must use this in our favor. The people must believe that their god is behind this uprising. God will reward them for their devotion and their sacrifice. Words, Nin-Nibru, words and beliefs are very powerful weapons, more potent than any sword or knife. Words evoke images for people especially those under the whip. When you were in the desert your thirst made you think of water and your eyes saw it even though there was only sand. Words can transform the lowly farmer into the courageous freedom fighter. We must show him his true destiny. The Persians know not of words. They believe that power rests in their weapons and numbers. But it is untrue. The ritual of our beliefs is the fuel behind our convictions. When played correctly, belief in our god will walk hand in hand with the desire for freedom and we will crush the Medes.*"

"Master, the Persian Empire is vast and powerful. Can we actually defeat such an enemy?"

The Priest became quiet for a minute then responded. *"Do you have faith, my student?"*

"Unquestioned, master"

"Do you believe that God is more powerful than the Medes?"

"God is more powerful than all men"

"We must be strong in our hearts, Nin-Nibru. We must accept our destiny and be bold in our behavior. The Persians have expected lambs and we will show them lions. We will not ride the Persians with force. We will make them believe that we are their allies. We will become a disease in their body. Now close your eyes Nin-Nibru. It is time to pray."

PERSIA

CHAPTER XV - HO OF SEBENNYTOS

The cave stunk of stale air and human excrement. The Persians had set up exclusive and spacious tents outside of the cave to house their great King. The Egyptian would not leave her hole in the mountain to satisfy the King, or for that matter, any man. He would have to bow to her wishes if he wanted to hear her predictions. Ho was considered a stolist, a lay priestess. She was versed in Egyptian magic but was never connected to a specific Egyptian institution or order.

When Xerxes entered the cave, he was surprised by the décor. It was immaculately clean and ordered. The walls of the cave were painted with detailed designs and hieroglyphs, none of which he understood. Once inside the cave, he was impressed by the drawings. They depicted unworldly scenes.

A bald and tattooed priestess met the King. She couldn't have been more than eleven or twelve in years. Xerxes was asked to wait in an area that was separated from the rest of the cave by large colorful tapestries. The cave was lit by numerous olive oil lamps. It created a surreal atmosphere as the light flickered, mixing with the colors and the smell. It almost made him nauseous and he struggled to settle his stomach.

On the tapestry that faced him was a large woman wearing leopard skin. It depicted a female who was communicating with the dead. The priest, who stood next to the naked woman, wore the side lock of youth and was pictured with part of his body in the world of the living and part in the underworld. The woman appeared to be negotiating between the two realms. Each tapestry that surrounded him told stories of the abilities of the priests to communicate with those who have passed.

Ho was considered a high priestess or one of the prophets of God. It was the pharaoh's decision to elevate her to that status and since she was his wife, it was a simple procedure. It was an unusual occurrence for a woman to obtain such a lofty position, but because of her abilities and influence, Ho was one of the few females to accomplish it. Ho was an expert in the Egyptian Book of the Dead. The manuscript was the map that Egyptians had to take to navigate their way to eternity. It was also called the Papyrus of Ani. It began with the legend of Osiris and ended with the funeral ceremonies. It was said that Ho had a relationship with Osiris, the lord of the hidden place. Ho often wore a white hat with colored feathers, like her lord, Osiris. Ho was also practiced in the Egyptian spells for protection of the pharaoh. But even though she was not considered a magician or an oracle, Ho was able to foretaste the future by communicating with the dead. She did not dispense evil spells and she was not revengeful. It was also said that Ho communicated with Sekhmet. Sekhmet was a revengeful goddess who drank the blood of mankind as a prelude to her desire for the destruction of mankind. But the legend goes on to say that Sekhmet began to drink beer to wash down the taste of the blood and became so intoxicated that she forgot about her evil plans and mankind survived.

As Xerxes sat, he noticed wooden wands laid out over one of the tables. He rose from his seat out of curiosity to study the wooden pieces. On the wands were many hieroglyphs none of which he could read. As he studied the finely carved pieces, his thoughts were interrupted by a sound from behind him.

"Do you like my wands?" Xerxes turned quickly to see a short woman standing by one of the tapestries at the rear of the cave.

"These are fine works of art." Xerxes said. Ho hesitated than began laughing. *"They are not art, my son, they are protective things."*

Xerxes looked again at the horn shaped pieces of wood with the many inscriptions. Ho left the tapestry behind and began walking towards the King. As she did, Xerxes realized that she might have been standing there for some time, camouflaged by her dress melting into the beautiful rug. As she approached, he turned to her and bowed.

"Mother," Xerxes avowed, *"I am humbled in your presence."*

Ho touched the King's head as she walked past him to sit on a stool that was in the corner of the room. The diminutive woman had her head shaven bald and tattooed with signs that honored her personal god Osiris. She wore an exquisite robe that was decorated with many amulets. On the top of her head were numerous blue tattoos. They were fine paintings, very exact in their depictions. One of her eyes was covered in red. The amulets that lay on a small table were of all shapes and sizes. Some were carved of lapis lazuli and some carved from carnelian and feldspar. But the most frightening of the amulets appeared to be carved from human bone. Ho immediately noticed Xerxes' fascination as she walked by him.

"You are impressed, my son, by my amulets?"

"I am, mother," Xerxes admitted.

Ho wore a large breastplate of engraved red carnelian. It held the carving of an Egyptian scarab and had jasper stones attached to the sides. But, she carried her most precious amulet in her left hand. It was a long walking stick that was adorned with bright blue lapis lazuli. The stones were quite pure showing only a few white calcite veins. She held it up to her adopted son and said, *"This was given to me by Shalinadone of Badakhshaw, a man who was much too taken with himself. It is quite lovely, is it not? After I arrived here* with your father, Darius, I traveled east to the rocky mountains of Badakhshaw by request of a local chieftain, Shalinadone. I contacted his lost mother in one of his dreams and could clarify a problem he was having with his warring brother. Shalinadone gave me this amulet to protect me on my future journeys. I have grown accustomed to carrying it. It seems to hold great magic, as it has saved me on at least two occasions."

Ho rose from her stool and approached Xerxes now standing with his mouth unconsciously hanging open, his eyes focused on the amulet.

"**Here,**" Ho handed the walking stick to her son. Xerxes took it as if he were handing a delicate piece of crystal. "*Don't fear, it my son. It is quite magical, but it serves only to protect, not to harm. I give it to you for you are planning many adventures that will require your protection. You will notice that on the top of the stick is the ankh. The ankh sign represents life and protection for the Egyptian. The ankh combined with the lapis gives this stick great power. When you are far from your home, if you pray on this amulet, I will appear to you in your dreams and help you to solve your dilemmas. But be careful, my son, for you are not to let this stick fall into an enemy's hand. It will carry your essence and the memories of your*

369

father and his father, and if it is possessed by others it will be used to your detriment. If you lose it, I will not be able to help you then. This stick is an ushabti. It is an amulet that directs you to a path. That path will lead you to your ancestors. This ushabti is called the Answerer. You can call on your ancestors to work for you by using the ushabti properly. It is a gateway, my son, but not one to be fooled with."

Xerxes fell to the floor in reverence. It was an unusual position for the King-god. Showing deference was not one of his strengths. *"Thank you, mother, I will treasure this prize. Please teach me the prayers that release its magic."* Ho turned and made her way back to her perch. She turned back and repeated her warning. *"Do not lose the Answerer, my son. Later I will teach you about its power."*

Ho, again, sat in the corner of the room. Xerxes still shocked by the enormity of the gift that his mother gave him, remained silent for a few seconds. He then seemed to regain focus and maintained, *"Mother, I need your special skills. Before I leave Susa, I must seek the advice of my father and grandfather."*

"You seem afraid, my son. I have not seen such emotion in you before."

370

The King stiffened at the comment. *"I am not afraid mother, I am unsure. I do have some questions about the best way to proceed. My father made few mistakes in his life and I need his advice."*

The old woman looked at the young monarch with loving eyes. His comments took her back to her husband. *"You are correct, my son, your father, Darius, made few mistakes. But he also had sound advisors."*

She turned with a giggle, *"But in the end, he didn't listen to me and he paid for that with his life. The Answerer had foretold treachery but Darius chose to ignore its warning."*

Ho seemed dysphoric with her memory. She had never missed anyone as much as she yearned for Darius. She walked a few steps and returned her attention to her step-son. *"The process is simple my son. But you must consider, for there is pain involved in revelation. You must die before you can be reborn. We are most alive when we are suffering. Think for a moment and be sure you want to walk the path that leads to the underworld. Consider also that some walk this path and never return."*

She now stood, her mood switching from nurturing to very solemn.

The young King seemed to contemplate the warning. In watching his step-mother's face, Xerxes was now more uneasy about his direction than he was fearful of the hidden one, Osiris.

Finally, after what seemed like an eternity, the young King said, **"Yes, mother. I am sure; I need to travel to the underworld."**

"Good," Ho said with a wry smile. **"Good. You know my young son; I've always admired your courage. You should know your father admired it as well. That's why you are King of Kings, and not one of his other sons."**

"What?" Xerxes responded.

"I know that your father was not one to offer praise. But he was proud of you."

Ho continued, **"Tonight, after we eat, you will drink the special potion and rub the holy mushrooms on your skin before you sleep. You will have written down your questions to your father and grandfather. You will lie with the Answerer as you sleep. The answers to your questions will come to you in your dreams. When you wake, you will tell your dream to your scribe. Remember all the parts of your dream, my son. Even the smallest of detail can change the** message. *When you come to me in the morning, I will interpret what your father said to you."*

Ho slanted her head and walking away whispered, *"that's if he chooses to respond to you at all."*

"Thank you, mother."

With her back turned, Ho raised her hand and said, *"now, my son, go back to your tent and return to me after sunset."*

****

His knees and hips hurt as Penish had spent the last two days riding. More than that, the tracker, Sippar, was getting on his nerves. It became clear over the last two days that Penish and Sippar just didn't like each other. Penish had reluctantly given in to the tracker's instincts and headed north. It went against his instincts to go north, feeling that the old priest would head to the east and the Zagros Mountains. Up until this time there was no evidence that the old priest had headed in this direction. With each day, Penish's irritation grew. As sure as Sippar was of the direction they headed, Penish was increasingly doubtful. Both of their nerves were frayed this day as the sun began to set. They were finally entering the town of SAR-I Pul-I in lower Media.

The two men had agreed that they would rest here for a few days and attempt to ascertain how to proceed.

The town, although sleepy, was quite large as it sat at the base of the Northern Zagros at the border of Media and Assyria. Because of its location it housed many different cultures and political persuasions. Sar-I Pul-I was a very diverse place with clear neighborhoods and diverse factions. The Persians were not favored here, as the city held a large minority that favored both the Assyrian and Babylonian cultures. Finding people who would betray a Babylonian priest would be a tricky undertaking especially in this political atmosphere. Although Penish had both silver and gold to tempt people to provide information, these were religious and superstitious people who were generally unwilling to lose their place in the afterlife for a handful of gold. But then again, Penish knew that everything had a price. Every man has his weakness, he thought. If a man couldn't be bought, he could be intimidated.

Sippar was much more comfortable in this city than Penish was. In fact, he knew that being seen with the Persian could undermine his ability to secure information from the populace. Because of that he informed Penish when they were approaching SAR-I Pul-I that when they arrived in the city they would be separating for their time there. Although he understood the rationale, it still bothered Penish that people could find him distasteful. Sippar knew that he could get more information on his own. Besides, he was sick of the Persian. He considered ending this relationship, not returning to his service, although he also knew that Penish had a violent and revengeful reputation and he didn't need more enemies, especially such powerful ones. Even though his fear of the Persians was palpable it wouldn't take much for Sippar to abandon this ship. Although he was never a supporter of the Medes, Sippar was always able to tolerate and get along with them. This Penish, and his insufferable talk about the superiority of the Persian, had begun turning Sippar's stomach. He even considered cutting the Persian's throat in the middle of the night.

Without Penish's knowledge, Sippar had sent advanced men into the city. These men left Susa two days before and now Sippar had a planned meeting with them to help in the search. Tracking was not just instinct and observation, it was knowledge and gossip. The street for the underground rendezvous was in the poorer section of town. It was a neighborhood that was dominated by Assyrians who were generally cool to the Medes. The Assyrians were a harsh people who were hardened and paranoid by nature. Sippar went to a local hash house to meet his contacts. The two men who were the advanced scouts were cousins and Sippar had used them before. Tarqu and Maltai sat in the back of the large room somewhat obscured by the hashish smoke that hovered like a cloud over the small tables. The two cousins were quite different from each other, both in stature and temperament. Tarqu was usually the spokesperson of the two, although when Maltai commented, Sippar learned that he needed to pay attention. After a time alone and surveying the situation, Sippar sat with the men. He had taken extra precaution to make sure that he wasn't being followed as he made his way to the meeting place. He knew that he was smarter than the Persians, so he wasn't worried about spying eyes.

The cousins looked as if the hashish was affecting them, as their eyes appeared heavy and red. Tarqu began the conversation *"Welcome Sippar, we have much to tell you."*

The tracker sat quietly and tried not to stare at Tarqu's black teeth. Tarqu continued. *"The priest was definitely here, my friend. Your instincts to send us in this direction were true again."*

Sippar did not change expression as Tarqu continued. *"He travels with three* other men. They continued north from here. My people believe that their destination is Ashur."

He hesitated and then said to Sippar, "*Our behavior has been weighing on our minds. My cousin and I will not continue. We will not help you and the Mede dogs anymore.*"

Sippar smiled and admitted, "*I understand your feeling, my friend. I, too, despise the Medes. But we must do what we must to survive. Our time will come again when we can throw the dirty, shit eating Medes out of our lands.*"

Maltai took out a very large knife and placed it on the table. This action was usually a challenge, but Sippar knew that he was just trying to make a point. The knife was followed by a handful of silver pieces. His voice was gravelly and low as he murmured, "*We were offered this to help the priest.*"

Sippar's eyebrow's rose as he stared at the quiet cousin. "*We were told that we could satisfy the Persian's search and protect the priest at the same time. We were promised much more if we help these men.*"

Sippar leaned forward in his chair placing his elbows on the small table. Then a small smile appeared on the corner

377

of his mouth. He turned his head to the man sitting to his right and he declared, *"Tell me more. I have interest!"*

****

Xerxes returned to the cave after resting in his tents. He sat in the cave naked with only a small loincloth around his private areas. The King felt very vulnerable sitting with sparse clothing in an unusual place without weapons or guards. His legs were crossed in front of him as he waited for his mother to enter the area. He carried the Answerer to the meeting. The amulet gave him a strange sense of reality. He had never felt this before. It was if it were real and unreal at the same time. There were few men who Xerxes feared. But here, he feared a piece of wood.

In front of him on a small mat were many olive oil lamps. He had been given a special liquid to drink and was instructed to concentrate on the flames of the candles. The strange liquid burned as it went down the King's throat, but it was unusually compelling. He was also given a mixture of mushrooms and a liquid that he was instructed to rub on his body.

Ho had told him that the first step in connecting to his dead relatives was first to be able to see the colors in the flame. Ho had lectured him about the power of the fire. *"Each **flame** **is** **different**. **The** **color** **betrays** **its** **power** **to** **you**. **Each** **flame** **has** **different** **origins** **and** **different** **intensities**. **Some** **are** **hotter** **than** **others**."*

Ho explained to her step son: *"**the candles I use in these rituals are pure. They have all four of the colors of fire in them. The ability to see and meditate over the colors brings the power to the person. It takes great concentration to see the colors. The drink will help you to relax and let go of the material world.**"*

*"**Remember, my son, that to reach your ancestors you must let go of yourself. You must lose your existence and become part of the flame. Concentrate on where the colors meet, for they are the doors you are pursuing. The steps are simple my son. I cannot travel with you, you must make the journey alone. When you feel fear, you know you are on the correct path. Engulf yourself in the confluence of colors. The more you let go, the wider the doors of eternity will open for you.**"*

To add to his confusion, his step mother had explained that the area where colors of the flames met was the door to the dark underground. The King was asked to concentrate on the flames and try to distinguish the colors between the sections of the flame. Between the drink that he consumed, the fragrances in the room, the background chanting, and the special ointment that Ho's slave had placed on his eyelids, the King was falling into a deep trance. He was having trouble keeping his eyes focused on the flames. As he sat, a slave in the background repeated that he was getting tired. She asked him to let his head rise to the sun and his body to enter the flame. His head began swimming and he was struggling with keeping himself upright. His skin was beginning to itch and burn from the mushroom mixture.

Before he entered this cave, Xerxes was asked to disrobe and was washed with natron water. The purification ritual took almost an hour and two slave girls covered his cheeks and upper body with red ochre. His finger nails were colored with henna turning them orange. He was asked to lie on his stomach as one of the slave girls placed a substance on his back in three separate places. She then lit the substance and it burned for a minute. Xerxes noticed the flame but felt no heat on his back. The flame finally burned out with no marks left on the King's body. Small pins were placed in different places on the King's back. The last part of the ritual preparation was a special tattoo which was placed on the back of the King's neck.

As Ho entered the area, the great King was only semi-conscious as he struggled to keep his eyes even half open. He seemed to sway, apparently having increasing trouble maintaining his equilibrium and moving to the incantations. Ho sat next to him and began chanting quietly into his right ear. The right ear was the key to consciousness in her religion. As the melodious chanting continued, the King seemed to sink deeper into the trance. As he did, Ho began to put an open flame on his forearm. Xerxes didn't seem to feel the burn as his skin began to crackle. Ho began talking to Xerxes and offering suggestions to him as he continued to stare into the flame.

Xerxes seemed to rise slightly in his sitting position. His voice was shaky but he almost seemed excited and said, *"it is dark. I am afraid. I can see somebody, mother."*

His voice was shallow and monotone.

"Yes, my son, I know you can - keep the image - stay focused. Bring the image to you. Let yourself merge with the image."

The image was fuzzy as it seemed to materialize in front of the King. Xerxes was having trouble keeping his eyes open and his mind on the task. The apparition appeared to float above the great King, hovering over his head. The ghostly specter appeared to reach down and touch the top of the King's head then immediately reached for the Answerer. Xerxes shivered as sparks seemed to pass down his spine. Xerxes bent his head back and started to chant along with Ho. Then his voice disappeared and his lips continued to move as if he was speaking to someone who was invisible to everyone else. The figure was now moving closer to the King and then seemed to enter his body through the top of his skull. Xerxes' eyes closed and he appeared to have a seizure as his entire body began trembling uncontrollably. He lost control of his bowels and a small puddle appeared under his seat. Ho sat next to her adopted son and smiled as the King lay down and appeared to fall into a coma. But it was not a quiet rest as Xerxes continued to moan and chant with his eyes closed and feeling continual movement under his skin. At intervals, his body spasmed. The Answerer began to glow with a blue light and the King's hand that held it shook as if it was burning.

The great King was now sweating profusely even though it was cool in the cave. Ho stayed close keeping a hand on her son as he tossed and even let out an occasional shriek. This unearthly dance continued for over an hour until the King finally fell into a deeper oblivion.

Xerxes slept the best part of the night and next day. His slave girls were instructed by Ho to continue to wash his body. The servants were told that the King was no longer in this world and his body had to be kept clean for his return from the underworld. His sleep was so deep that the servant girls at times appeared afraid that he left the world of the living. They were seen listening to his chest, searching for a beat.

When Xerxes finally opened his eyes he was drained of energy and dehydrated. Ho gave him another potion that would refresh his body and allow him to regain his strength. Six hours later the King finally sat up and felt invigorated. Within minutes Ho was at his side.

"My father was unable to attend to me so my grandfather, Cyrus, appeared in his place. I was told my father was fighting devils. Cyrus the Great appeared in a yellow robe but his arms were made of fire. When he touched me, I felt as though my body was burning. I looked and my arm was burnt. A bull appeared and my grandfather tended to it. My grandfather called me to the bull, but when I approached, the animal became angered so I walked away. My grandfather then approached me and gave me a goblet and forced me to drink from it. It was filled with the bull's blood, and as I

drank, it covered my entire body. I felt as if I had grown horns. My head hurt terribly..."

Ho interjected, *"Good, my son, this is a good omen."*

Xerxes continued, *"But mother, then something very strange happened. The bull walked over to me and urinated on my leg."*

Ho smiled and put her hand on her son's head. She then pronounced, *"you're tired my son. You must rest. This evening we will repeat the dream letters. But rest well, my son, because this evening will be more difficult for you. Your first experience was good but your ancestors have more to tell you."*

Xerxes anxiously interrupted. *"Mother, what messages did my first dream letter say?"*

"It is incomplete, my son. You will need to be patient and wait until the message is complete. But be encouraged, for seeing your grandfather during first experience is very hopeful. Your grandfather spoke very strongly about your future but he left some things short and unfinished. Was there anything else that he said?"

"I am remembering one other image from my grandfather."

"An important dream, my son."

"Mother, I saw two eagles. They flew around the world and passed over Persia landing in Greece. I chased the eagle mother, but they flew past Susa."

"Go to sleep, my son, and dream again."

Nin-Nibru entered the eternal city in the middle of the night. He had ridden for two days and was physically tired but emotionally excited. The city was asleep as he made his way silently through the alleys. Nin-Nibru was very careful as he skulked his way, for he knew that Persian spies could be everywhere. The Persians were entrenched in Babylonia and Nin-Nibru had to be careful with whom he trusted. He knew these alleys well, as he grew up playing in many of them. He had a sense of comfort as he made his way to his destination. The house that the young man was seeking, belonged to one of his mentor's old friend's, Belshimanni.

Nin-Nibru found the house and waited in a side alley. After a few minutes, he decided that enough time had passed to assure that he wasn't followed. There was no moon out this evening and the young acolyte silently entered a back doorway.

Nin-Nibru had worried that Belshimanni had animals that would warn people of his approach. But as he silently worked his way through the house, he was not confronted by any non-human sounds. He silently approached the room in which Belshimanni slept and took out his large knife. He walked into the room and took a deep breath. He bent over and quietly placed the knife under the older man's throat. Belshimanni woke with a jolt and Nin-Nibru put his finger up to his lips, urging silence. Belshimanni's eyes were as wide as melons. Finally, Nin-Nibru whispered: **"Do not speak, old man, or you will lose your throat to this knife."**

Belshimanni was too scared to try to speak as his eyes widened again in fear and sweat appeared on his dark forehead. Nin Nibru placed his mouth up against the man's ear. **"I am sent here, old man, by my master, the great Priest, Ningizzida. He needs your help."**

Belshimanni weakly nodded his head in affirmation and the young man cautiously removed the knife from his throat. Belshimanni wiped the sweat from his face and quickly rose from his mat. Nin-Nibru motioned the man to follow him into the adjourning room.

When they arrived there the young man spoke first: **"I must know, Belshimanni,"** *Nin*-Nibru asked with seriousness in his voice. *"Will you support the great priest?"*

The young man's look was stern as he moved closer to the trembling older man.

"The road ahead will be hard old man. The entire 2000-year history of Babylonia is in front of us. I must know if you stand with us!"

The old man slowly placed his right hand on his forehead signifying his allegiance to the old priest. Nin Nibru smiled at the gesture understanding its significance. He placed his hands on the old man's shoulders and smiled.

"The Sheshgallu told me that of all the men he knew in Babylonia, you would be the most trustworthy."

He smiled as he professed, *"He was right. We have much to talk of, my new friend."*

Belshimanni smiled, finally appearing calmer and responded, *"I am devoted to Ningizzida. He is our only hope for salvation and liberty."*

Nin-Nibru again smirked. *"Before we plan, I have to do a favor for Ningizzida. And we will plan for the revolution."*

Nin-Nibru left Belshimanni's home the next evening. He had slept for ten hours and felt energy returning to his body. He waited purposely until the city was quiet and mostly sleeping. Again, he crept slowly through the streets. He arrived at Shamah-eriba's home and sneaked into the back of the house as he had done a few nights earlier with Belshimanni. Shamah-eriba's wife and children were asleep in the front room and it didn't take Nin-Nibru long to tie them with the rope that he brought. He thought that it might bother him to bind the children, but he finished it without any emotion in a very methodical fashion. The Sheshgallu had told him that he thought Shamah-eriba was the traitor who betrayed him to the Medes. Nin-Nibru would take it on himself to even the score. He found Shamah-eriba in a room off the kitchen. He hadn't decided beforehand how he would end his life. When he saw the dread in Belshimanni's eyes he found that he enjoyed seeing the distress. He quickly decided that he would slowly torture Shamah-eriba. He wanted to repay the agony that Ningizzida suffered in Susa. He also wanted to find out whether Shamah-eriba had any co-conspirators. He quietly entered the room where Shamah-eriba slept. He stood for a minute or so watching his prey and visualizing the outcome. When he finally acted he let loose a barrage of blows immediately crippling his adversary as he

388

hammered his legs and knees. With Shamah-eriba writhing in pain he again took out rope and tied him up to immobilize his body. He covered the man's mouth with a scarf that he wore. The man's wide eyes betrayed his fear and pain. He kept his eyes fixated on Nin-Nibru pleading with his tears.

Nin- Nibru sat quietly on the side of the mat and waited until his breathing settled. He waited for his heart to stop pounding from the rush or the adrenalin. He took a few deep breaths and prepared himself for the next part of his revenge. He put his face within two inches of Shamah-eriba and exalted, *"you **betrayed our master**,"* as he roughly slapped the man's face. Shamah-eriba looked up with surprise as he attempted to understand the man's anger towards him. Nin-Nibru calmed himself again and threatened, *"**I will kill your family unless you tell me the truth.**"*

He waited while the man processed his demand. ***"Do you understand, pig?"*** He demanded as Shamah-eriba's eyes again widened. He nodded his head in affirmation.

"Good, I will remove the scarf. If you scream I will cut your wife's tongue out."

Nin-Nibru removed the scarf and he could see the man's face trembling in fear.

"Now tell me, who helped you betray Ningizzida"

"What?" the man pleaded. *"I did not betray the Great Ningizzida."*

Nin-Nibru slapped the bound man again.

"Liar," Nin-Nibru shouted, *"Liar!"* he bellowed again. *"Hit me all you want, but my mouth tells the truth. Ningizzida is my master as well. I did not betray him."*

Shamah-eriba was completely at the mercy of Nin-Nibru, which provided all the motivation he needed to lie but Nin-Nibru seemed to believe what the man was saying. It left him ambivalent and confused. But he didn't expect that this would be so difficult. When he entered this house, he was convinced that Shamah-eriba was the traitor but now he was reconsidering that conclusion. He leaned over the prone man and questioned, *"if you are not the traitor, then who is?"*

He grabbed the older man by the collar and lifted him off the mat. He stared into his eyes and repeated his query. *"Who, then, was the traitor? Who told the Medes where Ningizzida went into the* desert? There were only three people who knew where the master was. If it wasn't you or Belshimanni, then it had to be the other priest, Manishtusu."

Shamah-eriba was quiet as the man held him up. After a minute he responded to the accusation. **"When the great priest was kidnapped by the Persians, Manishtusu immediately took over the church and began making changes. Although many people assumed that the Sheshgallu would never return, we did spend many hours praying for his safe return to us. Manishtusu joined us in our vigil initially, but then excused himself claiming that he had business to attend to."**

Nin-Nibru was confused. He didn't have the insight that his master possessed, the intelligence to solve the puzzle, or the experience to be able to tell the difference. He was caught in this dilemma without a good way out. If he let him go and he was wrong then his master would be in danger again. And yet there was a part of him that felt this was an innocent man quivering in front of him. He looked down at the prone man and did the only thing he could reason. He reached down and cut his throat. The blood spurted on Nin-Nibru and its force stunned him. He cut again, this time deeper, almost beheading the man. He was caught in the blood trance and all he could imagine was beheading this man. He cut again, but this time his knife caught on the man's spine. Nin-Nibru had to use all his strength to finally break through. Shamah-eriba's head finally rolled off the mat. Nin-Nibru sat exhaustedly with his legs straddling the man's chest. His mind was blank. He found that he had almost stopped breathing during the butchering. When he calmed he looked up to the sky and prayed that his god understood why he had taken this action. Nin-Nibru knew that since he didn't know who to believe he had to kill both men. Finally, after sitting in this position for a few minutes he rose and quietly left the residence. He had walked almost three blocks when he finally realized that he had to clean his face and change his clothes. He really didn't recall leaving the house or how he got to the place he now stood, but his consciousness was finally returning. He felt faint at the experience. Nin-Nibru had killed before, but his sense was that he just killed an innocent man.

****

It was his third day of dreaming and the great King was physically and emotionally exhausted. He had to rest because today was the day he and his entourage were returning to the palace to prepare for the council meeting. He was resting and trying to regain his strength. He was also waiting for his mother to return and give him her final interpretations. On the second day of ingesting the special drink Xerxes was nearly psychotic. He began having visual hallucinations, seeing symbols floating over his head. They seemed not to have a purpose, although his mother sat next to him as he announced the things that he saw.

Xerxes only recalled part of the things that he saw. He was waiting anxiously to hear what advice his great ancestors had for his future. Finally, after a time, Ho appeared. Her head was recently shaved again and she smelled of incense and oils. Her red and yellow gown flowed down over her body and her makeup was heavy and colorful. She slowly walked over to her son and sat with him. She placed her hand on his face cupping his jaw. She then took a jar that she carried and sprinkled some of the water on her son. She finally spoke. *"My son, your wanderings through the underworld were complex and I can only give you some vague direction. Some things are even beyond my understanding."*

"Tell me what you see, mother."

Ho closed her eyes and began to chant. She finally stopped and appearing to be in a trance answered, *"your future will lead you to islands. Your enemy awaits and he will be consumed with fire. Your feet are solidly planted in the ground but you must be very careful of the wind. This is important for the wind and the water hold your fate. You must be careful, my son, for there are enemies within the Empire that are planning to send you to your relatives. This is your fate."*

"But mark this, Xerxes. Your danger waits in water. You will be lured into the water, so be careful."

"Your first blood will not cause much pain. You must follow the eagles. You must go to Delphi and listen to the great Oracle. The center of the world has the ears of the god. The gods call you, my son."

****

The young priest didn't see it coming. He had just finished his prayers and was returning to his study in the immense church. He didn't see the man hiding in the shadows when he entered the great study. The strike was quick and silent. There was no explanation, no discussion, just swift justice. Unlike his previous assassination, this one was quick and effortless. The priest died without knowing either his assassin or the reason that his life was being sacrificed. As the lifeless body lay prone in front of him, Nin-Nibru bent over and prayed to his god. He was sure that his faith would lead him to correct decisions and that his effort this day would finally clear the slate for his master. The message needed to be sent to the entire Babylonian community that not only did the Sheshgallu return, but that all those who stood opposed would pay with their lives. Unlike his last effort, this killing seemed to invigorate him. Ningizzida taught him to write ancient ciphers with his enemy's blood next to his lifeless body. These cryptographs were ancient Babylonian and announced the coming of the messiah.

Before he left Nin-Nibru bent over the dead Priest. He took out his small wooden cup. He held the cup next to the priest's neck and cut a slash into the dead man's throat. The blood began to flow and Nin Nibru patiently filled the cup with the priest's blood. He then looked to heaven, said the appropriate prayer and drank from the cup until it was empty. He would inherit the dead priest's power. Manishtusu, the priest who betrayed Ningizzida to the Persians, was dead.

PERSIA

CHAPTER XVI - THE
COUNCIL MEETING

Artemisia waited patiently in her chambers. The Warrior Queen was still having difficulty accepting Xerxes' decision to exclude her from the attack on Egypt. Although the great King tried to persuade her of the importance of the excursion to Delphi to consult the great

Oracle, the Queen was still not convinced. The King also knew that the Warrior Queen had a strong reputation throughout the Hellenic world for being fierce, incorruptible, and relentless. Of all the Levantine peoples who ruled the seas, the exploits of Artemisia stood out. The King was hoping that in the negotiations with the Greeks, the violent competitiveness of the Queen would rule the day and persuade the Greeks to succumb and quietly bow to the rule of the Empire. Such a conclusion would save Xerxes a tremendous amount of money and effort. He was depending upon the fact that Artemisia was an imposing figure. He believed that her status, and the fact that she was so striking, would impress the Greeks. Xerxes also believed that men were at a disadvantage negotiating with a beautiful woman. Their thoughts could wander away from the task at hand as they stared at the attractive face.

There was another reason that the King wanted Artemisia to go to Delphi. The Greek gods! Xerxes knew that in the complicated assemblage of deities that the Greeks worshiped, there were a few that stood above the others. Zeus was the patriarch of the Greek gods, but his daughter the goddess Athena, was almost as powerful as her father. The Greeks, especially the Athenian Greeks, worshipped the daughter goddess. She was their patron saint. Xerxes realized that the human embodiment of the Greek goddess was the Warrior Queen, Artemisia. When the great King heard the Greek story about the Athenian goddess, the first thing that crossed his mind was the uncanny resemblance between Athena and the Warrior Queen. And now he could send this human replica to negotiate for Persia.

Even though the Queen would not be involved in the Egyptian excursion, her Phoenician brothers would. She now waited to consult the Phoenician generals before the council would convene.

When the two men entered the room, the Queen appeared surprised. She had expected the general King from Tyre, but had not expected the other man. Merbalos, the general-King from Arwad, was a surprise. Her eyes widened with joy when she recognized the large dark man. She jumped up from her chair and rushed to greet the two men. Merbalos put his large arms out to greet Artemisia. He hoisted her off the floor with ease as if he were lifting a young child. As quickly as she rose the big man put her down.

"My friend, it's been much too long since I've seen you," the Queen observed.

"Well little one, I've traveled far for this meeting, but to place my eyes on

you makes the god - cursed desert pleasant. Like a flower rising from the wasteland," Merbalos said with a smile. The Queen then turned to the other man, whom she also knew for much of her life. "Matten, it is good to see you, as well, my brother."

Matten, only half the size of Merbalos and smaller even then Artemisia, was himself a dramatic presence. He had the reputation of being a shrewd politician and adequate warrior. Matten was actually Matten III, as his family had ruled Tyre for generations. He wore his favorite purple robe and had a red and blue tunic that hung past his thighs. Matten was a very business focused individual who spent little time in small talk. With his fiery eyes he looked at Artemisia and spoke, "this great King of Kings is stupid. Why would he waste your talents in a diplomatic mission to Greece? He is overconfident in his troops."

Merbalos smiled again and turned to the smaller man. "Quiet, my friend. Remember where we are. The walls can hear everything that you say."

"I don't care," Matten blurted out, "Stupidity is stupidity, either in the desert or on the oceans. Don't waste your most precious possession in useless talk."

Artemisia, turned away from the two men and spoke, *"my brothers, let us talk in the gardens. It is safer in the wind."*

The three sovereigns walked for quite some time in silence after arriving outside and then Matten began the discussion. *"My information tells me that Xerxes has had contact with the Athenians and has come close to an agreement for them to join the Empire."*

He hesitated and then continued. *"It seems to me that the great King has second thoughts about his own ability to dominate the Greeks. He seeks diplomacy when he should be seeking dominance."*

"Remember," Artemisia added, *"this is a young and inexperienced King. He has never been involved in conquest. He doesn't know the feeling of subjugation. He relies on his advisors for their expertise."*

"I understand that," Merbalos warned, *"But if his negotiations fail, he will need all of the Levantine strength to conquer the Greeks. The Persians win their battles by numbers. At Marathon the Greeks outsmarted them even though they were outnumbered."*

"I have found out that the Persians have already made allies of the

Carthegians and with those in Thessaly."
Matten added.

"It does not sound like he is a man who is depending on negotiations."

"Yes," Artemisia revealed. "He also sends engineers to bridge the Hellespont and build a sea approach to the Greek islands."

"We must conclude that the negotiations are a diversion as he prepares for war with Athens," Matten offered.

"So, what is my role?" questioned Artemisia.

Merbalos focused on Artemisia's eyes and responded, "Your role, little one, will be most important for us. You must be our eyes and ears. You will be in the heart of the enemy's land. You will need to determine their strength and their resolve. If we are to stick with this Persian monarch we must have our own intelligence. Although the Greeks are only adequate sailors they are very clever, whereas the Persians are blunderers and subject to impudence. They seek to overcome by numbers, not by intelligence. The Greeks will attempt to deceive them again."

He continued, *"**We will go to the great council meeting. We will listen and help the King conquer Egypt. But we will need to determine whether we will follow him to Greece.**"*

Artemisia bowed to her friend and mentor. But even though she appeared to be accepting this as her role, she had already formulated a plan of her own. She would go to Delphi. She would bargain with the Greeks and consult the great Oracle. But her goal was not to attain the Greek's submission, it was to subvert it. Artemisia wanted a fight. She wanted to taste the Greek blood. A victory over the Greek navy would make her and her brothers the seafaring equals of the Persian's land army. Artemisia knew that the triumph over the Greeks would cement her legacy and could even put her on an equal level to the Persian Monarch. Whereas Xerxes could rule the land, she and her Phoenician brothers would control the seas.

★★★★

Penish was finally tired. He, Sippar and their small entourage had left Sar-I Pul-I in the middle of the night. Almost immediately they had encountered a dust storm on the northern trek to Ashur. Penish pushed the small caravan in the hope of quickly recapturing the priest and returning to Susa to receive his just rewards. He could feel the gold and

402

silver in his hand that he knew he was guaranteed if he completed his mission. As the group trudged through the storm, Penish fantasized about how to spend his money. He wanted very much to complete this assignment quickly so he could appear at the great council meeting with the great priest bound in chains. He also envisioned bursting into the council meeting being followed by the chained priest. He imagined the stunned faces of the council members when they realized who he was bringing back. It would be a grand entrance. Through the dark and sand drenched nights he kept envisioning the wealth and acclaim that would follow him upon his return. But, in truth, he also wished to see the King's eyes when he walked in with the old priest in chains. He knew the King depended on him and he wanted to justify his trust. ***"They will write songs about me,"*** he thought.

The trio had set up a camp about a mile outside of Ashur to plan their personal assault on the hiding place of the old man. Sippar's spies had already identified where the priest was hiding and gave details about the hut and the possibilities of who could be guarding their prey. Having the military background, Penish had favored a direct assault on the hut, overwhelming the inhabitants with their surprise. But Sippar was strong in his protest of such a plan. He argued that the priest would be heavily guarded and even though they had surprise on their side, they would still be at a disadvantage with a head-on assault. There could be upwards of twenty men in a hut of that size and their small group of five would be at a severe disadvantage.

Sippar's suggestion was to wait in ambush outside of the hut while they set it on fire. The flames would force the defenders into the open and make them easy pray for their arrows. Penish thought for a long period over such a plan and had difficulty arguing against it, as it seemed to offer more positives than negatives. He finally had to succumb to the logic. In trying to escape the flames the defenders would be so worried they would be totally surprised by the ambushing arrows. The old priest would be in the open and easy pray for the band.

On the next night the small group made their way into Ashur, located the house, and the trap was set. In the early morning during the darkest part of the night, the small group outfitted the outside walls of the house with scrubs and other flammable substances to make the fire rapidly rise. The inhabitants would need to escape quickly, and the group would stand by the door and pick them off, one by one. The archers took up their position on both sides of the

404

house. Their orders were to delay their shooting until all the men exited the house so no mistakes were made. Penish wanted to make sure that the old priest didn't become a victim of the assault. He wanted him alive.

Penish himself lit the fire. As expected, the flames quickly shot up the sides of the hut. Before anyone could turn his head, the hut appeared engulfed by the blaze. The men were vigilantly watching the front of the structure but nobody emerged. Before long it appeared that the structure would become a tomb for anyone that was inside. The men stood dumbfounded not sure what to do. In reality though, there was nothing they could do. They could only watch as the flames continued to percolate.

Before long other people began to gather to watch the fire. Penish's men kept them at a distance, claiming that the area was restricted. When the fire burned itself out, Penish's men searched the ruble. They found the charred bodies of three men not the twenty they anticipated. Although their faces were burned beyond recognition, part of the robe of one of the men was recognizable.

"This looks like a priest's robe."

One of the searchers said excitedly. Penish came over to the body to inspect it further. It certainly looked like a robe that the Sheshgallu would wear.

"It is a priest's robe, but how do we know that this is the old man?"

Penish bent over and put a rag on his hand. He reached down to the body's arm and lifted the charred limb. With his other hand he took the hand of the corpse noticing two rings on the fingers. He recognized the rings, as he had studied them when he first captured the old priest. He signaled for one of the men to bring over a pouch that he had tied to his horse. Penish took out a long dagger that was attached to his lower leg. With a quick movement, he cut the burned corpses hand off, placing it in the pouch. He repeated the procedure on the other hand leaving the sacred rings on the charred hand to prove its authenticity. After closing the bag, Penish stayed in his crouch for a few minutes contemplating whether he really believed that the old priest was dead. After a time, a smile emerged on his face and he stood. He turned his head and looked at Sippar almost begging for confirmation. The tracker looked back at Penish and nodded his head in affirmation.

Sippar came over and inspected the severed hands more closely. He also took some time and examined the robe that lay almost unburned on the ground. Finally, he turned to Penish.

"The gods are with you. There is no question, my friend. You have completed your task. You have captured the old priest. It is a shame that we couldn't bring him back in person for the King to piss on. But the great King will still wear the priest's rings as a sign of his dominance. I have heard the tales of these two rings. It is believed they were given to the priest by God himself. Look here. One has a red stone and the other a blue one. The legends tell of these two stones. The writing is old. I cannot read it. But I am sure these are the old priest's rings. You have killed the jackal."

****

The great King knelt in front of the sun disc. He had left his private apartment that was situated by the northern edge of the temple before the sun showed its imposing face. He left his room almost two hours before his meeting to assure himself that he would have enough time to satisfy his god before his triumph. Behind him stood his servants, his loyal Calah and a Zoroastrian priest, who was one of the hereditary of priesthood from the western portion of the Empire. These holy men were born into the priesthood so they were considered closer to God, being viewed as his children. The belief was that virgin maidens were impregnated by the god's servants to create this priestly caste. When a virgin woman became pregnant, she was removed from the general population and cared for by the priests. If she was lucky enough to give birth to a male child, she was praised and given a prestigious position in the temple. Female children, on the other hand, were considered bad omens from the god. On their tenth day of life, when their ears opened to the delight of the world, they were sacrificed to appease the angry spirits. Also on the tenth day following birth, the male children were castrated to assure their reliability and commitment.

Xerxes had made sacrifices over the last days to the earth and to the wind. He drank out of the large sacred silver goblet, the bottom of which was shaped as a combination of a horned deer and a winged bird. The wine tasted good to the monarch for if one could finish the entire amount without breathing, it foretold success in his upcoming meeting. The wine especially brewed with a mix of herbs, blood worms, and grapes. Drinking a small amount of the concoction was an accomplishment but finishing the large silver goblet was a herculean task. The night before Xerxes prayed to the Answerer. Following that, he again had vivid dreams of his grandfather, Cyrus the Great.

Xerxes struggled to keep his thoughts focused on the prayers, but his mind eventually drifted back to the agendas of the meeting. This would be the first time that all the allies would gather together since the death of Darius, Xerxes father. The young King had a legacy to uphold and his future depended on his ability to win over the trust and confidence of the allies. They needed to believe in him, and for that, Xerxes had to believe in himself. He had a specific design for the council meeting and the diversity of the participants would make the task more difficult. To secure peace in this vast Empire the young King had to come across as strong and decisive. Their men would have to support him without question, for if there were hesitations about his leadership, provinces would rebel as quickly as rotten dates falling to the ground.

Xerxes knew that his allies were like wild dogs. They could smell weakness and hesitation. They would only follow a strong alpha male. Every man in the great council chamber was a proficient and skilled leader of people. Many were Kings in their own right, or were at least, accomplished warriors. None were as young or as inexperienced as Xerxes, and he knew they would look at him differently after they worshipped his father Darius. As of this date he had accomplished nothing. He had conquered nothing nor created any great political revelation. His father, Darius was not only a great conqueror, but also an adept politician. In many ways he was a legal genius, creating a series of inventive laws. Darius introduced coinage to the Empire and increased trade by stabilizing the monetary system. He expanded the Empire east to the Indus river; north, conquering the Saka tribes; and west, into Macedonia. Darius built the great temples at Susa and Persepolis and built a great temple to Amun-Re in Egypt. He sent the Jews back to Canaan and even helped them to begin rebuilding their temple. Xerxes knew that his father was more than a ruler to many peoples: he bordered on being viewed as a deity. Even with his reputation and accomplishments, Darius himself had to deal with numerous internal revolts. The Empire was not a stagnant entity but was alive with stirrings, uneasiness and chaos. At best such a vast system could only become a partially domesticated animal. One never knew when the rebellious head would reappear.

Xerxes placed his hands on his forehead. He was still on his knees as he prayed: **"Ahuramazda, God who made the earth and who made man. I worship the earth to give praise to your**

410

righteousness. Your earth gives us our sustenance and every day we walk in your shadow. I worship the waters which are derived from Ahura and give us life itself. Between your two mothers, the earth and water, we worship your greatness. I am Xerxes Ahuramazda, your loyal subject. I rule the greatest Empire of your world and devote my prayers to your greatness. Many men believe in false deities, they follow the lie. I am Xerxes, the great King, son of Darius, an Achaemenid. I am from the great Persian seed. Now, Ahuramazda, as I begin my great journeys to spread your word, I promise to vanquish all other fake gods. I will force all the peoples of the world to bow to your greatness. I promise, Ahuramazda, that if you walk with me on this journey that I will spread your greatness. I have contacted my ancestors and they have decreed that my quest is just. I know my father, Darius, sits in your council. I want both you and my father to be proud of how I will spread the word."

In times of hesitation and self-doubt, Xerxes wondered how he could follow such a man as his famous father. This day would be his first true test. Behind the King of Lands, Calah stood next to a naked slave. Xerxes was still bent in front of the famous sun dial with Calah closely watching his master. The servant felt that the King was hesitating and losing his purpose. He slowly looked at the naked slave standing next to him. He reached up and touched the man on the shoulder. The slave cautiously moved forward and approached the kneeling monarch. He slowly walked up to the King, leaned down, and placed his mouth next to the King's ear and whispered, *"**Remember Marathon!**"*

★★★★

Demaratus was finally feeling that his time was arriving. He had been exiled from his beloved city, Sparta, because of the deceit of the other Spartan King. He had to prostrate himself in front of the egocentric megalomaniac that was the Persian King. He had to be given a new province to rule by the young King, and the people of his city looked at him as a usurper. Since he'd been in this new Empire, Demaratus felt as though he had earned nothing. Everything has been given to him by the generosity of others. Being given things was not in his nature, taking was. But the time for his emergence and eventual revenge had finally arrived. He was preparing to enter the great council chamber and sit with many Kings and warriors. He rationalized to himself that he was returning to his proper status. But deep inside he knew that Egypt would be his proving ground.

Since arriving in the Empire, Demaratus had prepared for this. From his first day in his new province he had begun training troops. It was very difficult instilling Spartan discipline in these barbarians. Demaratus was brutal with discipline. He greatly rewarded hard work but bordered on viciousness with his punishment. Demaratus worked long hours, but he also knew that he could only approximate the strength and discipline of the Spartan soldier. He had amassed a small army of about 2500 men who he considered elite troops. Of course, these men could not stand up to Spartan warriors, but Demaratus had every confidence that the Egyptians would be no match for his elite troops. He also believed, although would never say it in public, that his crack troops were superior to the Persian Immortals. Egypt would be the testing ground for Demaratus, his troops, and his generalship. By proving his worth in Egypt, he was sure it would reserve him a prominent place when the real fight began. Demaratus believed that if he could spearhead a successful invasion of Greece, his true worth would be seen. When the Persians finally triumphed, the young King would reward him by reestablishing his rule over both Sparta and Athens. On a nightly basis he dreamt about his eventual success. The vivid nature of his dreams had convinced him that this vision would come true. The gods, he believed, were on his side. He would leave Egypt in triumph, or he and his troops would not return.

The Spartan King had travelled to Susa for the great council meeting with 25 of his elite troops. They would serve as guards for him as well as confidants. He believed them to be fiercely loyal, as he had created an intricate system of payback and payoff for the families of those loyal to his rule. Supporting Demaratus meant you would eventually be wealthy.

Demaratus had heard that the young King was planning on sending an envoy to Greece to secretly meet representatives of Athens. He suspected that the King was attempting to "buy off" the Greeks in exchange for their submission. When he was told of this rumor, he mused to himself, that he was surprised that the Persians hadn't learned anything from their horrific defeat at Marathon. Demaratus knew that the Persians had thought they had bought Athens before their invasion at Marathon. They placed all their faith in this clandestine arrangement only to be betrayed by the clever Athenians. Demaratus would not let history repeat.

However, with all this intrigue, Demaratus was fearful of the Oracle at Delphi. It was a true wildcard for him, and its message to the Persians could shift power in many separate directions. Because of its renowned reputation to have the ear of the god Apollo, the Oracle had the power to inspire or to deflate. The Oracle could foretell the outcome of any invasion and thereby possessed great influence. There were times when his home, Sparta, had attempted to "buy" the Oracle's influence. It ended up costing the city large amounts of money and provided little support. Apollo had proven that he would foretell the future, no matter what the gift for his advice was.

Demaratus also knew that the Persian monarch was a fiercely superstitious man. No matter how great his anger, if forewarned by the Oracle of impending disaster the monarch would probably reconsider the importance of his revenge. If Persia never invades the Greek Isles, then Demaratus would be stranded in this godforsaken place forever. It was a fate that he couldn't live with. It was hard enough living with the insult of banishment, but not returning in triumph would leave him forever cursed. He believed he would walk through the underworld, forever to be mocked by the gods. If Persia did not attack the Greeks, Demaratus made a promise to himself to end his puny life. Better to die by your own sword than to live in such humiliation and dishonor.

The great young King stood in all of his glory by the great throne. The throne had been built by his father to honor the majesty of the Empire. Fire alters burned brightly on both sides of the throne. Behind both fires were raised inlaid designs. On the right was the man-bull with the colors of his face standing out against his jet-black body. On the left side of the throne was the sculpture of the great Persian lion, the representation of the Empire. Behind the great throne stood an enormous monolith dedicated to Darius. On the monolith there were inscriptions that spelled out all the triumphs of the great King. Behind and next to the great monolith stood three columns of the Immortals. The Immortals were dressed in their long, blue-gray robes with their fluted hats. They all carried their war spears and shields. They were both stylish and imposing. Next to the Immortals stood the servants and slaves. They too wore their finest regalia, for this all-important event.

Two steps behind Xerxes stood the Patischorian. This man was the royal bearer of the family battle axe. Xerxes himself carried his long bow in his right hand and the Answerer in the left. The King stood stoically in the center of the platform which was raised about four inches above all others. For this event the King had new tattoos on his face ringing his eyes in black and red. The shape of the design made him look more sinister and emphasized his dark complexion. The King's beard was braided with gold colored feathers.

To the left of the great King, and about ten feet in front of him, stood the high generals of Xerxes' army. In the front was Mardonius. Next to him stood Tritantacechmes, one of the men who Darius trusted to outflank opponents. Now in charge of his own Immortal's battalion, Smerdomences stood proudly in his new regalia. In order of seniority were the rest of the senior officers: Masistes, Gergis, and finally Megabyzus. To the right of the great King were the admirals of the Persian Navy. Bowing to the King were the three great admirals, Ariabignes, Prxaspes and Zephan.

The King stood silent, more reminiscent of one of the magnificent statues that flanked the hall. In front of him lay Sameron. Sensing the importance of this moment, the lioness looked regal as she showed her canines and growled with a deep moan. She was also adorned in fire red regalia. The King slowly looked around the room, not settling his eyes on any one individual. He looked as though he was distant, staring through people. He slowly raised his right arm and pointed to the heavens.

417

"I am Xerxes, son of Darius, the unquestioned ruler of the Archimedean dynasty, the greatest Empire on earth. I am the hereditary heir of Cyrus the Great, and my father, Darius. I am the ruler of lands, ruler of peoples, and ruler of Kings. No mortal in the world can attain my status."

Almost on cue, Sameron snarled again, verifying the status of her master. Xerxes smiled to himself approving of his pet's presence and her perfect timing. Xerxes stepped forward and motioned for Calah. Calah followed his master as Xerxes walked slowly past the Immortals. He stopped and reversed his direction approaching his generals and admirals. He stood in front of them and again raised his arms. *"Our destiny has arrived. This will be our first step. Providence is on our side. Our god has spoken to me. My ancestors have shown me the path of the truth."*

He raised the Answerer and with it pointed to the fire behind the throne. On cue, the fires sparkled and seemed to explode to the ceilings. At this sight the military men erupted, banging their spears on the ground. Now the King focused on the eyes of his generals. He met each of their gazes one at a time. He held the stare with each man proudly focused on the young King. He wanted to impose his will on these men. He had to put his faith in them and they had to trust his vision and follow his will without question. Xerxes thought he could tell by his stare which of these men would pledge their loyalty. His face was stoically stern as he met each set of eyes and moved on to the next. The great King then walked slowly back to his throne. He stepped up to the mantel and turned and sat on the throne. He was quiet and controlled. He looked to Calah and exclaimed, ***"Allow the allies entrance."***

Calah took two steps forward and raised his walking stick. Slowly the large wooden doors the height of three large men, swung open. A very large man clad in pelts of wolf skin lumbered forward. The man came from the rugged mountains near the Xantos River. His name was Arbaces and he was the Lycian King. The Lycians were earthy and rugged people who were prone to tall tales as well as detailed and convoluted myths. The Lycian delegation entered the great chamber after their warrior King. In the tradition of his people, Arbaces pounded his great club before bowing his head to the Persian King. Xerxes smiled slightly at the gesture and Arbaces summoned his people. The delegation bowed in unison and they moved towards their place in the great hall.

It was ironic that the Lycians were followed into the great chamber by Mazaeus. Mazaeus was the King of the Cilicias. He came from the capital of Tarsus and he represented both Cilicia Trachea and Cilicia Pedias. The capital of Tarsus was bounded by two great walls of rocks referred to as the Cilician Gates. Mazaeus himself had a very colorful history, as his family clans were pirates before becoming royalty. For many years the Cilicias and the Lycians were unfriendly. But here in the great hall, in front of the Persian King, they were forced to act like brothers.

The Cypriots and Macedonian delegations were next, and they took their place after paying their respects to the great monarch. They were followed by the Dorians and the Ionians. The Ionians were now allies of the Persians even though it had been their revolt against Persian rule that had been the causative factor in Darius' invasion of Greece. Darius had concluded that the Greeks were behind the Ionian revolt. His anger at the Greeks led to the battle of Marathon. The army was set to punish the Greeks for supporting the Ionians in their revolt against the Empire. Athens had supported Ionian independence, for these people were descendants of the migrants from the Peloponnesus. Their language was even a Greek dialect.

Hanno of Carthage was next to enter and present his delegation and gifts to the Persian War Lord. He was followed by Thorax of Thessaly. Demaratus was next on the agenda and Thorax made him very anxious. He had been told that the man was to be at this gathering, but even though he was an ally, Thorax didn't trust another King from the Greek Peninsula. He was fearful that whatever the plans were for an invasion of Greece, the Athenians would have forewarned knowledge of it. Even though he was anxious, he kept his composure when he met Demaratus two days before the meeting.

Demaratus was followed by a Babylonian delegation and then a large contingent from Assyria. The Hebrews were also represented at this grand council meeting, as a group from Canaan also had a place in the hall. They were followed by representatives from the Aegean islands.

After the Aegean islanders, the Phoenician Kings were admitted to the meeting. Their delegation was also large and they were attired in their beautiful purple robes. The two great Phoenician Kings walked together to present their delegations to the King of Lands. Together in unison they patiently walked, as if their entrance should be applauded by the other delegations. They both stopped a few feet from the lioness, ignoring her growling as they approached. They bowed in a coordinated fashion. Then, without warning, a disturbance erupted at the entrance to the chamber. Two of the guards that stood by the door immediately reacted. As they approached the cause of the uproar, the King strained to see what the commotion was about. His hand automatically went to his sword hilt. All the generals and admirals reacted, but it was Demaratus who forcibly moved to stand in front of the Monarch with his sword raised.

The two guards approached the area of the pandemonium and were summarily thrown back. As they tried to regain their standing positions, the Phoenician delegation began to separate creating an opening for everyone to see. And there she stood. Her head was raised and she had two blades drawn. Her eyes were aflame and she had both swords out in her extended arms facing the two prone guards.

Xerxes began to smile at the sight. Artemisia then looked directly at the King of Kings, and with a sardonic note shouted, *"You will now see me, King of Kings. The Warrior Queen, Artemisia, the ruler of the vast oceans, has arrived."*

Whenever Artemisia entered a room there seemed to be a change in the atmosphere. Firstly, she was a female among men. But more than the shock of her gender, Artemisia was awe inspiring. She walked with a regal step and held herself as if she was above any of the other participants. On this day she was clothed in a fire red outfit with bright yellow armbands. Her hair was colored with purple strands. As she walked past the other delegation's heads invariably turned to notice her. There were more open mouths as she strode forward. It was only the Warrior Queen that could outshine the grandiosity of Susa itself. As was custom, Artemisia walked straight to the pulpit where Xerxes sat. But unlike the other Kings she did not bow to the Great Lord. She slowly approached him and then, arriving within feet of the throne, bent over and began stroking and talking to the lioness, Sameron. Artemisia had hidden in her belt a small piece of fresh meat which she gracefully placed in the lioness' jaw. The immense creature seemed to smile at the treat and she snuggled to the Queen's face. Unbeknownst to anybody, the Warrior Queen had been visiting Sameron daily, bringing her treats and becoming friendly with the great beast. Artemisia was aware of the importance of entrance and she had been preparing this little stunt for almost ten days. She knew that the lioness would be laying in her position in front of the Persian Monarch, and that her place there was ostensibly to separate

the King from others. Artemisia wanted
to breach this chasm and give the message
that the Persian monarch had an equal at
these proceedings.

When the Warrior Queen bent over and
was so easily welcomed by the lioness,
others in the room seemed to be stunned.
There were whispers that she must have
been a sorceress and somehow mesmerized
the great beast. In truth, it was simple
training. Ah, but what a grand entrance
this woman made. Stealing the thunder
from all the other dignitaries and
monarchs left a satisfactory feeling
within the Warrior Queen. It was almost,
she would later admit, as satisfying as
destroying an enemy's fleet.

After her show, Artemisia looked at
the young monarch and smiled. Xerxes
couldn't help but be impressed by the
woman's guts and gall. He knew that he
made the correct decision to choose the
Warrior Queen to head the delegation to
Delphi. This event only confirmed his
confidence in this extraordinary woman.

The Queen seemed to sense that she
shouldn't push her diplomatic victory any
further, so she bowed low to the King and
retreated to her place in the
delegations. Xerxes waited for the buzz
to stop. He then stood and walked down
off the pulpit. He scanned the great
gathering. This was the largest

gathering of powerful people that the world had ever seen. And he, Xerxes, stood at the head of this assemblage. He took a few more steps forward. The electricity in the room was palpable. All of these people had achieved greatness. Many were deceitful and manipulative, but they all were shrewd and powerful. And to be sure, none of them were afraid, even of this great King. The air was filled with anticipation. The King was majestic in his regalia, bright red robe with yellow stripes. His posture was straight and unflinching. His eyes distantly gazed over the assemblage.

Xerxes took a few more silent steps. Then he lifted the Answerer. **'We sit here as friends and allies. Many of the people in this room represent historical enemies. For generations we have spilt each other's blood. For years we have cursed each other and put spells on our families."**

His face contorted as he raised his voice and fisted his free hand. **"We have created a great Empire. But I fear my friends, that our destiny is not yet complete. There are peoples who mock us. There are peoples who spit on our traditions and build temples to their hatred of us."**

Xerxes was working himself up into frenzy. He was almost shouting his message, and those around him were frozen to see the quick conversion of this young man from a controlled, stoical figure to a screaming, sweating preacher. He shook his fist in the air and he traversed the gathering. *"My ancestors are screaming to me every night. Screaming! They call us coward for allowing the enemies of the Empire to live without punishment. Many of you can still taste the blood of our brothers who left us at Marathon."*

Xerxes calmed. He turned suddenly and slowly walked toward the assembled Immortals. The soldiers, the cream of the Persian Army, stood in their finest regalia, gold braided jackets with bright green undergarments. They were all armed to the teeth, brandishing their Persian swords and their individualized shields. They were impressive in their status. The great King stopped when he was halfway down the line of assembled soldiers. He looked at the delegations. He began to speak. *"Almost twenty days ago I received word that our garrison at Memphis had been overrun by the rebellious factions in Egypt."*

His face turned serious and angry. *"My father treated the Egyptian satrapy and the Egyptian people as if they were his born children. He created a new legal system for them and built them a great* temple to their god, Amun-Re. He sent our engineers and builders to create a waterway from the Nile to the Great Sea. It reached from Bubastis to Bitter Lakes. Many Persians bled and died for their Egyptian brothers."

He hesitated. "**And now we are repaid by the murder and enslavement of over 80,000 of our brothers in Memphis. Our generosity and compassion for our Egyptian brothers has been paid back by treachery. We opened our hearts and were treated with disdain. The time has come my friends to repay blood with blood.**"

In unison the massed delegations stood and voiced their approval that echoed around The great hall. All the assembled Kings and delegations began shouting at once, calling for Egyptian blood. The King let the masses continue their chanting.   He had stationed people throughout the great hall whose job it was to encourage such behavior from the allies. He smiled to himself and enjoyed the cry for Egyptian blood. The response was exactly what he wanted, but more than that, it was exactly what he needed. Finally, he stepped back onto the platform and the voices began to settle. "*I have seen it, my friends. I have seen the future and we must retake our destiny.*"

Xerxes now raised both arms above his head and the allies again began cheering. At the same time fires began rising at various places on the stage. The ram was brought in and with a smooth, athletic swing, Xerxes beheaded the animal. He held the head in the air and the assembled delegation exploded in approval.

PERSIA

CHAPTER XVII EGYPT

He was hardly recognizable as he sat on the bed. His clothes were torn and tattered and his long hair had been completely shaved off. He now had a cane, and whenever he left his modest dwelling he covered his head. Ningizzida had arrived back in his beloved city of Babylon almost a week before. He and his entourage had sneaked into the city in the middle of the night during a rare rain storm. He had decided it was best to hide in plain sight. When people passed him on the streets, it appeared as though he was a cripple, always having a few people help him get around. In truth, the old priest was heavily guarded, but the protection was cleverly disguised. The only person who was consistently in his company was Nin Nibru, who was now firmly implanted as the silent leader of the resistance against Persian rule. The message was spread that the next great Babylonian dynasty was just over the horizon. All communication in the underground was in the ancient Sumerian language, a tongue that only a handful of outsiders could speak or understand.

In a very short time, Nin Nibru had been able to put together a huge organization of resistance. The plan was to keep quiet and benign until it was time to rise up against the oppressors. But even though Nin-Nibru was seen as the orchestral genius of this revolution against Persian rule, only a few knew that the conductor of the rebellion was the Sheshgallu who stayed completely in the background.

The rumor of Ningizzida's death had circulated around the city as quickly as the eastern winds swirled through the desert. As the population heard of the great man's demise, a general sense of melancholy seemed to settle over the vivacious city. There were ceremonies, ablutions and sacrifices at all the churches in the area. In one of the largest temples of Babylonia, a statue of

Ningizzida was raised, next to Marduk the worshipped deity.

Ningizzida did not allow the sadness to linger. Within days of the news of his death reaching the city, Ningizzida began having his minions spread the tales of his extraordinary powers that were witnessed within his life. He wanted the image of the dead Ningizzida to become larger than life in death. The story of how he rose above the ground and was surrounded by divine light, leading to his escape from the Persian jail, became a widely repeated tale. Songs were written about it and within a very brief period, Ningizzida had become god-like, the new Gilgamesh, one third human and two thirds god. Not many men throughout history were able to orchestrate their own legacy, and yet this ancient man and his disciples carried out the charade.

Ningizzida's most flowery story had to do with his ability to tell the future. It was said that before the great priest died in a fire, he had been meditating in the desert when God appeared, arising from a rock to reveal the future to him. As Ningizzida prostrated himself before Marduk, the god reached out his hand and touched the priest on the head. Then, in a low but rich voice, God revealed the future to the priest.

"The Persian yoke will be removed from my city. You have pointed the way my son but I cannot let you remain for the final moment. Your return to my breast will hearken a new day for Babylonia. Your sacrifice will lead to a new light to shine on the land. But tell the people to be careful. They will all be asked to stand for their belief. Many will die and you will return to earth. You will rise again from the underworld to lead your people to their ultimate victory."

The story of the resurrection of Ningizzida was born.

On this day, Nin-Nibru reviewed how the stories were being received with the now legendary priest. The priest usually enjoyed hearing about his supernatural exploits, but not today. Although it was out of character, Ningizzida did not want to discuss rumors and story mongering on this day. He did not want to discuss rumor and folk tales. He wanted to focus on the future. He wanted to talk about the strategy for the upcoming revolution. He was very detail oriented and wanted his young protégé to repeat the plans.

"Is Belshimanni ready?"

"He is, my lord," Nin-Nibru said in a serious tone.

"Does he understand that he will need to visit the Persian King after we take control and that he will need to be strong and convince the King that the revolt is in his best interest?"

Ningizzida appeared more anxious than usual today. The seeds were already planted to put in motion the second part of his plan. He knew that there was no turning back. His city would either become free to be ruled by Babylonians again or would burn under the Persian anger.

****

The Persian ruler was tired. His unbending energy was drained from his cathartic presentation at the council meeting. He was very proud of the way he controlled his passionate burst during his first encounter with the allies. After his opening foray he allowed the emotion to cool in the room before laying out his thoughts about reconquering the renegade province. The King allowed each of the delegations to discuss their ideas about the strategy to bring Egypt back into the Persian bosom.

Xerxes believed that the Egyptian magi were responsible for his father's death. He was convinced that the Egyptians poisoned his father, although he didn't have a clear understanding why they would

433

have taken such a drastic and suicidal approach. After all, his father treated the Egyptians with great respect. He married an Egyptian showing the ultimate respect for their culture. The idea that these people murdered his father angered Xerxes beyond his understanding. His father's philosophical approach was to allow the different peoples of his Empire religious freedoms. Xerxes now believed that it was this approach that indirectly led to his father's demise. He reasoned that such freedom gave the wrong message to the Egyptian priests, telling them that the Persian King was weak and not committed to his own beliefs. Xerxes vowed he would not make this philosophical mistake. A strong local religion was a powerful political force to keep in place. It was a way of controlling them. When he reconquered Egypt he would teach them respect. They would bow to the Persians.

Xerxes was tired and hungry. Two slaves entered his quarters as the young King slumped on his bed. He was both emotionally and physically drained. Between his three-day hallucinatory experience with his step-mother and the build up to the council meeting, Xerxes was physically and emotionally spent. The slaves carried a feast into the King's chamber. It consisted of roast lamb, numerous vegetables, and sweet wines. Unlike other days when he was drained and would launch into his meals, on this day, he was almost too tired to eat.

As the King slowly moved from his bed, one of the slaves dropped to his knees and began holding his stomach and screaming in pain. Xerxes immediately rose, finding unknown strength, and ran to the door to summon help. The slave couldn't move as blood and vomit flowed out of his mouth. Help arrived very quickly but the slave was already dead. A second slave began swearing as white foam appeared on his legs. Calah was immediately on the scene. He looked down at the man and dropped to one knee examining the corpse.

Xerxes stood stunned by the event. The slave who died in such agonizing pain was the man whose job it was to taste the King's food before he ate. Xerxes eyes were wide as the realization passed through his mind that this had been a failed attempt on his life. He looked down at Calah with fear and rage in his face. He lifted the small man off the floor and stared into his face. *"What is this, Calah?"* The young King asked, *"I don't know, lord,"* he responded, almost stuttering.

"You don't know?" the King asked with concern.

"I will find out, lord," Calah assured, as Xerxes shook him and then put him down.

"I will find out Lord, I swear on my soul."

Calah left the room with a silent smile to himself. He didn't need to investigate what happened with the King's meal for he already knew. A week before, Calah was approached by a man while he shopped in the city. The fellow, a former confidante of the man-servant, indicated that he represented a religious leader from Babylonia. When Calah inquired about the identity of the man who sent this envoy, he was told his name was Nin-Nibru. Calah hesitated for he had heard of this man. It was a new name that only entered the rumor mill a few weeks previous, as if he arose magically from the desert. Calah was intrigued, as the word about this Nin-Nibru was too extraordinary to believe. Supposedly he was the heir apparent to the dead renegade priest, Ningizzida. There even gossip that Nin-Nibru was directly responsible for the death of Manishtusu, the great priest's original acolyte.

The man who approached Calah said that Nin-Nibru wanted to speak with him directly on a matter of great importance. He offered wealth, almost beyond reason, just to listen to this man. Being a man with many expensive tastes and inquisitive instincts, Calah couldn't refuse. Besides the financial aspect, the curiosity was too compelling.

The meeting was held in the back room of an opium den in the early hours of an unusually cold morning. Initially, Nin-Nibru was shrouded, covered with a hood. He attempted to disguise his voice as he spoke. Nin-Nibru knew that he was playing a very dangerous game, as the man he spoke with had the ear of the great King. The King, Nin-Nibru knew, was revengeful and vindictive, and could crush him without a second thought. He needed to ask this servant for his help without insulting him or pushing him too far out of his loyalty comfort zone. There were also unspoken questions as to whether Calah was just there to spy on him. He stared at the man servant of the great King for a while before gaining enough gumption to speak. He first tried to read Calah's intent with no success. Was he here to hear the proposal? Or was his presence just a prelude to arrest? When he finally spoke, Calah was already feeling a little woozy from the smoke that pervaded the room. Choosing this space was not only because of its hidden milieu, but the old priest behind this intrigue knew that the opium smoke would give Nin-Nibru an edge. Nin-Nibru swallowed hard but began the conversation. *"My friend, I am here to ask for your help."*

Calah almost looked like he would tip over as he held his hand up to his head. But even though his eyes were already turning red, he declared: *"I am not your friend; I am here because of curiosity about your growing reputation."*

Calah was clearly having some trouble focusing his eyes. His pupils were dilated and his eyes were tearing heavily. Even with the distraction, Calah went right to the point. He wanted no pretense. Calah continued: *"Why should I not return to my master and have his guards come and cut you into little pieces?"*

Nin-Nibru swallowed his fear and put on a stoic expression. He knew that this meeting was in truth a fencing match, and he had to plant his focus on the end result. He looked directly at Calah and without hesitation upped the ante: *"You still can, if you'd like. I will wait here for you to call them. I do not fear death. Killing me will only seal your fate in perdition."*

Calah smiled at the man who sat opposite him. He knew immediately that it would be difficult to intimidate this man. Finally, he sarcastically commented. "*I knew your master before he became a god.*"

Nin-Nibru responded: "*You should not make fun of greatness.*"

"*Ah, yes,*" Calah answered "*I hear these exaggerated stories about your master and the extraordinary powers that he gained. They are embellished and embroidered like fine cloth and hard to believe.*"

Nin-Nibru hesitated and straightened his back. He watched his words closely. "*I was with my master and was witness to many of the amazing powers that he possessed. You should not suppose that the stories are embroidered. Although he never claimed to be divine, I believe that he was closer to god than any man.*"

Calah wanted to smile but the seriousness of the way Nin-Nibru presented this information made him wonder. The opium smoke, of course, added to his uncertainty. Without thinking he pronounced, "*but I also understand that he has died. Is it possible for a god to die?*"

Calah giggled now being overcome by the smoke. But he regained his composure and continued, "*tell me, my friend, if your master is a god, can he return from the beyond?*"

Nin-Nibru said nothing but smiled at the man servant. But in the silence, Calah had an epiphanic thought. Maybe Ningizzida really wasn't dead at all. He really didn't know why he reached this possible supposition. He couldn't speak after the realization. If true, this religious conspiracy changed everything. For many years Calah was a silent follower of the old priest. He was a true icon to the servant. Although for most of his adult life he had served the Archimedean dynasty, he was born and raised in a small village near Babylonia. Pondering this new conclusion Calah seemed to vibrate a little. After a couple of minutes he finally demanded, *"so tell me, why are we meeting tonight?"*

The introductory moves were over. The game was now on in full glory.

As he walked out of the King's room, Calah recalled this secret meeting with Nin-Nibru. He couldn't tell the King that he himself had put the strong poison in the food. He was very cautious that he was not seen with the potion. Nin-Nibru had given the servant the poison at the end of their meeting. To his own surprise, Calah didn't feel any strong emotions at this betrayal. Of course, the poison was not meant to kill the King. He had to be meticulous in his timing. It was designed to kill the servant and make the King think that there was an active underground seeing his destruction. Calah was not told the intention behind this deception, but he trusted that it would serve the old priest's purpose. The King would be probing for answers and explanations to what happened and Calah already had the predetermined script memorized. He just had to wait a few days and reveal to Xerxes what he "uncovered" about the assassination attempt.

The King was leaving in two days to repossess the satrap of Egypt and Calah would speak with him before the army departed.

★★★★

Demaratus was ecstatic. He had been chosen by Xerxes to lead one of the three armies that would sweep through Egypt and meet at Memphis, the Egyptian capital. This was a great honor, as Demaratus was the only "outsider" to be in the vanguard of the attack.

Demaratus had risen during the council meeting and boldly claimed that his troops could outperform any of the troops that would be gathered in the Egyptian reconquest. His brazen boast turned heads and led to some mocking under the breath of some of the participants. The King stood with a doubting look on his face. His response to Demaratus revealed his irritation at the bragging Spartan. He pointed his arm at the Greek and rose from his throne. *"What do you say, King Demaratus?"*

"My King, my troops are well trained and will rival the feats of any of the men in the Empire!"

Xerxes stared at the Spartan in disbelief. He put his left hand on his hip and unsheathed his sword with his right hand. Demaratus bowed to one knee at the sight of the King's movement. *"My lord, I swear here in front of all these gathered dignitaries, that the troops under my leadership will reach Memphis before any other Persian unit."*

There was a hush that swung through the great room in reaction to the bragging Spartan. Then, as all eyes were on the Greek, the King stepped forward. He now lifted his sword and pointed it at Demaratus. *"This might be a costly wager for you, my friend."*

He walked past the bowed Demaratus and spoke to the council. *"Demaratus has challenged the Immortals. He has now bet his life on his army's efficiency."*

The council erupted in applause as the King laid out the extent of the Spartan's boast.

The King's own cousin, Mardonius, would lead the first army of Immortals. And even though Mardonius was scheduled to be the first into Memphis, Demaratus and his elite troops were expected to be close behind. But now, Demaratus had to outplay Mardonius and beat his army to Memphis. He knew that he and his men might be the first to attack an entrenched enemy, as the King would not want to waste his elite troops in a potentially difficult fight. Demaratus and his troops would be tested and given the task of challenging the enemy's strength. And yet this was the place that reputations were made or heads were lost and Demaratus knew it. He was hoping that a good showing in Egypt would place him in a leading position when the King decided to attack the Greeks. It would also affirm the King's trust in him and prove his abilities. The third army in the Egyptian offensive would be the new corps of Immortals being trained by Smerdomences. They, too, would be tested in this campaign and they had to earn their stripes for the upcoming invasion of Athens.

The two Phoenician Kings would support the ground troops with their ships.

****

Artemisia met with the two Phoenician Kings, Merbalos and Matten, after the council meeting. Neither man was impressed by the young King. Matten commented that the Persian monarch reminded him of a wind from your ass. A strong smell that quickly faded. He stared at Merbalos and commented, **"my face felt his presence, but my body showed no movement."**

The implication of the comment was that there was a lack of substance in the Persian's comments. More so than that, Matten was losing confidence in the King's ability to lead the Empire. He turned to his friend again and admitted, **"if I feel this way, then others in the Empire will also sense his weakness."** Artemisia turned to her friend and asked, **"what scares you about this man, my friend?"**

Matten thought for a moment, **"His decisions are guided not by wisdom but by emotion. It is dangerous to follow a leader that is blinded by revenge. He will make mistakes moving forward when he should outflank. He is blinded by his hatred... the Greeks are clever."**

He looked directly at Artemisia and asked: **"Do you believe that any of the King's generals can outsmart the Greeks?"** Artemisia didn't have to answer. She just turned away and strode to the edge of the room. She had her own concerns about the young King's judgment, but even with her brothers she chose to keep her inner thoughts quiet. Ever since the young King made his decision to send her to Delphi, the Warrior Queen was concerned. Matten followed her and even with her back turned to him he began to speak again. *"The Egyptians are fools. They surprised the garrison at Memphis and slaughtered the Persians. This young King has a taste for blood. He will feast in Egypt. But dining on Egyptian blood and destroying the Greeks are two different meals."*

Matten turned away from the Warrior Queen but he continued his evaluation. *"The Persians will roll through the desert in Egypt. But they will pay for this victory."*

Matten smiled as Artemisia turned to face him. Before answering his own statement, Matten walked a few feet looking at the ground. *"The Egyptian victory will give the Median King a large sense of false confidence. He will believe in his own invincibility. Between his exaggerated sense of his own troops and his blood vengeance he will be like a wild bull."*

Artemisia couldn't keep herself quiet any longer. With her face distorted and her voice raised, she sarcastically spoke, *"and with all this, I will be*

445

stuck in Delphi, speaking to a false God."

"And negotiating," Matten sarcastically remarked.

Artemisia turned with a smile on her face and looked at Merbalos. *"Tell me, my brother, what will the god have to say to the Queen of Halicarnassus? Do you think Apollo will compliment me on my outfit?"*

Merbalos laughed while looking at the Queen but warned, *"Careful, my Queen, the Oracle is not to be laughed at."*

The Queen, becoming serious questioned, *"Tell me more of what you know of this Oracle."*

Merbalos thought for a moment and then responded to the question. *"I know precious little, my Queen. But what I have heard is that unlike many false soothsayers, the Oracle is very accurate. Most people believe that it is a divine connection to the truth of the future."*

The Queen did not laugh or even smile. She seriously considered this possibility. With a sly look she turned to her brothers and stated *"then I will be honored my brothers, to speak with Apollo. But he will be more afraid of me than I of him."*

She half smiled at her friends and in a proud motion commented, *"I hope he is honored to speak with me!"*

* * * *

Matten was prophetic in his strategic evaluation of the Persian advance into Egypt. It took Xerxes and his Army only four weeks to advance from the Jewish capital of Jerusalem, through the Egyptian defenses, capturing the capital of Memphis. To his credit, Demaratus engaged the heaviest resistance, but his troops were extremely disciplined and outflanked the Egyptian defenders. In many ways Demaratus' Spartan trained troops outfought the two armies of Immortals at every opportunity. It led Xerxes to wonder whether his Immortals were merely reputation with little substance.

Demaratus' troops were late arriving at the outskirts of Memphis. They had engaged and swept through a large contingent of Egyptian national guards a few miles from the city. They were ambushed, being caught off guard as they rushed to the capital. Demaratus' second in command and three of his lieutenants were killed in the attack before the Spartan trained troops regrouped and slaughtered the attackers. Demaratus himself got caught in the blood rage hacking an Egyptian for minutes after the man had perished.

Demaratus' ferocious troops approached the outskirts of the capital as the sun began setting. He was told by his scouts that both contingents of Immortals were preparing to wait for the morning to coordinate their attack on the heavily fortified city. Demaratus' men were now tired, having engaged in forward fighting advances.

The ex-Spartan King knew that opportunities were fleeting and if not seized, would disappear like a whiff of smoke in a strong wind. He immediately called his two most senior generals to his council.

Siementus III entered the tent first. He bowed to the ex-Spartan King and then straightened, lifting his knife and placing it under his chin. It was an ancient Spartan tradition of placing the knife under your chin as a sign that if the King preferred, you would gladly cut your throat. The second general, Ukinow, also performed the same ceremonial greeting in front of his King.

"I am proud of both of you. You have shown your valor."

Both men bowed their heads in appreciation. *"But we are not finished.*

I will not allow the other armies to embarrass us at the last minute. We will conquer Memphis tonight."

Siementus III straightened at the thought and his eagerness was obvious. Ukinow on the other hand, seemed to back away even though he didn't move. Demaratus immediately picked up the attitude shift. He moved toward his general. *"What is the problem, my friend?"* Ukinow shuffled his feet. His uneasiness was obvious.

"Lord, our men are tired. We can wait for the morning and still reach the heart of the city before the Immortals. It will allow our men to eat and rest before the big push."

There was quiet as Demaratus began pacing. The emotions on his face were palpable. Demaratus stopped and faced his general. *"I understand your hesitancy, but you will put your army in position to advance. Our time is now not tomorrow morning."*

Again quiet. Then Ukinow stiffened and staring at his King in the face said with confidence, *"lord, I believe this strategy is ill advised."*

Demaratus moved closer to his general. He stared into Ukinow's eyes.

"Take out your scabbard, Ukinow, and place it under your throat."

Ukinow swallowed, the poise suddenly leaving his demeanor. He slowly reached for his belt and removed his knife. He hesitated for a second, hoping that the King would change his mind, but Demaratus stood silently staring down the general's eyes. Ukinow's hand began to shake as he held the knife on his neck.

"I am waiting, general."

Ukinow continued to shake as droplets of blood appeared on his neck. Demaratus continued to stare. Tears appeared on Ukinow's cheeks. Finally, after a few seconds, Ukinow closed his eyes and cut deeply into his skin.

The remaining general, Siementus III, looked stunned at the death of his comrade. Demaratus stared at Siementus in silent question. The general paused and then bowed at the King, indicating his submission to the King's plan.

The Spartan walked toward the bowed man and spoke: *"since I arrived, Siementus, you have been at my side. I raised you to your position because of your bravery and your strength. Ukinow saved his honor even though he was a coward. He showed me his fearful side. Do you have anything to say?"*

450

"No, lord, except that victory will be ours."

"Good, Siementus, good. Remember, Ukinow, although he was scared to attack the city, he was a loyal soldier. He will be remembered as a devoted, brave man. Do you agree?"

"I do, lord."

Demaratus smiled and stood face to face with his general. He began, **"Prepare your troops, Siementus. You are now second only to me. We will dine tonight in the Egyptian capital. You and I will share Egyptian women tonight."**

Rather than approaching the city from the north, Demaratus decided on a unique strategy. He marched his troops west, past the miles of necropolis tombs that marked the western outskirts. Demaratus decided to attack the city from the south hoping to surprise the defenders. He figured that the Egyptian spies would concentrate their attention on the two Immortal armies that stood at northwest and northeast of the city. He reckoned that the defenses in the south would be less concentrated than those in the north. When he marched past the Colossus of Ramses and an alabaster Sphinx that marked the outskirts of the city, Demaratus knew that he was fundamentally

451

wrong. The southern defenses were not less concentrated then those in the north. No southern defenses existed and the army marched unattended through the heart of the city. When the Immortal generals heard that Demaratus was attacking the city from the south, they rallied their troops into formation and hastily advanced towards the city once known as Ineb-Hedj (the White walls). With the realization that the enemy was already in their midst, the Egyptian defenses evaporated like smoke in the wind.

Although the victory was generally easy, Xerxes did not like what he witnessed. Twice he called Mardonius and Smerdomences before him to question strategy. It appeared to Xerxes that even with heavier resistance, Demaratus' troops advanced more uniformly than the Immortals. What impressed Xerxes even more was the Spartan's enthusiasm to take on the more intense fights. He seemed to have endless faith in his troop's ability to outmaneuver and outfight any resistance. And this last strategic coup engineered by the Spartan trained troops to conquer the city made the Persian King furious at the hesitancy of the Immortals' leadership.

After their destruction of the Persian garrison within the white walls of Memphis, the Egyptians were so stunned by

their victory that they reveled in their
success.   Their defenses were weak and
not organized throughout the country.
Somehow, they believed that the threat
from the Persians was over.

   Memphis was an international city with
large minority populations of Jews,
Persians, Libyans, Greeks, and
Phoenicians.   The Persian garrison at
Memphis had been undermined from within.
In the middle of the night traitors
opened the gates of the garrison allowing
the Egyptians to kill many of the
Persians while they slept.   The Egyptian
Magi who were behind the uprising made
the situation worse by not taking any
prisoners.   They were brutal in their
slaughter.   They sacrificed the
prisoners to their god, Ptah. Xerxes was
told of the massacre and it led to one of
his famous temper outbursts.

   Now Xerxes sat in the great central
palace in Memphis. He had never traveled
this far from Persia before and he was
taken by the magnificence of the Egyptian
monuments.   As his troops approached
Memphis he visited the Great Pyramids.
The Persians constructed mausoleums to
their dead rulers, but Xerxes had never
considered such extensive monuments to
the dead.   Xerxes stood for hours
admiring the Sphinx. He tried to imagine
the magnitude of the ruler that had such
a statue erected to his greatness.

The palace in which he now sat was flanked by six beautiful statues of past pharaohs. But the most dramatic statue was the Colossus of Ramses that sat at the beginning of the causeway that led to the palace. The statue was over 25 feet high and superbly sculptured.

This great city rivaled the beauty and regale of Babylonia. It was located at the confluence of three trade routes and was a very valuable staging point for trade. Memphis was also the center of both the lower and upper Kingdoms of Egypt. Before it was called Memphis, it was called Ankh-Tawy, meaning "*that which binds the two lands*". Memphis was also the most religious city in Egypt devoted to the cult of the god, Ptah. Ptah was the creator god of the deities of the Egyptian cults. There were offshoots of the religions with prayers to Ptah's wife, Sekhmet, and their son, Nefertem. Memphis was also the showplace for the most beautiful temples in all of Egypt. They were numerous, varied and dissimilar, depending on which of the trinity was worshipped.

★★★★

It was unnerving but the King felt different sitting on this throne in this ancient city. The heritage of these peoples made his own Archimedean legacy look primitive. Xerxes was stage-struck by the longevity of these people. He could almost taste the history. He seemed to sense the importance of the pharaonic line, and more importantly, this realization put his Empire in perspective. Xerxes had always thought that his heretical line was beyond historical comparison. But here in the land of the pharaohs, the Archimedean heritage paled in comparison. Xerxes was energized by the experience. The grandeur of the pyramids, the spectacular Sphinx, the Colossus of Ramses, all combined to put the great King in an almost mesmerized trance. But even with their 2000-year history, it was Xerxes who sat on the throne of pharaohs. It was Xerxes who now ruled this wondrous land. It was Xerxes who put down the rebellion and brought the Persian splendor back into its god given role. No pharaoh sat on this throne. This land would not be ruled by those of Egyptian blood. A Mede sat on this throne and would rule this land. The pharaohs had lived their time and given way to a stronger seed. And that stronger line was Persian.

While sitting on the great throne Xerxes became aware of the real driving force to subdue the Greeks. Up until this point he had believed that his motivation arose from revenge. The crushing defeat that Datis had bungled into at Marathon was always on the King's mind. But he now realized that this wasn't about Marathon at all. At the same time he realized that this wasn't about the death of his father, Darius, either. Xerxes now knew what this driving force was all about. This was about Persian destiny. While sitting, his mind wandered back to his experiences in the cave of his mother. She herself was Egyptian, and she knew that the Persian destiny was to rule the world. He recalled his hallucinations and visions while under his mother's spell. With vivid clarity he recalled his ancestors lining up and showing him the roadmap to his future, to the Persian destiny.

Xerxes also knew at that moment that he didn't need to conquer the Greeks. It they bowed to him, and presented him with water and earth, he would accept their bloodless submission. Destiny had to be served and it was more important than revenge. If it could be heralded in in a bloodless submission and with proper reverence, then it could be accepted. Or if the Greeks were stubborn, it would be forced on the stupid and unwilling. In either case the Persian destiny could not be blocked. God willed it and it would occur. Xerxes prayed to the gods, and the Answerer for the insight. His victory was foretold.

It was then he realized the incredible metamorphous that was occurring. If wasn't until this day, sitting on this foreign throne, that Xerxes became a true King. For the first time he understood the purpose of life and his role in it. He knew his place in history and what he had to do. Up until this epiphany he had merely been a descendent of his great father. Now the transformation had occurred. The butterfly had shed its cocoon and with it, its pretense. His internal difficulty and hesitancies were over. He was Xerxes, the greatest King on earth. He was now, truly, King of peoples, King of lands, King of Kings.

His daydreaming trance was broken by a young servant entering the throne room. The servant approached the King and immediately fell to his knees. It took a minute for Xerxes to refocus himself. When he did he smiled at the young man prostrate in front of him. He was different now and others would notice it. For the first time in many years Xerxes felt that he had nothing to prove. He looked down at the young man and summoned him to rise. The servant looked up at the young King and exclaimed, *"my lord, there is someone here to see you!"* The King looked past the servant uttering, *"where is Calah?"* The servant again bowed his head and replied, *"I am sorry, my lord, but my master, Calah, asked me* to take over his duties while he accomplished a mission."

"What mission?" Xerxes quickly asked, "I don't know, my lord. My master did not brief me on his tasks. He just told me to serve you with my life."

Xerxes immediately switched his focus. "Who is here to see me?" The servant looked at the King and responded, "It is one of your generals, my lord. He calls himself Demaratus, lord, and he brings three prisoners with him."

In all his regalia Demaratus strode into the throne room. He seemed to clank as his bronze armor rubbed against itself. Behind him, bound in chains, were three men. They could barely walk, and their faces were bloodied and bruised, obviously the result of intense interrogation. Demaratus strode triumphantly toward the King. Xerxes rose immediately upon noticing him and walked forward to meet him. He ignored the men who had been forced to their knees and pounded the shoulders of the soldier that stood in front of him. Demaratus spoke first. "My King, I bring to you for your judgment the men that were behind the revolution in this satrap."

Xerxes continued to ignore the prisoners as he spoke.

"My friend, when I first met you I doubted some of the stories that you told of the Spartan military skill. But what you have done here has been exceptional."

Demaratus bowed his head in recognition. Xerxes then pointed to the men that were on their knees in front of the King. He looked at the servant and declared, *"Tomorrow, in front of the Egyptian court, I will consider the fate of these rebels. Remove them from my sight for they stain my eyes."*

He turned again to the ex-Spartan King and smiled, *"tonight, we will feast the triumph."*

Xerxes was still basking in his new-found sense of his own omnipotence when Calah reappeared in the Egyptian palace. When he entered the King's residence it was obvious that he was deep in thought. The King raised his head when his servant entered his presence. In a very serious manner the King spoke. *"Where have you been, Calah?"*

The servant looked surprised by the question

"My lord, I have been doing your bidding."

"My bidding?" Xerxes asked.

"Yes, my lord. I have been investigating the event that happened before you left Susa."

One could see the immediate recognition at the task that the King had given him. *"And, Calah, what have you found?"*

"My lord, I have some truly unfortunate and confusing news."

Calah appeared contemplative but was obviously hesitant to divulge the information that he had uncovered.

"I am waiting, Calah," the King replied. *"My lord, the words that I need to say are not coming easily to my mouth."*

The King became quite serious, but again insisted. *"I said, I am waiting, Calah, for your revelation."*

His brow was now folded.

Calah again looked directly at his monarch and swallowed deeply. He knew that this was be a very anxious moment for him. His life stood in the balance. If the great King did not believe his conclusion, Xerxes could explode with rage and take it out on him. Calah could feel the sweat beading on this chest and back. Calah's throat suddenly felt as dry as the desert within which he stood. He silently cleared his throat and began to speak. *"My information, Lord, is that you have been betrayed by one of your closest associates."*

Xerxes visibly tensed at this information. He stood to receive the rest of the report.

"My lord, the governor of Babylonia appears to be behind the attempted poisoning."

Xerxes seemed to fly, as he jumped up at the report. *"What?"* He almost screamed. *"It can't be. Zopyros cannot be involved in any conspiracy. His father was one of my father's most trusted allies. It is impossible that he turned so far against my dynasty."*

Xerxes looked with anger at his man-servant. *"This cannot be true, Calah. Your information is wrong."*

Xerxes turned suddenly and took two steps towards his bed. He turned again quickly and he pointed to his door and bellowed, *"leave me, Calah. Take your lies and leave my eyes."*

Calah bowed his head and began to walk away. As the King sulked a slave entered.

"Lord, there is a messenger from Susa. He begs to have an audience with you."

With disdain the King barked at the slave. *"I am in no mood for trivialities. Tell him to give his message to Calah."*

"Lord, he indicated to me that the message he has is for your ears only."

The King stepped forward slapping the slave hard in his head bringing blood to the man's lip. The slave hid his pain and quietly licked his lip, wiping the blood away. *"I am sorry I troubled you, Lord. I will send him away."*

Xerxes stood in front of the slave as the man backed away.

"What is your name?" The King inquired.

"My name is Psusennes, Lord."

"Where are you from, slave?"

"I am Egyptian, lord," the small dark man said. Xerxes was impressed by the way this small man held himself. Xerxes continued his query, *"How did you rise to this position?"*

In his mind Xerxes couldn't comprehend how an Egyptian could be in the presence of the great King, especially without others around. *"Lord, when your courageous troops liberated this city I was bound in chains in the center plaza. I was against this illegal revolt, and because I stayed loyal to your dynasty, I was punished by the Magi cult. My family, Lord, had always been influential within this city. The renegade priests turned us into slaves. I am sorry to say, Lord, that one of my jobs was to burn the dead bodies of your murdered soldiers from the garrison in this city."*

As he spoke, Psusennes spit on the ground mentioning the Magi. *"Your general, Demaratus, found me in chains and decided to elevate me to be your slave."*

Psusennes hesitated and bowing his head continued to speak. *"If you are angry with me my Lord, my unworthy life is yours to take. I swear to you this day, my Lord, my allegiance and my loyalty."*

Xerxes seemed to be in a brief stupor as he stared past the slave thinking. Finally, his eyes refocused looking at Psusennes. *"Repeat your name,"* Xerxes demanded. *"I have forgotten it already." "My name lord is Psusennes." "Psusennes,"* the King murmured to himself as he turned away from the slave. *"Psusennes, do you wish to prove your loyalty to me?"*

"Ask, lord, and it will be carried out."

Xerxes dropped his knife on the floor in front of the slave. Psusennes looked inquisitively at the weapon lying in front of him.

"Pick up the knife, Psusennes."

Xerxes pushed a small table to the man. *"Place your left hand on the table."*

Psusennes immediately obeyed.

"Now," Xerxes went on. *"Cut off the smallest finger on your left hand off with the knife I provided."*

The slave didn't blink. He took the knife in his hand and with a quick stroke chopped off his pinky. To the Great King's surprise there were no screams, no show of any pain. The slave reacted as if he was being asked to drink water out of a cup.

"Rise, Psusennes. You are a slave no more. You have shown the strength that rests in your heart and your loyalty to me. Go out and purchase a fine set of clothing from a local merchant, for tomorrow you will be involved in a ceremony at my new court."

Psusennes had but a cloth over his left hand and picked up his cut off finger. As he left, Xerxes called after him. *"You mentioned an envoy from Susa. Give me a few minutes then show the man in."*

Psusennes began backing away from the King, obviously still in distress and Xerxes reminded him, *"make sure, Psusennes, that there is no one around listening to this conversation. Take care of your hand and remember about tomorrow."*

Xerxes moved back to his chair. He sat again, fading into a daydream, trying to sort out the information that Calah had told him just a few hours earlier. Could it be true? Could Zopyros be behind the attempted poisoning? Loyalty was such a finicky beast, worse than any cat he owned. But like cats, Xerxes mused, it can be purchased for the right price. There was a venal nature to all. For the right price, Xerxes, knew, he could purchase any outcome. People were fickle in their worship of their god, Xerxes thought. How can I assure their loyalty to me? His mind switched without notice to the Greeks. They, too, like any other men, could be bought. Was the Warrior Queen the right person to tempt them? What would they want in return for their loyalty?

His mind raced back to Babylonia. Zopyros. What would have been his purpose? If he didn't know better he would have believed that cursed Ningizzida was behind such an attempt on his life. He bristled as his mind went back to the celebration, when the priest embarrassed him in front of the ruling Babylonians. It came to Xerxes that the goal of the priest all along was not to embarrass him, but to expose his weakness and entrench the priest's control over him. He cursed again to himself.

But, Zopyros! If his attempt had succeeded, what would he have gained? Did he hope to expand his rule past Babylonia? Why would such a loyal man have turned against his King? Xerxes could not recall insulting the man or even having bad thoughts about him. Xerxes cursed to himself. The Babylonians were trying to take advantage of him and it raised his irritation. He was in Memphis with the army and they were stirring up trouble behind his back.

Xerxes was becoming agitated with his thoughts. He took a drink of tea and attempted to slow his heart rate. He finally accepted his own rationalizations. Remember the gods. The gods have supported him and he now had the magic Answerer. The gods must have stopped the assassination attempt, and with their intervention had proven again that they favored his dynasty and his realm. Rather than have the assassination attempt create doubt, Xerxes knew that it had to invigorate him. Between his Egyptian victory and his ability to survive the murder attempt, the young King was finally feeling royal and much more than that. He was feeling indomitable. For the first time in his young reign Xerxes was feeling in charge of his own destiny. The only stain, the only black mark, was this Zopyros allegation. As he thought in contemplation, his silent meditation was broken by Psusennes reentering his chamber. The now freed slave was as silent as he could be, but the movement in the room caught the King's attention. When Psusennes realized that the King was paying attention to him he began to talk. *"My eminence, the envoy from Susa awaits."*

Xerxes pondered Psusennes. He stood without emotion as if nothing had happened within the last few minutes. Xerxes straightened himself and gestured for Psusennes to let the envoy in.

Psusennes turned and motioned to the door. A man entered and walked towards the King, and in an obviously deferent manner fell to his knees. As he did, Psusennes bowed and backed out of the room. The man on his knees finally raised his head and said, *"great King, my master, Queen Artemisia, sent me this great distance to give you a message from her. It is urgent and I'm happy to be able to relay the information in person."*

Before he could go on, the King held his hand up and demanded, *"What is your name, messenger? I have seen you before."*

"My name, great King, is Nabu-na-id. I am the warrior Queen's trusted eunuch."

It took Nabu-na-id almost an hour to accurately reveal the Queen's messages.

****

The next morning was an exceptionally hot day in the fertile Egyptian delta. One sweated even standing still. Xerxes had the Egyptian court assembled in front of him to hear his decrees. There was an air of anticipation and anxiety among the peoples of this city. After all, this was the core of the revolt against the Persian King. He now re-entered the city and people were unsure about the extent of his punishment. There were many rumors flying around, ranging from the young King leveling the city to ashes, while others were less ghastly.

Xerxes himself knew that the Egyptian populaces were not warlike people. They were mostly farmers and herdsman. His father had taught him that they admired strength and would probably not rebel against being ruled. **"The generations have turned them into dogs"**, Darius had told him. The magi and priests, on the other hand, were stubborn and very self-centered. More than once during the history of this great culture they had brought a pharaoh to his knees. Xerxes concluded that he needed to deal harshly with the renegade priests so that their spirit could not be transmitted through the people of this land. He could not show personal weakness or sadistic over reaction. He wanted Egypt to again become a quiet and docile satrap of the realm. His Kingdom collected a large amount of tax from these "sheep".

Most importantly Xerxes had learned that the Egyptian people were very spiritual. Their lives were ruled by their ritual and their belief. And the first task of the great King was to make them believe.

Xerxes wore a white outfit fitting tightly around his waist. He loved showing off his muscular physique. His muscles were accentuated by the oils that were applied. His outfit had a gold shaft that hung to his knees. He was naked from the waist up with only arm and wrist bands to cover his upper body. His wrist and arm bands were made of Lapis Lazuli, a deep blue stone that shone brightly against his sun darkened skin. Half of his head was shaved for this occasion, and this hair hung down from the right side of his head, again ornamented with Lapis stones and ribbons. He carried a large staff of gold and wood with the sacred Egyptian ankh on the top. For this event he left the Answerer behind. It made him anxious not to hold it. Behind him was carried a large tapestry with the pictures of two regal lions each facing away from each other. They sat back to back with the sun rising between them.

Xerxes entered the courtyard walking slowly and showing no facial expression. Amassed in front of him was a majority of the population of this great city. It was a mandatory event. There was a buzz from the crowd until the young King raised his hands to the sky. **"I am Xerxes, son of Darius. I am here to reclaim my city and my peoples. You were my father's children and now you will return to my gracious protection. My very mother came from your stock which makes me also from your womb."**

Xerxes knew that this was a blatant lie. Ho was his step-mother and had no blood connection to him. But he needed to use the association to achieve his objectives. **"You are all my brothers and sisters and I am your protective lord. From this moment on, I will be known as**

Pharaoh Momus the Second, when I am in my Egyptian capital."

A spontaneous cheer arose from the masses. In fact, Xerxes had placed stooges amongst the people, who, at certain times, would act to fuel the mob mentality. **"Now that the disease has been removed from the body of our people, peace and harmony will be restored. I know the people of this city have remained loyal and were not part of the infection."**

He hesitated as another cheer rose.

"I am Xerxes. I am Pharaoh Momus the second, of the greatest lineage the world has known!"

Xerxes looked to heaven. Suddenly a falcon appeared overhead. The bird screeched as it circled. The crowd was transfixed watching the bird circle and finally it put its wings together and streaked to the newly anointed Pharaoh. It suddenly stopped and gently landed on Xerxes outstretched arm.

Again, the people began waving their hands over their heads. But this time, when the Pharaoh raised his amulet above his head, they all fell to their knees and began shouting "Horus, Horus"

"This amulet is sacred among the people. It attests to my power," The Pharaoh pronounced.

At this point the three bound magi were brought into the square. They were raised onto a platform so all could see.

"These men are not who they have claimed to be. They follow the lie. They are not hem-netjer (servants of God). They are not the prophets as they have maintained. Amman Ra does not support them. He rejects them as usurpers."

The Pharaoh raised the amulet and the head of the first bound magi seemed to jump off his shoulders and roll toward the crowd. No guard had moved, no sword had been unsheathed. The crowd gasped in unison, lifting their hands to the air and bowing to the Pharaoh.

"I am Pharaoh Momus the Second. I am Man-God."

With this next pronouncement, the second magi's head flew off his body with blood spurting in every direction. What type of divine intervention was this, the people thought.

"I am today, yesterday, and tomorrow. I am the past and the future. I am Pharaoh Momus, the brother of Amman Ra. I

472

am what you were, what you are, and what you will become. I am Pharaoh forever."

He pointed to the third magi, sitting with an astonished look on his face having watched his two fellow priests beheaded in front of him with no effort. The Pharaoh just pointed his amulet and their heads seemed to just leave their bodies. The Pharaoh looked down at this third priest. He raised his amulet a third time, but the magi's head remained on his shoulders. The crowd seemed to hold their breath in anticipation.

"I am Pharaoh Momus. The guilty will be punished and will walk the underworld for time everlasting."

Xerxes pointed the amulet to the third man and within an instant he seemed to burst into flames. His screams filled the great courtyard but they died as quickly as they began. Even in the bright sunlight of the Egyptian morning, the priest's fire appeared to light the city. The Pharaoh raised both his arms again and said, *"I am the zero point. The chaos of the void starts and ends with me. Ptah has explained the Zep Tepi the genesis story to me and we are one."*

He hesitated as another cheer arose from the masses. *"I am Pharaoh and I have returned to my people."*

Xerxes, the new self-proclaimed Pharaoh of Egypt, waited for the crowd to settle. He then said, **"Sekhmet and Nefertem are both false deities. They are part of the lie. It is Pharaoh's decree that all of their temples and monuments should be either destroyed or rededicated to Ptah. They shall not be worshipped anymore. It is now decreed."**

The Pharaoh again waited a few minutes for the population to ingest the new decree. He continued with all the confidence of a great leader. **"I am Pharaoh, I have the ear of Ptah and we are brothers. Together we will guide our children"**

The Pharaoh again raised his staff and held it up to the morning sun. He turned and made a signal and Psusennes appeared from the background. He was almost unrecognizable in his new outfit. He had chosen red silk adorned with yellow beads. Psusennes' head was now completely shaven. In fact, all the hair on his body was shaved and his chest held the great amulet tattoo.

The Pharaoh raised his staff again as if he were creating a new world order. Psusennes dropped to his knees in front of the Pharaoh and the living God placed his staff on Psusennes' head. He made a grand sweeping gesture and said, **"This man that is now before you has made the**

474

42 declarations. From this moment on he will become my voice in this great land. I raise him to a prophet. He is a servant of the living God. It is Pharaoh's decree that Psusennes is now the great chief of all artisans."

The Pharaoh hesitated again. His eyes wandered across the masses for a second and then he spoke, *"his words should be heard as my words. His steps should be seen as my steps. His decisions are my decisions. Although my brother, Achaemenes, will be the new governor of this satrap, Psusennes will be his head priest. I am Pharaoh and I am God and I decree this truth!"*

PERSIA

CHAPTER XVIII -
ECBATANA

After his dramatics in Memphis, the great King decided to allow his Immortals to finish the cleanup in Egypt so he could return home. Before he left he was assured that the Immortals had retaken Elephantine in southern Egypt, essentially ending the rebellion. Xerxes himself had cut the head off the serpent by executing the religious leaders and his troops buried the body. But Xerxes left Egypt a troubled man. His Immortals had not performed up to his high expectations, and the troops led by Demaratus outperformed them at every turn. When he was a young boy, he had always heard of the reputation of the Immortals as fearless warriors without equal. Although the Immortals he did accomplish their goals, they did not appear as disciplined or as organized as he had hoped. When Xerxes decided to lead the troops to Egypt he had first gone to his teacher, Hamath, to seek advice. Hamath had a reputation of being a courageous warrior and leader. His strategies were legendary. Some believed that without Hamath, Darius, the King's father, would not have been able to conquer as much land as he had. "The Great Teacher", as Xerxes came to know him, had an uncanny ability to anticipate the enemy's strategy. Hamath had urged the young King to accompany the troops and prove to the masses his omnipotence.

Although he personally felt more in control of his Kingdom, Xerxes now had to seriously reconsider his Greek expedition. The young King had lost his black and white understanding of the world and the grey that he found in its place troubled him. As he passed Tyre on the way back to Persia, he thought about how much easier it would be if Artemisia could secure the submission of the Greeks without him having to take his massive army to that peninsula. He was realizing that his rule did not have to be dominated by blood to be effective. And although it would have been obvious to most, to Xerxes it was a revelation. If the Athenians fought anything like the ex-Spartan King proclaimed they could, Xerxes would have to reflect on this approach. He was taught not to be a fool. His father, Darius, was a strong and assertive leader, but he was not impulsive or impetuous. Even though his blood burned for his rightful revenge and the conquest of Egypt excited him, Xerxes felt as though he was now sober, not stained by the intoxication of blind rage. But his new revelations had created questions about the attack on Athens. Before conquering Egypt, the King was committed to another direction. He wanted to crush the Greeks. Now the decision wasn't as simple, as weight had to be given to preserve what was his.

After days of back and forth in his thought process, Xerxes called Hamath to his council. The great teacher looked the same to the young King as he remembered from his childhood. Xerxes had not seen the man for a few months, but every time he saw him his mind drifted back to his childhood.

Hamath was not a particularly large man but he seemed to have a presence about him. He seemed to demand attention. Xerxes was always aware of this about his teacher but he could never put his finger on what that meant or the reason for its truth. Hamath was almost the only man who appeared to evoke this type of reaction in the young King. He walked into the small room where the King sat and his face told nothing of his emotions or his feelings. Hamath had always practiced his empty stare. Over the course of his long life the great teacher felt that others inability to read his emotions was one of his greatest attributes. He saw the King, but Hamath showed no reaction. Xerxes watched him enter and he knew that the great man was happy to see him. Although others were confused by Hamath's icy stare, Xerxes believed that he could read through the iron mask to interpret the message in the emptiness.

Xerxes smiled when he recognized his teacher, *"Hamath, I am honored by your presence."*

The great man bowed and spoke, *"No, young lord, it is I who is honored. As always, I am at your service."*

Xerxes walked to the great man and put his hands on his shoulders. The two men slowly leaned forward and touched foreheads. For at least ten seconds the two men stood with foreheads touching. The King then backed off, and as he withdrew he began to speak. *"I have learned many things, my teacher, since I have become King."*

He turned in a pensive retreat. *"I cannot trust many people and my insights have left me questioning many truths that I have held. The certainties that I knew as a child are now less pure. And with each turn of the wheel of history my balance is undone. Hunting is simple, my teacher. You stalk and you kill."*

"Not so simple as your words suggest," Hamath retorted. *"You must plan to stalk. Much insight is needed to find the pray. You must put yourself at an advantage when the pray is located. To kill the pray you must anticipate and react. Not simple at all."*

The King raised his right hand. He showed it to his teacher with his fingers outstretched. *"I have grown up, my teacher, and the world is different than I expected. There are few definitive. There are only questions. My feet now walk with hesitancy as the ground is forever moving."*

Xerxes gazed out over the desert. After a moment he smiled again and turned to his teacher. *"But Hamath, I have been very disappointed in the Immortals. While I was growing up I believed that the Immortals were invincible. The Immortals were not as efficient as the Spartans. Their generals hesitated and their men were more show than substance. I fear now that my childhood conclusions were only an illusion of youth."*

The King suddenly had a more serious look. *"I need your advice. Suddenly I have hesitation about taking a large army to Athens.'* The great teacher smiled to himself and turned toward the young monarch.

'Are you afraid of the Greeks?"

The King turned quickly to his teacher and anger burned on his face as his cheeks turned red.

"I fear no race, Hamath."

"I know, young King, I know. But my question was not whether you, personally, are afraid of the Greeks. Are you fearful that your army will not defeat them?"

The King turned aside and began walking to the window. *"My army performed poorly, Hamath. Only the Greek, Demaratus, performed up to my expectations."*

His face changed expression. *"I am almost ashamed, Hamath. We conquered and yet I am humbled."*

481

The teacher looked the young King in the eyes.

"Remember, lord, a victory against the Greeks will depend on preparation, information and strategy, not on pure strength."

The King turned. *"Also,"*

Hamath remarked, *"Your navy will have a big part in the victory. You must continually supply your army as they move"*

The King's face softened. He jumped on the last comment *"So, you think we can destroy the Greeks?"*

Now it was Hamath's turn to have his face soften.

"I think you can defeat the Greeks, my Lord. But remember, there is another matter. To take an army and navy the distance that is required for the victory will cost a large sum of the treasury. And even in victory there will be a heavy price to pay."

He then hesitated to let the young monarch digest that information.

"It would be much less expensive but would take almost as much skill to buy their allegiance."

Again, the teacher hesitated. *"I heard that you are sending Artemisia to meet the Greeks."*

The King nodded his head in confirmation.

"I have some ideas to complement this approach and improve our chances for success."

The young King was contemplative. He turned to the teacher. *"I am concerned, Hamath. I am interested in your wisdom. We do need to discuss your thoughts about Delphi and our diplomatic mission."*

"I will tell you everything, my King."

"Good, Hamath, Good."

He turned again and smiled, walking up to his teacher.

"Hamath, I need you to do something special for me."

"My life is yours, my Lord. Since you were a young child it always has been and you know that."

Xerxes smiled again *"You will accompany the Warrior Queen to Greece."*

"What, my Prince?" Hamath responded in startled shock.

"Hamath, your hearing is fine. You see, I need someone to carry out the secret negotiations while Artemisia makes a mockery out of the public talks."

"Lord, if you think she will make a mockery why do you send her in the first place?"

"She is a great warrior, but her judgment can be tainted by her lust for the fight. Hamath, with her brash appearance and her blustery exuberance, she will make your secret discussions that much more successful. Besides, I think Artemisia would rather bloody the Greeks than listen to their words. It wouldn't be beyond that woman to undermine the talk only for the opportunity to take her ships to Athens and dominate their weak navy. It would be like a hungry dog among the chickens."

Both men laughed, but Hamath turned serious.

"You know, to conquer the Greeks you will need that woman. Some call her undefeatable."

"Exactly, Hamath. Precisely why I send her to Greece. She will also be scouting. I need to know the souls of those people, and who else but my greatest ally to do such an evaluation."

Hamath smiled at the young Monarch. *"You know what she will say, lord. All else pales in comparison to her. Whereas Demaratus will tell you only of their strengths, Artemisia will tell you only of their weaknesses."*

The King smiled as he listened. Hamath went on. *"Yes, I have heard of this Demaratus. He was a King in Sparta. He says that the Spartans are the world's fiercest warriors. They live to fight, he says. Supposedly they are hard men who have no mercy for others. I would like to meet one before we confront them."*

"Aha," the King shouted. *"So you are now looking forward to going to Delphi. Good, good. I knew you would change your mind."*

He turned away from Hamath, and smiling to himself mentioned, *"I have heard that the Spartans will also be at Delphi."*

The King turned pensive. He looked directly at his teacher.

"I have another problem, my friend."

485

Again, he took two steps away from Hamath.

"When I was readying to go to Egypt there was an attempt on my life."

Hamath dropped to his knees in horror. He did not want to embarrass the King by letting him know that he had already heard the story.

"My servant vowed to find out the source of the attempt. In Egypt he came to me and told me he believed that the Babylonian governor, Zopyros, was behind the poisoning."

Hamath looked surprised at this piece of news. Xerxes had not remembered ever seeing that expression on his teacher's face. Xerxes went on, *"but then I received an envoy from Artemisia bringing into question the information that Calah uncovered."*

Hamath thought for a few minutes. Then he said, *"so, my lord, this boils down to which person you trust the most?"*

The servant entered the King's sleeping quarters. He was out of breath, obviously running to deliver the message to the great King. He was also anxious because he knew that he might have to wake the Monarch and he didn't want to fall out of favor from such an event. When he arrived at the chamber he was surprised that the guards were both standing. He approached the first one with his urgent request to enter the King's quarters. He was told that his request would be presented to Xerxes but that he would have to wait for the King to be engaged in other business. Before the servant reluctantly took a seat outside of the King's chamber, he pleaded with the guard that his information was pressing and that the King needed to know what was happening. The servant was obviously shaken as he sat waiting. He was sweating and was trembling throughout his body. He tried to breathe to control his heart from jumping out of his chest. It took almost an hour but eventually the King's door opened, and a beautiful woman strode confidently out. She clearly wasn't a slave or a servant girl. She was browned skinned and statuesque. She strode confidently from the chamber as a high official or a general would. He tried hard but couldn't stop himself from staring. Luckily for this servant, this woman didn't stare back, but only kept her vision in front of her. He didn't realize who the viper was that he was watching.

The guards bowed in deference as she passed. The woman strode passed where the servant sat and seemed to stop for an instant as she began moving by his place. He wasn't sure, but he thought he sensed a smile on her lips as she hesitated. The servant got the feeling that the woman already knew the information that he was about to relay to the King. Of course that was impossible, but there was something about her that was bewitching to the man. After she passed his position the servant couldn't take his eyes off her long legs as she slowly walked away. Then without warning she stopped and turned around catching his stare. The servant put both hands over his face fearing that he would be severely punished for the transgression. He didn't see the Warrior Queen smile as she continued to leave.

It took a few minutes for the flush leave his face. Suddenly the King's guards were standing over him urging him to rise, that the Monarch was waiting for him to deliver his message.

The servant flew off his chair almost jolting himself toward the King's chamber. He then straightened himself, composed his racing heart, and walked into the King's chamber. The servant had trouble focusing on anything when he entered the room. He immediately threw himself to the floor as if he had done something wrong. He almost crawled forward as the sweat covered his back. When the servant finally looked up it appeared as though the King was oblivious to his presence. He was unsure on how to proceed - should he speak or keep silent until he was spoken to.

After almost two minutes the King broke the silence, *"I am waiting on you."*

"Lord, there is an envoy here from Babylon."

The King appeared distracted. After the servant spoke Xerxes stood and paced slowly in front of the prostrated man. The King then stopped and directly asked, *"why is it important for me to speak to a Babylonian?"*

"Lord, my master is Nin Nibru, a religious leader of my people."

"Your people?!" Xerxes now appeared agitated and the servant immediately felt the wave of emotion that came from the man standing above him.

"Your people, Lord! I mean no disrespect by my words, lord. I am only a poor man who serves his master."

The King suppressed his anger and consciously withdrew his emotion from the discussion.

"What is your name, servant?"

"My name is Bit Sa'alli, lord"

"Well, Bit Sa'alli. I have heard rumors about your master, Nin Nibru. Tell me why he deserves my attention."

Bit Sa'alli felt the pressure of his statements fall directly on his head. The servant was poorly trained, but he did understand that he was in jeopardy. *"Lord, I am not a philosopher. I have never learned to speak well."*

The King reached down to the man and lifted him off the floor. He held the smaller man up to his face.

"I will cut your throat now Bit Sa'alli. I am the great King. You have no allegiance but to me. Your master means nothing here. Either I hear from you or your blood will wash my floor this evening."

Bit Sa'alli was now visibly shaking. He tried to steady himself and began to talk, *"Nin Nibru is a holy man lord. He is one of the apostles of the great teacher, Ningizzida."*

The burning in the King's chest and stomach became alive. He could taste the bile in his throat at the thought of the rogue priest. The King put on a bland face and hid his hatred. He swallowed hard and attempted to downplay his true feelings. *"Ningizzida, I have also heard this name. But I thought he was dead."*

"He is lord, but my master is one of his former students. He saw the prophet Ningizzida, rise to heaven."

"Prophet? Yes prophet!" the King sardonically remarked. Xerxes gathered himself again. He smiled to himself as he knew that the hands of the prophet were kept in a box in his palace at Susa.

"Sa'alli, tell your master I will see him this evening. But remind him that I am the only prophet of God. All others bow to me. I am Pharaoh".

****

Nin-Nibru was prepared, or at least he thought he was. This was the moment he had trained for since he converted to the cause of the renegade priest. The trap was set. Nin-Nibru expelled the anxiety from his body and his mind. His teacher had him practiced in the meditation of nothingness. He had spent the last few hours in deep thought, releasing pressures and cementing the internal understanding that his time in the limelight had arrived. Ningizzida had assured him that their secret remained intact. But even with the assurance of the great man, Nin-Nibru couldn't help but feel deep in his heart that their

491

charade would be discovered. He worried that he would present himself to the King and the monarch would see through him to the truth. As the anxiety rose, he again pushed it out of unconsciousness. Nin-Nibru couldn't afford to think about how this day would end. He needed to focus on his performance in front of the great King. It was up to Nin-Nibru to convince the monarch of the great deception. The first part of the plan, the poisoning at Susa was successfully achieved. The poison was supposed to fail. It was a planned miss. The second part of the plan was to leak the information that the assassination attempt came from the governor of Babylonia. This was a very tricky part of the ruse. The conspirators knew that the governor was a friend of the King and his betrayal would be a hard pill to swallow. It was part of Nin-Nibru's performance to solidify the conclusion that the King had been betrayed by a friend.

There had been other things set in place to convince the young King of the truth of this deception. A document had been generated and released to spies indicating that the Babylonian governor had grandiose plans. Was it believed? Nobody knew. The conspirators had tried to gain information about their success without finding out anything. They also knew that they had an ace in the hole with the King's personal servant spreading gentle and delicate musings in their favor. But was it enough? Nin-Nibru did not know. He went deeper into his meditation. Clear your mind, become nothingness. He drifted farther and farther into the void letting his consciousness fade away. Throughout his training, Nin Nibru had difficulty with the meditative experience. He felt it was like trying to catch the wind. There were days when the young acolyte struggled with even a shallow trance. But today on the most important day of his life, he seemed to be hitting his stride. He was descending deeper than he had ever had. All sights and sounds seemed to vanish as the nothingness overcame him.

In such a state time had no meaning. Nin-Nibru had no sense of how long he was in his stupor when the servant entered his chamber. When he regained his senses, climbed the ladder back to reality, he realized that he was drenched. It was if he had swum through a river. He called for a servant to bring him fresh clothes to change into when he brought his message before the great King. It was time and Nin-Nibru was ready.

Calah led the young acolyte into the great chamber. Outside of the room the two men had exchanged quick glances. Nin Nibru walked as straight as he could even though his legs trembled. He was clothed in the most formal of outfits. He wore a dark black robe with two stripes of gold that fell from his shoulders to his knees. He tried very hard to maintain his outward composure, not wanting the King to see his tension. As he walked he was having some difficulty focusing, not really noticing the other people who were in the room.

He approached where the great King sat and bowed down, dropping to one knee. He stayed with his head down and waited for some sign that he should rise. No such indication came and Nin-Nibru stayed in the prone position. When he finally raised his head, he noticed that there were five Immortals standing behind the monarch. Although he hadn't considered it before, he didn't understand why the situation made him anxious. Although he tried to keep his eyes in front of him, he scanned to the sides of the great King. His biggest shock came when he noticed the tall woman standing to the King's right. Her black hair was pulled back and she wore both a large scabbard and had a pearled knife exposed at waist level. Nin Nibru had heard of this sea witch. The rumors about her had spread through the Mesopotamian area like wild fire. But in truth, little was known in Babylonia about the Warrior Queen.

Calah broke the silence. *"Lord, may I present to you the priest's representative from Babylonia, Nin Nibru."*

Xerxes remained silent at the introduction. Calah continued, *"Lord, Nin-Nibru would like to offer you a tribute to your greatness and the loyalty of the new rulers of God's city."*

Again, Xerxes looked like a frozen statue staring past his servant.

Calah turned and motioned towards the door and a series of slaves entered the great chamber. With them they brought a large box. As it was hauled in, Nin Nibru stood and faced the great King. He began to speak even though there was no indication that the King was ready to hear his presentation. *"Lord, I am Nin-Nibru and I would like to present myself as a representative of your great city of Babylonia."*

Xerxes finally changed his expression and looked directly at the young priest. He slowly stood and in a tempered fashion began to speak.

"You are a priest?"

"I am, lord."

"Did your lord, Zopyros, send you here?"

"No, Lord, Zopyros did not send me. He no longer leads the great city."

Xerxes took a step forward as his face tensed. *"What happened to my governor?"*

"Lord, I am sorry to report that Zopyros betrayed the Empire."

Nin-Nibru paused as if expecting a tirade from the King. But to his surprise the young monarch just stared through him. He continued. *"Belshimanni, one of the great leaders of our elder's council, exposed information that implicated Zopyros in a plot to assassinate you. Thank god it failed. Zopyros had distorted visions of his own importance, and he believed that if you were removed from the head of the Empire, he could establish a new Assyrian dynasty. Zopyros then approached Belshimanni to gain his alliance. But Belshimanni was loyal to your Kingdom. He outmaneuvered Zopyros and was able to undermine this coup attempt. Belshimanni was supported by loyalists who stormed the palace and took the renegade prisoner. Belshimanni then assumed control of the city and reaffirmed the loyalty of the new government to you, lord."*

"So why is Belshimanni not standing in front of me. Why does he send a priest?"

There was stillness in the chamber as many of those present tried to digest the information that they had just received. Xerxes broke the silence with a stern question. ***"Where is Zopyros?"***

Nin-Nibru swallowed hard before answering.

"Lord, Belshimanni could not allow a man to live who would attempt to take the life of our beloved King."

"Zopyros is dead?" the King asked.

"He is, lord."

Xerxes walked forward toward the young priest and pointed to the cedar box that was placed on the floor. He walked over to it and summoned a slave to attend to him. Without words he pointed to the box indicating that he wanted it opened. The slave bent over and removed the wooden pegs that held the top in place. As the top was lifted off the slave gasped while looking into the opening. The King showed no affect, keeping his face emotionless to not betray his inner rage.

Xerxes turned to the young priest. ***"Who ordered the execution of my governor?"***

Nin-Nibru felt his heart sink. **"Lord, the high council of the city recognized the danger of this traitor and decided it was the only true punishment for his crime. My Lord, Zopyros, declared a new Babylonian Empire. Belshimanni reacted quickly to squelch the uprising before it gained a footing with the people."**

"I see, so Belshimanni is a hero!"

Xerxes said as he turned away from the young priest. As he did, Artemisia took a step forward from her background position and seemed to stare through the priest. She then smiled as she quickly retreated behind a large hanging scroll behind the King. Quite descended over the gathering until the Warrior Queen emerged a few minutes later. With Artemisia walked an obviously tortured and beaten man in heavy chains. His face was swollen with large welts and his own blood covered his clothes. Artemisia almost dragged him to the front of the King. She grabbed his hair and lifted his head up to the young priest. Nin-Nibru recognized his friend, Belshimanni.

Again, the priest could feel the blood rushing to his cheeks as he recognized the bound man. Next to him, Calah took a noticeable step backwards, responding to the surprise appearance. Artemisia seemed to be enjoying the play as her

498

smile widened. Her right arm was on her sword head as she held the hair of Belshimanni. Xerxes finally demanded, **"I will ask again, priest. Who ordered the execution of my governor!?"**

Again Nin-Nibru felt shaky. His mouth became so dry that he was having difficulty formulating words. Then, sensing the anxiety that the priest was feeling, Xerxes began to approach the young man. He knew the man would not answer his question for it meant his immediate death. He walked to within a breath of the priest and hissed, **"You were introduced to me as Nin-Nibru. But what was your given name?"**

"My name, lord, is Nin-Nibru."

The King's hand was quick as he backhanded the priest across the mouth. Nin-Nibru backed a few steps from the assault. There was an obvious tremor to his voice now, the controlled presentation quickly vanishing.

"Did you not hear my question, priest? What was your given name?"

Nin-Nibru dropped his head and in a low voice in a whispering tone muttered, **"Jehoash, lord."**

"Jehoash, an Assyrian name. From what family do you come?"

Xerxes was not pacing back and forth in front of the priest. It was as if the Priest had become a child, as he appeared to retreat into his own body, shrinking in front of the assembled nobility and the Man-God.

"My family name is Gaseen, lord."

"Gaseen," Xerxes mouthed. *"Is that not a trade name?"*

Jehoash shook his head in affirmation.

"Well, the son of a tradesman becomes a priest and reaches the highest levels of government in God's city. Tell me Jehoash, how does this happen?"

"I found God, Lord."

Xerxes smiled and winked at the Queen. *"You found God or you met God? Did you find a man that rose out of a dungeon being carried by celestial light? Yes, I've heard these absurd child's tales."*

The King turned away again, not waiting for a response. *"Tell me priest. Why did you change your name? Were you trying to hide from something?"*

Nin-Nibru was so anxious he could barely speak. He knew that his life was hanging in the balance and quickly slipping from his control. Seeing Belshimanni in chains really threw the priest into internal disorder. He wasn't prepared for this circumstance and his logic now escaped him. After the King asked about his name, Nin Nibru just stared into space, apparently just drifting away. The King did not back off as he verbally continued to press the young priest.

"Are you a liar, priest? Have you lost your tongue, son of Gaseen?"

Xerxes quickly turned. With a very fluid movement he knocked the priest to the floor. Nin-Nibru was stunned as he sprawled over the floor. The King bent down over the priest. In a hushed voice he said, whispering into his ear, **"I know the truth, priest. I know that the pig, Ningizzida, is behind this. Do you really think that this charade could fool an Archimedean? I know when you breathe and I know when you shit. My ears are everywhere. Your life is over, priest. It is time for you to pray to your god and hope that he offers you salvation for these sins."**

Xerxes rose and turned to Artemisia. He pointed the Answerer in the air and with a fluid motion, Belshimanni lost his head. The cut was so clean and sharp that little blood was splashed. The body seemed to hang in space for a moment and then toppled over. A smile covered the warrior Queen's face as she returned the blade to its holder.

Xerxes again turned to the prostrate priest.

"How you die priest, is up to you. Either you decide to be truthful with me and I will have the Queen make it quick and painless, or if you maintain this fairy tale, the pain will burn through your body for an eternity. You will cry out for mercy and all ears will be deaf. I will burn your body from the inside out."

Xerxes withdrew from the man allowing him to consider his death. Nin-Nibru shook noticeably. Sweat flowed from his back and face. His mind was lost as he couldn't clear his thoughts. Xerxes waited and then reproached the young man lying flat in front of him.

"Tell me, priest, who was behind this illegal revolution?"

Nin-Nibru was now noticeably crying with his emotions out of control. He started shaking his head in denial of the question. Xerxes pulled his head up from the floor and it was covered with tears and mucus from his nose.

"I asked you a question, priest. Who was behind this revolution?"

He now yelled at the priest repeating his question. Nin-Nibru shook his head. Finally, he sighed, *"Lord, the revolution was carried out by Zopyros."*

Xerxes threw the man's head down and it bounced off the floor. He was clearly frustrated, but he seemed to restrain himself as he turned back to the priest. Nin-Nibru's head was now split open from the contact with the floor.

"I will not ask again. Tell me priest. Who else was involved in this conspiracy?"

The priest denied any knowledge of such an event. Xerxes turned to Artemisia and shook his head. The Queen drew her sword and walked to the prostrated man. In a single motion the sword went toward his neck, but it seemed to stop in air, only drawing a drop of blood. With her foot she came down on the priest's hand, pinning it to the floor. A slave simultaneously appeared from behind the scrolls bearing a brick bowl. He casually, but with apparent purpose, walked to the prostrated man and sat by his pinned hand. He took out a red-hot spike from the bowl and stuck it under the priest's middle finger nail. There was a heavy moment of silence and then Jehoash let out a blood curdling scream. His entire body shook with pain as the slave inserted another spike under another finger. The entire entourage in the room seemed to wince and many turned their head at the sight. Again, Xerxes approached the man. This time Xerxes was clearly in more control. He leaned down and spoke to the priest.

"Nin-Nibru or Jehoash, whatever you call yourself. The pain will continue. All I need from you are names of the conspirators and this will end."

Nin-Nibru was only barely hanging onto to awareness. He was having trouble formulating any response to the question as his consciousness seemed to drift. Xerxes bent again to speak with the man. *"I am growing tired, Jehoash."*

The Queen removed her foot from the man's right hand and stepped over the now barely moving body. She looked at the monarch and uttered,

"He is barely alive, my Prince."

Xerxes looked frustrated. He looked at a slave and pointed to him.

"Bring water and throw it on him."

504

The slave followed the King's order and Jehoash jumped when the water hit him. His eyes fluttered and it almost appeared as though he was having a seizure. Again, the slave again threw water on the prone body and again the priest shuttered.

Jehoash turned his head almost unconsciously opening his eyes for a second as the King bellowed at him. He seemed to look at the King's servant, Calah, as he stood near the event. The gesture by the priest didn't go unnoticed, as Artemisia glanced her head in the direction that Jehoash looked. Her eyes met Calah's and she saw fear. The Warrior Queen smiled to herself in recognition of what had just happened. She raised her sword and pointed it at the small servant. Calah seemed to congeal with her movement. She looked again at him with her gaze stiffening.

"You are the conspirator," the Queen accused, again stepping over the fallen priest with her sword raised leaving it pointed at the servant. Xerxes looked stunned at the possible revelation as the Queen drew closer to him. Artemisia towered over the small man, having to lower her sword to his eye level. She was smiling by now and Calah was now obviously anxious. He looked at the King in a pleading fashion.

"Lord, I resent this accusation. I am your most loyal servant. I have always been loyal to both you and your father."

Xerxes appeared confused not knowing how to respond to this accusation. Artemisia looked at the monarch with a questioning glance.

"Who do you trust?"

Xerxes recalled his teacher, Hamath, asking him

He finally looked to some of his present guards and they approached Calah, and through his piercing protests dragged him off. The Queen appeared disappointed and stepped back toward the prostrated, almost unconscious priest. Xerxes walked over and kicked the priest. There was little movement from Jehoash. He looked at Artemisia and cocked his head. The Queen walked over and nonchalantly plunged her sword through Nin-Nibru's chest.

"You realize," the Queen remarked facing the young monarch, *"that the renegade priest still lives."*

Silently Xerxes turned away and spit on the ground. Calah was killed in a most brutal manner. Long hot spikes were pieced through his body and his internal organs burned before his skin.

****

Hamath walked through the hall approaching Xerxes' sleeping chamber. He had heard about the incident with the Babylonian earlier in the day but all he knew were rumors. He found the King sitting on a stool toward the corner of the room. He appeared pensive as the great teacher entered the room.

"You are troubled, my King?"

"I am troubled, Hamath, I am troubled. The last few months have been difficult for me."

Hamath stopped surprised by the honesty of the young monarch. He waited for the King to say what he needed. But after a minute, Hamath became a little concerned as Xerxes just stared off passed his teacher.

"My friend, I learned many things growing up. They aren't what I expected."

He looked at his teacher with child-like eyes. Xerxes continued his expose.

"You taught me about power. I particularly remember you explaining to

me about boldness. Do you remember, Hamath? I had just lost a sword fight with one of the slaves. I could not have been more than eight or nine. After the fight my pride was hurt. I remember trying to hold back my tears at the defeat. You told me that when someone hesitates, either in a fight or in a political battle, the enemy gains the advantage. You convinced me, Hamath, that in any situation, daring movement disorients your opposition as hesitancy empowers them. We sat outside one night as the clouds gathered on the horizon. You asked me how the storm was like a warrior."

The King smiled
to answer your inquiry. I finally said that the storm is like a warrior because of their dark foreboding natures. You laughed at me Hamath. Do you remember? You laughed out loud. I thought my answer was the only possible one but you knew better. I stayed angry at you for a long period of time. Do you remember what your answer was, my teacher?"

"I remember, Lord. I told you that the lightning struck without warning. It burned everything in its path. It attacked decisively."

"Yes, Hamath. You also said that nobody remembers the rain. You always

508

remembered the thunder and lightning. You see, my teacher, I do remember what you have taught me."

Xerxes again appeared dysphoric.

"Do you remember it all, Hamath? You once took me out to watch a family of lions. We stayed out for two weeks living in the trees. I smelled worse than the beasts when we returned. We watched the lions stalk, we watched them feast. You had me describe how their hierarchy worked. You pointed out how they exploit fear in other animals and within the pride itself."

Xerxes paused, then continued, "I have found Hamath, that I am much more comfortable in battle, either with the army or in competition. When one fights it is clean and pure. A winner and a loser. But politics, my teacher, is not for lions but for rats and scorpions. My generals might disappoint me with their lack of skill, but they don't betray me or the Empire. In politics, you never know who is a rat or who a lion."

Xerxes looked at his teacher and put his arm on his shoulder.

"At least I can always trust you, my friend."

Hamath crossed his arms over his chest. He began to pace in front of the monarch.

"It is a bitter lesson, my Prince. Trust is like the wind. Its direction and force is always changing. You must be very careful whose hands you put your fate into. Most men are weak my Prince. Remember that. They make decisions out of fear, not dedication. Many men wear ceremonial masks to cover their own fears and truths. The Babylonian priest thought that by changing his name, he would change the man. He did not."

Having known Xerxes from his youth, Hamath was one of the few people allowed to call Xerxes, Prince. Xerxes had always heard the term from his beloved teacher so it never registered as anything but normal. But if another used the term, swift justice would follow.

Hamath continued. *"The servant, Calah, is a snake. Even when your father was alive, there were rumors of his treachery. I'm glad you removed this vermin from our Empire. My Prince, our people have been betrayed many times in our history."*

Hamath changed the direction of the discussion.

"My Prince, I am glad that you are sending Artemisia to negotiate with the treacherous and deceptive Greeks. The Greeks promise much and deliver little. They undermined your father in the Ionian revolt and further embarrassed us at Marathon."

"I know Hamath, I know. It eats at me every minute of my life. I can taste their blood in my mouth."

"Be careful, my Prince. It is easy to allow your anger to control your decision. It would serve the Empire well if we didn't have to take our armies to Athens. I know you have begun the preparation for the assault. But such a war will bleed our resources. You know, my King, that my specialty is war. But there is more to rule than forceful power. Many of our satraps have begun testing our resolve. If we must take our army so many miles, other parts of the Empire could be lost. They will take advantage, even though I have no second thoughts that you have the will and the soldiers to defeat the Greeks. But I believe, my Prince, that we will be stronger by negotiating peace with them."

"This is difficult for me, Hamath. Anger is strong within my bones. I fear that if we don't bloody them they will think we are weak."

"You have shown your strength in Egypt and you will again show it in Babylonia. The Greeks will hear about the superiority of your army. Do not make decisions out of fear, my Prince. One tree will burn but the forest still stands. You must make choices with the forest in mind, not just one tree."

Xerxes thought.

"I understand, Hamath, I understand."

After a few seconds, Xerxes asked, *"Hamath, I know I asked you before but I am still uncertain. Tell me again, what do you know about Delphi and the Oracle?"*

The great teacher's face became very serious.

"My Prince, I know some people who have visited the great oracle. They say that the priestess sees the future. It scares me, Lord. I can't touch it, but from what I hear, the god, Apollo, speaks through the priestess. I believe this to be true, Lord. I am glad I am going with the Queen to see this phenomenon for myself."

Xerxes quieted. He had decided to confide his strategy to his teacher before leaving Susa, but even so he was hesitant. He walked over to Hamath and took him by the shoulder.

"I am also curious about this Greek named Themistocles. I hear of his great leadership. I need to know about his spirit if he leads the self-righteous Greeks. But, Hamath, before we discuss this, I have some other business to complete."

Xerxes motioned for a slave. The man rushed into the room and fell to his knees. Xerxes didn't wait for the slave to rise. *"**Send for my generals, Megabyzus and Mardonius.**"*

PERSIA

CHAPTER XIX - THE EMISSARIES

Ningizzida had just heard the news about Nin Nibru. He mourned deeply for his student. The man had saved his life and brought him back into prominence. He knew immediately that the plan had failed and that the revolution would be crushed. Even though his people were totally in command of all the strategic positions in the city and the surrounding area, the priest knew that they could not stand up to the power that the Persian King would bring against them. He was brazened but was no fool. His only hope was deception and subterfuge. Ningizzida slipped into a quick depression with the death of his acolyte. For two days he almost became catatonic, not being able to move or ingest food. One of his other students became so concerned about his condition that he drenched his teacher in ice water in the hopes of lifting him out of his stupor. Although he exploded with anger, Ningizzida eventually was in his student's debt for not letting him fall too deep into his darkness. With the unsuccessful ruse, Ningizzida knew that he had to move his infantile government into underground exile. The Persian horde would be falling on his beautiful city and would, without mercy, purge any of his followers.

Although the priest would not admit it privately, he had considered what to do if his plan failed. The satrap of Babylonia bordered the river Euphrates. He had previously hidden in the high country north of Babylonia in Assyria. But he suspected that his government would be searched for in that area. So Ningizzida's plan was to lead his people

south along the Euphrates to the holy
city of Ur. He would lay a fake trail
north through Sippar to the ancient city
of Ashur. He knew that the followers he
sent north would pay for his deception
with their lives. He was hoping that
their sacrifice would lead the wolves
away from his entourage. Their sacrifice
would be worth their lives if their death
assured that the rest of the government
would escape. This meant that Ningizzida
was back to square one. His anger and
resentment of the Persian King grew
geometrically after the death of his
acolyte. He berated himself for not
poisoning the young King when he had the
opportunity. Another foolish and deadly
mistake. He did not think there was room
in his heart for more hatred than he
already felt for the young monarch. But
he had learned that there was plenty of
room left. He could taste the foul
flavor of bitterness in his throat.
Ningizzida swore to himself that the
Persian King would not get away with
this. But just what was he angry at?
Was he angry that he could not wield
power or upset that the King outsmarted
him? The priest really didn't care. He
was frustrated and he wanted to cause
pain. The pain he wanted to create could
only be satisfied with the King's blood.
Now the priest had to also think about
his people. He would abandon Babylonia
in the hope that the Persians would not

take their vengeance out on innocents and raze the city itself.

He sat by himself looking at the horizon. He looked east towards the King's residence. In a soft voice he breathed, **"it is not over, Xerxes. You think that you have won but you haven't. My victory is only delayed. I am an old man, but I will outlive you. I will have you before I die. I swear it!"**

The priest raised his hand in a fist. He shook it at the sky.

* * * *

Mardonius was the first of the generals to arrive at the King's residence. Mardonius came before the King, being humbled by his less than stellar performance during the Egyptian campaign. Mardonius had put down rebellions before. He made his reputation putting down the revolt in Lydia and restructuring the Ionian peninsula after its failed rebellion.

This general had a long and detailed history of great successes and spectacular failures. Before Marathon, Mardonius had gained the confidence of Xerxes' father, Darius, and was given a fleet to lead the Persians against the Greek isles. His entire fleet was destroyed in a storm off the coast of

Mount Ethos.   Twenty thousand Persians were lost in that storm and Darius relieved by Mardonius, of duty. Darius believed that the gods had turned away from Mardonius.   Darius replaced Mardonius with two generals, Datis and Artephemes.   For their failure at Marathon, Darius blamed Mardonius, even though he was already relieved. Datis immediately lost his head.   Darius couldn't disconnect the colossal collapse on the Marathon beach from Mardonius. Xerxes' father was so angry at the failure that if Mardonius wasn't the son of his closest friend and relative, Gobryas, Darius would have executed the general upon his return. Darius settled for expulsion from the military.   When Xerxes became King he bowed to the pleas that came from many of his relatives to reinstate the old general.   After what occurred in Egypt, Xerxes was now second guessing his decision.

Even though retaking Babylonia was an easy assignment, Xerxes was not going to give it to Mardonius.   He wanted Mardonius at this meeting so that he could humble him in front of the other generals.   He knew that Megabyzus was going to be the general to retake the pearl city.   Xerxes wanted to see Mardonius' shame of not being chosen. He would not make an overt issue of the disappointment that he felt in Mardonius. He would just stare at the general while he made the decision. Xerxes knew he didn't need words to make his point. He knew Mardonius would not show his disillusionment in front of the King. But he also knew that the general would be bleeding inside by the unspoken insult.

When Mardonius entered the King's chamber, Xerxes pointed to the chair by the side of his bed, indicating that he wanted the general to sit. There was no verbal acknowledgment of his arrival, just the gesture. The general felt the affront immediately. He could feel the blood leaving his face in his humiliation. Mardonius knew exactly what was happening the moment the young King motioned for him to sit. Xerxes purposely asked his servants to have Megabyzus wait while Mardonius waited in his chair. While he sat the young King just paced in front of him with his back to the general. Finally, Megabyzus entered the chamber. The King immediately walked over to him placing his arms on the general's shoulders.

"General, you are welcome to my home"

Megabyzus fell to a knee for an instant and pronounced, ***"My Lord, I am at your service." "As you know, General, the Babylonians have betrayed the Empire. I believe that the revolt is led by the religious wing of the city."*** Xerxes fisted his right hand in front of the general's face.

"I have had my fill with these religious zealots. Both rebellions have been fermented by these misguided men. It is time for punishment. I want you to level the wall of the Pearl City. I want all the religious leaders in the city sacrificed for this stupidity. This needs to be a public display, as I want others in other cities to receive a message." Xerxes continued his pacing. *"I want their churches razed, their gold statues of their gods melted down, and the booty returned to me in Susa."* Megabyzus bowed to the King. Xerxes now raised his voice to emphasize his desire.

"General, I want no doubts. They are to suffer. I want no questions as to who is in control of this satrap. When I visit general, I want not to be able to recognize this city. Do you understand my orders? I want you to take every able-bodied male to serve as we march to Greece. But make sure to spread them among the legions. I don't want them to organize. Do you understand?"

"I do, Lord."

Xerxes turned to Mardonius and with a wave of his arm dismissed both men. Megabyzus strode out of the room with his head high and with confidence.

Mardonius, on the other hand, seemed to have legs of lead. Xerxes smiled to himself watching the departure, although he wasn't sure if the punishment was enough for Mardonius. Hamath had once told him that punishment doesn't change a man's ability. If he's just a poor general, then no chastisement will improve that. His father concluded that Mardonius made too many mistakes. Xerxes now questioned his decision to reinstate him.

****

The Gardens at Ecbatana were the summer residence's most attractive feature. There were, in truth, two separate garden areas. The first was a place with a small pond centering its beauty. Around the small pond were beautifully sculptured bushes with wood paths weaving between the numerous flowers and blooming plants. As balanced as this area was attempting to create equilibrium between positive and negative energies, the true marvel of the area was the unequalled stone garden. This idea was supposedly brought by traders from the east. The stone garden was composed of sand, rocks, and patterns drawn in the sand. It was a compelling place as it drew the soul towards tranquility. When in Ecbatana, Xerxes relished his time in the gardens. He would disappear for hours in the stone garden, often meditating for hours on end.

On this day the King had called a meeting in his favorite sitting place.

The area that the King chose was completely flat with three prominent vertical rocks dominating the landscape. The center stone was the most attractive and persuasive. When entering this area it was difficult to remove one's gaze from the stone. It was said that it was placed in this garden by the gods. Around the center stone was virgin white sand that stretched for almost twenty feet. The bareness of the area was undeniable and compelling. There were concentric circles drawn into the sand around the centered rock. Outside of the twenty-foot circle of sand were three wooden benches. One was positioned facing the rising sun. The second bench was positioned to watch the setting sun, and the third bench faced the north star. Outside of the benches were rings of colored sand with designs that took slaves months and months to complete.

The young King had entered these garden hours before the sun rose. On this day, the King had ordered his emissaries to meet with him in this quiet place. He had finalized his thoughts about the journey to Delphi. He knew that the meetings to be held at Delphi would shape the future of two continents. If played correctly the Greeks would be bought off. Xerxes would not have to empty the treasures of the Empire to revenge himself against them. More so, they would accept the Persians as their masters. They would have to present the traditional signs of subservience, sand, and water. Xerxes knew that the Greeks were a proud people and his goal was to offer them limited freedom within the Empire. They would be able to govern themselves if they paid homage and taxes to Susa.

Artemisia was the first to arrive in the garden. She sat on the bench opposite the King as he sat with his eyes closed. She knew that she would have to wait for the King to return from his stupor. Artemisia worried that the King's spirit left him during his meditations and she came early to try and see if she could observe his spirit return to the body. Artemisia was drowsy and daydreaming when the King suddenly opened his eyes. He seemed to know that the Warrior Queen was sitting opposite him as he smiled when their eyes met. Xerxes rose and slowly walked to the Queen.

"Are you ready, my Queen?"

"I am, Lord. Our journey to the Oracle is already planned."

"You know that Hamath will be accompanying you."

"I know, Lord. But I'm unsure what our different roles are."

Xerxes smiled to himself. *"My Queen, I want you to be the one to speak with the god. Their god, Apollo, has had many encounters with the other Greek gods. I am told of their stories and myths. In their Trojan conflict, one of his adversaries was with the goddess, Athena."*

Artemisia looked strangely at the great King.

"Lord, do you believe that these priestesses at Delphi actually communicate with the god?"

Xerxes straightened himself and looked directly at the Warrior Queen.

"I do, Artemisia. I do. My mother, Ho, also believes. Do not underestimate the power of the Oracle, my Queen. If we gain the approval of Apollo, then Greece will submit without a fight."

Xerxes refocused his eyes on the Queen. His eyes narrowed as he was making his point.

"*Apollo controls Athens and Sparta. They listen to this Oracle. If the god gives them confidence then they will take many chances. If the Oracle turns against them, they will become discouraged and make our job much easier. If the Oracle is on our side, many Persian lives will be spared. Be careful, my Queen. Your job is to convince the Oracle of our invincibility. But you will be treading a very fine line. You cannot appear too masterful, bringing the wrath of the Oracle. You cannot appear too weak or the god will think us unworthy. You will take many chests of gold and silver to offer to Apollo.*"

"*I understand my role, Lord. But the silver and gold will serve better elsewhere. Just speaking with me is enough of a gift for Apollo.*"

The King laughed at this comment before becoming serious. Xerxes placed a hand on the Queen's arm. **"*You must control your famous temper and your aggressiveness. This is a mission for control not for antagonism.*"**

Artemisia felt her hand tighten around her sword as she did not like the King lecturing her. She maintained an external calm, not allowing the King to read her underlying feeling. The Queen had her own idea of what her job was in speaking with the god. After the King was finished, Artemisia bowed slowly to the Monarch.

"Go finish your preparation, my Queen. Know that our Empire rests on your shoulders."

Xerxes stepped forward and placed his forehead to touch the Queen's forehead. In a soft tone he said, *"remember, my Queen. Strength doesn't just come from advancing. Giving ground can lead to an advantage as easily as taking a step forward. Go with power, my Queen."*

As the Queen was leaving the stone garden she almost ran into Hamath. The two warriors bowed to each other in mutual respect.

"It brings me comfort to know that you will be traveling with us, my Queen."

"I feel the same, Hamath. Your presence at this diplomatic foray is comforting. With you at the negotiations, our chances of success rise significantly."

Xerxes watched the interchange although he was too far away to hear discussion. He purposely stayed away from the duo hoping that their alliance would begin now and end with diplomatic success. He turned his back on the pair and walked carefully to one of the large stones standing in the northeast corner of the circular garden.

When Hamath arrived, King Xerxes had a smile on his face.

"My teacher, my entire Kingdom is depending on you. When I was young I placed my life in your hands. Now, I place the Empire there as well."

Hamath remained silent and stared at the Monarch.

"Hamath, you will be the chief negotiator at this meeting. I have received many messages from the powers in Athens. They have assured me through these emissaries that they are open to a negotiated settlement."

"Do you believe them, Lord?"

"I have already learned, Hamath, that you can't believe anything. It will be up to you, my friend, to strip them of their deceit and ascertain their underlying motives. You will negotiate, but you also will be my eyes and ears in the enemy's camp. You will have to read these people, Hamath. All your experience and brilliance will be tested by these Greeks. So far, these people who consider us barbarians have outsmarted our best military minds. But

now our time has come. They will outsmart us no more. I won't allow it, Hamath. I won't allow it. They will either submit to us with earth and water or they will be crushed. Hamath, I want to have a negotiated peace, but I am also not afraid to take our army into their peninsula. Two names to remember. If you hear the name Themistocles be wary. They boast of a new type of ruler called Demos, some nonsensical way that the common people vote for change. Stupid! But I believe that this Themistocles is the King and the decision maker. Be careful of his snakes and ploys, my emissary. He cannot be trusted. Also, be careful of the representative from the aristocrats, for they betrayed us at Marathon."

Xerxes again hesitated before he continued. He then instructed, "make sure, my teacher, that these people understand the consequences of failure at these negotiations. Make sure the Athenians understand that their city will burn if I have to visit their land."

Xerxes again became pensive. "If you must, kill these diplomats before you leave, but be safe and return to me. A representative from Sparta will also be present. They are a warrior people. Gauge their strengths and weaknesses. Also, you are to speak with men from a city call Aegon. They are the traditional enemies of Athens and might lead to alliance."

The King became meditative. "*I've heard of this man, Themistocles. He has sent messages but they are somewhat confusing. I don't think he will be at Delphi but his representatives will. You will need to judge these men, evaluate their strength of spirit. As you have taught me, my master, you can defeat weapons, but the spirit is more difficult. Their strength or weakness lies in their resolve.*"

"*And in ours, Lord.*"

"*Yes, Hamath, in ours as well.*"

Xerxes walked to the teacher, his most trusted confidant. He looked him in the eye and again put his hand on the man's shoulder. He then touched his head to his master's forehead.

"*I trust you more than any man alive, my teacher. I give you complete command of this delegation. You are negotiating for the Empire. Any choice you make will be my choice. Your voice is my voice.*"

Hamath left the stone garden and the King slowly walked back to his meditation bench. The young King sat and closed his eyes. As he sat a figure approached him from the palace. The man walked slowly towards where the young monarch sat. He didn't appear in a hurry and he certainly didn't appear to be trying to hide his approach. He walked to the King and silently stood by the sitting sovereign. He waited statue like while the King remained in his trance. Finally, Xerxes opened his eyes and stood facing the man.

"Ummanaldash, we have not spoken for days."

The eunuch bowed his head to the King. *"I have a special assignment for you."* The slave bowed to the monarch. *"Ummanaldash, you've heard about our mission to Delphi. There will be high level negotiations with the Greeks. Hamath will handle those negotiations. Artemisia will consult the great Oracle."* Ummanaldash was stoically focused on the King.

"But your job, Ummanaldash, will be to handle the secret negotiations. The Greeks will be sending people who will stay out of the light. They will carry with them the ability to make proposals and accept payments. You will be able to be more direct with these people than Hamath will be with his opponents. They will test you, my friend. They will send false messages and try to tempt you. They will seek to get you to betray everything you believe in. You have passed many tests in your life, my

friend, but this ordeal will test even you. You know what you must accomplish. I have faith in your manipulative skills."

Xerxes walked to the eunuch and again, as he did before, stepped up to the man and placed his forehead to Ummanaldash's. In a voice just above a whisper the King murmured, **'before you leave, Ummanaldash, I want you to contact the guardians of the secrets."**

With the mention of the guardians Ummanaldash clearly tightened. The King went on. **"I don't trust this Greek, Themistocles. He must be eliminated. I want the Sand Dancers to take care of the situation. Take care of this, Ummanaldash, before you leave. Pay whatever you need. Make sure you emphasize the need for success. If you cut the head off the snake the body will die. In Delphi our contact will be a man named Eudox. Be careful with him, he has the ear of this Themistocles, and therefore the mind of a snake."**

The eunuch walked slowly away from the King. Xerxes watched him leave. After a few steps the King turned and walked toward the center stone. He stopped by the edge of the concentric sand circles. Had he made the correct decisions? He knew he was taking some chances. He had never liked the brotherhood of the Sand

Dancers. They were called guardians, but in truth they were heartless assassins. But they were trustworthy in their occupation. His innate sense was that Themistocles could be bought. That meant that he couldn't really be negotiated with. Self-centered people couldn't negotiate for a country. Xerxes wanted someone who would bow to his power, not a leader who was so nationalistic that he resisted subservience to the Archimedean dynasty. He wanted the Sand Dancers in reserve, just in case. He didn't require total dedication, just enough to bow to him. He needed this to make up for Marathon and satisfy the debt that his father, Darius, had left him. If he could get the Oracle to support his superiority it would dramatically affect the negotiations for Hamath. He believed the god could also be bought. It would be a game of momentum, with the talks at one level having a gravitational pull on the other levels.

The King took a deep breath and looked to the rock. The dye had been caste. There were still preparations before they left. The King had played his cards. Now it was time to let the gods and fates finish the game. He had consulted the Answerer and hoped that he understood the messages from his ancestors.

Xerxes, the King of Peoples, the King of Nations, the King of Kings, the

Pharaoh God-Man Momus II, brother of the god, Ptah, had set the wheel of chance in motion. The zeitgeist was turning, history was on the verge of being written. The structure of reality was evolving. He was preparing for World War I.

The King smiled as he looked to the heavens. The day appeared brighter to him than before. The time was now and he held the future. Xerxes smiled and walked back into his abode satisfied in himself, and in his belief in his God, and his ancestral destiny.

* * * *

END BOOK I

PERSIA: PRIDE & POWER
THE STORY CONTINUES
IN BOOK II:

Greece

With regard to ancient mythological power, Dr. Donner is releasing a series of novels called, "*The Great Persian Saga*".

The first book in this series, **PERSIA- PRIDE AND POWER**, takes place in Persia circa, 500 B.C. This novel focuses on the great Persian dictator, Xerxes, and his hatred of the Greeks. Xerxes also confronts a rogue priest named Ningizzida, who haunts him as much as the Greeks. Artemisia, the greatest female warrior of all time, comes to Xerxes defense, as he faces external and internal threats to his sovereignty.

Book II of this saga, **"GREECE"**, occurs during the same period as the first book. "Greece" centers on the Greek hero, Themistocles, and the birth of democracy. Themistocles struggles against aristocratic forces within Greek society as well his own hedonistic addictions, to press his egalitarian principals. The book brings a new perspective to Greek myth, spanning the Greek pantheon and examining the Gods' motives. As Greek society evolves, the Persian hoard awaits on the horizon set to destroy the Greeks and their fledgling democracy.

Book III of the saga, **"THE GREAT ORACLE AT DELPHI"**, takes place at the mythological "center of the world". As the novel opens, the Greeks and Persians converge on Delphi to seek out the Delphic Oracle for insight into the future regarding the threat of war between them. The Delphic Oracle made prognostations about religion, philosophy, life and death, and history in the ancient world. Although the Delphic Oracle wields significant influence over generations of Kings and entire civilizations, the Delphic Oracle does not seek to interfere in the affairs of men and women. Instead, the Delphic Oracle defers to the Greeks and Persians to interpret the wisdom of the God Apollo to determine their fate.

Book IV of the Saga, "PRAY TO THE WIND", finds the Persians invading the Greek homeland. It is the time of the battle of Thermopylae, as well as the destruction of the Acropolis. In the aftermath of the battle between tyranny and democracy, Dr. Donner explores the emotional toll on Artemisia, Themistocles and Xerxes, their relationships to each other and historical legacies.

OTHER BOOKS BY JEFFREY DONNER

If you enjoyed this book, you would probably love some of my other books:

Descent Into Madness

Boundaries of Hell

BOUNDARIES OF

HELL

EMERGENCE OF THE BEAST

A PSYCHOLOGICAL THRILLER

Book II: Descent Into Madness Series

DR. JEFFERY DONNER

www.ingramcontent.com/pod-product-compliance
Lightning Source LLC
Chambersburg PA
CBHW051932020726
47501CB00001B/83